SUPERWORLD

SUPERWORLD

—— BOOK 2 ——

BENJAMIN KEYWORTH

Podium

In loving memory of Alison,
Who believed in me
And listened to my stories
When they were still in my head

Copyright © 2022 by Benjamin Keyworth

Cover design by Podium Publishing

ISBN: 978-1-0394-1476-1

Published in 2022 by Podium Publishing, ULC
www.podiumaudio.com

SUPERWORLD

DAWN SERVICE

"Superhumanism and the New Social Contract"
Amanda Watson, PhD, Oxford University

Abstract

This paper analyzes historical and political trends in the era following the widespread acquisition of superhuman abilities ("post-superhumanism"). After clarifying key concepts and establishing the position of nation-states pre- and post-Aurora, it examines the forms and extent of societal evolution across a range of countries and government systems. Overall, this paper will conclude that inalienable individual empowerment has resulted in a shift toward greater personal freedom and self-determination, as well as an intolerance to exploitation, and that additionally, after an initial period of adjustment, the instinctually cooperative and stability-seeking nature of human beings has prevented empowerment from creating lasting states of anarchy.

Extracts

[32] . . . dubbed retrospectively as the "Year of Chaos," the approximately thirteen months in which countries without exception struggled to adjust to the implications of a superhuman population. A detailed time line of events throughout this period is beyond this paper's scope, but general features included a sharp increase in both crime and arrests; escalation of existing national, ethnic, social, and religious conflicts; state of emergency declarations; statistically significant spikes in accidental and criminally related deaths; and the international reinstatement of capital punishment. Of important note, however, is that actual revolution, as opposed to violence and

minor loss of territorial control, predominantly occurred in nation-states without an existing democratic or representative structure . . .

[67] . . . conversely resulting in a long-term decrease in rates of violent crime. Arguably, while superhumanism increases the individual capacity for destruction and criminality, it also increases the capacity of would-be victims of crime, as well as society as a whole, to resist and respond (Kennedy 1985). As the portion of the population inclined to engage in criminal activity is proportionately smaller than those inclined to obey the law absent clear injustice or need (Shelley and Black 1977), the effect of empowering the former appear to have been outweighed by the empowering of the latter. Furthermore, the random and untelegraphed nature of superpowers introduces an element of unpredictability into committing crimes against the person; as Sir Lee stated in the 1982 congressional hearing (Shelley and Black 1977, n7), "a superhuman could rob a bank, were it not for the fact that the tellers and every customer there will have an ability of their own . . . [T]he danger of robbing an old lady in a dark alley rises exponentially when you don't know what powers the seemingly harmless hide . . ."

[104] . . . reflected in the inevitable collapse of totalitarian states. Regardless of whatever ideals these oligarchies espoused or whether they were feasible in theory, the reality of a sizable underclass visibly exploited by a small elite could not withstand the superhuman advent. With conventional military means of control no longer viable against an empowered population, minority-led dictatorships lacked the tools with which to enforce compliance with their regimes . . .

[112] . . . unclear whether these collapses are due to more than a residual "bad taste" left by previous communist ideologies. It is argued (Moore et al. 1995) that communism as a societal concept provides little incentive for individual distinction and accomplishment, making it fundamentally incompatible with a superhuman world where differences are not only apparent but abundant. This assertion is naturally contested (Jokovic and Noble 1994), but it seems less controversial to propose that humans inevitably gravitate toward a stable and cooperative societal structure, wherein still lies the potential for recognition of personal talent, achievement, and skill . . .

[127] . . . a much greater apprehension on the part of governing bodies towards the populations which they governed. While equality of outcome does not seem necessary (Walsh 1985), there seems to be, as a requirement of stability, at least a general perception of equality of opportunity and governance "for the people." Systems that promote or permit substantial and debilitating corruption or inequality are inevitably rejected and destroyed by a superhuman population that, for the first time in human history, possesses power greater than or equal to any state-funded military . . .

[139] . . . the conclusion being that humans, as instinctually social creatures, are in the majority drawn to cooperative social "contracts" of nonviolence and mutual trust with those around them, so long as their personal beliefs are able to be represented, or at least heard. There is a natural gravitation toward systems that maximize general safety and individual freedom while unduly sacrificing neither, and the increased power wielded by every person has not fundamentally altered this inclination or the societal equation sufficiently to result in long-term anarchy . . .

[151] . . . quote: "[I]t is disparity then, that is the enemy of progress; disparity, not power. Prosperity persists so long as power cannot be concentrated disproportionately in the hands of the few. It is this concentration, therefore, that signals the advent of tyranny; that must be averted before it elicits the death of liberty, and heralds the coming of doom . . ."

Her name was Cassandra Atropos, and she left neither body nor mourning nor name.

She'd had friends once, a family. A white-walled cottage in Thessaloniki, a collection of orchids, a ginger-haired cat, a guitar. All long-since sold or repurposed or forgotten, save for the cat, which still prowled the Macedonian alleyways, irritated and unaware that its mistress had died. Unintentionally, this was her strongest remaining connection. Cassandra had not been a good friend, a good sister, a good relative. She had not been much good at anything once telepathy came to her, and her composure had slowly been eroded beneath wave after wave of thought. She'd hated herself for it, but the truth was inescapable—some people were just born sensitive, eyes too open, nerves too raw. She retreated from society, then solitude, then sanity, and at no point was it enough.

She'd prepared to end her life feeling like a failure for her failings, and most of all for giving up.

Of course, no one knew any of this. Nor would it ever be discovered. By the time she blew herself to pieces, five years after the date on her death certificate, Cassandra Atropos was a memory faded into acceptance to all those who had once known her, and her disappearance would be marked by neither notice nor suspicion. The life she had lived and the end she had chosen would never be connected, the only potential link residing solely in the mind of a young human, who held such secrets ever-tightly to his chest. It was a mystery none would ever solve, a guess nobody could ever make.

Though it did not stop them trying.

In a farmstead in rural Albania, men and women in black clothes donned white full-body safety suits and stepped gingerly into a ruined basement, to scour among rocks and ash. They found only meaningless pieces: bits of bone, wood, and tooth, residue and marks for calculations, which together added to nothing beyond chemicals, temperature, and yield. They searched with superhuman eyes and heightened senses, with fine telekinetic fingers and the power to separate earth on command. And all of it, in summary, amounted to the same forensic dead end: there had been a woman, she had waited, and she had blown herself up.

Eventually, the Ashes would give up their searching. Eventually, they would one by one grimace and shake their heads, pack up their equipment, and leave the mystery of the dead "clairvoyant's" identity and motivations in a pile on a laboratory bench—less an autopsy than a jigsaw, where the pieces were incinerated and no one knew what the picture was supposed to be. All that were left were guesses, and arrangements for a burial beneath an anonymous tree.

And finally, when no one was left to see it, for a man who would be king to look down upon Cassandra Atropos's ashes and seethe with silent rage.

How dare they still deny him? How dare they make him wait? No longer. He had spent too long on fruitless searches, hunting dreams of endless sight. No. No more patient waiting, no more appearances and charades. The cogs were in motion and soon the reckoning would come. He would burn down Dawn and everything he stood for and grind his legacy to dust.

You achieved nothing, he told her ashes on their cold and silent slab. Keep your name, your face, your secrets. They were meaningless, as were you, as were all of you. Go, you filthy gnats—throw yourselves against my tempest, smear your blood across my stone. You failed to keep my birthright. You failed to take my prize. You prevented nothing.

The pale smile faded, and he left the remains of Cassandra Atropos alone to their eternity.

He had what he wanted.

"Mr. Callaghan. Thank you for coming."

They always started these meetings the same way, Matt mused internally. By thanking him. It was a neat little psychological trick, he supposed, a little bit of predispositional politeness to make you feel like your existence was appreciated and your attendance was optional. Like you had some choice in goings on.

Across the table from him, Director Daniel Winters leaned forward, his kind, diplomatic eyes staring at Matt over entwined fingers. Hillary Cross sat to Winters's left, and to his right a third woman who Matt didn't recognize, with long curly black hair, tan skin, and thick eyebrows. They were in a room on the third floor, some kind of boardroom that wasn't normally utilized by students, with a long oval table ringed by identical yet surprisingly comfy office chairs and a smartboard on the far wall. Most of the chairs were not in use. Matt was the only one sitting on his side, and Winters and his two companions were the only ones sitting on theirs.

Across the table from him, Winters's face moved into a mask of genuine concern.

"How are you?"

A potentially loaded question, Matt thought wryly. Physically, Matt was the same as ever. Still a regular-sized, brown-haired white boy, his burns from being almost incinerated completely healed and his new haircut from having his hair singed almost unnoticeable. Emotionally, well, honestly, better than he could have been. Two weeks had passed since the incident in Albania, and while Matt probably should have felt a bit more traumatized, apart from a little difficulty sleeping and occasionally having dreams about eyeless women, he was sort of . . . fine? He'd talked to the Legion's resident psychotherapist, a nice man by the name of Peter Elmwood who used lots of nautical metaphors, and he had engaged in therapy honestly, if with a little massaging of facts. The fundamentals had remained unchanged; he'd been kidnapped by a crazy person, she'd said a bunch of crazy things, then she'd blown herself up. It had been, naturally, a distressing experience. But when the moment of danger had come, Peter and Matt had reflected, Matt hadn't frozen, and once he was out of it no residual fear or lingering existential dread had shown up. Matt's mind was just kind of . . . resilient. He didn't not trust people. He wasn't afraid of the outside world. He just maintained a strong personal preference for not being blown up.

After three sessions, the psychologist diagnosed Matt as extremely well adjusted, made some pithy remark about king tides, and discharged the supposed clairvoyant back into the wild. Morningstar Academy, perhaps smelling his less-than-enthusiasm, had offered him telepathic counseling, too, but Matt had politely declined that idea, thank you very much.

"May I introduce Ms. Hosseini, from legal. She'll be taking notes." The woman in her mid-forties smiled and spread her palm over a blank sheet of paper, into which burned rows of thin, curling characters. "We've read your report."

"Report" was a strong word for it, in Matt's opinion. "Vaguely coherent essay minus all the incriminating bits" was probably more accurate. He'd have given it a B.

"Firstly," said Winters, straightening slightly as he fixed Matt with his movie-star gaze, "may I commend you on your bravery. You stepped into a difficult and distressing situation, and you handled yourself admirably. That is to be commended. Well done."

For what, Matt scowled internally. All he'd done was get kidnapped, hide behind a table and shout a lot. Nevertheless, he kept his face deliberately blank and received Winters's praise with a serious nod.

"We're all familiar with the details," Winters continued with only a quick glance either side of him. "But still, it would be appreciated if you could recount your experience. So we can make sure we haven't missed something. Get the story straight from the horse's mouth."

Matt was unshaken, and as always, perfectly prepared.

"We landed in Buzahishtë," he stated, his pronunciation flawless. "Will Herd teleported us about half a mile out. We identified an abandoned farmstead nearby and approached cautiously on foot. About a quarter mile away, I sensed that Jane and I should go ahead, and that it'd be dangerous if the others accompanied us. Natalia Baroque sensed not long after that there was someone hiding in a nearby structure and she alerted Jane. We proceeded with caution. We found explosive traps buried in the ground and wires designed to cut speedsters. Jane was able to disarm them before they could do any harm."

Cross let out a small sniff, but otherwise remained silent.

"About five minutes into the ruins, I sensed that I needed to be alone to lure out the other clairvoyant. I sent Jane away to make it look like I was vulnerable. The other clairvoyant sprung her trap, a literal trapdoor. I knew I was standing on it, but still, I was glad I was wearing armor."

Winters gave him an approving nod. "And then?"

"The trapdoor led into a nearby basement," Matt continued. "The other clairvoyant was there, waiting. She had clearly gone mad." He shivered, perhaps unintentionally. "She'd self-mutilated her eyes."

There was a brief silence across the room before Matt continued, veering sharply from the truth. "She was younger than she looked in the briefing. Shorter, too, maybe five six, and had lost a lot of weight. Her hair was completely brown. And her face didn't look like it had in the photo."

"Prosthetics," Winters nodded, as though Matt's words were putting everything in place rather than deliberately trying to obscure any attempt at piecing Cassandra's identity together. "What did she say to you?"

Matt shrugged. "Nothing coherent. Mainly 'five billion souls, five billion souls,' over and over and over. Then she said something about the crossroads of destiny compounding over and over and . . ." he squinted, pretending to try and recall, ". . .'no mistakes, no mistakes ever'? It was just rambling. It didn't sound coherent."

"Did you get her name?" Cross demanded.

"No," Matt lied. "Like I said, she was barely coherent. Sometimes it felt like she saw me. Other times she barely knew I was there."

There was a pause as the Cross and Winters exchanged glances. Matt continued after a moment.

"I tried to introduce myself, to explain who I was, that I wasn't going to hurt her. But she just kept rambling. And then she opened her robe, and I saw that she'd rigged herself up with explosives. That's when I started calling for help."

"Which Miss Walker was able to respond to," Winters said, nodding. The director paused. "Could you see what was distressing her? The clairvoyant I mean." He fixed Matt with a piercing gaze. "What was compelling her to take her own life?"

"Honestly?" Matt answered, and it was indeed honest. "Not even a little bit, no. It was clear something was upsetting her. She kept talking about love and destiny and seemed to think someone was after her. Frankly?" He shook his head. "I think she pushed herself too hard. She got too good at seeing the future. I think in the end, she saw all her life's possibilities and just, I don't know . . . sort of lost her mind."

There were a few moments of intense, deliberative silence.

"That doesn't make sense," said Cross, her dour, chubby cheeks pursed into a scowl. "Why would contact with the Legion cause this kind of reaction? Why would our mere presence trigger such a negative response?"

To his surprise, before Matt could answer, Winters sprung right into his trap. "No, it fits, think about it," he said. "Every one of these clairvoyants we've tried to reach has been deliberately cut off from the world, isolated. Maybe it's a coping strategy, a way to minimize potential futures. No people to interact with, no destinies to become entangled. And then we arrive." He paused, musing, making a temple with his fingers. "With all modesty, the Legion stands to impact a large cross-section of humanity. Our actions affect the fate of nations, not to mention countless lives. Imagine the magnitude of anticipating that, of witnessing the ramifications of your every potential action rippling across the globe. The pressure would be enormous, the choices paralyzing. No wonder they go mad."

It seemed a different sort of madness, Matt knew, but he kept his mouth shut. Rule number one of being a clairvoyant, never interrupt when your client is doing your job for you.

"I don't buy it," Cross scowled, obstinate as always. "If that's the case, why haven't we seen the same effects in Mr. Callaghan? You've read the psychologist's report, he's perfectly well adjusted." She spat the words out like they were sour. "Why's he not going mad from this 'crossroads of destiny'?"

I'm right here, thought Matt, suppressing his irritation. Nevertheless, he was quick to speak.

"I agree actually," he said, before anyone else could properly react. "I'm concerned about my long-term well-being. If this is the effect being near the Legion has on clairvoyants, respectfully, I don't know if it's in my best interests to keep hanging around here."

Across the table from Matt, Cross narrowed her eyes and the legal lady, hands burning characters into a fresh sheet of paper, glanced over at Winters with a raised brow. To Matt's surprise and frustration, however; Winters did not even hesitate before shaking his head.

"Respectfully, Mr. Callaghan," he said, "I have to disagree. Matt. Look." He held out a palm to the folder in front of him, where Cassandra Atropos's picture stared out at them from the page. "Look at what happens to clairvoyants who don't get Legion training. Look at what happens when they try to go it alone. Your time here, I have to say, has yielded positive advancements. Well," he added, catching the incredulous look on Cross's face, "perhaps not positive in a traditional sense, but a far cry removed from the isolation and derangement these other clairvoyants seem to suffer. No. We've consulted with Selwyn, Mr. Elmwood, and Captain Dawn, and the verdict is unanimous. We've been lucky enough to catch you early before your gift grows overwhelming. For once, we have a head start. We can't throw that away. Least of all for your benefit."

"But . . ." Matt spluttered feebly, "all the futures . . . crossroads . . . destiny . . ."

"It's all about endurance, Matt, it has to be," Winters insisted. With each word, he sounded increasingly fervent, and Matt's protests shrank to smaller and smaller speed bumps. "These other clairvoyants, they were obviously retreating as their powers developed. By the time we approached them, later in life, they couldn't cope with the outside world. But they'd run away from what they could do, not toward it." He shook his head. "A speedster builds up to running. A strongman builds up weights. Even a technopath when they first manifest their powers can't stay connected to the entire Internet for more than a few seconds. There's too much information; it's overwhelming. But that doesn't mean it's impossible. That understanding, that filtration, the ability to process—that's something you build up to over time. Your clairvoyance is a muscle, and it may be that your future, nay your very life depends on us helping you exercise it."

Matt struggled not to slump and sigh. It'd been such a good excuse and Winters had swallowed it hook, line, and sinker, only to somehow swim so passionately that he'd dragged Matt further down. Jesus Christ.

Cross, however, was not so easily convinced.

"Daniel, respectfully," she said, turning to the director, "I still don't concur. Mr. Callaghan lacks the temperament to remain with the Legion. That is my formal assessment. Write that down," she said, firing a quick glare at the lawyer lady, who Matt saw barely avoid rolling her eyes.

"In terms of attitude, Hillary," replied Winters, his tone equally cool, "I have trouble debating against a competently and courageously conducted field operation. Don't you?"

"My issue is not Mr. Callaghan's courage," snapped Cross, eyeing Matt coldly. "Be that as it may. My issue is his commitment and his competence. He clearly does not possess the dedication needed to be an Acolyte, as evidenced by a mere glance at his attendance record. He is repeatedly delinquent. And the contents of his visions so far are so lackluster that I am beginning to wonder if he is being deliberately obstructive." And to Matt's horror, her expression infinitesimally slackened and her words began to slow. "Or, perhaps, if we are dealing with the same kind of clairvoyance at all."

Despite his calm exterior, Matt's heart skipped a beat. Somehow, in the course of simply venting her distaste for him, Cross had flown perilously close to the truth. Silently, Matt grit his teeth. She had been so close. So freaking, freaking close to just saying he wasn't worth it and kicking him out. Why did she have to go that step further? Why did she have to pry?

Stay hidden or the world ends.

Because now he was going to have to do something he really, really didn't want to, and after this there'd be no goddamn escape.

Death.

"Here," Matt said brusquely. He reached into his pocket, pulled out a piece of folded paper, and flung it across the table at Cross. The note slid to a stop an inch from the edge. "That came to me two nights ago. Take it, if you want to doubt my predictions. Use it for a new gym hall or something. A ladder maybe, to get the hell off my back." He stood up, scowling at the three professionals across the table. "I almost died for this place. I don't need this."

"You're absolutely right," said Winters, clambering to his feet as Matt turned to leave. He shot out his hand, almost as if he was afraid Matt would leave before shaking it, and to Matt's eternal chagrin he was forced by years of proper parenting to turn back sourly around. Winters clasped Matt's hands in both of his.

"I apologize, Mr. Callaghan. This meeting was intended to be a debriefing, not an evaluation." He shot a sideways glare at Cross, who had remained in her seat. The dour Ashes woman said nothing, having unfolded the piece of paper Matt had given her and staring, stunned, at the contents. "Your time here is greatly appreciated. I think that's all?" He glanced quickly at Ms. Hosseini, who nodded and moved to pack up her papers, before turning back to Matt. "Stay strong. Keep training. We here at the Academy are here for you. All of us." He shot Cross another glare. "If you need anything, please don't hesitate to ask. Our goal is to keep you a happy, healthy, valued member of the Legion's team."

I should be so lucky, Matt thought as he trudged from the conference room. Behind him, Cross remained silent, still staring blank-faced at what was written on the slip of paper. Matt's insurance policy. Cassandra Atropos's final gift: 4, 7, 13, 18, 21, 26, 32, 3.

"How'd it go?" Jane asked as he shut the dormitory door. The empath was splayed out on his mattress—they'd spent the morning before their interviews ironing out the kinks in their respective stories, and Jane had come to get Matt from his room after her own debriefing was over. She'd remained in residence, it seemed, and was lying on his bed bouncing a ball of ice off the ceiling.

"Fine," Matt grumbled. He dropped down into his desk chair. "Winters bought the line about undue clairvoyant pressure. Except then he took it one step further and concluded that if I don't get proper training, I'll go insane and hang myself. Now I have to stay not just for the Legion's improvement, but for my personal health."

"Told you, you should've pretended to be traumatized," said Jane, twisting the ice ball to spin on her finger. "Only thing Winters fears more than death is a lawsuit."

"Yes, well, we went over this," Matt said, vaguely irritated. "I don't like faking mental conditions. And I don't like the idea of having to pretend to have one for, I don't know, the indefinite rest of my life."

"Well, we all have to make our beds." Jane shrugged. She melted the ball back into her fingers and sat upright. "So . . . now that that's done, what're you thinking?"

Matt leaned over, massaging his eyebrows. Truth be told, he didn't know what he was thinking. He didn't know what he was supposed to be doing anymore. Definitely not going on any more missions. Probably trying his hardest to get expelled, except he'd just handed Cross a rock-solid reason never to do that. Goddamn lottery numbers. Matt had been carrying them around in his pocket for two weeks since he'd got back from Albania, and as much as he wanted to write off Cassandra's ramblings as insanity, he somehow doubted the oddly affectionate woman was attempting to screw him over from beyond the grave.

"I've been thinking more about what she said," he told Jane, dropping his voice a few notches—not quite a whisper, but just so there was absolutely no chance of carrying through the walls. "I don't think she was crazy."

"She escaped from a padded cell and gouged her own eyes out," said Jane.

"Yes," conceded Matt. "But in the moment, she definitely made it sound like it all made sense. Or at least made some kind of sense. I don't know. It all happened so quickly. It's hard to remember the exact wording."

"You seemed to remember the lottery numbers fine."

"Well, some things are clearer than others. Has word gotten out?"

"How the hell would I know?"

"I don't know," Matt grumbled. "You talk to people."

"I talk to Wally. Maybe Giselle. That's it."

"You are a useless social infiltrator. All right. Come on. Let's go over it again."

"Thousandth time's the charm," said Jane, rolling her eyes. Nevertheless, she leaned back on Matt's bed and let out a long, huffing sigh.

"All right," she said. "One: clairvoyants exist."

"Right. Except maybe they don't and maybe this lady wasn't one of them."

"Right, she'd just psychically . . . I don't know, imprinted off one. Or something. We actually have no idea."

"Clear as mud. Excellent. Continue."

"Disturbing fact number two: your application to the Academy was submitted by some weird, magical teleporting child."

"Or something that looked like one. At least that's what it claimed."

"Yes. Who also warned you about death."

"And the end of the world."

"Right."

"I'm not going crazy."

"No, you've been cleared by a psychologist," Jane mused. "And, well, a woman did blow herself up in front of you."

"In front of *us*."

"I feel like I was more of a bystander. I barely saw anything."

"No, she mentioned you by name."

"That's still unsettling. Still"—Jane straightened, flicking hair out of her eyes—"what the kid said seems to be kind of coming true."

"Kind of. But why me? Why are all these weirdos fixated on me of all people?"

"It's got to be because you're human," said Jane. "It's the only logical thing."

"You'd think so," said Matt, face twitching into a frown. "Except I don't really understand why, you know? Surely, if anything, I'm the person least likely to cause the world to be destroyed, not the most."

"Yeah, I don't get it either," agreed Jane. "But the message does seem consistent." She paused, kneading her palms. "I know we've already gone over this, but have you considered the possibility that she was legitimately schizophrenic? Cassandra? Schizophrenic and clairvoyant? They're not mutually exclusive."

"I've thought about it," admitted Matt, shaking his head. "But you didn't hear her. She answered everything I asked her. She seemed completely calm and in control. She wasn't worried." He paused. "And she was just so certain, you know? She didn't seem crazy."

"I mean, again, the eyeballs."

"True. It's a hard case to argue."

They lapsed into silence.

"The big thing's got to be the two people," Matt said eventually, clasping his hands behind his head and drawing a long, deep breath. "That's what I can't stop thinking about. That's what I don't understand."

"And there was definitely two of them," Jane asked, slightly squinting her eyes at him. "Two nebulous, nameless people she kept referring to, one who—"

"Was filled with bottomless love and the other who was just, you know, the absolute worst."

"Right." Jane paused. "So . . . we're thinking one of them is the child, right? The benevolent one?"

"Yeah, except it doesn't really line up with what she was saying," said Matt. "Like the way she talked about the good guy, it made him sound like he was a grown-up, that he was . . . I don't know, old and wise. And the way she described the bad one—*weak, pale little boy*—I mean the kid sure fits that description."

"So . . . the boy is evil," said Jane. "Except he's giving you warnings."

"Except are they even warnings," said Matt, pinching the bridge of his nose and closing his eyes, "or am I being manipulated?"

"Matt, I am so far out of my depth right now, I am an airborne submarine."

"All I wanted," Matt said through gritted teeth, his eyes still closed, "was to finish high school, go to a nice, semi-respectable college, and drink a lot. Why is that so goddamn hard?"

"The universe hates you. Come on." Jane got to her feet. "I've got to go. I'm missing too much class."

"You still care about class?" Matt asked her, opening his eyes and looking up. "We're looking at the end of the world here! Maybe. We almost got blown up!"

"That's literally what I signed up for." Jane shrugged, folding her arms into her sweater. "That's the Academy. Get beat up, get healed up. People trying to kill you is normal."

"It's not normal to me," Matt complained, pouting. "I want to go home."

"Well, it's not long 'til Thanksgiving. Everyone goes home then."

"Great. I meant permanently."

"I know." Jane made a face. "Come on. It's not so bad here."

"You're just happy you got to go on your first mission."

"I know," she said, grinning. "Only wish I could rub it in everyone's face."

"You have the purest motivations." Matt sighed and pushed himself to his feet. "Nuts to it. I'll go with you."

"What, to class?"

"No, you idiot, the buffet. It's almost lunch."

"It's eleven thirty."

"I said almost."

They strode across the room and Jane reached to open the door.

"Jane?"

"What." She turned to him.

"Thanks for saving my life."

The tall, bronze-haired girl flicked her hair over her shoulder and fixed Matt with a radiant, triumphant smile that stretched from her gray-blue eyes to her spiky tattoo. "You're goddamn welcome," she replied, beaming.

It was a surreal feeling, being back at Morningstar. In reality, Matt, Jane, and the rest of them had barely been gone two hours before they returned, burned, bloodied, and bewildered—but to Matt, it felt like he'd been gone a lifetime. It was weird how that worked. Days could fly by, weeks even, without feeling like any time had passed, but a few desperate minutes stretched out so distinctly inside your head. Yet for all the terror and excitement and for all his inability to forget, once Matt stepped foot back into Morningstar, it was like nothing had ever happened. Nobody noticed they'd been gone—nobody looked at him differently. He felt changed, or like he should be changed, or should be running around waving his arms and screaming at people—but nobody cared. Or more accurately, nobody knew.

There were debriefings, of course, and the psychologist. Matt took a little break from meditating with Selwyn, but then found he was both missing the big monk's company and bored with nothing to do. He kept on sort of waiting, eyeing off shadows and peering into silences, waiting for another sign of the pale child or another clairvoyant or another call. But nothing came. That was, it turned out, the worst part of living through terror—you couldn't help but keep expecting it to happen all over again.

Of the other Acolytes who had come with him to Albania, the only one Matt hadn't spoken to was Natalia Baroque. That suited Matt fine—he held no desire to converse with the pasty, raven-haired English girl, and she seemed to hold no desire to see him. The rest he'd talked to, separately and on the sly. James Conrad had been oddly positive. To him, it seemed getting face-to-face with a clairvoyant was an improvement, even if she had still blown herself up. Giselle Pixus had been more resigned about things, and they'd sort of talked their way around the topic over mimosas with Wally one night, and through that each established that the others were all right. With Will, there hadn't been much discussion—just a shake of the head when they were both standing in line for the buffet the morning after, and the teleporter muttering in discreet commiseration, "Freaking clairvoyants, man." None of them seemed particularly surprised by the outcome, and none of them seemed particularly disappointed in Matt. When a mission sucked, it seemed, you just put it behind you, notch the loss, keep clearing the board, move on.

Of course, none of them knew what had truly transpired. Matt had kept that between Jane, himself, and the dead.

"You're dead, Walker."

They were in the forest. The sky wrapped overhead in a gray and rolling blanket, bringing whispering cold, dimming the light. Branches rustled above them, the scent of pine needles crushed underfoot. Somewhere, a squirrel chittered, taking shelter against the wind. And a boy who looked like he should have been in grade school pressed a gun to the back of Jane's head.

"You're dead."

Jane closed her eyes, trying to block out the pain. Slowly, her gloved hand touched to her chest, then her side, then the back of her neck. When she drew back, it dripped thick with liquid, red and bright.

It was paint, she knew, but that did not spare her the humiliation.

"Get on the ground."

Jane did no such thing. Instead, she turned stiffly and walked to lean against a pine tree, careful not to wince at the bruises from where the paintballs had hit. The brown-skinned Acolyte boy, who looked like he'd hit puberty with the force of wet toilet paper, raised his faux rifle and flashed it menacingly at her.

"I mean it. I got you, Empath. Get down."

"Relax," snarled Jane. She pressed her back against the tree, the rough grate of scale-like bark. "I'm out."

This was a field exercise, a training session deep in the woods. It was essential, their instructor claimed, that they understand firearms—that even with their powers, they appreciate the damage a piece of supersonic metal can do and what a superpowered person could do with it. Thus, those in attendance had been split into two groups: one with functioning replica firearms, one without. The former to pursue, the latter to disarm.

It was an asymmetrical exercise. Intentionally so. Jane had been placed on the team of the hunted. That, too, was probably intentional.

Allegedly, Jane had teammates, but she'd seen neither hide nor hair of them since the whistle first blew, not that that surprised her anymore. She knew no one among those participating, and she expected nothing. The only surprise in the whole damn thing had been when the boy had phased out of solid rock and shot her square in the chest. Then once more in the side, thigh and back of the head, you know, just to be sure.

Even then, it was only the method of her defeat that surprised her. Not that it had come, or probably been assisted, or orchestrated.

She sat down on the forest floor, her back against the trunk. The Hispanic boy hovered over her a few feet away, gun still raised, seemingly unwilling to go.

"Take a picture," Jane said, her voice flat with ice and venom. "It'll last longer."

The boy hesitated, seemingly a little perturbed by the lack of resistance, of reaction. The barrel of the gun, which Jane now recognized as a Tavor TAR-21 from stripping and reassembling them all morning, dipped. Jane stared the pubescent man-child square in his puppy-fat eyes and resolutely didn't blink.

Eventually, the boy sneered.

"I got you," he repeated, and turned a shimmering translucent, phasing back into the ground. Alone, bruised, dripping paint, and shot, Jane rolled her eyes. The talisman she'd been holding inside her—the knowledge that she'd rode out with the Legion, that she'd up and donned armor, that she'd been on a real mission—was beginning to lose its spark. Reality was sinking in. Nobody knew what she'd done, and even if they did, it didn't seem like it mattered. Nobody outside of Giselle and Wally gave her the time of day, and most still actively loathed her. Every day that passed walked that one night of excitement further and further into nothingness—and dragged her closer and closer to the dulling, burrowing misery that loomed ahead.

The ninth of October was coming. There was nothing she could do. And so, Jane just sat and waited in silence in the dying forest light.

The night was dark and the halls were silent, and Jane Walker was alone.

An empty expanse of long, dim-lit room stretched out before her, haunting and still in the moonlight. Five rows of empty auditorium seats ran along the left side, facing the empty expanse and off-cream wall on the right. Junior Acolytes weren't supposed to use the gravity chamber unsupervised—the technology was complicated. But tonight, Jane just needed a place to be hidden, somewhere to push away what was eating her.

It was 2:00 a.m. The rain had stopped, and a white sliver of new moon was poking its head between the clouds. Jane couldn't sleep. Her insides gnawed with a sickly, nervous dread, the feeling of fearful surrealism that lingers a few minutes after waking from a nightmare. She'd tried to shake it, tossed and turned, but to no avail. The fearful energy wouldn't leave. And so, she'd come here, alone in the dark, to try and burn it out.

She approached the clear panel on the wall she'd watched the Ashes adjust a few times and set the gravity to two times norm. With a low whirring hum, Jane felt the machine that was the room start up, and a moment later an invisible weight pressed down upon her shoulders. She fell to the ground in the push-up position.

One. Two. Three . . .

The sound of her increasingly ragged breathing, her creaking joints, and rustling clothes as she pushed against the hardwood floor engulfed her senses. The giant chamber, usually filled with shouts and blasts and the crackle of powers, stood silent, save for her.

Fourteen. Fifteen. Sixteen . . .

She stopped, pushed to standing and broke into a run with only the smallest hesitation. Her bare feet padded quietly up and down the length of the room.

One. Two. Three . . .

It was a strange night. A restless night. A full moon, her grandma would have said, except it wasn't. She hadn't thought about her grandma in years, almost as long as she'd been dead. No room, she guessed, for sentiment.

Fourteen. Fifteen. Sixteen . . .

She was off and running again, the sweat from her forehead dripping into her eyes. This was why she'd come here—everything took more effort, sapped more thought. Her hand touched the far wall. She turned and turned.

One. Two. Three . . .

Jane ran back and forth, sweating hard but breathing steady, the laps blurring together, identical save for the dull ache slowly spreading through her legs and chest. She lost count around thirty, her mind blank and her eyes unfocused, seeing nothing but the unchanging floor.

Fourteen. Fifteen. Six—

A small, sudden noise from somewhere in her periphery snapped her out of her trance. Jane looked up—and immediately skidded to a halt, her red face blanching as white as her singlet.

"Don't let me disturb you," murmured Captain Dawn, his soft voice echoing down the chamber. He was standing at the other end of the room, his golden-gloved hands clasped behind his back, having appeared as if from nowhere who knows how long ago. Time seemed to freeze. The world around Jane narrowed and blurred, everything irrelevant except the white-and-gold figure framed impassively in the doorway. For what seemed like hours—but, in reality, was only a few seconds—she just stood there gawking, unable to hear anything except the erratic pounding of her heart.

"Are you all right?" Dawn asked, mild puzzlement blooming across his handsome face. A rush of panic surged through Jane as reality came crashing back in, and she became suddenly, painfully aware of how stupid she must look, standing with her mouth hanging open like she was trying to catch flies. Her jaw stammered open and shut, struggling to form words, to say any one of the million things that simultaneously seized her as being monumentally important to say, but unfortunately her brain seemed to have turned to mush and everything she could think of got all tangled up together, tripping over her tongue and catching in her throat. Dawn tilted his head slightly to one side, looking at her with an expression of some concern, and Jane resolved to commit ritual suicide at the next available opportunity.

"C-C-Captain!" she finally managed to get out, the word coming up like a hairball. "Wh-wh-what are . . . I mean I'm sorry I-I-I was just . . . I couldn't—" She jerked her hands half toward the door, half toward him in a strangled, manic gesture that she immediately tried to take back partway through, which communicated nothing to anybody. "How long . . . I . . . ah . . ."

"Jane," Captain Dawn said calmly, and Jane felt suddenly faint. He knew her name.

"Y-y-yes, sir?" she stammered.

"Breathe."

Jane drew in a long, shaky breath, feeling her chest expand. She closed her eyes and opened them again.

"Better?" asked the captain.

"Y-y-yes, sir. Th-th-thank you, sir."

They looked at each other, the hero with a small smile on his face, the empath clutching nervously at her arm and wishing she was wearing something other than a ratty singlet. A silence spread throughout the room and Jane wondered if it was awkward, if she was supposed to say something. Captain Dawn seemed in no hurry to speak.

"D-d-do you need . . . want the gravity . . . I mean, the room, Captain, d-d-do you want the room?" she stammered, then added hurriedly "Because if you . . . just say so, I can . . ."

"No thank you," Dawn replied. His eyes had wandered behind her. "Are you training?"

"Yes. I mean no! Not really, I'm not, there's not, like, an exercise, I'm just . . ." She laughed, an unnaturally high almost barking sound. Oh God, what was she doing? Please make it stop. "Uh . . . p-p-push . . . push-ups. Sir. I can't sleep," she added, as if that somehow made it better.

"I see," said the captain, his face deliberately blank. Jane couldn't tell if he was angry. She felt a sudden surge of panic swell up in her guts.

"Sir, I know I'm not supposed to be in here—" she started desperately, but before she could try to explain, Dawn cut her off.

"Why?" he asked. Jane blinked.

"Why, sir?"

"Why are you not allowed here?" He seemed genuinely curious.

"I . . . ah . . ." replied Jane, confused at the direction the conversation was taking and struggling to find a reply. "Because of the, ah, artificial gravity. We aren't supposed to . . ." Her voice trailed off.

"Ah," murmured Captain Dawn, glancing around the empty space as if seeing the weight pressing down around them. Then, without any sound or warning, he began to rise, floating gently up, his arms open, his palms upturned. Jane watched in wonder as he rose above her, detached, the golden waterfall of his cape waving softly in the dim light.

"You're right," he said finally, looking up at the ceiling. "The air is heavy here." Three feet above Jane's head, standing as if supported by some invisible platform, he glanced down at her and smiled. "The wonders of our age."

He floated back down, coming to land not two feet in front of her. Jane felt herself become very, very still.

"Why can't you sleep, little empath?" asked Captain Dawn. There was no hostility in his words, only honey and music. From up close, Jane could drink in every detail of his face—his emerald eyes, his perfect skin, his proud, defined jawline. A face she'd looked up at every night for years, but which was now somehow so different from the poster, so much more amazing in real life.

Jane struggled to form an answer, her cheeks flushing with an uncomfortable heat that had nothing to do with running. "I . . . uh . . . it's . . . just n-n-nerves. It's two days . . . I mean, technically tomorrow, now, is the . . . um . . . you know . . . the Darkest Day." She spoke the last part in a very small voice, averting her eyes.

"Ah," Dawn said softly.

"Not that I'd . . . not that you didn't . . ."

"Of course. A sad day for all of us."

"Yeah," Jane said ineffectually. She stole a glance up at the captain, whose face remained smooth and impassive.

"And this concerns you?" he asked after a moment's silence. "This drives you from your rest?"

"I don't know," she replied—but that wasn't right, and the truth gnawed at her chest. Dawn was watching her, she knew, as if able to see right through her evasion.

"I just . . . it's never a good day for me," she finally confessed.

"For any of us," corrected the captain. Jane blanched, horrified—here she was, talking about the Darkest Day being bad for *her* to Captain Dawn, the man from whom it had taken literally everyone.

"I'm sorry, I didn't . . . of course it would be—"

Dawn raised a hand, silencing her fumbling mid-sentence. "What is lost is lost," he said simply. "Grief cannot bring back the dead."

"I know, sir, I'm so sorry, I can't imagine what—"

"And nor can sympathy," he finished, ignoring Jane's fumbling. "Believe me, I have received enough of both over the years. So please, let neither sadness nor thoughts of the departed keep you from your sleep."

"Yes, sir," said Jane, lowering her gaze.

"There is a time for mourning, and a time for remembrance. This is neither."

"Yes, sir," she repeated. An uncomfortable silence stretched out between them. Jane could feel the man's eyes studying her face.

"Except that's not what's keeping you up, is it?" he asked after a while.

"No, sir," admitted Jane, feeling ashamed.

"Then what is it, young one?"

"People always want to . . ." She sighed, hating herself for voicing this aloud, especially to him. "To . . . I guess . . . get revenge. Around this time."

"Ah," Captain Dawn said quietly, "and they tend to seek you out for this revenge?"

"Yeah."

"And so, you are afraid."

"No," Jane lied, too quickly. On top of everything else, she didn't need Dawn thinking she was a coward. "I'll be fine. It'll be like every year, I'll just wait it out."

"Wait it out."

"Yeah. I won't be any trouble, sir, I promise. I'll stay in my room."

For a few seconds, Captain Dawn was silent, one arm across his chest, one finger pressed to his lips.

"The Academy holds a memorial service at sunrise, every year, on the Darkest Day," he said finally. "Few things are mandatory here, but that is."

Jane blinked. "I know, sir, but it's just . . . I thought that—"

"Why are you here, Jane?" Dawn's voice was soft, but his question was direct.

"I don't—"

"Why are you here?"

She hesitated. "I want to be in the Legion."

"Why?"

The empath fell silent. For what seemed like an eternity she simply stood there, staring at the ground, feeling the captain's gaze pressing down upon her. She knew the answer, of course, as she suspected did he.

"I want to be a hero," she said finally in a small, quiet voice.

"For how long?" Dawn asked simply.

"All my life," Jane admitted, and it felt stupid, foolish, beyond childish to say.

"All your life," the captain repeated, and to Jane's relief there was no mocking in his voice. She looked up to find him looking down, a strange, resolute expression on his face.

"And is hiding in your room, staying out of sight in the hope of not inciting fools to violence—is this what heroes do?" He said it without venom, but the words cut deep.

"No, sir," whispered Jane. She lowered her head, too ashamed to meet his gaze—but to her astonishment, Dawn's hand reached over and gently lifted her chin so that she was staring up into his eyes. The glove's fabric was soft, silken against her skin. All of a sudden, Jane's heartbeat was deafening.

"Do not hide what you are," said Captain Dawn. "Do not be ashamed. Embrace it. Be proud." He dropped his hand but not her gaze. "Heroes do not flee because their presence disquiets the world. Heroes do what needs to be done, because they must." He paused, his green eyes searching.

Jane's insides squirmed, but she couldn't look away. "But I'll offend—"

"Your presence does not offend me," said the captain, cutting over her murmured protests. "And if it does not offend me, then no one else can complain that it offends them. Offense is the problem of the offended. Don't let yourself be cowed by fear of fragile feelings. Walk openly, as is your right. Stand tall among your equals."

"But everyone hates—"

"They hate what they fear," Dawn said simply, his expression resolute, his voice unwavering. "What they cannot be. You are powerful, gifted, and those that are not will always hate you for it."

He turned away from her slightly, his eyes wandering off into nothing. "A hero is someone strong enough to change the world—strong enough to forge a path, to walk unburdened by doubt and the jealousies of those who cannot see beyond their own comfort. The world resents heroes—resents, or reveres," he added, smiling to himself. "But never let that stop you."

"I won't," Jane whispered, and this time Dawn smiled.

"Good girl." He touched her lightly on the cheek; her marked cheek. "You are an Acolyte. Never forget that. Now get some rest." He turned, his golden cape swishing behind him. "And I will see you at tomorrow's ceremony."

"Yes, sir," she said with a smile, but he was already gone, leaving her alone in the dark, weight lifted from her shoulders despite the gravity—the skin on her chin and cheek tingling where he'd touched her, her head hot and her heart hammering for reasons entirely unrelated to any workout.

"And then he said he'd see me tomorrow," Jane gushed. She looked eagerly at Matt, evidentially expecting a reaction, but Matt remained silent, his expression skeptical.

"It happened," said Jane, souring slightly, "I'm not making this up."

"I'm sure you're not," Matt replied with complete sincerity, but nevertheless keeping his real opinions to himself.

They were sitting at breakfast in the Grand Hall late the next morning, on the quieter end of one of the long tables. True to her word, Jane had gone back to bed after her meeting with Captain Dawn, for all the good it had done—she'd been too keyed up to sleep for several hours. But eventually, physical exhaustion had taken its toll, and she'd finally passed out just before sunrise and slept through her morning class. Right now, though, Jane didn't care. There were more important things than classes.

Matt had been surprised to see Jane enter the hall not long after him, and even more surprised when she'd made an enthusiastic beeline right to where he was sitting reading the paper—North Korea was being re-sanctioned, two senators had resigned following corruption charges, and Australia had elected their first invisible prime minister—and proceeded to unload on him the events of last night in a torrent of frothing excitement. To Matt, it was slightly unnerving—he'd never seen Jane this excited about anything. The way she was gushing over the finest details, running her fingers through her hair and almost bouncing in her seat made the empath seem less like her usual battle-hardened self and more like a schoolgirl who'd been front row at an NSYNC concert.

"You don't seem very excited," said Jane, who had no such problem.

"I am excited," lied Matt. "It's very exciting." He took a sip of orange juice and glanced discreetly out of the corner of his eye to check if she was convinced. She wasn't.

"But?" said Jane, crossing her arms.

"But nothing." Matt shrugged, putting down the glass. "I just think you're getting a little worked up over something that's not that big a deal."

"Not a big—not a big deal?!" spluttered Jane incredulously. "It's Captain Dawn!"

"Yeah, exactly, it's Captain Dawn. He lives here, doesn't he? Everyone's probably run into him at some point."

"Have you?" Jane demanded.

"No," Matt conceded.

"Exactly."

"Well, whatever. I'm happy that you're happy."

"Thank you," said Jane, although still somewhat irritably.

They were silent for a minute before Matt couldn't help himself.

"It's a little weird though, don't you think?" he said. "Isn't Captain Dawn meant to be a recluse?"

"Oh, so before seeing him was normal, now it's weird?"

"I'm just saying, guy sounds pretty friendly for a hermit."

"He's not a hermit," Jane hissed, scandalized. "He's in mourning!"

"What? For ten years?"

"You try having all your friends die, see how you feel!" Jane snapped.

"I guess," conceded Matt, perhaps feeling a little bad at his own heartlessness. "I suppose there's no way I can talk you out of going to the Darkest Day service now."

"No way in hell," Jane replied matter-of-factly, spreading strawberry jelly over a piece of toast.

"Even if I said that you being there is probably going to mean some sort of unpleasantness?"

"Nope," reiterated Jane, popping the toast into her mouth. "I said I'd go and I'm going."

"Right," Matt muttered under his breath. "Wouldn't want to disappoint the captain."

"What?"

"Nothing. Have you seen Ed by the way? He was supposed to be down here this morning."

"Nope," answered Jane, unconcerned.

"He's probably in the lab," said Matt, more to himself than anyone. "I should check if he's all right."

"He's fine," Jane assured him, dismissing Matt's concerns with a wave of her hand. "You worry too much."

"Someone has to," Matt muttered. He stood up. "Give me a sec to fill up a plate, I'm going to check he's okay."

"I'll come with you," said Jane, also standing up.

"What about classes?" said Matt, somewhat surprised. They started toward the buffet.

"I've already missed the morning ones. May as well take the day off." She watched as Matt filled a plate with food then fell into step alongside him as they strode back through the hall.

"Right."

"What? I want to be fresh for tomorrow."

"Fresh so that you look good, or fresh so that you're good to go when someone attacks you?"

Jane's only reply was a noncommittal grunt as they passed through the hall doors.

"Well, at least your celebrity crush hasn't completely melted your mind," Matt said ruefully. Jane simply rolled her eyes and started humming.

They arrived at Ed's computer lab to find the door closed and a fluorescent glow emanating from beneath the doorframe, despite it being close to midday. Matt sighed and rapped a knuckle on the wood.

"Ed, we're coming in!" he called. "Be decent!"

With only a quick, despairing glance at Jane, Matt turned the stainless-steel handle and pushed the door open, instantly engulfing the pair of them in a wave of stale air. Matt coughed.

"Jesus Ed, open a window." Over in the far corner, the genius's messy black mop peered out from behind his workstation, adjusting his glasses with one hand. The eyes behind the lenses were bleary.

"Hey," he said—his voice distant, somewhere between a sigh and a moan. "What's up?"

"You said you'd be down for breakfast," Matt reminded him, glancing around at the empty room illuminated by sickly, artificial light. "It's almost eleven."

"Oh," said Ed wearily. His head moved back behind his computer. "Sorry. Lost track of time."

"You don't say," muttered Matt, shaking his head. He strode over to the long window that ran down one length of the room and wrenched open the blinds. Natural light streamed in and Matt's fingers began fiddling with the latch.

"What do you do, just sit in here all day and fart?" asked Jane, wrinkling her nose. She flopped down into a disused office chair, obviously feeling no need to help. Ed, preoccupied with whatever was on the screen in front of him, declined to answer. Matt pulled open the window and a breath of fresh air seeped into the room.

"I brought you some food," he said, picking up the plate from where he'd set it down on a table and moving toward Ed's workstation. The genius grunted his thanks, and Matt took in Ed's disheveled clothes, unkempt hair, and the numerous empty cans of energy drink littering his desk.

"You pulled another all-nighter, didn't you?" asked Matt, already knowing the answer.

"Sleep is for the weak," murmured Ed, not looking up from the screen. His fingers tapped so quickly across the keyboard that the sound could have been mistaken for rain.

"Amen to that." Jane smirked, raising an imaginary glass.

"Don't encourage him," berated Matt.

"Sorry," said Jane, not sorry at all.

"Why were you up?" Ed asked flatly from over in his corner, still fixated on the computer.

"She had a sensuous midnight rendezvous with the leader of our esteemed institution," Matt answered before Jane could say anything.

"Captain Dawn?" Ed asked in disbelief, actually looking up from his screen.

"It wasn't sensuous; I wasn't rendezvousing," growled Jane, glaring daggers at Matt, which he parried with a broad smile. Although she didn't sound too unhappy at the insinuation. "I went for a run and bumped into Captain Dawn. We talked. That's all."

"They're getting married in the spring," added Matt.

"I can hurt you," reminded Jane.

"Who can't?"

"That's odd though," remarked Ed, his dark eyebrows furrowed, apparently oblivious to their back and forth. "Captain Dawn usually avoids people. I've been here three years and I've never seen him wandering the halls once."

"Yeah, I heard he was a recluse," said Matt, leaning on his heels, hands in his pockets.

"You guys are full of it," said Jane, rolling her eyes. "I see him all the time."

"All the time?"

"Well, twice," conceded the empath. "He was walking around that night I was in the infirmary."

Both boys stared at her. "You never told me that," Matt said, surprised and a little hurt.

Jane just shrugged, trying to appear nonchalant. "It's not a big deal. We chatted a little. It was cool. What?" She turned to look at Ed. "Do you think that means something?"

"It's just unusual," replied the genius. He adjusted his glasses and peered at the empath with newfound interest. "Most Acolytes never see him outside of the Darkest Day. Let alone get to talk to him, twice."

"Is that . . . do you think that's bad?" asked Jane, suddenly looking worried.

"Well, no." Ed blinked as Matt watched. "I don't know. Probably the opposite, maybe—by the sound of it, I'd say he's taken a liking to you."

"You think?" said Jane, and it wasn't difficult to hear the excitement in her voice. Matt rolled his eyes so hard the sockets hurt.

"So, what happened, Ed?" he asked, changing the subject. "What could possibly be so important that you'd just leave me hanging?"

"Sorry," muttered the genius. He shot one last curious glance at Jane before swiveling in his chair to face Matt. "I lost track of time."

"You know this isn't good for you, man. You need sleep."

"I know." Ed sighed. He lowered his glasses and pinched the bridge of his nose. "I just get caught up."

"Caught up in what? What're you doing?" Matt leaned over and glanced at the indecipherable jargon littering Ed's screens. "I swear to God if you've been up all night playing *Counterstrike*, I may have to call off this friendship."

"No. It's not, I wasn't, I'm-I'm-I'm," the genius stammered.

"Relax, Ed," said Matt, patting him on the shoulder. "I'm just giving you a hard time." He tilted his head slightly to one side, trying to make sense of the kaleidoscope of colors, code, and numbers that Ed had open on multiple windows. "But seriously, what is this stuff?"

The genius hesitated for a second then glanced at Jane, who was half-listening, half-rocking on her chair.

"It's fine, man, she's cool," Matt assured him. He looked over at the empath. "If Ed tells us what he's working on, you won't go spreading it around, right?"

Jane shrugged. "Who would I even tell?"

"Exactly," said Matt, turning back to the computers. "I'm your friend and she's got no friends, you can trust us."

Ed seemed to wrestle internally for a second or two before sighing. "All right," he conceded. "Fine. It's one of my major projects." He paused, then gave both of them meaningful looks. "I'm mapping the human genome."

Across the room, Jane made a face. "Didn't they do that already?" she asked insensitively. "What?" she added defiantly as Matt shot her a furtive "shut up" glance.

Ed brushed off the implied insult. "No," he answered with a patient smile—the kind an adult might have when explaining something basic to a child. "They've mapped the superhuman genome—at least a few of them."

"A few of them?" remarked Matt.

"We're all different—each power configuration is supported by a different genetic structure. But that's peasant stuff—point and click, rote learning." Ed's voice was gaining momentum, growing more excited as he carried on. Matt couldn't help wondering if they were the first people he'd spoken about this to out loud. "Any college lab can map a superhuman genome, given enough time. Why couldn't they, it's just note taking, the sequence is right there."

"So, what're you doing then," asked Matt, "if you're not doing that?"

"I told you," replied Ed, turning and smiling up at him. "I'm mapping the human genome."

A sudden, icy pit punched into Matt's stomach. "The what?"

"The human genome. The pre-superhumanism layout of DNA." He looked over at Jane, who had her head cocked and her eyes narrowed. "See, before the Aurora genetics as a field hadn't really taken off, at least not in terms of gene mapping. We were getting there—no disrespect to the old-world scientists—but it hadn't happened. And then after the Aurora hit, sure, we've come leaps and bounds—but everyone's superhuman. Now all our genes are different, all hodge-podges of unrelated code. Even as babies. Did you know that?" he added enthusiastically, all tiredness forgotten. "Even years before someone's powers manifest, technically you can tell what they're going to be just from looking at their genes." He scoffed, more to himself than anyone else. "Of course, at this stage it'd take years and cost millions, so why would you bother, but still"—Ed's eyes gleamed—"it's possible."

"But," he continued, unfazed by Matt and Jane's stunned silence, "here's the thing. We're all superhuman. A hundred percent. There's literally not a single scrap of original recipe human left on the planet. It's all lost to history, mutated by the Aurora before we could get a proper look. So that's it." He shot significant glances at both of them. "That's what I'm trying to figure out."

"What are you trying to figure out?" asked Jane, still a little lost.

"The human genome," repeated Ed, more excited than impatient at having to repeat himself. "See, I figure, the Aurora modified all our DNA into these crazy new structures, right? All these wildly different genetic codes? I mean, it defies science that our species can still procreate. Reproduction shouldn't work!"

"So that's your excuse," needled Matt, throwing up a smile he didn't feel.

"Shut up," scowled Ed. "Where was I? Oh yeah, the Aurora. The Aurora heavily changed our DNA—but it changed it *from* something, right? It took the colors and it spun them, but the picture we're getting now is still rooted in that first configuration."

"You're saying we're all human, deep down inside?" asked Jane, looking skeptical.

Ed turned to her. "I'm saying parts of us are. We all look the same, talk the same, walk the same. The building blocks are still there. And if we can identify those base codes, put them together . . ."

"We'd have the DNA of a normal human," murmured Matt. He understood what Ed was trying to do—and he found the staggering coincidence deeply, deeply uncomfortable, especially in light of recent events. *Stay hidden*, the boy's words whispered. Unbeknownst to Ed, the answer to the problem that had him working through the night was standing not three feet away, trapped in Matt's spit, blood, and follicles.

"How're you doing it?" Jane queried before Matt could say anything. She was looking at the genius with a sort of newfound respect—but her eyes flicked to Matt's in a way that told him she'd made the same dangerous connection he had.

Ed shrugged, oblivious to the meaningful look that had passed between Matt and Jane. "Well, I'm looking at various superhuman gene sequences," he said, rotating the computer screen so they could both see his windows of colors and code, "trying to find the common ground. It's not easy—a lot of trial and error, a lot of balls in the air, definitely genius work." He paused and looked back at them. "It's like having a whole gallery full of paintings and examining all of them to try and figure out what a plain white canvas looked like. It's time-consuming—frustrating too. You find yourself wishing someone had just kept a blank canvas around, instead of painting on all of them."

"Yeah," Jane agreed with a slightly nervous laugh.

"But why?" asked Matt. The cold feeling in his guts had not abated and it took considerable effort to keep his voice level. "I mean, why go to all the trouble? What's the point?"

Ed blinked, looking a little taken aback. "Science is the point. Discovery. Furthering mankind's understanding of the universe. What greater purpose is there?"

"So . . . there's no practical application?" said Matt, trying not to sound relieved. But before his icy dread could dissipate, Ed shook his head.

"I never said that," responded the genius. "There're loads of practical applications, if I crack it. No, not if"—he looked back at the screens in front of him, suddenly sounding confident—"when. *When* I crack it, there could be loads of potential applications."

"Like?" Matt asked, apprehensively.

"Well, permanent neutralization comes to mind."

"Excuse me?" said Jane, incredulous.

"Permanent neutralization. An anti-powers vaccine—something that strips someone of their abilities."

"Pretty sure that's against the Second Amendment," Matt said with a scowl. Ed waved him away.

"The Founding Fathers wrote the Second Amendment about muskets, not mind control," he dismissed.

"The Supreme Court disagreed. Powers are an inalienable right."

"It's true," piped up Jane, through a mouthful of toast. She'd started helping herself to Ed's untouched food.

"Only because we have no way of permanently alienating them," Ed retorted, "but we could. If I get this."

Matt couldn't believe what he was hearing. "You say that like being able to take away people's powers is a good thing!"

"Isn't it?" mused the genius. He offered up a pacifying hand at the look on Matt's face. "Think about how many people have to get the death penalty because we don't have the facilities to hold them."

"How many criminals, you mean," replied Matt. "And it's less each year."

"Still," said Ed, undeterred. "What if there was another way? A better way?"

"A way to strip someone of their fundamental rights?"

"More than killing them?"

"Criminals make their choice," said Matt, shaking his head. "They choose to commit serious crimes, the worst of the worst, despite all the systems we've got in place to help them. Telepaths make a hundred percent sure that someone is beyond saving before we resort to the needle."

"So they say," scoffed Ed, but Matt ignored him.

"But if you start throwing around an anti-powers vaccine, it's not just criminals who are going to get it. How long before governments start using it to control people? How long before the old imbalances return?"

"How would mapping the human genome even help?" asked Jane, who up until now had been watching the debate in deliberative silence. "I mean cool, you know what human DNA looked like. Whoop-de-doo. How does that change anything?"

"It's purely speculative," answered Ed, who was still glancing at the anger on Matt's face with some degree of confusion. "But in theory, if you could synthesize a replica of empathic binding—the process by which a blood-based empath absorbs and replicates new DNA at a genetic level—you could rewrite someone's entire genetic code and replace it with a human DNA sequence."

To both Matt and Ed's surprise, Jane laughed. "Yeah, that won't work," she stated, chuckling.

Ed appeared rankled. "What do you mean?" he said, slightly irritably. "Why not?"

"Hello?" Jane laughed. "Hynes and Calford? I thought you were meant to be a genius."

"I don't get it," said Matt, who genuinely didn't, glancing from one to the other. "What's Hynes and Calford?"

Jane turned to him, smiling and ever so slightly rolling her eyes. "Hynes and Calford were a pair of scientists who had the same bright idea Ed had a few years ago—mimic empathic absorption and use it to Velcro new traits onto criminals. Except they didn't use human DNA, they used neutralizer." She shook her head. "They thought it would be like having a little neutralizer running around the criminal's bloodstream stopping them using their powers, but all it did was give them cancer."

Matt stared at her, taken aback, unused to Jane knowing more about science than he did. "How do you know all this?"

Jane shrugged. "Just empath stuff. Keep my ear to the ground."

"Their formula was flawed," muttered Ed, arms crossed and defiant, "and their reasoning unsound."

"How so?" scoffed Jane, turning back to face him, seemingly unconcerned about going toe-to-toe in a scientific argument with a genius.

"They tried to put one power on top of another," Ed explained, adjusting his glasses. "And hoped the second would make the first go away. It's stupid, like trying to zero an equation by throwing in a random number and being surprised when it doesn't disappear."

"But adding in human DNA would be different?"

"Yes. Because instead of trying to remove a person's ability by counterbalancing it, you'd be negating their superhumanism all together."

"In English, please."

"Human DNA is the baseline for all of us," explained Ed, with only a trace of impatience. "It's zero. If you fold it into a superhuman genetic structure, it doesn't matter what that person is or does—the end result would be the same. It's multiplying by zero. Big number, small, doesn't matter—multiply by zero and you get nothing."

He paused. "Although," he admitted, "that's just the theory. I haven't even figured out human DNA yet. I could be completely off."

"I still think mimicking empathic absorption is a pipe dream," Jane said with a shake of her head. "Nobody's come up with a way to replicate any powers yet, let alone empathy. The technology's way off."

"Well, then, I guess that's the next step after this one."

"I still think it's a bad idea," Matt muttered. Ed turned to him.

"Think about the Black Death," said the genius. "Think about what he was able to do because we didn't have anyone who could stop him."

"Captain Dawn stopped him," interjected Jane, almost as a reflex.

"Yes, Captain Dawn stopped the Black Death," Ed said impatiently. "But not before the world was almost destroyed. Imagine if we'd had something like this back then! Imagine the lives we could've saved."

"The Black Death is dead," Jane said flatly. Ed just shook his head.

"And there'll never be anyone else like him? Never be someone who gets powerful and goes crazy? It's only a matter of time. We need to be prepared."

Ed turned back to his computer and his windows full of unsequenced genes.

"It's not enough to remember the Darkest Day," he said quietly, "not enough to remember those who died, to honor their memories. We have to learn from what happened, or they all died for nothing. We need to be ready. We need to make sure nothing like that ever happens again."

"They shall not grow old, as we that are left grow old."

Winters's electronically amplified words echoed out over the frosty moor—over row upon row of somber, silent figures, a regimented sea of black.

"Age shall not weary them, nor the years condemn."

The morning was cold, washed with the low, gray light of a sun not yet risen. A weak fog trickled through the grass, licking at the ankles of the assembled but held back by the heat of hundreds of bodies. There was no rain today. The sky stood blue and open, completely cloudless— though whether the result of good fortune or a weather-controller, Matt couldn't say.

"When the first light breaks the darkness, and in the twilight."

The rows were arranged in order of importance, with relatives, dignitaries, and the Ashes at the front, and then senior Acolytes behind them. Matt's place was in the very back. He had to crane his neck in order to catch a glimpse of the proceedings.

"We will remember them."

"WE WILL REMEMBER THEM."

The black-clad crowd echoed Winters's words, and from its head the man bowed his own in silence. To Winters's left, a long-nosed woman Matt recognized as the state's governor stood in equally somber colors and contemplation; to his right stood Captain Dawn, golden gloves clasped in front of him, golden cape brushing lightly on the ground, the only one not wearing black. Even from this distance, seeing him for the first time Matt understood Jane's infatuation. Stone-faced and silent, broader and taller than Winters by half, the captain was every inch the figure of a hero—a legend given life, a god in mortal form. Even without moving or speaking, power and authority seemed to radiate from him in waves. Although Winters led the service, not a single eye ever wavered far from Dawn.

"Evil," uttered Winters, no longer from verse, "does not discriminate. It does not hesitate. It does not waver at the pain it causes, the life it takes. It would inflict every loss upon the world so that it would be advanced a single step."

He was speaking from atop a small wooden platform, erected no more than a foot high in front of the memorial so as not to obscure the monument behind. An imposing slab of black granite some twenty feet tall, the memorial loomed over the assembled crowd, a somber backdrop to the service, the etched names of the Legion's lost inscribed over it in white, twisting lines, creeping vines of honored dead. Those who were meant to be there, those connected to the Legion past or present, stood in stiffly regimented rows before the stage, silent and respectful; but around this black formation floated a swarm of media delegations, abuzz with the clicks and whirr of cameras.

"Let us never forget that loss," proclaimed Winters, gazing out over the crowd. Down near the front, Matt could see the gigantic figure of James Conrad nodding, his head a full foot above anyone else's. "Let us never forget those who fought; those who fell; and those hundreds of millions of innocents who needlessly, senselessly died."

Matt turned his head discreetly to his left, glancing down the row at Jane, standing in the very backmost corner. Like many others, her eyes were closed, her head bowed—the black she was wearing a perfect match with her E. Somehow, they'd become separated in the service's assembling, but luckily the Acolytes around her seemed to be simply ignoring the empath's presence. Thankfully too, her position in the left rear corner of the service meant her tattoo faced inward, rather than outward to where the media's hungry cameras swept over everything going on.

"Ten years ago today . . ." Winters spoke as the lenses flashed and the crowd stood silent. "Humanity faced its Darkest Day. Evil drove us to the brink, and only the greatest good, in all of us"—he motioned to the immobile figure of Captain Dawn—"spared us from oblivion. What was lost that day can never be returned, can never be replaced—and must never be forgotten. It is up to all of us, every day, to remember. Humanity endures. The Legion endures. Our memories, our legacy, our good, endures."

"Lest we forget."

"LEST WE FORGET."

"Lest we forget," murmured Matt.

They stood for several more minutes as Winters respectfully stood aside and allowed the podium to be taken up by the governor, who iterated her own speech of memorial and condolences along much the same lines. Despite trying his hardest to listen, Matt found himself shooting discreet, nervous glances at Jane—checking, he supposed, that she was still all right, although God only knew what he was supposed to do if she wasn't. Thankfully, few people seemed to even realize she was there.

The governor's speech ended to polite silence. There was a glance, on her behalf and from Winters, at the statue-like figure of Captain Dawn. Dawn, however, remained unmoving, his hands clasped and his head bowed, a silent statue of gold and white shadowed by a black monolith bearing the names of his fallen friends. After a few seconds, Winters took the hint.

"Stand with us now, in five minutes of silence."

The first rays of sunlight peaked over the hills.

"Well, that was fairly painless," said Matt. The second the service had ended, he'd wormed his way through the dispersing crowd to her side, and the two of them had started briskly back toward the mansion. Jane merely nodded, unable to reply. There was a cold around her eyes and a tightness in her chest that prevented all words from coming out, which she wanted to keep Matt unaware of. Luckily, he seemed pretty oblivious, his head straining left and right surveying the surrounding people.

"Goddamn vultures," he swore, glancing over his shoulder at one of the camera crews pointed at the stage. A preened blonde woman in a newsreader blouse now stood in front of it with a microphone, no doubt relaying a live update back to audiences at home. "I didn't realize there was going to be so much press."

"Ten years," murmured Jane, finding her voice and keeping it level. "Significant anniversary." She agreed with his sentiment though.

"Poor Captain Dawn," said Matt. Despite force-marching them both across the grounds, there was genuine sympathy in his voice. "Trying to mourn while there's a hundred cameras flashing in your face." He looked behind them at the memorial. Unbidden, Jane followed his gaze. A herd of a dozen or so reporters had started clambering toward the front of the service, flocking toward the solitary figure of Captain Dawn, unmoved from beside the podium. Even from far away, it was obvious that they were scrambling for an interview, or at least a better shot of the grieving hero.

"No wonder he shuts himself away," murmured Matt, and Jane nodded in silent agreement. He shook his head in disgust. "Come on, let's get out of here before they get bored."

He took her by the arm and started leading her away, and uncharacteristically, Jane didn't resist. She was still preoccupied, looking over her shoulder at Captain Dawn, all alone on the stage. After a second, Dawn slowly glanced up, and to Jane's shock and amazement, even though they were almost back at the mansion, the hero somehow seemed to see her, staring back at him across the field. A small, sad, knowing smile crossed his face—nothing more than a greeting, a tiny token of acknowledgment, understanding, and maybe thanks—and Jane's heart leaped. The empath blinked and the moment was gone, the hero looked away—but she knew. He'd looked at her. Her specifically, not around, not just at anyone—her. Just her. She'd seen it.

But she wasn't the only one.

Fixated on his every move, analyzing the slightest change, the reporters and their television crews couldn't help but notice, not so much following as pouncing the moment Dawn's gaze moved. Their own eyes followed and an instant later their cameras swung, a dozen lenses twisting in to focus on her fleeting face and fleeing form.

Matt didn't see. He was still turned, his back to the ceremony, still determined to retreat unnoticed—but Jane knew. It was too late. They'd seen her.

The world knew there was an empath at the Academy.

THANKS

IN THEIR MIDST
LEGION OF HEROES DARKEST DAY TENTH ANNIVERSARY SERVICE
REVEALS SHOCKING SECRET
Salon.com, October 10, 2000
[8,921,120 views, 25,012 shares]

It was supposed to be a day of mourning, solidarity, and—most of all—remembrance. But explosive new photos taken at the Legion of Heroes memorial service for the victims of the African Devastation have uncovered a shocking secret Legion administrators have attempted to keep quiet.

>>Read More: Why the African Devastation Was Racially Motivated and What That Says about White America

Exclusive pictures from the service, intended to mark ten years since the empath dubbed the Black Death killed hundreds of millions of people, captured in attendance another empath who investigation has revealed has joined the Academy as part of the Legion of Heroes' rebuilding program. Head of Legion administration Daniel Winters has confirmed that the empath, Jane Walker, was allowed into the institution over two months ago after "demonstrating outstanding combat ability and offensive potential."

>>Read More: Ten Tips For Spotting Unregistered Empaths Near You

The Legion of Heroes has declined to comment on the security risk posed by the empath, or whether they believe she possesses a conflict of interest with the Legion's peacekeeping goals. Under antidiscrimination legislation, organizations are not allowed to exclude individuals, including empaths, from entry based solely upon their powers if a particular power is not a pre-requisite for membership, meaning the Legion of Heroes could have faced a lawsuit if they had not allowed Walker to attend.

>>Read More: Dawn's Dismay—Pictures of Our Hero Reacting to the Empath's Presence

Should Empaths Be Allowed in the Legion of Heroes?

Vote and comment below
Mini-Poll
[] Yes (0.81%)
[] No (99.19%)

Comments

Jackie Willcox 3h
Were is the goverment? Surly must be someone in power who can do some-thing abut this. As a mother I know for a fact that this empath is up to no good, you can see it in her eye she is only their to steel powers and their she will steel them all. This is disgrace I do not feel safe my children knowning that Legion of heros is not save anymore. Captain Dawn you must be strong and destroy empath threat as you did ago ten years ago so world can know piece . . . THANK YOU.
4,217 Likes
6 Dislikes
View all 72 replies

ImmunisEVIL
+Jackie Willcox Well said her here
984 Likes
22 Dislikes
View all 34 replies

SenseiChingaNaruto 5h
Empath do not respect Human Rights or Democracy and must be banned in civilized countrie
3,002 Likes
4 Dislikes
View all 80 replies

TheLastDefender 4h
Empaths Are Scum Of The Earth It Makes Me Sick Thinking She Is There Spitting On The Graves Of Everyone Who Gave Their Lives For The Cause If We Do Not Act Now This Will Be The New Normal Empaths Everywhere In Charge We The People At The Bottom Look It Up Open Your Eyes Sheep To The Truth
http://onegovtruth.org/africaconspiracy
1,612 Likes
101 Dislikes
View all 179 replies

Racquel Poison 59m
how can he tuch her dirtie filfth she probally got him in brain contrul
1,100 Likes
23 Dislikes
View all 150 replies

Xxgriffdog420xX 2h
Probably there 4 Cap Dawns power LOL gg earth screwd nice nowing all u fgts hope u lyk b slav empath dog illuminati y2k
2,010 Likes
5 Dislikes
View all 99 replies

Jeff Jones 6h
Once again woman given special privileges over man, only let in because she is woman, women rule while men drafted to wars, we are firefighters and coal miners, we get screwed w divorce, pay for wives personal needs and kids tuition, depression and suicide bc of this, domestic abuse is ignored when men are victims and men cant strike back, prostate cancer is ignored,

1 in 8 women get breast cancer and 1 in 7 men get prostate cancer but breast cancer is looked on more, 70% of the homeless are men bc women can just marry a men
103 Likes
567 Dislikes
View all 237 replies

Walter Knight
+Jeff Jones Shut up MRA nobody asked you go back to ur whole
512 Likes
47 Dislikes
View all 102 replies

MadMan87
+Jeff Jones LOL well done nice work FEM-ocrats girl power 4ever screw society amirite?
98 Likes
312 Dislikes
View all 37 replies

Anonimouse 10m
Empath, if you're reading this, do the world a favor and kill yourself
400 Likes
0 Dislikes
View all 5 replies

"We're trying to control the situation," said Winters. He sat with his hands folded neatly together on the desk, his face and suit framed by the black leather of his executive chair. "But I'm not going to lie, there's a lot of anger. In the last twenty-four hours, Morningstar Academy has received a lot of very . . . concerned correspondence."

Jane said nothing. She'd said nothing the entire time she'd been in Winters's office, her face set and her arms crossed. The empath had sat through enough of these conversations to recognize that her input was not required.

Winters's gray-blue eyes examined her. "You've hardly had a trouble-free time here. And with your record . . ." He trailed off, as if waiting for

Jane to supply a defense or explanation. When none came, he broke off his gaze.

"But then again," he continued, debating more with himself than her, "your comportment during recent . . . field exercises was nothing but satisfactory. And your other incidents, well, they could hardly be said to be outside the ambit of normal Academy activities. And events prior to your attendance, well, they're less relevant . . ."

"Am I getting expelled?" interrupted Jane, already knowing the answer and getting sick of Winters's rambling. She wasn't, obviously— even if Winters or anyone else wanted her gone, Captain Dawn wanted her here and his word was gospel. The administrator frowned.

"It's Academy policy never to expel anyone unless they've engaged in criminal conduct," he said.

"And have I?" she demanded.

"No," Winters conceded, although it didn't sound like much of a concession. "And I'm glad you haven't, because expelling you now would benefit no one."

Jane narrowed her eyes, suspicious at the finely groomed man seemingly being on her side.

"The Legion harboring an empath is bad publicity," explained Winters, rolling a pen between his fingers. "The Legion harboring an empath who then gets expelled is worse. Not only are we made to look fallible, but it then looks like you, in addition to having come here and learned our secrets, have become too much to handle and gone 'rogue.'" He used his fingers to put the last word in quotes. "To the man on the street, that's practically a template for supervillainy."

"Why is this even happening?" complained Jane, ignoring the supervillain remark. "You offered for me to come here in the middle of a public school. What, nobody told their parents? No media managed to find out about that?"

Winters fixed her with a blank expression and clearly barely restrained from rolling his eyes.

"There's the media," he stated curtly, "and the *media*. The first are professionals with whom an institution like the Legion can share a mutually beneficial understanding. The other are money-grubbing sensationalists who would sell out their own mothers if it would help boost views. You, Miss Walker, have drawn the attention of the latter."

Winters paused and pursed his fingers together in front of his lips, his pale eyes contemplating her.

"I want you," he said finally, lowering his hands, "to be aware of the . . . delicacies of this situation. The Legion enjoys a privileged place in the court of public opinion—a position we'd like to maintain. Right now, the world thinks you've managed to trick us into taking you"—Jane bristled at the accusation, but Winters raised a pacifying palm—"which you haven't, but which undermines our reputation, nonetheless. Our end goal is to develop you into an obvious asset, which removes the doubt from our credibility and reinforces our foresight." He paused, then said, in a somewhat conciliatory tone, "You handled yourself well in Albania. All we want is more of that."

Jane strained for a few moments. "So . . . what? Work hard?" she eventually replied, mentally sifting for meaning through the managerial jargon.

"And keep your head down," concluded Winters. "The quickest way this story dies is if we give it nothing to work with. All scandals are old news in two weeks."

He glanced idly down at a stack of papers arranged neatly on his desk. "The Academy will break for Thanksgiving in just under two weeks, as is our tradition, and—"

"Why?" Jane interjected. "Why is it tradition?" Winters looked annoyed at the interruption.

"Captain Dawn's late wife, Caitlin, considered it important," he explained impatiently. "She felt that it was nondenominational enough of a holiday not to alienate the Legion's many international members. She also just generally liked the idea, and any idea she liked Captain Dawn tended to like too. But the 'why' is less relevant"—he added, looking across the desk—"than the fact that no classes will be held for that period, providing all Acolytes with several days of free time."

"I don't get it," said Jane.

"Then listen," Winters replied curtly. "And if you stop interrupting, I'll explain." He clasped his well-manicured hands in front of his chin. "So-called 'photojournalists' have taken up residence outside the grounds—expecting to catch a glimpse of you, presumably, but nevertheless a nuisance for all of us. Captain Dawn has personally expressed his displeasure at their presence, and I have, on his behalf, conveyed to the major media outlets that anyone found violating Legion land or airspace forfeits their safety." He smiled wryly. "Not that they'll all listen, but it should give the Acolytes new targets for stress relief."

He raised a finger in warning. "Nevertheless, stay out of sight. The last thing we need is some new photograph of you from which the tabloids can run wild."

"They're trying to take photos of me?" balked Jane, appalled at this fresh hell. "Why? What do they expect me to do?"

"It doesn't matter what they expect," explained Winters with only a trace of impatience. "And what you actually do will change nothing. Any picture they get will tell a thousand words, and those thousand words will be written by a sensationalist who would claim that cows were cockroaches if they thought it would boost circulation."

"As most Academy activities are held away from the public eye," he continued. "I'm not overly concerned about your photographic safety during training. However, during the Thanksgiving break, I suggest you utilize your free time in an exclusively private capacity. For the remainder of this month, I want you unseen."

"That might be a problem," Jane replied dryly. "Considering I may occasionally need to step outside."

"Cover yourself up."

"I thought you said you didn't want me committing crimes," derided Jane. "Concealing my mark is illegal."

"That it is," remarked Winters, staring at her intently through narrowed eyes. "However, as a pyromancer, it is an essential skill that you be able to engulf yourself in flames. Should you choose to practice this skill in an informal setting, say, on your way between classes, the fact that it may—heaven forbid—obscure your identity could only ever be seen as unintentional and in the context, permissible, being incidental to your education." He paused. "Am I clear?"

"Nobody can see who you are if you're on fire and it's not your fault if Teacher told you to."

"More or less."

"Fine." She rose to leave. "Anything else?"

"One more thing," said Winters. He paused and leaned back in his chair. "Captain Dawn has asked me to pass a message on to you personally."

Jane's heart leaped at the unexpected news. "What?" she asked, throat suddenly constricted.

"He requests your presence at, quote, 'the same place as last time, midnight, Thursday after Thanksgiving,' " the administrator repeated. He folded his arms and looked at her with unspoken skepticism. For her part, Jane's mind was already racing in a dozen different directions, enthralled at the possibilities.

"Wh-wh-what . . ." she stammered, aware of the administrator's piercing gaze and trying to sound unconcerned. "What did he . . . did he say why?"

"No," said Winters, his mouth pursed slightly, "but from what I could gather from our brief conversation, I believe he wants to train you."

Jane's pulse was so loud she swore half the mansion could hear it. "Me?"

"Yes, you," said Winters, and even through her excitement Jane could hear the trepidation and displeasure in his voice. "And no, before you ask, I don't know why."

Jane didn't either but she didn't care. It took every ounce of her restraint not to run skipping from the room. "Is that all, sir?"

"For now," he said. Jane turned to leave, a giddy smile almost hurting her face, but before she could reach the door Winters's voice rang out. "Miss Walker."

Jane turned around. "Yes, sir?"

Winters stared at her impassively, leaning back in his chair, cool and composed. "If you even so much as think of trying to take his powers, I will kill you myself," he stated calmly, in the same tone one would use to discuss the weather. Jane recoiled, feeling like she'd been doused with ice water, but Winters did not meet her stunned gaze.

"That is all," he dismissed, before she could even open her mouth to reply, having already leaned forward and returned pen to paperwork.

"I always wanted a nice camera," crooned Giselle, holding up the brand-new, jet-black, top-of-the-line Canon in the light of the hall. "It's so pretty. I wonder how fast it can take photos."

"Probably not as fast as you can press the button," wagered Wally from the bench beside her, through a mouthful of sausage. "Careful running with it, you're liable to crack the lens."

"Duh." The speedster laughed. "I'm not stupid. It's the same as a phone."

"Though substantially cheaper," said Matt, and the entire table laughed.

Word that the paparazzi lurking around Morningstar's grounds were fair game had come down from Ashes administration almost as soon as word had got out that there were paparazzi lurking around the grounds to begin with. So far, Giselle was leading the scoreboard with a tally of six cameras, although Ryan Mitchell and his invisibility was a close second. Between spoons of mashed potatoes, Matt was in the middle of setting up an illegal betting pool.

"Winners on the same pick split the winnings," he explained to Odette Dodecan, who nodded her understanding and made a hasty fluttering of gestures with her hands. Matt gazed at the sign language blankly. "Ed?"

"She signed 'When do you decide the winner?' " answered the stubble-ridden genius beside him, not looking up from the book he was pretending to read while in fact covertly eyeing Giselle.

"Thanks. Sorry," Matt turned back to Odette, smiling apologetically. "My cousin's got hypervoice, you'd think my ASL would be better." The cute Greek girl just smiled and shook her head as if to tell him it was okay. "Pot matures once we go a whole week with no one finding any more paparazzi, first-second-third goes sixty-twenty-ten. You want in?"

Odette nodded emphatically and pressed Matt sixty dollars, pointing over the table at the dark shape of a familiar gigantic figure.

"James Conrad?" Matt let out a low whistle and wrote Odette's wager in his notepad. "Popular bet tonight, popular bet. Well, best of luck to you."

"Just because he made a ruckus," Ed grumbled to no one in particular. "Ruckus" was apparently the genius's preferred term for identifying a group of four photographers nested together in a patch of dense woodland and promptly charging through said woodland, scattering the unfortunate freelancers and the trees around them like a bowling ball through tenpins. Matt for one found it hilarious and enjoyed seeing the path of arboreal devastation now visible from the Grand Hall and listening to James's laughter as he pulled pen-sized splinters from his shoulders. Ed seemed to take a dimmer view.

"He could've hurt someone," the genius muttered sourly.

"Ed, relax, they're paparazzi, not people," replied Matt, feeling the satisfying weight of cash money in his pocket as Odette shuffled back down the benches toward her regular group of friends. Ed looked at him.

"Isn't this a little unfair?" he commented, indicating Matt's betting book. "You already know who's going to win."

"No, I don't," Matt replied honestly, then added less honestly. "My visions are vague. Big-ticket items. This is just little stuff. Harmless fun." When Ed didn't look particularly convinced, he raised his hands in mock defense. "And anyway, I'm not betting. I'm simply the facilitator. Impartial and unbiased."

"So, no hot tips then?" Ed half-joked.

"Shame on you," Matt chided him. "I cannot believe you would seek to corrupt my impeccable morality. Now are you going to use that big brain of yours to get in on this sweet, sweet action, or are you too smart to gamble?"

Ed hesitated, then reached into his pocket.

"That's the spirit," Matt said, smiling.

"Twenty on Giselle," the genius bet, quietly sliding the note along the bench.

"Putting your money where you'd like your mouth to be I see," Matt teased, low enough so as not to be heard among the noise of the hall but nevertheless causing Ed's face to turn a delightful shade of pink. He was saved the embarrassment of having to respond by Jane's arrival, which as usual triggered the customary recoiling and whispers from everyone nearby with whom she wasn't on first-name terms.

"Ah, the celebrity in our midst," he said with a smile, ignoring the muttering. "The patron of my industry." He nodded significantly down at the betting book. "Care to place your own wager?"

"No," Jane replied. She began helping herself to the dinner rolls on his plate.

"No, please, go right ahead, I didn't even want those," said Matt. Jane just grunted, her mouth already full of bread. "You sure you don't want to make a bet?"

"I said no," she snapped.

"All right, all right," said Matt, holding up his hands, trying to be placating. "What's going on? You seem more irritable than usual."

Jane swallowed a lump of bread. "Winters won't let me go outside unless I'm on fire," she complained, her face taunt and grumpy, before tearing at a fresh roll with her teeth.

"Well, see, that's not so bad, you're a pyromancer. If he told me that, I'd find it significantly more concerning."

"And I can't go outside during Thanksgiving weekend," she continued, ignoring his feeble attempt at humor.

"Why?"

"No classes during Thanksgiving," Ed answered, chiming in. "I'd guess he wants to keep her away from the paparazzi."

"You're not going home?" Matt asked, genuinely shocked. "How're you not going home?" When Jane only shrugged, he shook his head in disbelief. "Man, what the hell. My mom would murder me if I missed Turkey Day." He paused, waiting for a response, but none came, so he added, "Plus, you know, free food."

"All the food you eat is free," said Ed, squinting at him.

"Shush," shushed Matt.

"Thanksgiving isn't big in my family," Jane said, staring straight ahead.

"But you still do, like, dinner and stuff, right?" Matt asked her.

"Nope," grunted Jane, still just blank-faced and eating bun. "Never."

"Never, never?"

Jane shrugged. "Maybe once. A long time ago. I can't remember."

Matt shook his head, appalled—and then was suddenly struck by an idea.

"Come to mine!"

This actually made Jane break out of her thousand-yard stare and look at him, albeit as if he was insane. "What?"

"Yeah, come to mine. Spend Thanksgiving with my family!"

"I—" she started. Matt could already see the reflex rejection forming in her mouth, so he interrupted before she could get it out.

"Come on, I insist. You, your dad, your—" He paused, suddenly perplexed. "Wait, do you have siblings? You've never mentioned any."

"No," replied Jane, off-balance. "But I don't think—"

"Come on then, it'll be fun! Won't even be any extra cooking."

"No, but, I-I-I," Jane stammered. "I couldn't . . . no . . . I mean . . ."

"What?" said Matt, mildly reveling in her discomfort. "What possible excuse could you have? You already said you've got nothing to do for a few days. And there'll be no paparazzi at my house. Come on, what's the harm? Have a meal, get out of Morningstar, come meet my family, see where it all went wrong."

"Well, I don't . . . your parents might not . . . uncomfortable . . . empath."

"They already know I'm hanging out with an empath," Matt dismissed with a wave. "They're fine with it." *Fine-ish*, he added mentally.

"I . . ." Jane's voice trailed off, leaving behind only a pained expression. For a few seconds, she just sat in exasperated silence, eyeing Matt's unrelenting smile. Then she held her face in her hands. "If I say no," she despaired, "you're just going to harass me about this all month, aren't you?"

"Yup," Matt replied sunnily.

"Fine," groaned Jane. She pinched the bridge of her nose. "I'll go. But I swear to God, I'm not wearing any goddamn pilgrim's hat."

"Pilgrim's hat . . . ?" Matt murmured, glancing sideways at Ed. The genius just shook his head. "What do you think people do on . . . You know what, never mind." He turned to Ed. "You'd be welcome too."

"Appreciate the offer," replied the genius. "But I'm going to stay here, try and hammer out a few projects."

"What about your family?"

"Dad's in Dubai on business and Mom's on a cruise. We'll conference call."

"All right," said Matt, sounding skeptical. "But don't just stay locked in your lab for four days."

"No promises."

"I'm serious, man, you need fresh air occasionally. Sunlight. I'd hate to think what your vitamin D levels are."

"I take a supplement," Ed replied, already turned back to his book.

As October advanced, the first signs of snow began appearing around Morningstar's grounds, dusting the grass with frost and lending the trees the appearance of having been dipped in powdered sugar. Biting winds blown in from between the mountains howled and snapped at the Acolytes' exposed skin as they moved between classes, and there was an outbreak of thick parkas among the students—with the exception of Celeste, who forwent any protective clothing and instead waddled around as a variety of bears and the occasional caribou. Reluctantly, the cold turn found Matt scaling back his hiking and bird-watching activities, as even rugged up he'd often return to Morningstar to find a previously undiscovered cut or gash, probably inflicted by a stray stick, bleeding along one of his numbed and clumsy limbs. Not that there were many birds out anyway—the few that hadn't fled the snows seemed to have been scared away by the swarms of shutterbugs infecting the surrounding countryside.

In the weeks following the Darkest Day service, the plague of paparazzi stalking Legion land had not abated nor shown any signs of letting up. Indeed, on more than one time-wasting walk, despite not even looking for them, Matt had personally stumbled across several photographers—some slinking around through the snow, others perched in pine trees like big ugly birds with telescopic lenses, and all of whom inevitably fled for their lives as soon as they saw him. The third time he found one, Matt was tempted to call Giselle and unleash her on the fleeing fat man and his ugly camo jacket but refrained from doing so on the grounds that it might impair his impartiality as a bookie.

Despite the enjoyment many Acolytes were deriving from either repelling the trespassers or betting on those who were, a general irritability at the paparazzi's presence nevertheless spread through Morningstar like a slow infection. Exercises were being disrupted, lectures spied upon. Range practice had to be interrupted one morning to shoot down two photographers taking aerial shots three thousand feet in the air. The Ashes, in particular, were taking the violation of their honored institution very, very poorly, to the point where Selwyn was actually spending their morning meditation sessions astral-scouting the nearby countryside and relaying the location of any photographers he found. But no matter how many paparazzi they roughed up or turned away, there always seemed to be another one willing, eager, and stupid enough to take their place—and all, Matt thought sadly, for a picture of one girl who wasn't doing anything wrong, and who just wanted to be left alone.

True to her word, Jane had been following Winters's advice and engulfing herself in a veil of flames when walking between training grounds or moving anywhere she could potentially be seen, which on the upside insulated her from the cold, but unfortunately also equated any momentary lapse in concentration with the partial incineration of whatever she was wearing. Having to study and train with holes burned into your clothing would have been annoying enough for a regular person, but Jane didn't own that many clothes and it was only a matter of time before nearly everything she had was fire-damaged. Before long, feelings of paranoia, exposure, and vulnerability from being under constant surveillance permanently niggled at the back of Jane's head, chewing away at her concentration—and exacerbated by many of the other Acolytes, who blamed her for the whole situation. An Acolyte petition calling for Jane's removal circulated through Morningstar Academy, gathering more than a hundred supporters—inspired perhaps by an almost identically worded one lodged on Change.org the week before which had attracted more than 12 million signatures. Despite the numbers, the Ashes' response to the applications remained the same—a bluntly worded reminder that neither Acolytes nor the outside world had any say in who attended their institution.

This fact was not lost on Matt, who—despite his vain, now half-hearted struggles—continued to remain unexpelled. It seemed inescapable now—a week after he'd handed them to Cross, Cassandra Atropos's numbers came good, and the Ashes woman was able to walk into Winters's office the following morning and inform the administrator that Matt could have won 5 million dollars. Not that he actually did—Cross had expressly prohibited Matt or anyone acting for him from buying a lottery ticket, citing some high-minded concern about abuse of powers, disclosure obligations, and the Legion's public image. Matt, who would have liked 5 million dollars but recognized the inherent risk in winning it, suffered this further indignity in grating silence: on the one hand, glad that the numbers had worked out; on the other, feeling resentful and resigned.

What did it prove, beyond that Cassandra had seen the future? It did little to reveal the who, the how or the why of the woman's warnings, and seemed to achieve nothing besides turning Cross's attitude toward Matt on its head. This was ultimately a good thing, on balance—but Matt still couldn't help but feeling like, in buying himself some breathing room, he'd handed his assessor a rope to tie around his neck.

Not that he needed much help in that regard. If Cassandra Atropos had supplied the coffin, it seemed fate was content to supply the nails—because one by one Matt's stupid "predictions" kept coming "true." It was such a run of good luck, it was almost bad—a Kentucky senator was caught in a men's "health spa," a royal commission was opened into the Australian priesthood and to top it all off, Cross herself was asked to consult at an international audiovisual conference where she met a man who—against all odds—seemed interested in her.

"It was just like you said," she told Matt, uncharacteristically gushing, in the assessment the week after. "He asked me to dance. He was even wearing a white shirt."

Fancy that, thought Matt flatly, a man in a suit wearing a white shirt.

Matt smiled mechanically, inwardly struggling to think of a way out of this and to keep a lid on his looming despair. With Cassandra's ramblings and the child's threats looming over him, maintaining his deception would always be his top priority, but Matt couldn't help but fear that soon there wouldn't be anything he could do that Cross wouldn't excuse. Like Jane's paparazzi, the Ashes woman's probing, and her desire for a seer she could control, did not seem to be things that would be going readily away.

And so it was, with their respective specters looming over them, that Matt and Jane found themselves in the unusual position of being in the same mind about the upcoming break for Thanksgiving. For Matt, any excuse to get away from the Legion, even temporarily, was welcome, and though it pained Jane to pause her training and she hated the thought of being the scruffy tumor plonked uncomfortably in the Callaghan's Christmas card photo, she couldn't deny that there was some appeal in going somewhere there wouldn't be photographers hiding in the trees.

"Thanks, Will," Matt called as the teleporter gave the two of them a casual salute with his un-lead-barriered arm before disappearing in a waft of sulfur. They stood there for a moment at the end of Matt's street, ankle-deep in freshly fallen snow.

"Well, let's get to it," he said after a moment's awkward silence. He forced Jane a smile, but the empath just stood sour-faced with her hands in her pockets, the whiteness of her cheeks against the frozen backdrop bringing out the color of her eyes. "My house is down that way."

"Right," she grunted. They set off, side by side in silence.

"Are you cold?" Matt asked after a hundred feet or so. His down jacket was fantastically warm, but Jane was only wearing her normal hoodie, which upon closer inspection had several blackened holes in it. Matt also couldn't imagine her worn-out sneakers did a great job of keeping snow out.

"I'm fine," Jane muttered. Her arms had migrated from her pockets to across her chest.

"You could always set yourself on fire," Matt suggested. "Warm you up, make you feel more at home."

"Ha-ha," Jane replied without any humor. They walked in silence for another block.

"Is your dad coming?" Matt asked eventually, as the footpath and the houses lining it took a slight turn.

"Maybe," replied Jane stiffly, arms still locked across her chest. In truth, she hadn't told her father anything. Matt glanced sideways at her, seeming to sense the deception.

"Well, I think Mom might've called him from the phone book. You know, so he has the right address."

"Great," grumbled Jane, seeing an already bad idea taking a turn for the worse.

They walked some more.

"Just to be clear," she asked, "did you tell your parents about Albania?"

"No," Matt replied. "And I don't plan to. I've got enough to worry about without adding them to it. Besides, I signed an NDA."

Jane grunted. Winters had made her sign one too.

They kept walking.

"That's us," Matt said, pointing out his house as it came into view. The snow had the shrubs in the garden looking a little worse for wear, but someone—Matt presumed Jonas—had cleared the driveway to reveal the flagstones underneath. Jane looked on blankly as they approached.

"Nice house," she said, not sarcastically but without any warmth.

"Thanks," replied Matt, who'd settle for what he could get. They reached the front lawn and made their way to the porch. At the front steps, Matt noticed Jane was hanging back.

"It's okay," he assured her, walking backward and grabbing her by the wrist. Jane flinched at his touch. "They won't bite." He started once more doggedly forward, with Jane in tow. The empath resisted for a moment before giving up and letting herself be pulled to the front door.

"Powerless freak," she muttered under her breath, the skin-to-skin contact feeling solely like cold fingers.

"Shut up," hissed Matt. "None of that." His free hand rang the doorbell. From inside, there came the sound of movement, and the faux-clairvoyant dropped his grip as something ran scrambling and yelping toward the door.

The door swung open. "Woogie!" Matt cried, falling to his knees to hug the bounding, licking golden retriever as it launched itself into his arms. "Oooh, *¿Qué pasó, perrito mío? Te extrañé.*" The dog wriggled around, trying to get a clear lick at Matt's face.

"Woogie?" asked Jane, raising her eyebrows.

"Sarah named him; we drew straws," said Matt, rising from the over-enthusiastic mutt to hug his father, who'd opened the door from down the hallway. "Happy Thanksgiving, Dad."

"Happy Thanksgiving, Matty," Michael Callaghan, who was wearing a turkey-patterned apron, said with a smile. "So good to see you." He released his son and turned still smiling to the empath. "And you must be Jane. It's a pleasure to meet you in person."

"Hi," Jane said awkwardly. The man's eyes fell to the way her arms were locked across her chest.

"You must be cold, come in, come in, get warm," he proclaimed, ushering them inside. Matt bent and gave Woogie another scratch behind the ears then followed his father.

"Come on," he hissed at Jane's obvious reluctance. The empath was so uncomfortable she couldn't even muster a scowl. They crossed the threshold.

"Shoes off!" a woman's voice echoed from somewhere inside, and Kathryn Callaghan's head poked out from the kitchen. "Hi, Jane, lovely to meet you. Just so you don't get snow on the rug." Matt's mother's head retreated out of view. Matt chuckled to himself, and Jane followed his lead in bending down and removing their boots, discreetly maneuvering her socks while doing so to try and hide the holes. Her legs felt unusually stiff and jumpy—she didn't know why she was so nervous.

They walked through to the kitchen, where Matt greeted his mother, a slim yet intimidating woman with long brown curls, also wearing an apron, with a one-armed hug. "Hey, Mom," he said with a grin. "This is Jane."

"Three months," Kathryn Callaghan lamented, shaking her head at Jane with a look of mock despair. "Almost three months he's been gone, and the dog gets more of a welcome than me." Her face split into a warm smile. "It's lovely to meet you, Jane."

"Hi," Jane said awkwardly, wondering if that was the only word she was going to be able to say all afternoon.

From there, it was an endless parade of family, relatives, and assorted friends, coming up one after the other to affectionately welcome Matt and erratically acknowledge Jane. Several of Matt's aunts and uncles simply grunted and glowered at her, which Jane didn't take too personally, and his grandmother, having kissed her grandson on the cheek, stated primly that she was "welcome, so long as you behave yourself." Matt's younger brother, obviously wanting to be edgy, skipped greeting either of them to launch into a loaded interrogation about the Black Death, which earned him a telekinetic slap to the back of the head by his father. Matt's little sister, on the other hand, ran full pelt into her brother's arms, then promptly disentangled herself from the hug and starting tugging on the bottom of Jane's hoodie.

"I'm not supposed to ask about the E on your face," she informed her, little hands rocking behind her back. Then after a moment's contemplation added, "Did it hurt?"

"Yes," replied Jane.

"Does it hurt now?"

"No."

"You're tall for a girl."

"Thanks?"

"Can I have a piggyback?"

"Jane, how about you come in here and help me with the potatoes," Kathryn Callaghan called, leaning her head out of the kitchen and rescuing the empath from further discomfort. She smiled as Jane entered, seeing the shell-shocked look on her face.

"Just try and relax, sweetie. We're a noisy bunch. Here, are you any good with a peeler? Hope you're not too hungry, dinner's a while off."

Peeling wasn't one of Jane's talents, but she picked it up soon enough, moving on to washing, dicing, and greasing once it was done. To her

SUPERWORLD — BOOK 2

relief, Thanksgiving dinner needed significant preparation, and Matt's mother always seemed to have something else Jane could help with, keeping the empath occupied and sparing her from the gauntlet of familial conversation taking place in the living room. The doorbell rang and rang as more and more people arrived, and the noise of merry greetings wafted through to the kitchen. Matt ducked his head in once or twice, maybe to check if Jane was all right, but a short, funny look from his mother both times had him retreating back into the larger rabble where Jane could hear him fielding endless questions about the Legion, Morningstar, and Captain Dawn.

"Did your dad say what time he was coming?" Mrs. Callaghan asked, once the vegetables were all prepared and baking away in the oven.

"I don't know," Jane mumbled, running a scrubbing brush clumsily over a chopping board. It was technically the truth.

"Hmm," replied Mrs. Callaghan, sounding unconvinced and seeming, like her son, to have a knack for perceiving technicalities.

Finally, there was nothing more to be done in the kitchen, so Mrs. Callaghan sent Jane back out into the living room to be metaphorically eaten alive. She endured ten excruciating minutes of talking about fly fishing with a friend of Mr. Callaghan's who seemed allergic to eye contact before being cornered by that little rat Jonas, who wanted to know if she'd ever killed someone.

"Not that anyone's been able to prove," Matt interjected, hearing the conversation and siding over with a deadpan expression. He shot Jane a significant look. "But there have been . . . disappearances. People that annoyed her. Annoying people."

"Nosy people," added Jane, picking up what Matt was putting down.

"People who asked too many questions."

"Young boys, mostly."

"They just disappear."

"No one's ever found their bodies."

"But it's not like she can make acid and just, you know, dissolve people."

"Oh, wait." Jane laughed, then abruptly stopped and stared the kid straight in the eye. "That's right. I'm an empath. I can do anything."

Jonas laughed uncertainly, looking nervously from one to the other. "You guys are stupid," he said, but he moved hurriedly away regardless.

At the sight of his worried backward glances, Jane found herself genuinely chuckling.

"Food's ready!" announced Mrs. Callaghan, and there was a general rumbling of approval as everyone moved into the dining room, where the normal table had been buttressed by two folding ones to create a long, uneven surface running the length of the room, providing an unbroken view out the sliding doors and into the snow-soaked garden beyond. Jane ended up seated down one end with a spare space opposite her, while Matt sat a few places over. One by one, dishes of potatoes and gravy, peas and carrots, roasted parsnips, lasagna, salads, bread, and finally a gigantic turkey the size of her torso were telekinetically floated out of the kitchen by Mr. Callaghan and one of Matt's cousins. Once everything was on the table and everybody was seated, Matt's dad said a short grace, while his grandmother turned her hand to metal and sharpened the carving knife on her fingers.

"Dig in," ordered Mrs. Callaghan, and so the dishes were passed around for everyone to fill their plates. Jane held back at first but ended up going back for seconds and then thirds from the irresistibly delicious heap of turkey. Conversation buzzed around her, and despite a few underhand glances across the table, for the most part Jane managed to stay politely uninvolved. She began to suspect that the Callaghans might have forewarned their guests about her, for which Jane found herself feeling a deep surge of gratitude. This wasn't too bad. She could just sit here, full and warm, eating good food while watching snow fall in the yard and not having to talk to anyone.

Suddenly, the doorbell rang.

The babble of conversation momentarily stumbled into silence as two dozen heads, Jane's included, turned in unison toward the front hall. Down the other end of the table, Mr. and Mrs. Callaghan exchanged glances, and everything seemed to pause. But a second later, the moment passed and noise returned to the room as the guests picked up where they'd left off. Mr. Callaghan rose quietly from his seat, almost unnoticed, and set off to answer the door. Jane watched him go, a sinking feeling in her stomach.

"Hi!" she heard Mr. Callaghan say. There came a mumbled greeting in reply, followed by the sound of heavy footsteps moving down the hall. And then, with Mr. Callaghan at his back, Jane's father entered the room, and Jane knew that whatever part of this day she'd been able to enjoy was over.

He looked like he always did—a disheveled mess. A leather-skinned, sunken-faced old man, with bags under his eyes and dirt under his fingernails, wearing a dusty brown coat and blue jeans, both faded and frayed. His hair was knotted, his stubble untouched, and there was a glazed look in his eyes that Jane didn't need ten years' experience to recognize—she could smell the alcohol from across the room. Everyone looked at the newcomer in stunned silence.

"Hi," he muttered, and there was a half-murmured echo from those seated around the table that faded almost as soon as it arose. If Jane's father noticed the awkward silence, he didn't care. He said nothing further, only stood there, staring down.

Mr. Callaghan glanced worriedly from his wife to her father, then cleared his throat. "Ah, everyone, this is Jane's dad, um . . ." He glanced at him, unsure.

"Peter," murmured her father, eyes unfocused.

"Peter," repeated Mr. Callaghan, "well, welcome, I, ah . . . why don't you . . . I think there's a spot down there with Jane." He indicated the seat directly across from the empath. The sound of his daughter's name seemed to pull Peter Walker from his reverie. He looked up, his gray bleary eyes traversing the length of the table. His face momentarily hardened.

"Thanks," he muttered. He trudged over, the heavy clomp of his work boots the only sound in the room. Wordlessly, he dragged the seat out and slumped down into it, his hands laid in front of him. Jane sat opposite, her arms crossed, glowering.

The silence stretched outward, all eyes on the downcast, disheveled newcomer.

"I'm sorry I'm late," he murmured, not looking up. "The bus took a while."

"It's fine," Mrs. Callaghan assured him. She forced a smile. "I'm sorry we had to start without you. But please, dig in, there's plenty left." Jane's father nodded and without making eye contact reached out and began slowly filling his plate. Across the room, Matt's grandmother gave a small *tut* of disapproval, but Jane's father didn't seem to care or notice.

For a few seconds, there was only more silence and the sound of her father chewing. But then around the table, Matt turned to his mother and questioned what was in the turkey stuffing, an aunt asked Sarah about school, and two of Mr. Callaghan's coworkers started talking again about football. Slowly, the buzz of chatter began returning to the room as the guests lapsed back into conversation, with the sole exception of Jane and her father, who remained silent—the latter chewing with his head down, the former glaring at him, arms tightly crossed, her face hard and inscrutable.

The silence between them dragged on as the noise around them swelled. Finally, Jane broke it.

"Why didn't you drive?" she growled, low enough to be discreet. Her father didn't look up.

"It doesn't matter."

"You've got the truck; it would've been fine in the snow."

"I said it doesn't matter," he said harder, cutting her off with a look. It was the first time since he'd sat down that their eyes had met. He turned away after a second. "It's not important."

Jane opened her mouth to argue but was interrupted by a voice from the other end of the table.

"Well," announced Mr. Callaghan, rising to his feet and looking around at his guests with what was probably a genuine smile, "now that we're all here—and thank you all for coming—I think it's time for our annual Thanksgiving tradition." There were nods, murmurs of approval. "Each year," Mr. Callaghan continued, "we go around the room and get everyone to say a few words, just telling us what they're thankful for." He paused, still smiling. "I'll start. I'm thankful for my health, my family's safety, and that we can all sit here peacefully and enjoy such a fantastic meal."

"Hear, hear," someone called, and there was a smattering of applause. Mr. Callaghan smiled down at his wife.

"I'm also thankful I'm married to an aquamorph who can do all the washing up." The entire table laughed, and Mrs. Callaghan fixed him a withering look, triggering more laughter. Mr. Callaghan grinned and glanced over at his son. "Matty, your turn."

Matt paused for a moment before answering. "I'm grateful for friends, for family, and for free food," he announced, to general sounds of agreement.

"It's not free," retorted Mrs. Callaghan, shaking her head in mock disappointment. "Your father and I paid for it." There was more laughter.

"I'm thankful it was you and not me!" called one particularly fat uncle.

"All right, all right." Mr. Callaghan smiled, motioning down with his hands as the laughter subsided. "This is supposed to be serious. Let's have one of our new guests say something. Jane, what're you thankful for?"

All eyes turned to look at the empath, who recoiled slightly at being put on the spot. She strained her brain, trying to think. "U-u-um ..." she stammered, trying not to meet anyone's eyes, "well, um, I'm ... thankful ... for having me ..." There was a scattering of murmured approvals and nods. Jane took heart and continued. "Um ... I'm thankful for ... for I guess, getting to be at the Academy, for the opportunities I've, uh, I've been given, and, um ..." Captain Dawn's faced flashed momentarily into her mind. "Just ... yeah. That I get to be there. That they let me in."

Everyone around the table gave a polite round of applause—everyone, that was, except her father, who simply sat there staring at his hands.

"What?" Jane said as the applause died down. Her father just shook his head.

"Nothing."

"What?" she repeated, suddenly angry. "Spit it out."

"I didn't say anything," he murmured. The room had fallen silent, all eyes watching them.

"Jane, it's fine, that was lovely," Mrs. Callaghan said hurriedly, trying to force a smile. She shot a worried glance between the two of them. "Peter, why don't you tell us what you're thankful for?"

For the longest time, Jane thought her father wasn't going to speak— that he was just going to sit there, wordlessly, with that scrunched-up beaten look on his face, staring at his hands. She couldn't tell if he was lost in thought, a thousand miles away, or if he was still there figuring out an answer—or if he was just hallucinating, internally reeling from the drink. Finally, just when it seemed like he wasn't going to say anything at all—when Mr. Callaghan was casting concerned glances around the table, looking for someone to skip to, a way to break the awkward silence—her father sighed.

"What am I thankful for ... ?" he murmured, musing, weariness etched throughout his voice and face. Speaking more to himself than anyone. "What am I thankful for?" He paused and gave another sigh. "I'm thankful I have a job. It's not a good job—it's got bad pay, bad hours, and everyone there hates me, because my daughter's a—" He stopped and looked up at Jane with tired gray eyes. "But I've got a job, I guess. Pays the bills. Some of them. Pays rent, except when . . ."

He paused. Drew a deep, shuddering breath. "I'm thankful for the roof over my head," he continued. *Shut up*, willed Jane, *just shut up*. Everyone was staring at him, the room dead silent, but he just kept going. "It isn't much, but it's more than some have, I guess. Not nice like this though." His eyes wandered around the room, full of people and food, ornaments, pictures on the walls. "No friends or family, just me and . . ." He glanced across at Jane, and his voice trailed off.

"I'm thankful for my daughter," he picked up again. "Thankful that she's . . . she's healthy . . . and that . . . and that . . ." He shook his head, struggling to speak. There were tears in his eyes, and Jane would've given everything she had in that moment if he'd have just shut up. But he didn't. "She looks so much like her mother, and she—" He stopped, the words choking in his throat. His eyes shut tight and his hand moved over his mouth. "Sorry, I'm—"

"Don't," warned Jane. He looked up at her as she glared at him—and somehow the anger in her voice seemed to transfer through to his.

"I'm thankful for my daughter," he repeated, tougher, coarser, into the terrible silence. "Thankful that she gets to go off and play superheroes in a castle, while I'm down here, in the real world, working my ass off, trying to scrape by. I'm thankful she's out there having fun, throwing her powers around where everyone can see." His eyes had turned to hard lines and his words were starting to slur. "Never thinking, never caring that everything she does makes my life a little worse."

He laughed, high and cold, mirthless and terrible. "Because it's true! It's true! She gets in a fight; we have to move. She pushes some kid; I'm out of work. She gets on TV; I can't drive. Because, of course, it's only fair. See, she's my daughter, so while I'm up to my eyes scraping soot, they have to get together and torch my truck. She's has to be in the Legion, so I have to lose. It's only fair."

No one moved, and no one spoke, and Jane's father just kept on going.

"And I know . . ."—he scrunched his eyes shut, gritting his teeth, as though wracked by terrible pain—"I know it's not your fault, and I know you didn't ask for it, and I know, I know, but you still . . . you just . . ." His voice constricted and for a moment he seemed so frustrated, his hands clenched so tight around nothing that he couldn't get the words out. "You just can't . . . stay low, can you? Can't just let things be, can't keep your head down, always got to be out there, got to be pushing, trying to fight the world."

"I'm not just going to roll over and die!" Jane shouted.

"That's not what I . . ." her father started to shout back, but then he stopped himself, shaking his head, raising his hands. "Forget it. It doesn't matter what I mean. Doesn't matter what I say, does it? What I do, what happens to me. None of it. Nothing matters, so long as you get to play hero."

"Go to hell," Jane muttered, and she meant it. Her father gazed at her, black bags under his eyes, cracked lips taunt.

"You know what? We're talking about being thankful?" He shook his head. "I'm thankful that they took you. I'm grateful that you're gone." The words punched her in the guts, falling from her father's mouth like the tears from his scrunched-up eyes. "At least now I don't have to see your face. At least now I don't have to see . . ."

"Hey now, come on—" Mr. Callaghan started, but her father was still shaking his head, not listening, blocking out anything but his truth.

"Every day. That's what I'm grateful for. I'm thankful that I don't have to see it every day, that, that . . . thing." He pointed an unsteady finger at the mark on her cheek. "Every day. Reminding me what I lost, how he took her, how she . . ." He hiccoughed, choking. "How she died."

"She was my mother," whispered Jane, low and murderous.

"AND SHE WAS MY WIFE!" he roared, not just with his voice, drink and anger shaking his control, making the entire table jump. "And he killed her, killed a continent, and you walk around with his mark like you're, like you're . . . PROUD!"

"YOU DON'T KNOW HOW I FEEL!" Jane roared back, and she was on her feet, every muscle shaking. "YOU NEVER BOTHERED TO LOOK, NOT EVER, NOT ONCE!" She wanted to reach across the table, to grab him, to hit something, but her father was already standing up, stepping back, swaying unsteadily, his head shaking no-no-no-and-no in little twitches.

"I can't do this," he mumbled, red-eyed, constricted, bleary. "I can't. I can't. I just . . ."

He turned unsteadily to Mr. and Mrs. Callaghan. "Thank you for having me. You . . . you have a . . . a lovely home. I'm . . . I'm sorry. Happy Thanksgiving." He stumbled backward, his hands fiddling unsteadily with the sliding door. The latch flicked, the door slid open, and he staggered out into the snow, leaving heavy footprints.

"Dad!" shouted Jane, but he wasn't listening and he didn't turn around.

"Dad!" she called again—but he turned a corner and was gone.

For a moment, Jane just stood there, feeling everyone's eyes burning into her. They were all looking at her, staring, with disgust, contempt, and pity, and she had to . . . needed to . . . couldn't . . .

"Bye," she said abruptly, and before anyone could protest, she was striding off, away down the hallway, not looking at any of them, lacing up her shoes with shaking, raging fingers. There were wary footsteps behind her, but she didn't need them, she didn't need anything, she just needed to be out, needed to be alone . . .

She wrenched open the door and raced through, slamming it behind her and stepping out into the cold.

The dining room was completely silent, the echo of the slamming door still reverberating through the house. After a few seconds, Sarah started to cry. To his incredible credit, Jonas hurried over to wrap an arm around his sister's shoulders and tell her everything was all right.

"Who wants dessert?" Mrs. Callaghan asked, her voice unnaturally high. Matt swore under his breath, threw down his napkin and stood to go outside.

He found Jane two blocks away, sitting alone on the corner of a snowy curb, looking blankly off into the distance, unmoving. A silent statue of color, alone in a world of white. There was something sadly beautiful about it.

"There was still cake, you know," he said, trying half-heartedly to be funny. "And key lime pie." Her eyes flickered over at the sound of his voice, then flicked back, her face empty, the girl seemingly unable to even muster a scowl. Matt stood some distance away with his hands in his pockets, twisting his heels into the snow.

"Did you find your dad?" he asked, not sure which answer he was hoping for. Jane shook her head, as though it had been a forgone conclusion.

"He's psychic. He can feel when people are close. Stay away if he wants to." She sniffed, heavy, though her face was completely dry. Matt had never seen her cry.

There was a pause. Then Jane let out a tiny, exasperated sigh.

"What do you want?" she murmured.

"Nothing," Matt said truthfully. "Just wanted to make sure you were all right."

"I'm fine," she muttered.

"You don't seem fine."

"Well, I am," Jane snapped. "Just leave me alone."

"Are you sure that's what you want?" asked Matt. But a second after the words left his mouth, when Jane's head turned and she glared at him with real loathing and contempt, he knew he'd said the wrong thing.

"What do you think I want?" she spat at him. "Do you think I want to sit here and talk about my life, want you to take my hand and care and share and cry about my feelings? Go to hell."

"I—" began Matt, but she was already cutting him off, shaking her head.

"You don't know anything. Not about me, not about my life."

"I know what it's like to be different," Matt said quietly, truthfully.

Jane snorted. "You know nothing." She laughed, just like her father—cold and completely devoid of mercy. "You think you're alone, think you're hard-pressed, with your friends and your family and your dog and your stupid Stepford home. Oh, boo-hoo, you have to lie. Oh, boo-hoo, the world doesn't see you." She sneered at the dirt and the snow mixing on the asphalt. "I'd give anything to have what you have. Have people want to be around you. Care if you lived or died." She paused, staring straight ahead, kneading snow between her hands. "But I don't. And I never will. And you'll never know what that's like—not now, not in a million years. So, spare me your false pity."

There was a pause. When Jane saw he was still standing there, anger bloomed across her face. "Don't you get it?" she said bitterly. "Go away. Leave. I don't want your help. I hate you."

Matt said nothing.

"I hate you," repeated Jane, venom on her lips. "I've always hated you. Ever since you first sat next to me, ever since you . . . trying to make me feel like, like I could be normal, and . . . Ugggghhhhh!" she roared, clutching the sides of her head, auburn hair in her hands. "I can't stand it, I hate it, because I know it's not true, but then you worm your way into my head, and you make me forget and . . ." She opened her eyes and stared at the ground. "I know. I've always known. I don't get to be liked. I don't get to be loved. I get to be strong. That's what I get. Strong and great and powerful, and you and him and all your stupid little friends with your pathetic nothing lives, you can just watch me. Watch me change the world. I don't need any of you."

There was a blank, empty silence.

"I didn't know your mom died in Africa," murmured Matt.

"Well, now you do." Jane sniffed. "She was a wildlife photographer. She liked giraffes. She never had a chance. Are you happy?"

"No," he replied.

"Well, I don't care. Leave me alone."

Matt didn't move. Jane rolled to her feet. "Fine," she said, her voice hard, refusing to look at him. "Then I'll go."

"Where're you going?" he asked.

"Where I belong," she answered. Matt watched in silence as she pulled up her hood and walked away, hands in her front—watched as she kept walking, the snow melting where she stepped, across the street and down the road, until the white and gray swallowed her whole.

And then she was gone—the traces that she'd left already filling up with snow.

Ah, hell, Matt muttered to himself. He sat down on the cold, wet sidewalk and leaned his head on his hands. A few quiet seconds passed; then the sound of familiar footsteps padded up beside him.

"At least you still love me, Woogie," he murmured. The golden retriever yowled and flopped down next to Matt, laying its head on his lap. Matt scratched the dog behind the ears.

They sat there for a while, the boy and his dog, watching the world in white, the thick flakes falling from the sky, blanketing the world below. Snow made the world look peaceful, even if underneath it wasn't—but in the end you got cold and had to go back to reality. Matt didn't know how long he sat there, scratching Woogie idly behind his ears, but eventually he couldn't feel his legs, and he knew Jane wasn't coming back.

"*Vámanos, perrito*," Matt said with a sigh, pushing to his feet. "*Vamos a comer*." And so they headed back toward the house, to the warmth and friends and loving family, who he'd never really appreciated for most of his life.

FIREWORKS

https://en.wikipedia.org/wiki/Klaus_Heydrich

Klaus Heydrich
From Wikipedia, the free encyclopedia
The "Black Death (person)" redirects here. For other uses, see the "Black Death (disambiguation)."

Klaus Heydrich (June 17, 1933–October 9, 1990) was a German-born blood-based empath and mass murderer, posthumously known as the Black Death in reference to the medieval plague, as well as the Butcher of Africa. As the most powerful and variable empath in history, Heydrich was the cause of the African Devastation, which killed an estimated 400–500 million people after his defeat at the hands of Captain Dawn of the Legion of Heroes.

Early life
Birth and childhood
Heydrich was born in Berlin, Germany, on June 17, 1933, to German intelligence officer Reinhard Heydrich—a high-ranking Nazi official and one of the main architects of the Holocaust and founder of the Sicherheitsdienst—and schoolteacher Lina von Osten. His given name, meaning "Victory," was a tribute to the aspirations of the Third Reich.

As a member of the Nazi elite, Reinhard Heydrich was a German nationalist who instilled patriotic ideals and the doctrines of Nazism in his son, including the philosophies of natural selection, eugenics, and the superiority of the Aryan race. From a young age, Klaus was intelligent, cold, and unusually advanced, excelling at school—especially in science—and embracing Nazi teachings. Physically disciplined and a talented athlete, he reveled in exercising power or inflicting punishments on younger children or servants, and idolized his father.

Assassination of father, "death," and flight from Germany

On May 27, 1942, Reinhard Heydrich was attacked by the Czechoslovak government-in-exile and wounded, subsequently slipping into a coma before dying on June 4, 1942. The effects of this on the nine-year-old Heydrich were profound and caused him to exhibit bouts of irrational anger and depression. In the year following his father's death, threats in connection with those killed by Reinhard Heydrich were made against Heydrich's family, and subsequently a notice was posted on October 24, 1943, stating that Klaus Heydrich had died from a traffic accident—a deception now believed to have been instigated by Heydrich's mother to protect her son.

Little is known about Heydrich's subsequent movements and the remainder of his childhood. Conflicting reports have the Heydrich family fleeing Germany prior to the arrival of the Allied forces, with others claiming that they refused to leave and were subsequently incarcerated before being released. Several historians have postulated that Heydrich's 1943 death notice was not fake and that his identity was adopted by an unknown other, possibly even the secret son of Adolf Hitler (see: Black Legacy Conspiracy Theory) though this has never been proven. The commonly accepted theory is that at some point following the fall of the Third Reich, Heydrich and his family left Germany—according to some accounts accompanied by a small guard of SS troopers—and traveled to Argentina, where Heydrich spent the remainder of his childhood and adolescence.

Postwar

Heydrich spent the majority of his adult life in hiding, and the time line of his movements remains disputed. It is generally accepted that, by early 1960, he had abandoned his remaining family in Argentina and joined an underground group of Nazi loyalists in occupied Berlin. Heydrich engaged in small-scale resistance and sabotage, setting fire to foreign-owned businesses and murdering unsuspecting Allied soldiers. Several acquaintances from this period have placed him in Berlin when the Aurora Nirvanas hit the earth's biosphere and in the subsequent Six-Day Slumber that followed.

Post-humanism records of Heydrich, at this point an unknown and uncontroversial figure, have proved elusive. A barman in Munich made unsubstantiated claims that he served someone fitting Heydrich's description around August 1963, who lamented that "God had not seen fit" to grant him a power, suggesting that Heydrich may have initially struggled to uncover his empathic abilities. The only confirmed sighting occurred on November 9, 1969, when twins Franz and Ola Schmidt saw a man they would later recognize as Heydrich in the street during Captain Dawn's tearing down of the Berlin Wall. According to separately psychically verified accounts the twins, children at the time, stood next to Heydrich in a tightly packed crowd where he ". . . gazed up at Dawn with an expression that was at once awestruck and terrified." Ola Schmidt then held his hand, stating that she ". . . cannot remember the reason why . . ." and that ". . . he [Heydrich] didn't seem to notice anyway." This would be the last time Heydrich was seen in Europe and marked the end of any correspondence he had with his family or former compatriots. A private memorial service was held for him in Buenos Aires, Argentina, by his mother and sisters on January 6, 1975.

Africa
Pre-Legion Identification
Several events are known to have occurred following Heydrich's disappearance, although the order in which they occurred is unclear:
- Heydrich discovered the nature of his abilities as a blood-based empath and began accumulating and integrating powers.
- Heydrich absorbed the ability to regenerate cellular damage, decelerating his aging.
- Heydrich migrated to Central Africa through unknown means (possibly flight).

The motivation for Heydrich's migration to Africa has caused some debate. It is unclear whether his visit was intended to be temporary, or whether he came with an intention to stay to avoid detection or to exploit the unrest gripping the continent at that time. Regardless, once there, Heydrich began acquiring a vast array of powers from the African people.

Methods of Acquisition

Heydrich's exact method for acquiring the genetic material necessary for empathic acquisition is unknown; however, the extensive length of time in which he operated incognito implies a slow and methodical process, whereby a new power was acquired and then its utility mastered before the next ability was sought. Heydrich is believed to have progressed systematically between towns, cataloguing the powers of every adult and abducting any individual with an as-yet-unobtained ability. No trace of any of these abductees is ever believed to have been found, and they were often assumed to have run away by friends and relatives. Following these acquisitions, Heydrich, as a blood-based empath, would have required time to process, adjust to and integrate his new-found powers, leading to long periods of self-imposed isolation. To the best of current knowledge, this undetected cycle of stalk, kill, absorb, and process continued for up to two decades, and could have gone on indefinitely had Heydrich not become emboldened.

Legion Identification

On September 13, 1990, Heydrich arrived at Businga, Republic of the Congo, and entered the residence of local warlord Joseph Kony, whom he murdered along with approximately sixty others through the use of various abilities. Having assumed command of the town, Heydrich spent several days personally assessing every member of the population and executing approximately 320 people for being old, infirm, handicapped, homosexual, or otherwise possessing a quality he deemed undesirable. On September 16, 1990, Heydrich entered Bokoli, Kenya, and launched a similar "cleanse" before repeating the process on September 18–19 throughout Likimi province in the Republic of the Congo. On September 20, he returned to Businga and ordered the remaining townsfolk to spread to nearby areas and instigate similar "cleanses" of their own. When they refused, he massacred the majority of the citizenry and forced the remainder to accompany him to Bokoli, where he issued the same ultimatum, which was there accepted. On September 21, Heydrich and several hundred followers subsequently invaded the neighboring provinces of Binga and Lisala and killed more than a thousand "undesirables" before extending outward in their campaign.

On October 1, 1990, a report alleging Heydrich's actions was submitted anonymously to the Legion of Heroes, which due to a backlog in aid requests was not reviewed until two days later. On October 4, Legion members Justin Cleaver (Seventh Son), Samantha Del Lago (Nerid), and Goodluck Jonathan (Shadowsteps) were deployed to confirm the report's veracity and to locate and neutralize Heydrich. At approximately 9:00 a.m. on October 7, the three tracked Heydrich to the southern border of Chad, where they engaged in combat and were quickly overwhelmed. The deaths of Cleaver and Del Lago and Jonathan's call for reinforcements set in motion events that would ulti-mately lead to the African Devastation.

Death

For a summary of Heydrich's fight against the Legion of Heroes and a time line of the deaths of Legion members, see "Legion of Heroes."

Klaus Heydrich committed suicide at 8:48 p.m. on October 9, 1990 (Eastern Standard Time) following a protracted three-day battle with the Legion of Heroes and ultimate defeat at the hands of Captain Dawn. Heydrich utilized a combination of atomic destabilization, regeneration and cellular thermo-sinkage to infuse his body with explosive force equivalent to five thousand nuclear bombs, before "detonating" upon reaching critical instability. The resulting explosion extended from Libya to Zimbabwe and sent shock waves around the world.

For the African Devastation's immediate effects and global impact including seismic activity, emergency resolutions and countermeasures, see "African Devastation."

For permanent changes caused to geography, political landscapes and the environment including a list of extinct species, see "Post-Devastation World."

Aftermath and Legacy

Klaus Heydrich is the most prolific mass murderer in history, having caused an estimated 400 to 500 million deaths, approximately one-eighth of Earth's population at the time.

In the aftermath of Heydrich's geno-suicide, the Empath Control Con-vention was adopted by an emergency meeting of the UN General Assem-bly requiring all nations to regulate empath behavior. This move did not go far enough for some, who demanded international Empath Extermination Orders. The week of October 9 was designated as a seven-day remembrance period dedicated to Heydrich's victims (see: The Vigil), which is observed every year by folding paper stars and wearing black as well as with various memorial services. In the years following the African Devastation, Heydrich's name and his moniker the Black Death have become synonymous with the concepts of evil, sociopathy, empathic mimicry, and mutually assured destruction.

Matt woke up in his own bed for the first time in months. It was weird, he thought as he lay there, looking up at the ceiling—it felt wrong now. The mattress too soft, the pillows too firm. He wondered if it had changed, or if he had.

I don't think I'll go back, he mused after a couple of minutes laying there, listening to the muted sound of snow falling outside. Not today—not this week. Maybe not this month. What was the point? The only "learning" he was doing was in his morning sessions with Selwyn and missing them would be like forgetting to water a plastic houseplant. So, what was he rushing back for? Not Jane, who'd made it abundantly clear she didn't want him around. Visiting Ed in his computer hole? Seeing Giselle and sometimes Wally, maybe a few others? Creating more lies to placate Cross? Being terrified that at any moment he'd turn around to find another ominous warning or threat to his life?

He wanted to stay here. In this house, in this town. Go to a normal school, study normal things, live a normal life. He was sick of lying, sick of being afraid. He wanted to leave Morningstar Academy and never look back.

That's not smart, countered his brain. *Shut up, brain,* he pouted irritably. *Nobody asked you.*

The red face of his clock radio flashed ten and Matt knew he should get up. After all, he didn't want to be late for the long day of nothing he had ahead of him. He rolled out of bed and began shuffling towards the bathroom. Whatever else happened, he still needed to train his mind.

At least that wasn't completely pointless.

"Cumpletely pointlass," said Mac. His gnarled hand held her target sheet up to the light, his narrow eyes peering through the burn hole, a little left of center. "Ah teech you and ah teech you, scarface, and you still cannot hit tha side of a barn door." He let the paper go fluttering to the ground, shaking his gray head. "Ah told them. Ah told them Ash folk, no point en trainen an empaff. No in-ate ahbilitay. Jack of ahll traids, mastah of nun." He spat a hunk of black spittle into the dirt. Jane remained silent, her eyes fixed on the ground.

"What," said Mac, "no lip? No snappy re-tort? Ah tayk it back, gerl, mayhaps you are learnen somethen." He pressed a button cut crudely into the booth's wooden walls, and another target rotated up down the far end of the range. "Again."

Except for them, the range was deserted. A collect call from a pay phone outside a laundromat and two hours waiting in the snow had brought her back to Morningstar the day of Thanksgiving, but most of the other Acolytes hadn't been that quick to return. Maybe they were lazy. Maybe they liked their homes and families better than she did. Either way, it didn't matter. She was here, they weren't, and she was going to train. There were no formal classes on, but she'd make do. The facilities were there, and many of the Ashes lived on campus. And then there was Mac, who wasn't one of the Ashes, but who never strayed far either. Whether the old man didn't want to leave or had nowhere else to go to, Jane didn't ask, and Mac didn't share. It was irrelevant. He was there to instruct, she was there to learn, and even the constant stream of petty insults were just details.

"Watch you breathing," he muttered as she raised her arm and took aim once more. "You fire on tha in-breth or tha owt-breth, you gonna miss. And you miss ennuff for one day."

Jane breathed in, held steady, and released. Her fingertips sizzled, and a bolt of lightning shot straight down the line.

"Hmm," Mac grunted. He indented another button, and the target made its way the thousand or so feet along the length of the range. Mac held it up to the light.

Dead center. Perfect bull's-eye. Jane looked blankly at the grizzled old Southerner.

"Wipe thet smug grin off you face," he said, neither kindly nor unkindly, not even looking at her. "Don't mean nuthen. Aynuther twenny or so, an mayhaps ah start given you somethen difficul to shoot at."

* * *

"Another twenty or so," Kathryn Callaghan commanded. She stirred the pot of rice and onions with one hand and filled a saucepan with water from her own reserves with the other, somehow needing to look at neither, her gaze focused unwaveringly on the recipe book open on the bench. Matt grimaced and picked up another stupid carrot.

"How much are you making?" he complained, starting to peel once more with marked unenthusiasm. Strips of dirty orange skin littered the chopping board in a mound.

"It's kindergarten to sixth grade," his mother replied, sliding a heap of sliced vegetables into the heating water.

"At one picnic?"

His mom nodded, crossing the kitchen to idly refill herself from the tap. "Parents and kids."

"It's snowing."

"It's indoors."

"Won't it go cold?"

"Risotto is fine cold. Besides, there'll be pyros."

"Speaking of, how is Jonas getting out of this?"

"He's not. JONAS!" she called. "Come and help chop vegetables please!"

"I'm watching TV!" came the nasally reply from the living room.

"Matt, go and get your brother," Kathryn Callaghan said, sighing.

"Jonas," Matt called out wearily, trudging through into the front room. He paused at the doorway, looking down at the figure of his brother sprawled on the floor. "Mom says come help."

"I can't even use a peeler," the younger Callaghan blatantly lied. Nevertheless, he begrudgingly rolled onto his feet and stalked haughtily into the kitchen, not even bothering to turn off the TV. Matt quietly rolled his eyes and picked up the remote from where Jonas had left it beside the bowl of milky chocolate breakfast cereal his brother had been eating for lunch.

"All darkness yields before the Dawn."

Matt looked up at the TV to see the muscular fist of the animated Captain Dawn slamming into one of the Brothers Darkness. The cartoon shadows parted and there stood the hero of the era, pulsing with unstoppable light. As far as biographies went, it was impressive, Matt conceded. But the funny thing was, no matter how much of a courageous figure the cartoon captain cut, the rueful truth was that he looked even better in real life.

He looked even better in real life. On TV, in books, in her head—compressed into tiny pictures, something intangible was lost. Maybe it was his poise, his regal, solid stillness, or maybe his mere presence, his confidence, the air of true power. Jane's fingers were intertwining themselves nervously behind her back as the white-and-gold figure of Captain Dawn entered. It was all she could do to keep from bouncing uncontrollably on her feet.

She'd arrived early. Way too early, she realized, more than an hour—but what else was she going to do? Sleep? Impossible. Her body had been racing with nervous energy since Wednesday, and every second that brought her closer to this moment had only made the anticipation worse. She'd run through every way this could play out in her head so many times her fantasies were becoming difficult to distinguish from reality; her fears of messing up as real and galling as any actual failures. *Stay calm*, she said to herself, *stay cool. You are a warrior, calm and composed.*

Then he smiled his white, glorious smile at her and any composure she had melted, along with (it felt like) the muscles in her legs.

"You came," Captain Dawn said, and Jane was once again astounded at how such a quiet voice could carry so much force. He started forward.

"Of course," she replied, and it was all she could do to keep her voice from trembling.

"Good," said Dawn, and his green eyes sparkled. "Shall we begin?" He strode right past her, his golden cape rippling behind him. Jane quickly fell into his wake, and they moved together down the length of the long, dark gravity chamber.

"Here will do," the hero said quietly. They stopped and stood in still, cold silence somewhere around the middle of the hall. Captain Dawn turned and looked down at Jane, his handsome face smooth and impassive. He was at least a foot taller than her.

"I do not normally . . . teach," he said, and the words came out slightly oddly, like he was unpracticed in speaking. "I am not a teacher."

"I'm sure you'll be amazing," Jane gushed before she could help it. Immediately, she wanted to kick herself for interrupting, not to mention sounding like an air-headed moron. To her relief, Captain Dawn's only reaction was a small smile.

"Perhaps you should withhold judgment until after I have attempted teaching," he suggested with just a hint of a smirk. "Nevertheless, I thank you for your confidence."

He paused, breathing out into the cold night, and then continued. "You are strong, Jane Walker. You wield what you have borrowed better than many who were born with it." Jane felt her face growing hot from the praise. "But," continued Dawn, before she could completely dissolve in self-satisfaction, "you still avoid your greatest gift. You continue to shrink from your potential and pretend it does not exist, and in doing so you strangle your true strength."

He turned to gaze into the open space. "But first, a demonstration. Fly." He did not look back at her, nor did his voice waver. Jane hesitated for a moment. Then, sensing that this was all the instruction she was going to get, she took a step back and rippled her fingers. She pushed through with her arms and legs, and a second later flames shot down from her palms and feet, pushing her up into the air, where she held, hovering.

"Good," proclaimed Dawn, turning to watch as she floated five feet in the air, held aloft by pillars of flame. "But a question. Why do you use fire?"

"What do you mean?" asked Jane. Her flames flickered, and without even realizing it she began slowly sinking back down.

"I mean," the captain said plainly, "why only fire? Why not fire and lightning? Couple magnetic repulsion with thermal. Fire and ice? Heat the air below you, cool the air above."

Her feet back on the ground, Jane didn't know how to respond. "I don't know, sir, I just . . ." It took her a moment to gather her thoughts. "It's just how I've been taught," she conceded.

"And therein," replied Dawn, touching a knuckle to his lips, "lies the problem."

He straightened up, if possible, even taller and peered keenly down at her. The sigil on his chest, the breaking day, gleamed gold in the dark. "You have been taught your entire life by those unwilling or unable to accept what you are—a painter of color schooled in art by the color-blind, and subjecting yourself, nearly always, to their limitations. Well, no more. I am here, Jane Walker, to break you free of these restrictions."

"Sir," began Jane, "I—"

But Dawn overrode her protests with a glance. "We are here, young one," he said calmly, "so you may embrace that you are an empath."

For a few moments, neither of them spoke. Then, with a small, sad smile, Captain Dawn reached out and placed a steadying gloved hand on Jane's arms—which, she only realized now, were folded across her chest, holding her in place, trying to stop her shaking. "You have been told your entire life that what you can do is evil," he murmured, and there was kindness in his words. "But your power is nothing to be ashamed of. In fact, it is the opposite. It makes you great." He withdrew his hand, and Jane felt a painful longing, a cold absence, linger where it had been. "I hope this is something I can teach you."

The greatest man in the world took a step back. "Now fly—and this time, give it everything you've got."

"This is everything we've got?" Matt asked flatly, gazing at a breakfast shelf bearing one box of bran flakes and the ends of a loaf of whole wheat bread. Over at the table, Jonas grunted, not looking up from his phone.

Ding-dong.

"One-two-three-not-it."

"One-two-three . . . Goddamn it." Matt swung the door of the disappointing pantry closed and began trudging down the hallway with weary resignation.

A doorbell ringing at eight on a Sunday morning, he mused, was never a good sign. It was usually the police coming to inform you that someone was dead, or Jehovah's Witnesses coming to inform you that you were being alive wrong.

Although this morning, it was neither.

"Mr. Callaghan," said Cross, the minute he opened the door, her black pantsuit staggeringly unchanged. "I hope I find you well."

"Partially," Matt replied warily, unsure if he'd imagined the emphasis on the word *find*. He moved slowly outside onto the porch, closing the door behind him. His parents were still upstairs in bed, and Matt had a feeling he'd rather keep this conversation discreet. "What can I help you with?"

It had been two weeks since Thanksgiving break and two weeks since he'd last set foot in Morningstar. Two weeks, it seemed, was the point after which the Ashes cared about your absence.

The squat woman spread her hands wide and placating, the gesture making Matt secretly wonder what she could do with her powers. He'd never seen anyone change sound to light. "I'm simply here to inquire after your well-being, and to lock in the date when we can expect you back at the Academy." Her professional smile showed no sign of wavering. "For housekeeping and administrative purposes."

She's smooth, thought Matt. But so was he.

"Thank you so much for your concern," he said with a smile, maneuvering his features into an expression of submissive gratitude. "And I'm really sorry. I'll be back as soon as possible." Matt tried to make himself look pained. "It's just that we've been having . . . well, there's been some family matters. Unexpected. And I hate to take time off, but—" He sighed. "I really just need to be here right now."

He clasped his hands together and kept going before the Ashes woman could speak. "I'm really hoping it'll be resolved by Christmas. I promise, I'll be back right after that." Of course, his family was fine, but post-Christmas was the latest he could imagine they'd let him stay away.

Cross opened her mouth, possibly to argue, but caught herself, albeit with some visible struggle. Another two weeks or so, he could see her thinking, was not long enough to be called out as unacceptable—not in light of a family crisis—even though all up it would mean more than a month's absence. And it was partially over Christmas, which was when a lot of Acolytes would be away anyway—it was a difficult proposition to argue against. That was the trick, Matt had found: to use reasonable steps to achieve unreasonable outcomes. He looked at her, doe-eyed.

"Excellent," she said eventually, and only Matt's lifetime of reading faces revealed her smile as forced. "We'll look forward to seeing you on the twenty-sixth." She inclined her head toward him and turned on her heel.

"Thank you again just so much," Matt reiterated, slowly moving back inside, prostrating so low it was almost a bow. "Your support is really appreciated in this difficult time." He closed the door, still throwing gracious glances at the woman's retreating figure right until the door was shut, at which point he straightened up immediately and rolled his eyes.

"Who was that?" demanded Jonas, wandering into the hallway, his hand clutched around the last blackened Pop-Tart. "Your girlfriend?"

"No, I don't know, some girl from your year," Matt replied, brushing past his deodorant-deficient sibling. "Something about movie tickets? Anyway, it doesn't matter. I told her you had swine flu."

"What?" shouted Jonas, thoroughly incensed and now following his brother back into the living room, baited hard.

"Yeah, because you practice kissing on pigs. Don't play games with me, Jonas, we all know."

"Only you can know your destiny."

It was three thirty in the morning, the end of their third session in as many weeks. Jane panted softly, tired and flushed despite the cold and the company—Dawn his usual quiet, flawless, unshakable self. For more than three hours, they'd worked, Jane flowing from form to form, power to power, an endless stream of combinations and patterns. Training with Dawn was like . . . like nothing she'd ever experienced. There was no harshness, no violence, no pain—only movement, rhythm, an endless trance-like focus, engulfment in the moment. Their meetings were not drill sessions but dance lessons; private, intimate. Him leading with words, her following with form. There was no true fighting—the captain did not fight, had not once unleashed the power of Dawn in ten years, and barely ever before that—so all that was there of him was his presence. And still, it was exhilarating.

And now, they were done and sitting side by side in the grandstands together, alone—Dawn staring into the dark, Jane staring at Dawn, dwarfed as ever by the momentous shining figure beside her. As he spoke, she listened, drinking in his words in the cold night air.

"This world will always fear you," he murmured, his white and gold shimmering in the dark. "No matter your intentions, no matter how you try to save it. There is inherent taboo in doing what others cannot, a fear of potential by those who lack it. But it is wrong to give it credence."

He paused to look at her. "Does your power make you different?"

Jane hesitated, unsure what answer he wanted. "No," she said finally. "I'm no better or worse than anyone."

"Incorrect," replied Dawn, but it was a gentle rebuke. "You are different. But that is not bad."

He looked out across the empty hall. "Say there is an eagle, and below, a flock of sheep, jealous and berating it for being able to fly. Should the eagle land, to placate the sheep's bleating?"

"No," answered Jane.

"No," agreed Dawn. "Because even brought low, it is still an eagle, and neither the eagle nor the sheep will ever forget it. Nor," he added, "will its walking appease the flock. If anything, they will think the eagle mocks them and wish it harm. But if the eagle soars . . ."

"The sheep stop bleating?"

The captain gave her a wry smile. "No. The sheep never stop bleating. But now the eagle is too high up to hear their complaints." His gaze returned to the open, empty space. "Take pride in your gifts. Use them. Never be ashamed."

He leaned back slightly, then continued without looking at her. "An empath's greatest strength lays not just in their ability to combine and create, but to adapt. To take an enemy's power and turn it against them fast enough to overcome their advantage. Sadly," he said, chuckling, "this is one aspect I cannot help you with."

Jane laughed. "Yeah, I don't know how well teaching me to steal powers would go down with the papers."

"The taking is just the first step," said Dawn. The spark of humor had faded, and he had reverted to his usual expression—calm and distant. "The true talent is in mastering the acquired skill. Our whole world is a testament to the fact that simply being able to do something does not equate to being able to do that thing well."

They lapsed into silence. A slight chill was beginning to creep around the edges of Jane's arms and the tips of her shoulders, but she paid it no heed. Sitting here, listening to his soft, golden voice—she hoped she'd never leave. Even just being next to him, so close, feeling his presence . . . it was more than she'd ever dreamed of.

"Sir?" she asked eventually.

"Yes, Jane."

"How do you know so much about empaths?"

In the dim light, Captain Dawn laughed. "I have spent a lot of time thinking about them. Years, in fact." He paused and his green eyes grew distant. "That, and I have had more experience than most with the greatest empath who ever lived. In tragedy, certainly, and in pain. But we do not always get to choose the color of our lives. All we can do is reflect and learn."

Once more he fell silent, contemplating. Jane opened her mouth to press on, but then hesitated. She knew what she wanted to ask, but she was afraid to ask it. Her tired mind struggled to find the right words, struggled to decide if there was even a right way to ask what she wanted to know.

A small smile crept over the captain's lips. "A question restrained is an opportunity lost young one."

Jane bowed her head. She swung her thoughts around, trying to phrase what she wanted to say diplomatically, but in the end could only return to the raw truth.

"Were you afraid?"

For a few moments, she thought maybe Captain Dawn wasn't going to answer—maybe he was offended, maybe this was too personal, maybe she'd been too vague—but before she could try and clumsily retract her words, Dawn spoke.

"More than I'd ever been in my life," he murmured, and the way his eyes stared into the ether, she knew he was telling the truth—reliving it. "More than I'd let myself believe. Out of all of them, out of everyone I faced, he . . ." Captain Dawn's voice grew very quiet, to the point where Jane was almost straining to hear him. "He was the only one I ever truly feared."

He shook his golden head as if to chase away the memories. "I thought he was unstoppable," he told her, talking to her now, his words a bit clearer, a bit louder. "I truly did. How can you face someone like that and still believe? Still think you are enough? So many times, I found myself thinking, *This is it, this is the end.* I cannot match this kind of power. But in the end . . ." he trailed off.

"In the end, you did," Jane finished fervently. Captain Dawn raised his head slightly from where it had sunk down, smiling at her passion, the fiery support in her voice.

"Yes," he said kindly. "But it was close. So close. And the cost was so great, I swore I'd never let myself feel that fear again, never let myself be caught so unprepared."

The lines of his face hardened, and Jane swore she felt an energy, a breath of static, pass through the air. "Next time—and there will be a next time, Jane, of that have no doubt—I will be ready. Nothing will fall to chance. When the time comes, I will be ready."

"And I'll be right beside you, sir," she promised, and her heart leaped as he smiled.

"I wouldn't have it any other way, Jane," he said, and she knew he meant every word.

And for the longest time the hero and the empath simply sat together in silence, before finally, Dawn rose to leave.

"Merry Christmas," he murmured.

"Good Christmas?" asked Will, ducking under a snow-laden pine branch.

"Fine," Matt replied ruefully, struggling to maintain his balance in the foot or so of fresh powder. Every step he took caused his legs to sink down almost to his knees. Will, who was several inches taller, seemed to be doing fine, but it was taking all of Matt's concentration simply not to fall over every time he had to wrench a foot from the clutches of the snowdrift. "A lot of food."

They'd materialized at the edge of the forest that marked the boundary of the grounds. Any closer, Matt knew, and Will risked running afoul of Morningstar's Disruptances, which had—according to the latest email—recently been upgraded in light of the persistent paparazzi problem. Normally, Matt wouldn't have given the extended walk a second thought, but the combination of knee-deep snow and an upward-sloping hill was proving to be somewhat challenging. It was only a matter of time, he predicted pessimistically, until he misjudged his footing and found himself facedown making involuntary snow angels.

"How was yours?" he asked Will, half to keep up polite conversation and half to distract himself from his glumness at being back. At least he could see where he was going. The sky was blue, and the air unmoved by any thoughts of wind or snowstorms. If they'd warped right into a blizzard, Matt probably would have just given up and gone home, cover story be damned.

"Nonexistent," the teleporter replied as they passed through the last of the pine trees, and Morningstar came into view, pale and distant in the dull midday sun. "My folks are Muslim."

"And what are you?"

"Sick of shuffling through this goddamn snow."

"Amen to that," Matt agreed, catching himself mid-stumble as his foot disappeared into a deep powder trench. "Wish they'd relax the Disruptances."

Will shook his head. "Winters is nuts about security."

"Yeah, well, Winters can fly. I feel like the implications for the rest of us are kind of lost on him."

"Hey, man, preaching to the choir. You know how far I have to walk to practice every day?"

"You should get a toboggan."

"Then I would have to carry it back up."

"Get Winters to build a—"

He'd been going to say "chair lift," but at that exact moment Matt's foot hooked around something unseen, and he went crashing face-first into the freezing powder. For a moment, all he could see and feel was dark blue and cold biting away at his face—then a sharp pain and hot wetness started radiating from the front of his right leg, which he'd landed on heavily when he fell. Matt swore, his inventive curse words muffled by the snow, and craned his neck back up into the sunlight, spitting out a mouthful of slush.

"Watch yourself, man," said Will, sounding concerned as he bent down and grabbed Matt by the underarms, helping him up.

"Thanks," Matt snapped irritably. "I'll keep that in mind." He shook the flecks of ice from his hair and pulled his leg free from the snowdrift, stretching it gingerly out in front of him to get a better look. Sure enough, it was a mess. The force of the fall combined with the hidden rock he'd slammed into had torn right through his pants and left him with a messy-looking gash along his shin. Dark red globules of blood pumped through the tear, forming garnet splotches where they touched the snow.

"Owwww," Will whistled. "Damn snow."

"It's fine," Matt said through gritted teeth. "I'm fine. Let's just get inside."

"Dude, you should get that cleaned up," said the teleporter, surveying the wound. "You don't know what's in there, snow isn't clean." Matt opened his mouth to argue but then begrudgingly realized the older Acolyte was right.

"Fine," he answered, glaring. "Give me a hand." He wrapped an arm around Will's shoulders and put tentative weight on his injured leg. "Stupid snow."

They limped slowly back up the hill toward the mansion as a sort of ungainly three-legged-man, taking care not to fall victim to any more unseen obstacles. Luckily, whether due to gravity or thoroughfare, the powder got progressively shallower the further they went, meaning by the time they reached the front doors their boots were crushing little more than an inch of compacted ice. The moment they were inside, Will pulled Matt left toward the infirmary wing.

"Clumsy, goddamn idiot," Matt berated himself, looking down at his leg as they moved through the hallways. It was nice to be in out of the cold, but the newfound warmth of Morningstar was eating away at the numbness and pain was starting to sink in. "Shoot, hold on, I think I'm getting blood on the floor."

"Relax, man," Will assured him, maintaining pace. "It's cool. Everyone has bled on this carpet."

"Great," muttered Matt, watching the trickling wound. "Sanitary."

They pushed through the doors to the infirmary, Matt still shouldering his backpack.

"What happened?" asked Delores, one of the younger, more big-bodied healers. She looked up from her iPhone with a smile as they collectively limped inside and glanced at Matt's leg. "You do something stupid?"

"Tripped on a rock," explained Will, releasing Matt and straightening up.

"Neither stupid nor exciting," the medic tutted, placing a hand on her hips as she peered down to get a closer look. "Ah, come now, that's just a baby boo-boo." She flashed him a toothy smile that was in need of orthodontics and waved her hand toward the nearest empty bed. "Shoes and pants off, honey. Sit over there. We'll get you cleaned up in no time."

Matt dutifully did as he was told, moving to sit on top of the pristine bed sheets and awkwardly pulling off first his boots and then his partially ruined ski pants.

"Nice boxers." Will grinned at Matt's Star Wars underwear.

"Shut up," replied Matt, secretly glad he'd put on one of the pairs without holes in them. With his legs fully exposed, Matt was shocked at the size of the gash.

"How'd I do that on one rock?" he wondered, out loud and to nobody in particular.

"You're just special," Will answered, completely unfazed by the sight of blood.

"Suppose we've all got our talents," Matt agreed. His rueful contemplations were interrupted by Delores arriving with both fresh cloth and a clipboard bearing the requisite paperwork.

"Let's clean this up a bit, hmm?" she said. "Then we can get to the fun part." She grinned at Matt and handed him the clipboard, which Matt read while her gloved hands began dabbing gauzy fabric at the mess around his leg. He was about halfway through the form—trying to recall when he'd been vaccinated for HIV—when the sound of the infirmary doors opening caused him to glance up.

Matt's heart sunk. Jane. The empath strode through the door looking angry, defiant, and completely unchanged—save for what looked like a steel spike lodged in her side. Her eyes scanned the room, fixating first on the other healer on duty, who she nodded at in a no-nonsense, "here-I-am" sort of way. A second later, her gaze fell on Matt, sitting over bleeding on the bed. She froze. Their eyes met and for an instant, the empath's mouth opened a fraction—but then her face hardened, and she turned determinedly away.

"Lay down, Miss Walker," the other healer, a tiny woman with an aura of authority disproportionate to her size, sighed with familiar contempt. She shook her head, reluctantly rising from the lounge chair she'd been reclining in. "Over there, wherever you like. You know the drill."

"Almost done, honey." Delores smiled at him, oblivious to Matt's distraction. "Just about ready to close you up."

"Thanks," Matt muttered, glancing back down at his own injury.

Behind him, he heard Jane's healer clicking her tongue. "You're lucky this lodged in a rib. Half an inch lower and it would've gone in your kidney." A grunt. The woman's voice paused. "I'm going to pull it out, try not to scream." Another noncommittal grunt—

"Aaaand one, two, threeee . . ." said Delores. Warm hands pressed either side of his leg and Matt looked down to see new skin scabbing and blooming over the injured area, the wound repairing before his eyes.

After a few seconds, the gash was completely gone. Even the little hairs on his leg had grown back without so much as a scar.

"Good as new." Delores smiled as she put on a new pair of gloves to gather up the bloody gauze. Matt glanced over at Jane; in the time it had taken his leg to heal, the spike had been removed from her side and she'd begun having her chest pressed at by the healer. She was still in the exact same position, her back resolutely toward him. Matt hadn't heard her make a sound.

"Thank you," he told Delores. He forced a smile, trying not to let his irritation show. Matt got to his feet, hesitating momentarily as his mended leg took the weight, pulled on his ruined pants, and quickly filled out the rest of the questionnaire.

"Come on," he said to Will, not looking back. "Let's get out of here." He smiled at Delores. "Thanks again." The large healer winked at him. As they walked, the teleporter glanced over his shoulder at Jane, who was still silently pretending neither of them existed. He frowned.

"You guys have a fight or something?" Will asked.

"Doesn't matter," Matt muttered as they strode out of the infirmary. "It's fine."

"You sure?"

"Yes," replied Matt. "Totally. A hundred percent. I just need a drink. You know what?" He paused mid-sentence and stopped in his tracks, turning to Will. So help him God, he was going to get kicked out of this place. "I think we all need a drink. Everyone. The whole damn Academy."

"What do you mean?" asked the teleporter.

"I mean," said Matt, starting forward again at a brisk and purposeful pace, "it's almost New Year's Eve. Let's have a goddamn party."

"It's going to be quite a party," said Wally, lifting an avocado maki roll from the tray in front of them. "Outdoor dance floor. Fireworks. There's even talk of snow-based cocktails." He popped the seaweed roll into his mouth and glanced down his freckled nose at her with a meaningful look.

Jane wasn't sure she liked sushi. She'd never really had it before. Maybe once with Mom as a kid. But not lately that she could remember. She didn't know—something about raw fish and cold rice made her suspicious. But Will had bought it especially for Wally from some apparently great place in Japan, and he'd wanted to share, so she had to try and "appreciate" it.

"Jane?" the psychic asked, leaning over, trying to catch her downcast eyes. "Did you hear me?"

"I think I like the little fried shrimp the best," she replied, refusing to be drawn.

"Tempura," he corrected her. "And you didn't answer my question."

"What question?" Jane glowered. "There was no question. Matt's throwing a party. Big deal. What's it got to do with me? He can do what he wants. I don't care." She focused resolutely on the seaweed "food," refusing to meet Wally's gaze.

They were seated in their usual deserted Saturday classroom, their mental defense sessions over for the year—Jane's weary mind reduced to mush from another hour of psychic boxing. Wally hadn't pushed too hard this time—holiday spirit, she guessed—so her head felt less sickly and shambolic than normal. She was getting better, but slowly—Jane still couldn't keep Wally out in any meaningful way.

"You know what I mean," the psychic said, leaning back in his chair, waving his chopsticks around like a conductor. Even in the middle of winter, he still refused to wear anything but those stupid Hawaiian shirts. "Are you going to go?"

Jane just grunted and made clumsily for another fried shrimp thing, her chopstick skills lacking both practice and grace. Obviously, the answer was no—because what would be the point, because there was no point, because parties were stupid and a waste of time and so was everyone at them.

"Hmm," mused Wally, regarding her with a knowing gaze. After a pause, he asked, "Is there anything you'd like to talk about?"

"No," Jane replied, sounding more sour than she would have liked.

"Right," said the redheaded psychic, very skeptical. "Well, can I offer some advice?"

"No," she repeated.

"I'm going to anyway," he drawled, rolling his eyes. He paused and peered down at her. "You should apologize."

"I don't know what you're talking about," Jane replied.

"Right, which is why you're making that face," said Wally.

"I'm not making any face." Jane stated sourly.

"Matt will forgive you if you say you're sorry," the psychic pressed on, unabated.

Jane turned on him. "I thought we agreed you'd stay out of my thoughts," she snapped, dropping all pretense of not knowing what he was talking about.

"Yes, well, when people walk around shouting it sometimes carries through the walls," Wally said, his arms crossed, completely unapologetic. "And it's not my fault if I overhear things, especially when the walls are paper-thin."

Jane stayed silent, resigned to glaring.

"I'm not being mean," Wally said dryly, pointing a chopstick. "I'm just being honest."

For a moment, Jane contemplated feeling indignant, but victim was never a role she'd much liked. Besides, she conceded internally, it was hardly an insult to imply that her mental defenses were bad, since that was literally why she was sitting here in the first place.

"What else have you heard?" she relented begrudgingly.

"You mean apart from the existence of a secret little foray to the Balkans, which I definitely didn't already know about, and a whole bunch of very inappropriate thoughts about Captain Dawn?" He gave her a significant and somewhat disapproving look, and Jane felt her cheeks burn. "You know he's almost, like, sixty, right?"

Jane mumbled something indistinct, suddenly fascinated by the tray of gross sushi in front of her. Wally rolled his eyes.

"Uh-huh. Well, but hey, whatever. What goes on between you two is none of my business."

"Yeah, well, so is everything else," Jane retorted, still closely monitoring the seaweed.

"Nice try, but no," replied the psychic. "Look," he said, leaning forward. "Matt's a good guy. He's nice—I like him. And I think you like him too, actually, except you're too stubborn to admit it. But regardless, I think we both know he hasn't done anything wrong. And he's certainly not out to get you."

Jane just stared at the ground.

"Look," Wally said patiently, "these things happen. You were hurt, you lashed out, and now you feel bad. And"—he continued, overriding her protests—"you've spent the last few weeks going back and forth between trying to figure out how to apologize without apologizing and trying to convince yourself you have nothing to apologize for at all. And that you don't actually care."

Jane bristled and opened her mouth to argue but stopped at the sight of Wally's uncompromising frown. "Don't argue with me, Jane Walker," said the psychic, clicking his tongue. "I can literally read your mind." He paused, unaffected by her scowl. "I know what's been running around your head and not saying it out loud won't make it any less true."

They stared at each other for a few seconds. Eventually, Jane's glare succumbed to Wally's raised eyebrow.

"Even if . . ." she reluctantly conceded. "Even if that was true . . . which it isn't . . ." she added aggressively, managing to affect no change in Wally's expression. "Even if it was . . . I mean, I don't . . . what would I even say?"

"Hey, Matt, sorry about the other day, that wasn't cool."

"Seriously."

"I am being serious," said the psychic. "Just go up to him and say sorry."

"That's pathetic," argued Jane. "I'm not going to grovel."

"You're not groveling, you're apologizing," Wally replied with a touch of impatience. "It's what adults do when they make mistakes." He looked at Jane as if her thoughts were as plain as day. "Admitting you're wrong doesn't make you weak."

Jane shifted uncomfortably in her seat. It'd been easier when they'd been making fun of her fantasies.

"I . . . I don't know," she murmured. Her fingers intertwined themselves unconsciously in her lap. "I don't know."

"I think you do," contradicted Wally, though there was kindness in his voice. "And I think you'll regret it if you don't."

"You'll regret it if you don't," Matt assured him. "Come on, man, the whole Academy's going."

Ed said nothing but kept tapping away at the keyboard—though his typing was slow—for him—and half-hearted. He was listening at least, though his bleary eyes and sunken posture did little to instill a sense of confidence. But Matt pressed on, a valiant champion of positive peer pressure.

"It's New Year's," he said. "Everyone will be there. There'll be drinks and dancing and fireworks—well, sky explosions," Matt conceded, correcting himself, "courtesy of Chloe Gup, who can do, like, three different colors and apparently, like, eighty percent in the right direction."

"Oh great, fireworks," Ed droned, low and sarcastic. His eyes didn't leave the screen. "Loud noises and colors in the sky. How engaging. How unique."

"Come on, man," said Matt, frowning at him. "Don't be like that."

"Be like what?" mumbled Ed.

"All negative and stuff. Give it a chance. Have some fun."

"I'm a genius," Ed said in a dejected voice as he slumped back in his computer chair. "I'm too smart to have fun."

Matt shook his head. Ed had been this way ever since Matt had gotten back—distant and down, reluctant to talk or socialize or do anything that would involve him having to leave the safety of his computer room. In the month or so, Matt had been gone, the genius looked like he'd lost about five pounds. His face was gaunt and speckled with patchy, unkempt stubble, and his black mop of hair was in desperate need of a comb. Matt didn't know when he'd last gone outside—his clothes made it abundantly clear that he'd been sleeping in his chair.

"Ed, man, come on. Everyone will miss you."

"I don't know," Ed mumbled. He finally broke off from the screen, looking at Matt with a small, defeated gaze. His eyes still moved with their usual inherent quickness, but everything around them was heavy. "I don't think anybody cares if I'm not there."

"I care," Matt promised. Ed shook his head, turning back to his screen.

"Everyone will have fun without me."

"Everyone will have fun with you. Come on, man, why're you making this so difficult?"

"I just . . ." Ed protested. "I'm not a party person. These . . . these things aren't meant for me." He let out a long, heavy sigh. "I'm better off just staying here."

"Why?" asked Matt. "What are you doing here that's so incredibly important that you can't take a single night off? Is it the whole human thing? The gene-mapping stuff?"

"Well, yeah, a little bit," replied the genius. "But I've got other stuff too."

"Like what?" said Matt, folding his arms. Ed pointed at a small, thin, matte-gray coin about the size of the circle between a thumb and fore-finger that was sitting innocuously underneath his rightmost moni-tor. Smooth and rounded, it had raised edges and three tiny crystalline domes arranged in a triangle in the middle.

"Like that," he said.

"Okay," replied Matt, not sure if he was supposed to know what "that" was. He glanced at the innocent gray token. "What's that?"

"It's a telepathic enabler nodule," Ed explained. He paused, then see-ing the blank look on Matt's face, elaborated. "It lets a non-telepath enter someone's mind."

"Wait, what?" Matt exclaimed. He stared open-mouthed at the genius, who to Matt's disbelief did not appear in the least bit excited. "Ed, are you serious?" When Ed simply nodded, Matt struggled to respond. "Ed . . . I mean . . . holy . . . how long have you been sitting on this?"

"It's not that exciting," Ed mumbled. He made no attempt to pick up or move the coin, but simply looked at it with an expression of unenthu-siastic boredom. Matt couldn't believe his ears.

"Ed. Buddy. *This. Is. Huge.* How can you not," he faltered, at a loss for words, running his hands through his hair. "How are you . . . why are you so calm? This is incredible! Nobody has ever replicated a power before! This could be worth millions!"

"It's just the prototype," the genius said with a shrug. Matt couldn't understand how he could sound so disinterested. "I can't market it yet. There's still a bunch of problems."

"But . . . but . . ." spluttered Matt, still feeling like Ed was missing the enormity of his own invention. "But, I mean, it works?!"

"Well, yeah," said Ed. "Once. Then it burns out and is worthless." He shrugged again, complacent in the face of Matt's incredulity. "So I mean it's not special. It's not even really my own design."

"Well, then whose design is it?" Matt asked, gawking at the billion-dollar breakthrough sitting on a dusty computer desk like a disused pog.

"Viktor Mentok's."

"The Mindtaker?" said Matt, tearing his gaze away from the nodule and back to Ed. "How'd you get a hold of his stuff?"

"He was the Legion's genius," explained Ed, "back in the day. They kept a lot of his schematics after he went rogue." He glanced back at the screen. "His original designs were more centered around implants and motor control, but the underlying potential was there."

"Wow," wowed Matt. He leaned back, hands on his hips. "Still, Ed, that's pretty damn impressive."

"Maybe once it's finished," the genius mumbled. He looked up. "But now do you see why I shouldn't come to the party? I've got work to do."

"Ed . . ." implored Matt. On the one hand, he had to admit, it was incredible. But on the other hand . . . "There're more important things than work. Like you, buddy." Matt paused and shook his head. "What's the point of all this if you never give yourself a chance to be happy?"

"Bettering the human race?"

"You're part of the human race. Your first port of call should be bettering yourself."

"By being intoxicated and watching sky explosions? As opposed to expanding my knowledge?"

"Ed," Matt said with a sigh, "we both know you can argue circles around me. But don't think I don't know an excuse when I hear one." He continued firmly, because Ed looked like he was thinking of interrupting. "You don't want to come, fine, don't come. But don't kid yourself that it's because of work. Your work isn't going anywhere, man."

The genius said nothing, just looked straight ahead, staring blankly at the computer screen. He'd finally stopped typing. Behind his glasses, Ed blinked rapidly, and his head drooped.

"I'm a mess," he murmured.

"We'll get you cleaned up."

"All my clothes are ugly."

"You can borrow some of mine." Matt paused. Suddenly, he had an idea. "Look," he said, careful to keep his face honest, "I've been seeing a few things around you lately. You know . . . future things."

This actually made Ed glance up. "Yeah?" he said nervously—but maybe, just maybe, also a little hopeful. "Really?"

"Really, really," Matt lied through his teeth. "Now I can't say for sure. You know this stuff's always pretty blurry. But I can definitely, one hundred percent see you falling for someone, buddy." He paused to let the "prophecy" sink in. "And when you do, it'll change your life."

For a few moments, Ed was silent. He bit his lip. "You really see that about me?" he murmured.

Matt tapped his nose and gave him a knowing look.

"All I'm saying is, you know, man, this party, people are going to be there."

"Obviously. Human presence is literally a prerequisite."

Matt rolled his eyes and ignored his friend the dictionary salesman. "I'm saying, Ed, *people*." He paused and raised his eyebrows significantly. "Maybe people like Giselle. She's going to be there."

"So?" mumbled Ed, slumping back down over the keyboard. "She's out of my league."

"That's the only type of girl worth going for, in my opinion," replied Matt.

Ed's gaze was withering. "And how many girlfriends have you had?"

"How many girlfriends *haven't* I had? Well, technically, a lot," Matt conceded, but he continued unfazed. "But that doesn't change the fact that you're a great guy, who's probably going to be a billionaire someday, and if you like Giselle, you should just ask her out!"

"I don't know," mumbled Ed.

"What's the worst thing that can happen?"

"She breaks my neck at superspeed?"

"Okay, realistically what's the worst thing that can happen?"

Ed fell silent.

"I don't know how to talk to girls."

"Well, it's a lot like talking to people, since, you know, that's what girls are."

"I don't know how to talk to people."

"Right, you're smart enough to sequence a nonexistent genome, but you don't know the fundamentals of conversation. Just ask questions and pretend to be interested!"

"But what would I even say?" Ed asked, shifting uncomfortably in his chair. "All I really know about her is that we've got the same phone."

"Ed, man, come on, I'm sure you know—wait, why do you have a kinetic phone?" Matt asked, momentarily distracted. He'd seen Giselle zipping around the place texting on hers, but never imagined a non-speedster would need one.

"I'm a fast texter," Ed answered with a shrug.

"Like how fast are we talking?"

"Like non-speedster Guinness World record for a few years?"

"Wow. I mean . . . wow. There you go, that's impressive, talk to her about that!"

"You really think so?"

"Well, I wouldn't open with it, but I don't know, man. You're interesting! Is what I'm saying."

Ed shifted uncomfortably. "But what do I say then?"

"Jeez, Ed, I don't know," Matt said, exasperated. "Say 'hi, how's it going? What're you drinking? How's breaking land speed? Your shoes look nice, where'd you get them?' Then tell her about the amazing stuff you're doing, your dreams, your ideas, and then just say 'hey, I think you're really cool, do you want to go get dinner some time?' "

For a few seconds, Ed just sat, staring at the screen. Then finally, in a very quiet voice, he asked, "And you think she'll say yes?"

Matt threw up his hands. "Dude, honestly? I don't know. Maybe she will, maybe she won't. But"—he continued, before Ed could truly start to slump—"man, I do know one thing, and that's that you've got nothing to lose. I'm serious." He paused. "Maybe you tell her you like her, and she doesn't feel the same way. Or maybe you tell her, and she does! Either way," Matt said, and he looked Ed square in the eye, "you're no further away from dating her than if you stay up here."

Ed hesitated. He glanced at the screen, then up at Matt. And then, to Matt's amazement, he simply said, "You're right."

"I am?" Matt wondered out loud, taken aback. Then he added, "I mean, damn right I am!"

"I might as well try!" declared Ed, rising to his feet.

"That's my man!"

"My work can wait one night!" he cried, talking more to himself than Matt at this point.

"That's right! Well," admitted Matt, "unless something horrible happens to you tonight and you die leaving it all unfinished."

"Not helpful," growled Ed.

"Sorry," said Matt.

The night sky was clear. The moon shone bright and the snow-drenched world gleamed. Fires glowed, stars danced.

And Morningstar Academy celebrated.

Not just the Acolytes, who turned out in their hundreds, but some of the Ashes and tutors too. Warily at first, perhaps—to rouse, to monitor, to control—but in the end, the lure of merriment proved irresistible. It was New Year's Eve, after all, and, in theory at least, they were only human. *Human.* Matt's intoxicated brain giggled. *Shush*, said another smarter part, and so it did, the thought buried under noise and light and laughter.

There were so many people. He flowed through the crowd like water, between the rocks of those he knew and those he didn't, never staying anywhere for long, always being called over, being beckoned by another half-familiar face. Strings of colored lights were strung from walls to windows to trees, and man-sized speakers blared a never-ending stream of music. Matt couldn't quite remember whether this was his mix, but it didn't matter. Over near the speakers, the terra- and pyromancers had cleared a large, square dance floor in the snow, which pulsed and jumped with people, their movements mesmerizing. Everywhere there was people, laughter, drinks, red cups filled with green punch whose cloying fruity sweetness masked its potency—James Conrad's contribution, apparently a specialty, which, after about the fifth refill, Matt had to admit redeemed a lot of the strongman's negative traits. He kept on waiting for his drink to run out, but every time he reached the bottom, it somehow filled back up—or maybe some eager partygoer had put a full one in his hand, Matt didn't know. *I need to slow down*, he thought, feeling a sugary pain in his stomach as he wandered, breathing the night air deep, feeling the music in his ears, the company around him, and slow, warm happiness spreading through his fingers and toes.

With her back to the wall, Jane could see him. Standing in the thick of it—talking, laughing. So small, so uniquely vulnerable. How could he not be afraid of them, this drunken mass of the world's most powerful people, with nothing to protect him. He was stupid. She almost envied it.

She twisted her cold gloveless hands together, her fingers numb from standing in the dark, far from the crowds, the fire. She wasn't hiding, not exactly, but she hung back in the shadows against the manor's wall. She could see everything: Giselle laughing, surrounded by boys, Wally in animated conversation with Will, James Conrad making out with some girl. She even caught a glimpse of Mac, off to the side by a firepit, drinking from a silver hip flask and murmuring quietly to Cross. Everyone looked like they were having fun.

Hi. Matt. We need to . . I mean, can we . . . just talk, I mean, you don't have to talk, I just want to . . .

She kept forgetting her lines; or she hadn't forgotten, but she'd screw them up when she went to say them, she knew it. Stupid Wally, stupid . . .

I'm sorry. I didn't mean . . .well I meant, but not . . . what I'm trying to say is . . .

It was all the people. If she could just get him alone, where there weren't so many stupid people who would watch and laugh, she . . . she needed somewhere quiet, just to hear herself think, but the grounds were all pop music and bonfires and voices. Somehow, she'd never thought this part through—never considered that a party might actually have people.

You don't understand what I . . . I mean . . .You shouldn't have to understand . . . I just . . .

There. He was free. Breaking off, by himself at the edge of the crowd, slipping a little on the well-trod ice. Jane leaned forward; but then hesitated, struggling, stopped midway off the wall . . .

Come on, come on, before he—

Jane watched, shivering, as three girls drew alongside and pulled Matt toward them, something about doing their fortunes, cackling madly, one shimmering and pulling him into a literal bear hug. The tension sagged from Jane's limbs, and she slumped back against the wall.

Out of the corner of Matt's eye, he saw it. He was sitting by one of the firepits, cup in hand, while beside him Celeste's bear head lay drunkenly in her friend's lap, listening to a story about someone from some guy's high school who had fallen pregnant with twins. Maybe married a country singer—Matt drifted in and out. A young man with long, dark hair and beautiful almond eyes had brought out a guitar and was strumming some familiar tune, his fingers phasing in and out intangibly along the strings, sending haunting notes echoing out to be swallowed up by the sea of noise. There was Jell-O-shots—somebody had definitely said Jell-O-shots—and Celeste's friend was telling anyone who would listen that she was going to hook up with Natalia Baroque when she got back from London. But none of that mattered, because out of the corner of Matt's eye, he saw it.

They were all the way over the other side of the bonfire, the slightest bit separated from the party. Giselle Pixus, stepping out to warm her hands. And Edward Rakowski, coming up slowly alongside her. Even from over here, Matt could see him saying hi. Could see her smiling, see them starting to talk. See her reach out and brush his arm, the briefest, lightest touch. Saw Ed smile, and for the first time in who knows how long actually, genuinely laugh.

Go, you good thing, Matt thought, smiling, and he drained every last drop from his cup—because if Ed's courage wasn't something to drink to, then he didn't know what was.

Jane didn't know how long she'd stood there. A part of her, a stupid, irrational part, held fast to the belief that if she stood there, unsuccessfully, until the party was over, then somehow that counted. That she'd have "done her duty," so to speak and be absolved of the need to apologize.

She'd said it was stupid.

"Still trying to w-w-work up the c-c-courage?" asked Wally, stumbling up beside her. He was slurring but smiling, an arm slung over Will's shoulder. The teleporter grinned at him, perhaps a bit less drunk, and Wally grinned back before slowly untangling their arms. He slumped against the wall next to Jane, who'd seen them coming a mile away—hard not to with them lurching from side to side and Wally wearing his most garish floral shirt. She felt his reeling mind brush hers, not invasive, just sloppy.

"Honey, you just have to . . . you have to," Wally tried to say, but then stopped, ginger eyebrows furrowing in confusion. He turned back to Will. "What am I saying?"

"You just have to talk to him," the tall teleporter said with a grin.

"That's the one," nodded Wally, turning back to her. "Talk to him. Walk up, say 'Hey, Matt, let's talk . . .'"

"Or 'do you mind if we step outside'?" suggested Will.

"We're already outside," muttered Jane. The two men didn't seem to hear her.

"Can we talk in private?"

"Alooooooonnne."

"Where it's warmmmm."

"God, I could go someplace warm," announced Wally. "Screw this snow, bring me a beach." He pursed his lips, then shook his head and turned back to Jane, seeming to remember why he'd come over.

"Sorry," he mumbled, keeping his voice low. "Look. Let me go chat with him. Explain that you're sorry, that you . . . everything. You know. And then he can bring his cute butt over here and you can tell him yourself. What do you think?"

Jane wanted to say yes—but she couldn't. It felt so pathetic, like a six-year-old needing someone to carry messages across the playground. It was cowardly. Matt would never have done it.

So, she shook her head. A sad smile crossed Wally's face. He patted her shoulder, then turned back and looped arms again with Will. Jane watched the two of them wander off together toward the tree line, their figures fading into the darkness, alone, waiting for her moment, hating herself.

Matt didn't know how long he'd been out there. He remembered throwing back a drink with James Conrad; something about helping a large Mongolian man (with at least three other guys) back onto his feet after he'd hurled all over himself; fending off the advances of that healer Delores; and having a deep, animated conversation with a venomancer about Buddhism. But how that all tied together and in what order the drinks were keeping a mystery. All he knew now for certain was that he was dancing really, really badly.

Where was Ed? He'd seen him talking to . . . wanted to know how he'd got on with . . . Abruptly, Matt wrenched himself out from the mosh of moving bodies and stumbled between the firepits, scanning for his friend. "Wooo, Matt!" someone shouted, but he brushed the sound away as if it was a fly buzzing near his ear. He stopped by the bonfire, squeezing his eyes open and closed, trying to think straight. What was he doing? Why was he out here? Was he getting another drink? Something about Giselle . . . but wait, that couldn't be right, Giselle was there, he could see her, she was . . . laughing, a whirl of grace on the dance floor. But if she was there, where was . . .

In the darkness, he thought maybe he could make out his silhouette—his dark, messy hair, the slump of his shoulders, the paisley shirt

Matt had lent him. Matt saw him go, trudging back alone up the hill toward the mansion, and wondered if he should follow, if he should call out, make sure everything was all right . . . but then there was noise, and laughter, someone calling his name, something about the music, or shots, or dancing, and in his humming haze the thought of Ed slipped from his mind—dropped, misplaced, left laying somewhere in the snow. Matt's hand had somehow found another cup of that most excellent punch, and he was weaving back toward the dance floor, some commotion happening, people laughing and cheering, a wide space forming among the crowd . . .

It was a competition. A dance-off, the type of thing he thought only happened in movies. This short-haired Korean guy, a replicator, commanding the entire floor with a dozen copies of himself. People were whooping, clapping, because it was incredible, unbeatable—until Giselle Pixus stepped up. She looked down at the ground, and as the music started—some Spice Girls song—her feet began moving, tapping fast, then faster, then so fast they were a blur. And then, the movement began spreading up her body—her hips, her arms, her hands, swirling, swaying, mesmerizing. Suddenly, she paused, for only a fraction of a second right before the chorus hit, a single, breathless breath. Then the music dropped and suddenly there wasn't one of her, there were three, there was five, five hazy flickering images, illusions of unfathomable speed, all a microsecond apart so that when she danced, the movement rippled through them—beautiful, hypnotizing in its un-synchronicity. Even through the cloud around his mind, Matt couldn't avert his eyes, and when the music finally stopped and Giselle came to a halt, he found himself shouting, cheering, whistling his wild support along with everyone around him. She was laughing, exhilarated, red-faced and breathless, grinning from ear to ear.

He remembered wandering off after that, laying down somewhere, maybe, for a little . . . but then before he'd even really closed his eyes, a strong hand was shaking him awake, saying that he needed to get inside, come on, you can't sleep in the snow. The voice was helping him, holding him, almost carrying him, her voice familiar, as was the feeling of her hand in his as she dragged him along—relentless, firm, yet strangely warm.

* * *

"There you go," Jane muttered, ducking her head slowly out from underneath Matt's arm. The boy made a face and stumbled, sliding into the corridor wall.

"Wassda party?" he asked, more slur than words. He made a grab for a handhold that wasn't there but luckily Jane was quicker than an untrained drunk and managed to catch him before he fell.

"Keys," she demanded.

"Wha?"

"Keys," she repeated. "You idiot."

"Oh. Hi, Jane," he muttered. His hand fumbled around in his pocket, and it took a whole ten seconds to close around his keychain. "What you . . . what you want my . . . ?"

"Thanks," said Jane, snatching them out of his hand. She leaned forward and wriggled the key to Matt's room into the lock, which was made more difficult by the fact that she was also supporting most of Matt's weight.

"In you go," she announced as the door swung open into a breath of cold air. She hobbled the two of them inside with relative ease and flicked the door closed with her leg. The curtains were open, and the glow of the party fires was still bright enough to give her a general view around the room. She rotated her drunken cargo toward his bed.

"Lay down, shoes off," she commanded Matt, who instead collapsed, fully clothed, on top of his blankets. Jane rolled her eyes, and for a moment contemplated whether she felt regretful enough to remove Matt's boots for him. A second later, he began to snore, and she decided he probably wouldn't care. She sighed, gazing down at him, unconscious and asleep.

"This wasn't the plan," she muttered under her breath to him and to herself, but the fake clairvoyant remained blissfully unaware. Jane exhaled, somewhere between an irritable sigh and a groan. Well, there was no point in saying sorry now—the idiot wouldn't remember it. Still face down, Matt fidgeted slightly, murmuring something indistinct. Jane shook her head and, with only a single backward glance to make sure he was all right, padded softly from the room. She'd dragged him inside—maybe that counted. She'd ask Wally.

As she went to close the door, a roar of voices echoed in from outside—indistinct at first, but then louder. "SIX . . . FIVE . . . FOUR . . .

THREE . . . TWO . . . ONE . . ." and then there came flashes, bursts of light, and explosive bangs, intermingling with a chorus of cheers. Jane shook her head and smiled at the unconscious figure she'd pulled out of the snow.

"Happy New Year, dumbass," she chuckled, closing the door behind her.

The computer lab was dark, save for the glow of a single screen—an unrelenting torrent of white-blue light, illuminating the slouching body of the man before it. Edward Rakowski. Alone, like always. His fingers tapped and tripped along the keyboard, a sound as steady as rain and equally comforting. Everything else might leave him; nobody might want him. But his work remained. What did Mentok used to say? "My dullest thoughts are your epiphanies"? Arrogant, but accurate. Even after 5.6 standard drinks, Ed's brain functioned—he was still useful, still had purpose.

Even if he would always be alone.

Ed worked in silence—the computer an extension of his hand, the Internet an extension of his mind. Information, data, pieces, assembled here and there. Trivial and important, it all fitted in somewhere. Maybe he was an aberration in that regard.

He sighed, pinched the bridge of his nose. There were no breakthroughs coming tonight. He could feel that already. Still, there must be something to do, some minor goal he could—of course. Ed leaned back in his chair, fingers dancing, searching absentmindedly in pursuit of an insignificant task. On and on—through and through. Lists built, lists scratched.

Suddenly, he noticed something. Something odd. He shook his head as his mind processed the data and abruptly postulated an idea. A strange idea, an odd, bizarre suggestion, but yet . . . Alone, in the dark, Ed frowned. How peculiar. Surely, that doesn't . . . Yet even on a whim, worth investigating.

His fingers clicked from side to side, keyboard and mouse, further down into the rabbit hole. And slowly, a tightness spread throughout his chest. Trepidation. Dread.

There was no way. This couldn't be right.

But it was. One after the other, after the other, he found them. More and more of them. Dozens, hundreds. A thought became a question, became a hunch, because a fear, became a pounding, shrieking, terrible realization.

"Oh God," he whispered as panic flooded screaming through his mind. He raced into his email, his fingers trembling, his arms shaking—

And then suddenly he stopped.

Frozen.

Paralyzed.

Unmoving, unblinking. His eyes wide, terrified. Still, completely still—save for the slightest, momentary twitch.

Then the twitch stopped, and he stood. In a single, fluid motion, Ed rose from his chair, reached over, and turned off his computer. He turned and calmly walked across the lab and out the door. He strode briskly through the darkened corridors, past the closed-off rooms, the sleeping students. He turned up the stairs, moving quickly, with purpose. Around and around and around, up and up and up, until he reached the mouth of a bare and barren stairwell, having come as high as he could climb. Ed pushed open the metal door and stepped out, barefoot, into the cold.

Without a single word or sound, he walked slowly across the rooftop, further and further forward, until he was standing on edge of the building looking out into open space. His eyes were wide, his pupils desperate and frozen—and yet he never glanced down. His arms remained loose, relaxed by his side. He didn't shout or cry, didn't call for help. And he only hesitated, ever so slightly, when he took that final step off and out into nothingness.

At 3:54 a.m., Edward Rakowski walked off the highest point of Morningstar Academy.

Bzzzzzzz.

In the darkness, Matt groaned. Barely conscious, his hands fumbled down the length of his pants into his pocket, his fingers grasping clumsily around the cold metal of his phone. Begrudgingly, he pulled it out. Head still face-down in his pillow, he dragged the phone up until the screen was right in front of his eyes, which recoiled and stung at the sudden assault of light. Through bleary delirium, Matt tried to focus, to make sense of who on Earth was messaging him at this ungodly hour . . .

Ed (1)

Matt blinked, slow and painful, his dry tongue moving gingerly over parched lips, his head pulsating dangerously. His fingers stumbled through the unlock pattern, his eyes reluctantly adjusting to the glare, groggily taking in Ed's text. He groaned—what was this? Stupid Ed. Matt's eyes drooped. His vision blurred, and his head rolled back onto the pillow, the phone slipping from his grasp as he retreated into unconsciousness. It dropped onto the carpet with a muffled thud and lay there as the sound of Matt's snores filled the room. Forgotten, the light from the screen faded into darkness—still showing a final message.

A single word.

Dawn

A DEAD MAN'S WORD

"Fragile Minds and Fallen Angels: The Viktor Mentok Story"
The New Yorker, August 23, 1994

Selected extracts from the new biography by Miles Green
$29.95

It is typical to view hell as a place of fire. But to the people of Stalingrad in the winter of 1942, hell was the cold. Cold, which never abated, which wasted extremities, froze provisions, took people you cared about in the night. It is difficult for us now, with modern comforts and fire so easily conjured, to imagine this kind of cold. To imagine the hell that was Stalingrad, the greatest and possibly deadliest battle in pre-superhuman history.

Viktor Mentok was born and orphaned in Stalingrad. His father fell to the fighting—one of the millions who gave their lives to halt the German advance, his mother, a month later to the frost. The young Mentok, only ten at the time, could easily have perished there too, but he did not. Instead, he became an errand boy for the Russian defenders, running messages and relaying orders through the type of devastation no child is equipped to see. Even then, his uncle Ivan Mentok, a former Soviet rifleman, recounts, he was resilient, determined to do his part. No one can flourish in a place like Stalingrad—they can only endure.

It is difficult to reconcile the photograph of the bright-faced, underfed boy that Ivan Mentok hands me with the grim, weathered guise of the Viktor Mentok lead away in chains from an Oklahoma courtroom at fifty-eight,

convicted of 14 counts of abuse of powers and 212 counts of mental violation. This Mentok's nose is bent and prominent, his overarching eyebrows
thick and dark, his lips sallow and his eyes almost black. He is, to the tabloids' delight, the splitting image of the Russian supervillain he has been
made out to be—a hunched, sour-faced old man who sits silently in the
docks, unmoved by tear-stained testimony from witness after witness about
how he used them, controlled them, violated their bodies and minds. He is
as cold and unfeeling as his Stalingrad upbringing—the child inside him
long since dead.

At least, that is what the papers would have us believe. The truth, I think,
is not so simple. . . .

And so on a hot August morning in 1969, a lone Russian by the name
of Viktor Mentok strode unannounced into the Legion of Heroes camp and
impatiently offered those assembled his services. With a generation of "Red
Peril" still firmly entrenched in many minds, the arrival of this young, self-
proclaimed "genius" was met with suspicion and surprise. So far, the newly
formed Legion had struggled to bring in members. Few, if any, had sought
them out, let alone arrived from nowhere looking to swear allegiance on their
doorstep. But Viktor Mentok was different. He claimed he'd anticipated the
emergence of something like the Legion and was adamant in his belief that
it was mankind's best hope in these turbulent times—which, he assured the
Legion, would not end without intervention. . . .

And throughout it all, Mentok remained tireless. When he was not coor-
dinating operations or on the frontlines in Siegfried, his iconic twelve-foot
suit of mechanized armor, he was hard at work in his laboratory experiment-
ing, innovating and calculating the Legion's best response against rising
threats. . . .

Yet despite the Legion's many years and successes, the death of Captain
Dawn's wife, Caitlin Reid, seemed to invoke a darker change in Mentok. He
became markedly more pro-active, outspoken in his advocacy of intervention in a larger number of situations on ever less substantial grounds. When
his calls were not heeded, he grew increasingly isolated, withdrawing into
his research. Caitlin's accident and its random, almost trivial nature were to
Mentok tantamount to a personal failing—a failure to protect a woman he
had respected, admired, and maybe (in his own platonic, yet doggedly loyal
way) even loved from a pointless, unnecessary death. If a life as vibrant and
wholesome as Caitlin's could be snuffed out by an unemployed drunk in a

Chevrolet, how could anything the Legion did matter? People could be liberated from tyrants, protected from psychopaths and malicious regimes—but it was meaningless, Mentok argued, if the Legion could not save people, save society, from their own poor choices. . . .

The morning of February 5, 1989 brought snow—and the discovery of an empty room. Reclusive as he'd become, Mentok's disappearance was not noticed until Harsheel Singh came calling with a bowl of lamb madras, having not seen Viktor for several days and concerned for his well-being. When, exactly, Mentok had departed Morningstar was unclear—he left no note, no clue where he was going. In fact, the only indication the Legion had that their comrade had not been kidnapped was that, along with his files having been wiped, an additional administrator account had been added to Morningstar's security servers for Elsa Arrendel. Talks of a search party were shortly dismissed, with the White Queen stating in no uncertain terms that the Grandmaster obviously did not want to be found. His quarters were sealed off in case of return, and as weeks turned to months, the Legion came to muse that Viktor Mentok's disappearance was simply as sudden and unexpected as his arrival. . . .

But they were wrong. Late in the evening on January 9, 1990, in the small town of Athens, Ohio, Viktor Mentok pushed open the door to Copperfield's Bar, produced his Legion of Heroes insignia, and proclaimed to the gathered crowd that their town had been infected by a bioengineered plague. In addition to closing the roads, he told them, he would have to administer protective implants to everyone, and quickly, before symptoms manifested and the disease became untreatable. The townspeople, alarmed but moved by the urgency of these claims as well as Mentok's fame, did not hesitate to submit to his demands, and without resistance allowed themselves to be affixed with small metallic devices, embedded in the backs of their necks. By the time they realized their mistake, it was too late. . . .

Captain Dawn entered Athens alone—his first departure from Morningstar in months—insistent that he face his former comrade alone, that the reports were wrong. Once in the town, to his surprise, he found no dead, no destruction, no signs of disaster. But his relief soon turned to shock as every person in Athens greeted him in unison—their bodies, implanted with neural override receivers, under the complete and total domination of Viktor Mentok. He had created a prototype for utopia, Mentok told Dawn through a thousand, united voices, a place free from violence, mistakes, or malevolence, where everyone would always be safe. . . .

Dawn's report lacking detail, it is difficult to know the exact circumstances of Mentok's surrender. Some say he submitted after his central control console was destroyed, others that he voluntarily relinquished control after realizing that forcing the Athenians to fight placed them in the same danger he was trying to prevent. Some say he simply spoke to Captain Dawn and, when their conversation ended, allowed himself to be arrested rather than fighting his oldest friend. Regardless of what transpired, the town was released without casualties and Captain Dawn emerged with Viktor Mentok in custody, alive . . .

Though unharmed, to those who knew him, something in the man now being dubbed the Mindtaker had broken; something had changed. At first, they simply believed it was emotional—guilt, depression, the burden of failure—but as time went on it became apparent that something deeper, something worse, was afoot . . .

Scarlett syndrome: a degenerative disease of the mind, which had only recently been identified as occurring in as many as one in ten geniuses. Still widely misunderstood, doctors initially viewed the disorder as an abnormal form of dementia—only to later realize that the brains of those afflicted were not breaking down, but speeding up. . . . In essence, like Logan's disorder, the problem stemmed from the power growing erratic, strengthening even, to the point of detriment. . . . Mentok's intelligence, instead of settling, was accelerating, his thoughts getting faster and faster—until his brain became too fast for his body . . . a disability that would render him comatose, paralyzed by overthinking and disconnected from the real world. . . .

In light of his condition and in consultation with Captain Dawn, Justice Karim's decision came after only a day's deliberation. Viktor Mentok, the Mindtaker, would be relinquished to medical custody . . . a new section, built primarily with a sizable donation from the Legion of Heroes, of the U.S. Penitentiary Administrative Maximum Facility in Fremont County, Colorado (unofficially known as ADX Florence or Supermax). Dubbed the Nightingale Wing, the purpose-built facility would serve as the ailing Mentok's resting place for the remainder of his days . . . stripped of control of his body, an ending of bitter irony, for a man who once stole control from so many others. . . .

* * *

It took Matt Callaghan a few moments to work out whether the knocking he was hearing was real or imagined. He'd been in the middle of a dream where Giselle had turned out to be a bunch of hamsters taped together, except he was trying to explain to her that that was Celeste's power—except he wasn't sure anymore, since Celeste was the name of the pogo stick Jonas had gotten for selling so many marbles to Fiji. And now there was this tapping. None of this made any sense.

"Uggghhhh," he moaned, but either the person on the other side of the door didn't hear him or somehow his inarticulate grunt didn't get his message across. The knocking persisted. Matt strained open his eyes.

"Wait," he mumbled. Who the hell was battering down his door so early? What was even the time? He looked blearily around for his phone and found it laying on the floor. Matt reached down. Eight fifteen. "Come on," he moaned, "don't be ridiculous."

Matt groaned and pushed himself up off the bed into a sitting position, the movement triggering a chain reaction of discomfort, from sloshy nausea in his stomach to a searing headache across his forehead. He put his face in his hands, trying to block the painful brightness of morning out of his eyes, torn between the distinct feeling that he was about to hurl and that his brain had become detached and just slammed into the front of his skull.

Knock-knock-knock-knock-knock-knock.

"I'm coming!" he barked at the door. Matt climbed unsteadily to his feet, the room spinning, his body swaying slightly on the spot as his hungover brain readjusted to the concept of gravity. Sluggishly, he took mental stock of his situation—he was in his room, alone and still fully dressed, with sore legs and teeth in desperate need of brushing. And with some absolute sadist hammering away at his door. He started begrudgingly across the room, spouting a low torrent of swear words.

"What?" he shouted, wrenching open the handle. "What the fu—"

But his words stopped short when he saw the look on Jane's face. In an instant, the haze around Matt's mind parted, and cold dread pooled in his stomach. His heart sunk.

"What?" he whispered, suddenly afraid.

* * *

There was barely a body to move. Just pieces, broken beyond repair.

Jane hadn't wanted to let Matt see, but he'd insisted, adamant. Maybe a part of him didn't believe, couldn't believe until he saw it with his own eyes. But by the time they got down there, it was all in a black bag anyway.

Matt let out a low moan, the sound of a dying animal—his breathing coming in short, sharp bursts. For a moment, Jane thought he was going to do something stupid, going to run at the police, the Ashes, the medics behind the yellow tape. But instead, he just stumbled. His legs gave way, and Jane caught him before he hit the ground.

And then he began to cry. Openly, sickeningly cry, sobbing in the cold, while all she could do was stand there, holding on to him, and stare numbly at the blood upon the snow.

"It's not your fault," Jane murmured. Matt didn't look up. Didn't say anything. Just stared at the table through red and empty eyes. A pile of bacon, waffles, and hash browns sat in front of him, going cold. Her doing. She'd thought his favorite breakfast might cheer him up, at least a little. But the plate remained untouched.

"It's not your fault," she repeated.

"You keep saying that." Matt's words hissed through clenched teeth. Jane saw his eyes once more begin to water and his head began to rock. He wouldn't look at her. "But I still . . . I . . ."

It was still early. There hadn't been any official announcement about Ed's death, but the news of his suicide had spread regardless. The stories were all the same. Edward Rakowski had gone to the New Year's Eve party. He'd spent a while talking to Giselle Pixus, nobody knew exactly about what—it didn't really matter though. Ed had asked her out—Giselle had said no. Gently, Jane had heard, but the rejection had still been too much for Ed to take. He'd left the party, sat alone in the computer lab, then climbed to the top of Morningstar about four o'clock, and thrown himself off. Everyone agreed it was a sad, senseless waste.

And it still wasn't Matt's fault.

"You couldn't have known," Jane promised.

"I could've guessed," Matt replied. "I should've . . . I didn't . . ." The words faltered in his throat. His face crumpled and fat tears leaked out his eyes, his back beginning to heave with silent sobs. Jane just sat there, a painful tightness in her chest, not knowing what she was supposed to do.

"Eat something," she suggested. But Matt couldn't seem to hear.

The usual noise and energy of the Grand Hall had been subdued by the news of Ed's passing. A sense of shock and quiet lay over all present, leaving the open expanse feeling cavernous, and everyone inside it seeming small. Conversations were quiet, contained to little clusters of people, many wearing black. Even those that would normally have been staring at Jane with open contempt only managed it half-heartedly today. Ed hadn't necessarily been popular, but he'd been a senior and well-known. And the loss of anyone there was a loss of one of their own.

For Jane, it was just such a stupid shame—the pointlessness, the waste. She'd liked Ed, kind of. Well, she hadn't disliked him, which was much the same thing. And she'd respected him. He'd always struck her as meaning well—never been cruel or treated her like a monster or an idiot, which was sometimes worse. And he'd never seemed suicidal—although maybe that was the thing with depression, the ones who didn't let on were the ones in real danger. All over a girl. That was the saddest part. A whole life lost over something as petty and pointless as a crush.

The one, tiny bright side, in all the horribleness, was that whatever stupid rift had existed between her and Matt was gone. In truth, Jane had never really ended up saying sorry, but it didn't matter anymore. It was small, and it was selfish—but even if the cause made her sad, a part of Jane couldn't help feeling glad at this one, bittersweet piece of good.

There was the sound of tapping on a microphone.

"Ladies and gentlemen . . ." Winters's voice echoed humbly out through the speaker system, and Jane glanced up to see the man standing behind the lectern, his face downcast and tired. "As many of you may be aware, we have suffered a terrible tragedy this morning . . ."

Beside her, Jane felt Matt climb to his feet. He stepped over the bench, not looking at Winters, and started moving toward the exit. Jane whispered after him, unsure where he was going or if she should follow. But whether he couldn't hear her over Winters's echoing words or didn't want to, Matt didn't turn around. He simply kept walking, head down and shoulders slumped, out the main doors and into the lonely hallways beyond.

* * *

Matt sniffed, the sound falling frail and dull, swallowed up into nothing. His room was still, quiet, cut off from the outside, from the people and their world. Everything the way it had always been—books and pens still scattered across his desk, bedsheets tangled and unmade. Particles of dust hung suspended in beams of sunlight let in through the closed windows, clothes lay haphazard on the floor. None of it mattered. He stood, a cold, empty statue, unable to think or care or feel anything but this horrible, oppressive silence around him, ready and waiting to swallow him whole.

He couldn't stay and listen to Winters's speech—he just couldn't. He couldn't sit there and listen to the man drone on about what Ed had been like, what he'd represented about the Legion, what he'd meant to "them." It would all be nothing, sweet, meaningless nothings, praise and platitudes for a person none of them had ever properly known. Ed was—had been—modest, shy, and distractible. He'd been way too susceptible to peer pressure and way too good at video games. He'd liked peanut butter on his pancakes and hated dancing. He'd been socially awkward and scared of talking to girls. He'd been Matt's friend.

And now he was gone.

Matt clenched his teeth and gripped his face tight as a fresh wave of misery engulfed him. Why hadn't he noticed? Why hadn't he known? He'd seen Ed heading back, seen him leaving—why hadn't he gone after him? Why hadn't he followed, found him, made sure he was all right? He could have talked to him, could have stopped him, could have stopped . . . could have . . .

Matt's vision blurred, and alone in the silent room his shoulders once more started to shake, his breaths sucking in through wretched sobs. Stupid, stupid, stupid idiot, stupid, stupid drunk—you were supposed to be there for him. You were supposed to be his friend. He kept replaying it in his head, seeing it over and over, the moment when he should have done something, when he saw Ed walking away, when he should have realized something was wrong . . . And yet again and again, unchangeably, the truth was that he didn't follow—didn't call out, didn't even message . . .

Somewhere, underneath the waves of rolling, smothering despair, a tiny, niggling thought, a faint, hazy memory, snagged in the corner of Matt's mind. Hang on, there . . . there had been a message. Some kind of

... he'd been ... wordlessly, his sobs stalling into hiccups, Matt's hands moved from his side, down his leg, his pocket, unconsciously mimicking a blurry recollection of something ... something he'd forgotten, lost in his drunken stupor, something he'd dismissed as a dream ...

No, it hadn't been a dream. It'd been real, Ed had messaged him, texted him something ... something about ... without even thinking, Matt's hands were clamoring for his phone, his messages—

And there it was. The last entry in a conversation chain dating back months.

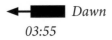 *Dawn*
03:55

Matt stared at the screen. He blinked. Then he blinked again. He drew back, then leaned in, squinting, rereading, wondering if he was going insane. Slowly, beneath the blanket of heavy misery, some part of him awoke. The gears in his mind began to turn. His sobbing dried to sniffing, then to silence. The tears stopped running from his eyes and his mouth turned in a small frown. He glanced up and around, then back down at the text, his brow furrowed.

Something wasn't right.

Quietly, almost discreetly, despite being completely alone, Matt clicked on the Lock button and slid the phone back into his pocket. He stood for a moment, stock still, his brow furrowed, staring without seeing, pulling his pieces back together. He needed to think, he needed to be able to think, unhindered for a moment by grief. His eyes narrowed and almost unconsciously he felt his breathing slow and steady, his years of mental discipline corralling and compartmentalizing. The blurring fog of sadness thinned, and a sharpening sense of disquiet began permeating through Matt's mind—a nagging unease, a floating suspicion, forming at the hard edges of his brain.

Something wasn't right.

He found Jane where he'd left her, sitting picking at some breakfast, her bronze hair hanging free from its usual tie. She glanced over at him with a mixture of relief and concern when he moved silently into the seat beside her.

"Funeral's on Thursday," she told him without any prompting. A single glance at the stage told Matt that Winters's speech was over. Good. "They're going to have the service here and then . . ." Her voice trailed off, her head cocked slightly to the side as she saw Matt wasn't listening.

"What's wrong?" she asked. Matt didn't reply but merely shook his head, distracted. He stared straight ahead, one finger on his temple, the other on his lip, his brows furrowed, his mind churning. Jane hesitated.

"You okay?" she asked, but Matt just nodded without sparing her a glance. A few seconds passed, the only sound between them the undulating murmur of the crowded hall.

"Don't you think it's weird?" Matt said finally. He dropped his hand from his face and turned to meet Jane's eyes.

"Think what's weird?" she replied.

"Ed. That he'd just . . ." The words caught on Matt's tongue, and he swallowed before forcing them out. "I don't know. Up and kill himself."

Jane blinked, slightly taken aback. "I don't know," she admitted after a moment's hesitation. "I mean, it's the worst, but it happens. And it sucks, but—"

"No note," Matt interrupted. He kept his voice deliberately low and steady, so as not to attract attention, but the intensity of his gaze never wavered. "No goodbye. No nothing. All over one girl. That doesn't strike you as strange?"

"Matt . . ." Jane's voice was hesitant, and Matt could see the pity forming in her face. She thinks this is grief, he realized—she thinks I'm trying to find an excuse. To her credit though, Jane didn't let her reluctance to hurt his feelings keep her from speaking her mind. "He clearly wasn't in a good place. He was a genius, and you know how they . . ."

"What? How they what?"

"Well . . . you know . . . how they're like. They get all wrapped up in their own thoughts and . . ." She tactfully paused. "Well, it takes its toll." It was the closest she'd ever come to sounding sympathetic. But Matt shook his head, brushing away the suggestion like it was a fly.

"He messaged me," Matt persisted. He glanced subtly at the many Acolytes around them, making sure no one was eavesdropping. "Early this morning. Must've been just before—before it happened."

"What?" Jane frowned. "What'd it say?"

Matt opened his mouth to tell her but paused as one of the Ashes—a fair-skinned weather controller—walked behind them. He waited until they'd passed then continued, keeping the inflection in his voice deliberately low and casual: "Dawn."

"Dawn what?"

"Nothing," said Matt. "Just one word: Dawn."

Jane's mouth twisted into an expression of confusion. "I don't get it."

"Exactly."

"No, I mean, why? What does that mean?"

"That's my point: I don't know," Matt replied. He shook his head. "But don't you think that's weird?" He leaned in closer, focused, staring at her. "Ed could've written anything. Why would he send that? It's not like he was in a rush, he had the whole rest of his life to go and off himself."

"Well," Jane said with a shrug, "he was a genius, who knows what . . . ?"

"Right," Matt interjected with some frustration. "He was a genius, and he knew me, which means he would've known I'd have no idea what this meant."

"It's not one of your . . . I don't know . . . Did you guys have like secret gaming codes?"

"No," Matt replied irritably. "Because we're not six."

"All right." Jane scowled defensively, holding up her hands. "Just a thought." She hesitated. "What are you getting at?"

"I don't know," answered Matt, which was only half-true. He paused, and for a few moments, they just looked at each other. Suddenly, what he was implying sunk in. Jane's eyes widened and instinctively she recoiled.

"You're not saying he was—"

"It doesn't strike you as odd that . . . ?"

"Come on, you can't seriously think—"

"I don't know what I think." Matt cut her off. "But something doesn't feel right." He unconsciously glanced down at the phone in his pocket. "If Ed was going to kill himself, this isn't what he'd do. He wouldn't just abandon all his work. He wouldn't leave without saying goodbye. And his last act on this earth wouldn't be sending some stupid cryptic text."

"Yeah," said Jane. "But that doesn't mean he was—"

"Think about it," Matt hissed, leaning in closer. "What if Ed was in danger? What if he was, I don't know, attacked or something, and the only thing he had time to do is send out a single message telling everyone who attacked him and—"

Instantly, Matt knew he'd made a mistake. Jane's face hardened and her eyes narrowed.

"If you're even suggesting Captain Dawn . . ." she began, her voice and the indignation in it both rising.

"No, *shh!*" hushed Matt, waving under the table at her to keep quiet. His eyes darted around the room. The noise of the hall meant that it was unlikely anyone would be able to casually listen on their conversation but only so long as Jane didn't start shouting. "Not so loud!" Jane glared at him, eyes ablaze.

"Captain Dawn would never . . ." she hissed.

"I'm not saying that, I'm not saying that!" Matt hissed back, waving her down. Privately, he cursed himself for being so stupid as to ever imply any wrongdoing by Jane's superhero crush. "Maybe he meant 'Go get Dawn for help.' Or 'Dawn is in danger, look out.' "

"In danger, in danger from what?" Jane scoffed.

"I don't know!" Matt despaired through gritted teeth. "Whatever was after him, whoever threw him off the roof!"

Jane leaned back, her arms folded across her chest, her face hard and skeptical. Matt took the fact she wasn't arguing as a sign she was considering what he was saying, and that he should continue.

"As a final word, it makes no sense," he insisted, pleading at her with his eyes. "But as a message, a warning . . ." He let the sentence trail off, the idea hanging. Jane chewed her lip.

"What time did you get it?" she finally asked.

"The message?"

"Yeah."

"Five to four. Says it right there on the thing."

"And you just, what, forgot?"

"I was asleep," Matt snapped.

"Passed out more like," Jane countered. But she didn't say it with much venom, instead seeming distracted, her eyes wandering off into space. Matt pressed on.

"Did Winters say what time it happened?" he asked, shooting a furtive glance up at the stage and the now empty lectern.

"No," she replied. "But I heard around four." She absentmindedly picked up a butter knife from the table and began twirling it between her fingers. They lapsed into silence.

"I don't know," Jane admitted eventually. "None of the cops have said anything. Nothing about this looks like foul play. All you've got is one weird message." She paused and turned to look at him. "You don't want to believe that your friend could do something like this, I get that. I really do. But the thing about people is that they always let you down."

"I'm not saying he didn't kill himself," replied Matt. "I'm not saying it was murder. All I'm saying is maybe, maybe, this is worth looking in to. Haven't there been enough weird things going on lately? All that stuff with clairvoyants and threats? Please," he pleaded, "I just . . . I just want to be sure. For Ed." He fought to keep his voice steady.

Jane's face softened. "Sure," she said, unfolding her arms. "Sure. We can check it out. It's just . . ." she paused and grimaced. "Well, how? Where would we even start?"

Matt hesitated, considering. "Ed's computer," he said finally. "He spent most of his time there. He was there before he died. Maybe it'll have something." He glanced at her. "What do you think?"

Jane shrugged. "Better than nothing." She blinked in surprise as Matt swung his legs out and over the bench. "What, now?"

"We've already wasted enough time," Matt replied shortly. He got to his feet.

"I've got class," complained Jane, but after a moment's hesitation she likewise followed his lead, albeit semi-reluctantly.

They walked side by side out the hall and up the stairs leading to the upper levels. With most people either already at breakfast, training, or nursing hangovers, the corridors were nearly empty.

"You sure Ed would want us snooping through his stuff?" Jane asked as they reached the third floor. But when they rounded the off-shoot corner that led to the computer labs, the irrelevance of her concern became apparent. The door to Ed's IT room was already open, the doorway bisected by a line of yellow plastic tape, beyond which were swarming several police and technicians.

"Better us than them," Matt muttered, slowing to a walk as an officer in a windbreaker strode past them carrying a thick, heavy-looking black case. He glanced over his shoulder at the "POLICE" emblazoned on the man's retreating form. Cautiously, Matt approached the open doorway and stole a quick glance inside, poking his head underneath the yellow "POLICE LINE" tape. The familiar waft of stale heat that greeted him was somewhat diluted.

There was about five people inside going about their various business, more than he'd ever seen in the room at once. One policewoman was standing on a chair in the corner, examining the security camera, while a man leaned over the rows of free-use computers, leaning down one by one, pecking at the keys—a third was on her hands and knees, gloved hands picking through the wastepaper basket, while a fourth, a large stony-faced man, stood cross-armed against the wall keeping watch. The fifth, a lean-built tech with wire-framed glasses, was seated in front of Ed's setup. None of them seemed to notice Matt's head protruding discreetly through the doorway. Matt leaned back, then glanced behind him at Jane, who had fallen silent and was still standing a few feet away with an expression of extreme reluctance. His foot already halfway inside, Matt nudged his head, beckoning her to follow, but Jane vehemently shook her head.

"Come on," he mouthed, understanding full well her hesitation but having no time for it right now. Jane gesticulated furiously, her exact words unclear but her overall message abundantly obvious. Matt shrugged as if to say "well, I'm going," and Jane rolled her eyes upward in despair.

"I am not missing class to get arrested!" she hissed.

"You won't get arrested!" Matt hissed back, but she waved him down, shaking her head in violent jerks. "Fine!" he whispered. "Go!" Matt shooed her away and, ignoring Jane's look of despondence and doom along with her flurry of half-whispered swear words, ducked under the plastic tape.

Seeing the room properly hit Matt harder than he'd been expecting— the sight of Ed's desktop, the mess of equipment, his empty chair, looking for all intents and purposes like his friend had just stepped out and would be back at any moment. Grief reeled through Matt's chest, threatening to spill over and out of his control. But he held himself firm and kept his feelings of sadness locked away in a corner of his mind, where they belonged for the moment. He moved cautiously forward into the occupied room, filled with renewed purpose.

"Hi," he announced. Five pairs of eyes swiveled around at the sound of his voice. Matt stopped, about a foot through the entrance, and gave a short, weak wave. "I . . . sorry. Is this a crime scene?"

The police officers and technicians exchanged glances, then one by one looked up at the stony-faced man for guidance. The big sergeant shrugged and uncrossed his arms. "We're just taking a look," he said, his voice deep but not unkind. "We'll be out of your way soon."

"Oh no, I-I-I don't mean to—" stammered Matt, feigning nervous reluctance. "I can go, I-I-I just . . . it's just he . . . Ed . . ." He let himself tear up a bit. "He was my friend." He gave a long, wet sniff. A look of sympathy passed between the officers—and as it did, Matt's keen eyes spotted something inconspicuously tucked away underneath the corner of Ed's right monitor. Taking care to appear miserable, Matt started to shuffle forward.

"I just can't . . . I can't believe he's gone," he whimpered. He moved with heavy footsteps, glancing longingly around the room, until he just so happened to be standing beside Ed's station. He gave another, hearty sniff. "I don't know why . . . I don't—" And then suddenly, his face scrunched up and Matt collapsed, doubling over with grief, throwing his hands out onto the desk to stop himself falling. The technician working on Ed's terminals recoiled a little at the sudden movement, but a few seconds later as Matt sucked in shaky, shuddering breaths, he felt the man's hand patting reassuringly on his back.

"Hey, buddy, it's okay. I know it's tough," soothed the tech. Matt squeezed his eyes tighter and clenched his teeth, drawing his face into an expression of miserable despair as he held on to the computer desk for support, feeling the small coin-sized disk with three tiny crystals in the middle pressing into his palm.

"I'm sorry, kid," the sergeant's voice came reluctantly. "But you're not supposed to be in here, we're still—"

"No," sniffed Matt. "I know, it's okay, I'll go, I just, I wanted to . . ." He straightened up, wiping his (in reality, tearless) eyes on the heel of his right hand. His left hand moved glumly into his pocket. As did the disk. "I guess . . . I didn't know . . . just to say . . ." He deliberately choked up again on the word "goodbye."

"Ah, don't worry about it, Sarge," the tech said. "Nothing's doing here." He glanced over at the policewoman down by the trash can. "Amira?"

"Nothing in the trash, sir," a woman's voice confirmed. Then, a touch more sympathetically, "I don't see the harm." The officer at Ed's desk leaned over, catching Matt's downturned eyes with a kind smile.

"You said you guys were friends?" he asked. Matt nodded, sniffing. The tech glanced at his commanding officer. The sergeant sighed and nodded reluctantly, refolding his arms. The tech indicated to the seat beside him. "I'm Officer Warbrook. I'm really sorry for your loss."

"Your loss," the Acolyte mumbled. He pinched one of the earplugs and started twisting it into his ear. His taller friend stayed silent, distractedly thumbing the edges of the long diamond blades coming out of his forearms, his expression subdued, distant. Half a room over, Jane's eyes stayed fixed on the ground, her fingers going through the motions, tightening the buckle firm beneath her chin. A few feet away, four Acolytes stood distracted, their backs to her, helmets still in their hands. The live-fire exercise they were walking into seemed a world away.

"Has anyone seen Giselle?"

"God, can you imagine?"

"Such a waste."

"You don't sound surprised."

Alone on her bench, her armor fastened, Jane said nothing, staring without seeing at the white plaster of the changing room wall.

Over the next hour and a half, the various members of the police unit one by one packed up their work and filed out. Eventually, all that remained was the quiet, muscular sergeant and the technician assigned to Ed's computer—who still sat, as he had the whole time Matt had been there, with one hand on the tower, staring mutely as a bunch of jargon flashed across the screens. Finally, in answer to some unspoken question, he twisted around to face his superior officer and just shook his head. The large man grimaced, walked over, clapped Warbrook on the shoulder, and left without another word. The tech turned back to the screens, a look of dull resignation on his clean-shaven face.

"Find anything?" Matt asked. After spending ninety minutes sniffing quietly and appearing miserable, he figured it was safe to chance a question.

"Nothing, actually," replied the tech, appearing glum. He turned back to the screens, which resumed their black-and-white garbled flashing. There was the sound of soft padding on the carpet outside the computer labs. And to his surprise, out of the corner of his eye, Matt saw Jane's head poke tentatively around the doorframe. Matt nodded discreetly inward.

"Can my, ah, is it all right if my friend comes in too?" he checked, throwing Jane a small, encouraging nod. Officer Warbrook just shrugged, not looking up.

"May as well." He sighed, indifferent. "Not like it'll change anything at this point." Matt shot Jane a significant look and flicked his eyes pointedly at the seat beside him. When all she did was twitch in his general direction with an expression of pained indecision, he scowled and furiously yet discreetly beckoned Jane forward with his hand underneath his chair. Fuming, she entered the room, head crocked back and hackles raised like at any moment she expected to be pepper sprayed in the face.

"Hi . . ." she muttered, sounding obviously forced. Her clothes were drenched with sweat, and the left side of her hair was matted with what looked like blood—although whether hers or someone else's was unclear. Warbrook glanced up and did a slight double take the moment his eyes reached her E.

"Hi . . ." he replied, equally wary. "You're the, uh . . ."

"One of Ed's friends," answered Matt, trying to sound his most sympathetic and sad.

"Right . . ." said the tech, reluctantly drawing his eyes back to the screen. He glanced sideways as Jane took a seat beside Matt and shuffled his chair a fraction of an inch to the left. "Well, I guess sorry for your loss too."

"Thanks," Jane replied dryly, pointedly ignoring his unease. Matt frowned slightly and tried to steer the conversation back to the matter at hand.

"So, what's going on?" he asked, careful to keep any curiosity out of his voice. "What are you trying to do?"

Warbrook sighed and tilted up his glasses to rub his eyes. "I want to have a quick look through the deceased . . . I mean, your friend's . . ." he amended sadly, "files. Just to be on the safe side."

"Why?" Matt said quickly, sitting up a little straighter. Maybe he wasn't the only one who had suspicions. "What're you looking for?"

His hopes, however, were immediately dashed. "Nothing in particular," replied the tech, looking glum. "Hate mail, bullying, death threats—the works. Just standard procedure." He sighed again. "Not that I'm expecting anything. From the sound of it he was"—he paused and coughed, catching himself—"ahem, I mean your friend was, um, pretty unhappy on his own."

Matt suppressed a flare of anger. "So, you haven't found anything?" he asked, biting back an irritable reply. He shot Jane a discreet glance. "Nothing unusual?"

Warbrook leaned back in his chair, linking his hands behind his head. "Well, that's the problem," he admitted, sounding defeated. "I haven't found anything at all." He paused and stared at the screens, now returned to black, shaking his head. "I can't get in."

"What do you mean?" said Matt.

"I mean, it's encrypted," replied the technician. "Everything's encrypted. I can't break through."

"But you're a technopath," protested Matt. "Can't you talk to machines?" He'd assumed that's what Warbrook had been doing for the last hour and a half, with his hand on the computer tower and his eyes twitching.

The technopath grimaced. "Normally, yes. But this genius knew his stuff. It'd take me a week to get in."

"So?" Jane said with a shrug. "Take a week." Matt was inclined to agree.

But again, Warbrook shook his head. "It won't make a difference. It's rigged to blow. Not literally," he added quickly, seeing them both recoil. "I mean, the hard drive is programmed to completely fragment if it isn't logged into every twenty-four hours." He paused and tilted his glasses up onto his forehead, looking resigned. "Which means in a week, everything will be gone."

"Wait, what?" cried Matt. He stared desperately at the blank screen, almost expecting to see a ticking clock. "Well . . . well, what about afterward? Can't you salvage it? Put it back together?"

"Sure," snorted the tech. "If I worked nonstop. For about twenty years." He tilted his glasses up onto his forehead and pinched the bridge of his nose. "I'm sorry, guys. But your friend obviously really didn't want anyone looking at his work. Tomorrow this'll just be a mess of ones and zeroes. It'd be like trying to rebuild a house from sawdust. Not that I'm giving up, but . . ."

Warbrook pushed back his chair and stood up, yawning. "I'm going to get coffee," he told them. "Back in a sec. I'd say don't mess with anything, but really"—he shrugged—"what harm can you do?" He meandered across the room, hands in his pockets, and ducked under the drooping police tape, leaving Matt and Jane sitting together in silence, Ed's screens looming in front of them—the glowing doors to a digital vault.

Waiting silently for a password.

The pair exchanged glances.

"Try it," nodded Jane. Matt nodded back. He leaned over Ed's desk and maneuvered the mouse around, bringing up the blue log-in screen. His hands moved slowly to the keyboard and carefully typed "Dawn." Then, not daring to breathe, he hit Enter.

There was a beep and the box flashed red with the words *Incorrect Password*.

"Yeah, like it was ever going to be a four-letter word," Matt muttered.

"Did you do the capital?" Jane asked him.

"Yes of course I did the capital!" Matt snapped back. They both stared at the unyielding screens.

"Try it without the capital. Or all capitals!" she suggested. Matt tried both. Unsurprisingly, neither worked. There was a lengthy pause.

"We knew him though," muttered Jane, her narrowed eyes staring at the monitor like it was an enemy in need of punching. She glanced down at the Matt's hands, hovering over the keyboard, then back up at the log-in screen with grim determination. "Maybe we can guess it."

"Jane, he was a genius," Matt replied, slightly impatient. "His password is going to be twenty-four random characters with no pattern or connection that no sane person could ever remember. It's not going to be something you could guess."

"Is there a hint?" Jane asked, stubborn as ever. Matt moved the mouse around the log-in menu. There was no hint. Jane cursed.

"Obviously, he's not going to need a hint, he was a—"

"Genius, yes, thank you, I got it," Jane snapped. They stared in silence at the screens, the small white password box still sitting there, taunting them. Matt clenched his teeth in frustration.

"It could be right there," he fumed, fixated despondently on the monitor. "The missing link, everything we need, right there in front of us."

"Not to mention all his research," lamented Jane. "So much work, all going to waste."

"You'd think somebody who was going to kill themselves would've made plans for that," Matt pointed out. Jane grunted noncommittally.

They sat in silence staring at the screen, racking their brains in vain for ideas, until Warbrook came back a few minutes later with his coffee.

"No change?" he asked without any preamble. They both shook their heads, and he sighed. "Ah, well. Wasn't really expecting anything, but you never know." He shuffled back down into the chair and gave Matt an apologetic look. "You're welcome to stay as long as you like, but I don't think we're getting much further than this."

"No, it's fine," said Matt, sounding as disheartened as he felt. "We'll get out of your hair." He stood up and Jane followed suit. "Thanks for letting me sit in."

"No problem," replied Warbrook, sounding genuinely sorry. After a moment, he reached into the front pocket of his shirt and pulled out a business card. "This is my number," he told Matt, handing him the little slip of cardboard. "I know it's not much, but if there's anything else I can do, let me know. It's really awful you have to go through this."

"Thanks," Matt repeated, not sure how that was supposed to help and still feeling down—but he pocketed the card regardless. He and Jane left the computer lab in silence.

"Well, now what?" Jane asked.

A full day had passed. They were sitting in the Grand Hall, eating lunch—Jane stabbing aggressively at pieces of schnitzel, Matt largely devoid of appetite. It had been more than twenty-four hours since they'd woken up to the news of Ed's death, and the idea that the tragedy was anything but self-inflicted was seeming less and less likely. The police had packed up and gone, having recovered nothing from Ed's computer but nevertheless having swept both roof and grounds and finding nothing to indicate foul play. The full report was due in a day or two, but Matt already knew what it would say. He'd looked around the roof himself—albeit under close supervision—and sweet-talked one of the medical examiners who'd been first on the scene. Everything pointed to the same conclusion: Ed had been working in his lab alone, gone up to the roof alone, and jumped straight off, alone. He didn't know enough about footprints and blood-splatter analysis to debate the police and paramedics' conclusions—and besides, what reason did they have to lie? It was all consistent. Matt had exhausted every avenue he could think of, run down every so-called "lead." Jane had helped as best she could between training, which continued unabated even in the face of tragedy—but Matt could tell she was only doing it as a favor to his feelings. Which was kind of sweet actually, if not a little belittling.

Of course, Matt had to keep reminding himself, there was still the text. But even he was starting to doubt whether that actually meant anything. The fire in his chest was fading, a part of him slowly turning toward the sad, miserable truth that everyone but him seemed able to believe. His friend had killed himself. Sometimes life sucks. And he couldn't do anything but try to move on.

I'm so sorry it has to be like this. A dead woman's words echoed in his mind. *For the pain you're going to go through. We both are.*

"I'm going for a walk," he answered. He put down his unused spoon, the bowl of pumpkin soup untouched, and pushed away from the table. He could feel Jane's eyes on the back of his neck as he left, but if she had something to say she didn't say it, and she didn't try to stop him. Matt pulled on his coat and scarf and set out into the snow.

Maybe he was wrong, Matt thought, as he moved between the pine trees—maybe the message had been some kind of genius thing. Maybe Ed had had one of his moments and just assumed Matt would get his meaning. Maybe it wasn't a warning; maybe it was meant to be comforting: I'll be with you in the dawn, or something poetic like that. Or an acronym: Don't Anybody Worry Now, Damn Acolytes Were Nasty, Deer Always Want Nuts. Except Ed had never much struck him as the poetic-nonsense type.

Matt sighed, his breath steaming in the cold air as he stepped over a downed log, boots compacting the snow, hands nestled firmly in his pockets. It was mercifully clear—no wind, no clouds. He didn't know how long it'd last but he wasn't headed anywhere particular. He'd set out west, where the snow from experience tended not to be quite as deep, but without any goal in mind. He'd been this way before, to pick plants or look at birds or something stupid—but today Matt just walked for the sake of walking.

He trekked for what could have been an hour, until the cold began nipping around his heels and Matt realized he should start heading back. As if on cue, a light dusting of flakes began to fall, their tiny white bodies nesting momentarily on his shoulders and hood before melting away into nothing. Yup. Definitely time to go back. Miserable as he was, Matt had no desire to be stuck in a snowstorm. He turned and trudged back in the direction of his own tracks, mutely remembering coming out here once before, to get herbs for that stupid tea that'd made Ed sick. His eyes prickled and a heavy tightness squeezed across his chest.

Preoccupied as was and with his hood up around his head, Matt barely had time to register the sound of running footsteps to his right before a gray-white figure came hurtling out from between two trees and almost bowled him over.

"Hey!" shouted Matt, stumbling backward, barely scraping out of the way before the runner barreled into him.

"Whoa!" yelled the stranger, skidding off sideways, almost falling into the snow. The man—because Matt could see now it was a man, a sullen-faced, mousy-haired man in his mid to late thirties—held out a hand and steadied himself on a tree trunk, breathing heavily. "Sheesh. Sorry. Didn't see you."

"Yeah, me neither," replied Matt, with some hesitation, naturally wary of strange men who came running at him in the middle of the woods. The stranger glanced around them, bent over, resting his hands on his knees and panting a little, oblivious to Matt's misgivings.

"You see a kid go past here?" he asked, the words whistling out from underneath a thick brown mustache. Matt shook his head.

"No," he answered, distrustful. This guy seemed sane enough, but that was probably how the more successful serial killers operated. "No kids. Just me." He glanced as discreetly as possible around him to see if there was a stick or other some other potential hitting implement nearby, just in case the need arose.

"You didn't see where he went?" asked the man, sounding confused. He turned his head from side to side, squinting between the trees. "I don't get it. I chased him for like ten minutes. Shouted, I-I-I could've sworn he was right there." As he continued to look around, Matt took in the stranger's strange appearance. He was dressed head to toe in patterned snow-camo—which might have explained why Matt hadn't seen him sooner—with worn black boots and a gray hood hanging loose behind his neck. There was dirt under his fingernails, a day or two worth of stubble on his chin, and small brown hairs making their way out of an uneven nose. He was also clutching a chunky black camera in one hand, but the man almost looked like he had forgotten he was holding it.

"You lose your son?" Matt asked with trepidation, still leaning back and away from the stranger. The man scoffed, still peering around him.

"Do I look like I have a son?" he asked. Matt had a feeling that question was supposed to be rhetorical. "Nah, nah," the man kept on, sounding distracted. He shook his head, still throwing the odd glance from space to space between the trees, "I'm only thirty-two."

"Okay," said Matt, a bit perplexed, unsure how deeply he wanted to investigate this rabbit hole. "So . . . who's this kid you're after?"

"Hell, if I know." The photographer shrugged. He straightened up slightly, rubbing the small bald patch on the back of his head. "I was just minding my own business back at the tent when I see this little boy running between the trees." He paused, shaking his head. "Couldn't have been more than ten. All pale and stuff. Blond, blue eyes."

Matt's breath stopped in his chest.

"What?" he whispered.

Death stalks Morningstar.

"Yeah, and so I mean I was worried," the stranger continued, oblivious to Matt's sudden vertigo, the hammering in his chest. "It's cold, the kid's in a T-shirt and shorts. I figured maybe he's just started 'porting, maybe he's lost. I'm not a monster."

"Where did he go?" Matt demanded.

The man shrugged. "I don't know," he replied distractedly, craning his neck to look around. "That's what I'm saying. I mean I'm just out here taking photos and—"

Suddenly, he stopped. His eyes swung back to Matt and he let out a low groan, "Oh, screw me. You're an Acolyte, aren't you?"

"And you're paparazzi," said Matt, his voice turning colder.

"Oh, come on," the photographer moaned at the contempt in Matt's tone. He gingerly held up his hands. "Don't say it like that. It's just a living, man. You know how it is." He winced, scrunching up his face. "Please don't hurt me."

"Give me one good reason why not," Matt growled as he glared daggers at the man, voice dripping with fake confidence.

"Come on!" the photographer pleaded, his hands still raised. "I've only been here a week! A buddy of mine, up in Boston, he said they're paying two grand a piece for a shot of the empath girl, and if I just lay low enough, I—"

"You take any photos?" snarled Matt, cutting him off.

"Only a few," the stranger pleaded. "And they're nothing, all crap, I swear." He wilted under Matt's fiery gaze. "I promise! Look, I got nothing, I'll show you, I . . ." He held up the back of his camera eagerly, showing Matt the small preview screen. "See? Look, it's nothing, just some people training . . ." He started flicking through. "These guys walking around . . ."

A sudden idea struck Matt. "Hold on," he ordered. "Were you here on New Year's Eve?"

"You mean when you guys had that big party with all the drinking and the fireworks while I froze my ass off in the freaking snow?" the man replied, sarcastic despite his situation. "Yeah, I think I saw that one. Looked fun."

Matt's heart skipped a beat. "Did you take any pictures?"

The photographer blew a huff of air between his teeth. "Well, of course, I took pictures, that's what I'm—" Halfway through the sentence he seemed to realize what he was saying. "Sorry," he whined. "I'm sorry I'll . . ." Even in the cold, Matt could see sweat beading on his forehead. "Just let me go," he begged.

Matt pushed forward, ignoring his pleading. "How much did you get?" he demanded.

The man winced. "All . . . of it?" he squeaked, squeezing out the words and squinting his face as though he expected Matt to lunge and hit him at any moment. "People drinking, people dancing, the fireworks going off, that big guy making out?"

"What about later?" Matt urged, dropping all pretense. "Did you see anybody on the roof?"

The stranger blinked. "What, you mean the jumper?"

"Yes!" Matt shouted, wide-eyed. It was as if someone had shoved an electric wire into his spine; every muscle went tense. It was impossible. "You saw someone jump off the roof?"

"Well, of course." The photographer shivered, his teeth starting to chatter in the cold. "Not much moving that time of night. Hard to miss." His eyes narrowed into a shrewd expression, and his raised hands drooped slightly. "Why do you care? What's it worth to you?"

"What's your life worth to you?" growled Matt, scrunching up his face and rising as tall as he could. He took a step forward, and the paparazzo's hands shot back up at lightning speed, swindling ambition instantly replaced with cowering remorse.

"Okay, okay, point taken, we're cool, we're cool," he pleaded, wincing in preemptive pain. "Please don't hurt me."

"Tell me what you saw," commanded Matt.

"What's there to tell?" whined the stranger. His hands trembled as he stepped backward, putting his back up against a tree. "A little before four, it's quieting down, I'm thinking maybe I'll pack up, but then there's movement on the roof. I swing the lens around, and there's this scruffy Jewish kid going toward the edge. Wham, bam, thank you, ma'am, straight off, straight down. Barely even flinched." He paused, recoiling slightly at the look on Matt's face. "I got the whole thing, see for yourself." He held up the back of his camera again looking eager. "Frame by frame. Shot for shot."

Matt didn't hesitate. "Give me the photos," he demanded. He took another step forward and was glad to see the photographer quail. "All of them. Every one."

"Okay! Okay. I will, I will, just . . . just hang on." The photographer's fingers fumbled hurriedly with the clasp on the bottom of his camera. It swung open, and he removed the memory card, gingerly holding it out with a trembling hand. Matt snatched it away in an instant, stuffing the card into his pocket, not daring to hope, not daring to believe. "It's worthless, anyway," the man spluttered, drawing his hand back to his chest and nursing it like it'd been burned. "I mean sure, yeah, there'd be an audience, no doubt, but nobody'd touch it, it's against the law. Government won't let you run stories on suicide." He almost sounded mournful at the fact.

Matt ignored him, heart hammering in his chest. "You have half an hour to leave," he told him. "After that, I come get you."

"You got it, Boss," the photographer assured him, scrambling backward, almost tripping over his own feet. "I'm out, I'm gone. You'll never see me again. Nothing is worth this."

"Or hear from," added Matt, breathing hard. His eyes darted around him, searching for some explanation, some reason or setup. He couldn't believe it. This was insane. "Or about. You tell anyone, I'll know it was you. One word and I'll hunt you down."

"Not a word," swore the man, stumbling backward, trying to face him as he ran away. "I promise. I'm quiet. I'm gone." He bent low, shaking, sweat dripping from the tips of his mustache—then he turned and ran, pelting back off into the woods from whence he came. Matt watched him disappear back between the trees, and then the second he was gone, he took off running, racing back along his trail of footprints, heart pounding in his chest.

Jane had just stepped out of the shower when the hammering started. By the time she'd managed to pull on a clean set of clothes and rubbed her hair vigorously with a towel, Matt, redfaced and breathless, had almost broken down her door.

"The hell's wrong with you?" she'd meant to say, but before she could get a single word out, he'd grabbed her hand and practically dragged her around through the corridors and into his room. If anyone else had manhandled her like that, their teeth would have been all over the carpet, but in Matt's case Jane just went along with it.

"Shut the door," he'd rasped as soon as they were inside. He doubled over, hands on his knees, panting, hair damp and half frozen with a mixture of sweat and snow. So, Jane did, then sat and listened as Matt told her his story.

"Unbelievable," Jane muttered.

"I know," Matt said breathlessly, his eyes wide. They both stared at the photographer's memory card as it sat, tiny and innocuous, on the desk before them. It'd been several minutes but Matt was somehow still short of breath.

"No, I mean I literally don't believe it," Jane replied. "It can't be true."

"Jane, it happened." Matt sounded pained.

"I'm not calling you a liar," Jane promised. "But it's too much of a coincidence." She looked over at him, shaking her head. "Of all the places you could go, you just happen to go to this one particular piece of nowhere where you just happen to wander into this photographer. This photographer, who also happens to be chasing your ghost boy, through the exact same middle of nowhere."

"That's what he said," whispered Matt.

Jane leaned back in her chair, running her hands through her hair. "I don't get it. I don't understand. Who the hell is this kid? What does he want?"

"I don't know," murmured Matt.

"I mean I thought maybe when he said 'death' he was talking about the clairvoyants, but you think he was trying to warn you about . . . ?"

"I don't know," Matt repeated. "I don't know, I don't know, I don't know."

They lapsed into silence, but after a few seconds Jane pressed on.

"So, this kid is real," she said. "And he appears and leads this paparazzi guy, possibly the only person on Earth with photos of Ed's suicide, right to you, probably the only person who'd hear him out instead of kicking his ass. The suicide that you are the only one in the world investigating. Right when you're thinking of giving up."

"I'm not saying it's not insane," Matt muttered, shaking his head.

Jane threw up her hands. "It's not insane," she cried. "It's impossible!"

"Improbable."

"Whatever." Jane scowled. She paused then shook her head. "Clairvoyants," she muttered. "It has to be clairvoyants, somewhere, somehow. It's freaking Albania and the farm and the trapdoor all over again. It's the only explanation. You're being played."

"Or being led."

"Led to what?"

"I don't know," Matt said quietly. His eyes lingered over the memory card. He paused, then turned back to her. "But I'm still going to look at the photos."

"Well, of course, we're going to look at the photos," Jane snapped. "Obviously, at the very least, we're going to look at the goddamn photos. Destiny be damned." She paused, flicking her hand at the computer stored beside his desk. "Do you have one of the . . . the thingy . . . card reader?"

"Yeah," replied Matt, "I think. I've never used it. But I think the computer Ed . . ." His voice trailed off and his eyes dropped.

"Well, what are you waiting for?" Jane demanded, not from her own impatience, more to pull him out of his thoughts. "Put it in. Let's have a look." Matt nodded quietly and reached over, pulling the laptop up and opening it on his desk for them both to see. He typed in his password then slid the card in the side. They watched and waited.

"Just remember," Jane muttered as the circle scrolled, "this could be a trick. Someone could be trying to play you."

"Thank you, oh Master of Psychological Warfare."

"Oh shut up."

The card loaded and the usual window popped up, asking what they wanted it to do. The pair exchanged glances—so far, so normal. Matt clicked to view files. Sure enough, it was photos—lines and lines of photos, hundreds, maybe thousands. All of Morningstar or the Acolytes or the grounds. Matt's mouth twisted in a small grimace, and he clicked on the first one, opening a slideshow.

"Snow," he muttered, clicking quickly through. "Snow, snow, mainly snow. There's James Conrad . . . Dr. Lum . . . Bianca . . ."

"He got one of me," Jane commented, peering at the bright orange figure captured mid-motion on the screen. "Over on the north end. Except I'm on fire; he mustn't have realized who it was."

"Otherwise, he would've gone home and got paid," murmured Matt, continuing to scroll through the images.

"Exactly." She shook her head. "How the hell did he get so close?"

"I don't think he got close," Matt muttered. "I think he just had a really good lens."

"Should've taken that too. Might've been worth something."

"Too late now." They flicked through the photos in silence, as the colors darkened and the New Year's Eve festivities came into focus.

"I don't remember half of this," mumbled Matt.

"You need to drink less," prodded Jane.

"I'll never drink again," he said quietly, and she could hear real sadness in his words.

"Hey," Jane said. She grabbed the sides of his head and turned it so she was looking Matt squarely in the eyes. "No matter how this turns out, it'll never be your fault, okay?" She paused, staring intently at him. "Okay? Hear me? This. Is. Not. Your. Fault."

"Thanks," he murmured—although Jane knew he was just saying it to appease her. Reluctantly, she let him go, resisting the urge to hug him close or subtly electrocute his stupid guilty brain. They went back to the pictures, Jane still discreetly watching Matt's miserable expression out of the corner of her eye.

They sat in silence as one by one pictures of the party clicked across the screen.

"Oh, that's cool," Jane said, pointing in spite of herself at a picture of Giselle dancing.

"Yeah, it was—how'd you miss that?" Matt asked.

"Too far away," Jane replied, pulling a face. She bent in a little closer. "I mean, look at her, she's ridiculous, you can really see why Ed—" She suddenly caught herself before she could blurt out any more, shooting Matt a guilty glance. "Why Ed, um, thought she was going to break land speed."

"Nice save," he muttered dryly.

"Shut up."

They kept flicking through. The pictures grew bright: people cheering, longer shots, fireworks over the manor. Then, as if they were fast-forwarding through a movie, frame by frame the crowds started to disperse. The fires went out. Acolytes left, wandering together in couples and droves. One by one, the lights flickered and died, first inside Morningstar, then out.

And then it happened. Matt clicked past a picture—and suddenly, there was Ed. Small and distant, a speck on the top of the photograph. Beside her, Jane felt Matt stiffen, heard his breathing become shorter and faster. The next shot zoomed closer, the photographer obviously zeroing in on the movement, the outline of Ed's body more visible now as he walked across the rooftop. Closer still—they could see his hands and hair. His shirt fluttering in the breeze. Closer now, just as he reached the edge, the shadows on his face, his eyes. His wide, terrified eyes. Jane suddenly felt sick. Matt was right—something was wrong. Why did they look like that? What was wrong with his eyes?

And then Matt moved forward again, and the picture changed, and Ed's tiny frame was falling, the camera zooming out, trying to catch him as he plummeted. It took three frames for him to hit the ground. And then there were only pictures neither of them needed to see.

"Close it," muttered Jane, but Matt wasn't listening. Instead, he clicked back through the stills of Ed's descent, one by one—until the raven-haired genius was back standing on the ledge, perched precariously over the drop below. Matt paused and leaned in, his brow furrowed. Jane followed his eyes, and this time she saw it.

"Is that blood?" she whispered. She leaned in too, so close her face almost brushed the screen.

"His nose," pointed Matt. "He's bleeding from his nose." Jane followed his gaze. Matt was right. If you weren't looking for it, if you didn't squint, you'd never see it. But even in the darkness, even from this distance, the crimson tracks running down over his lips were unmistakable. Edward Rakwoski had been bleeding profusely from his nose.

Right before he threw himself to his death.

Jane's eyes widened. She turned to Matt.

"You don't think," she murmured.

"Yeah," Matt whispered, pale as a ghost, "he's possessed."

"It all makes sense," said Matt. He ran his hands through his hair, his eyes unfocused, pacing the room, his fingers trembling. "It's the perfect crime. What better way to hide a murder than to make it look like suicide?"

"We don't know that," Jane muttered, stock-still, staring. "We don't know anything." But said aloud, the excuses sounded weak, undermined by the hammering in her chest.

Matt didn't hear her or he chose to ignore. "Psychic possession can trigger bleeding," he said. "Ears, nose, eyes, anywhere with fragile capillaries. The increased pressure on the brain triggers—"

"I know about the goddamn bleeds!" Jane snapped. She pinched the bridge of her nose and took a deep breath, trying to steady herself. "But . . . making someone off themselves? Over . . . over this, this device? Over one invention?"

"Not just any invention," Matt replied, still pacing. "A way to give non-psychics psychic powers. Can you imagine? It would've been a disaster for them! Worse than Psy-Block, worse than any court ruling, worse than anything that would've stopped their abilities. The second this device went public, every natural-born psychic in the world would've been out of a job." He turned to her, the words tumbling out unstoppable, a fever, a cascade. "Suddenly, they're not special anymore, not valuable—the monopoly is broken, the industry collapses. Who needs to pay a psychic a hundred and fifty K when you can buy telepathy from Wal-Mart for nineteen ninety-five?"

Matt shook his head bitterly. "It probably never even crossed Ed's mind. He just thought he was designing some new technology, when to a psychic he was threatening their very identity."

"But how would they have even known?" Jane asked angrily. "It wasn't like he went around blabbering about his work, how could they have even known what he was working on?"

"He told me," Matt replied, shaking his head again. "I didn't even think, I told him he should talk about it, said it was cool. God, maybe he listened. Maybe he told Giselle and then she told someone—maybe they overheard. Maybe someone illegally read his mind." His expression darkened. "Or Cassandra. Cassandra was a psychic. Maybe she knew, maybe she read a clairvoyant's mind and then she . . ." But even as Matt articulated the idea, he seemed to realize it didn't make much sense. The words died in his mouth, then he paused and shook his head. "It doesn't matter. One way or another, a psychic found out what he was up to."

"And they killed him to keep it quiet," muttered Jane, going along in spite of herself. "Took control of his mind, walked him up to the highest point of Morningstar, and made him jump off." She gritted her teeth, wanting to slam her fist into the wall.

"Those monsters," muttered Matt. He turned on his heels, striding back along the length of the room, head trembling as he paced, hands balled into fists. Jane had never seen him so agitated. "Those clever"—he swore heavily—"monsters. It's so easy to pull off, so easy to fake. Because it's the stereotype, isn't it?" He laughed, a cold, mirthless laugh. "Oh, poor unstable geniuses, so erratic, so prone to depression, unable to cope with their own thoughts. Nobody thinks twice when one of them kills themselves. Nobody bothers to take a closer look, do anything more than feel bad, because why would they, everyone knows that's just what geniuses do. Not to mention it's hard to check a brain for psychic tampering when it's splattered all over the ground."

"It all fits," agreed Jane. "Except—" She hesitated. "What about the message? That still doesn't make sense."

"Yeah, it does," countered Matt. He knelt back in front of the computer and clicked through the pictures on the screen. "Look," he said, pointing to the picture of Ed suspended in midair. "There. As he's falling. On the side of his body. See that light?"

Jane peered close. "Looks like a snowflake on the lens," she said, looking up. Matt shook his head.

"Look again," he assured her, moving through to the next frame. Sure enough, the tiny speck of white, no more than a few pixels, moved too. "It's his phone. His kinetic phone."

The penny dropped. "Holy crap," whispered Jane.

"Yeah," Matt nodded fervently. "I'm willing to bet anything that whoever was inside his head bailed out at the last second. Maybe they didn't want to feel what it was like to die, maybe Ed was fighting them. Either way, between leaving the roof and hitting the ground, Ed regained control."

"Anyone else would've panicked," said Jane, staring at the picture in awe.

"But not Ed," Matt agreed. "He's faster than that. He knows he's going to die. He works out he's got two, maybe three seconds. Not enough to save himself—"

"But enough to send a message," Jane added softly, not daring to believe. "If you were a world-record typist. Just one word."

"Exactly." They looked at each other, a shared mixture of horror and revelation mingling on their faces. But then the barb of an unpleasant thought creased Jane's forehead.

"But why 'Dawn'?" she asked, frowning at the tiny scraps of light in the photo. "Why that?"

Matt paused, following her gaze. "I don't know," he admitted finally. "That's the one bit I still can't figure out. Why 'Dawn'? What's he got to do with all of this? He's not a psychic and he's already worth billions—"

"Which he uses for the good of mankind," Jane interjected.

"Which he uses for the good of mankind," Matt repeated, for some reason sounding slightly annoyed at this important clarification. "Which means it's not like he'd be in it for the money."

"Dawn wasn't involved," Jane insisted, adamant. "So, it's got to be a warning. Or a call for help. It might not even be referring to the captain."

Then she paused. "What about the kid?" she asked, almost reluctantly. "Where does he fit in?"

Matt hesitated. "I don't know," he admitted finally. "But whoever he is, I think he's on our side." He bit his cheek. "He warned me Morningstar was dangerous. He led me to the photographs. He told me I needed to stay hidden—maybe he meant from psychics." He stopped, then turned to Jane. "I don't know what Cassandra was trying to tell us. I don't know whether she thought he was good or bad, whether they're enemies or on the same side. I don't even know if there are sides. I don't know who he is or what he's doing or why the hell he can't just be direct, but the more I think about it, the more I just can't shake the feeling that maybe he's trying to help."

Jane's face creased. "Assuming it's all real," she said, "assuming this isn't some trick."

"Which brings us back to square one," Matt said bitterly, slumping against the bed. But Jane shook her head.

"Screw square one," she countered. "This is real, this is big picture."

"Huge picture, actually," said Matt. "There're millions of psychics." He paused and shot an unwilling glance at the laptop's screen. "And you're right. Every one of those pictures could be Photoshopped. This whole thing could be a setup."

"To frame psychics?" Jane said, frowning. "Why?"

"I don't know," Matt admitted. "I don't know who or how. It could all be fake, we can't . . . I mean we still can't properly rule out suicide." To Matt's credit, he didn't hold back from voicing the idea, but his mouth did twist like he'd swallowed sour milk.

Jane considered for a moment, then shook her head. "We're not locking anyone up," she said. "We're not going to the police or pointing fingers. Right now, all we're doing is digging because either way, something weird is going on."

"Right," Matt murmured. For a second, the two of them just sat, still and silent, staring at the screen.

"So, what now?" Jane asked eventually. "Any ideas?"

Matt paused and chewed at his knuckle. "We need more to go on."

"Like what?"

"Like what happened in the lab."

"How the hell are we meant to figure that out?"

"There were cameras."

"Right," grimaced Jane. "And Acolytes don't have access to the security feed."

Matt's gaze flicked to her, and the corners of his mouth twitched.

"No," he replied, eyes gleaming. "But the police do."

"Detective Warbrook," Matt mumbled. "I'm so sorry to call you like this, I hope this isn't a bad time . . ."

"It's just officer," Warbrook replied, although he didn't sound too unhappy to be addressed by the title. On the other end of the phone, Matt silently smirked at the compliment implied in his "mistake." "It's good to hear from you, buddy. How can I help?"

"It . . . it's not . . ." Matt stammered, weaving the technopath's business card between his fingers and pretending to choke up between words. "I mean, I don't know if you can . . ."

"Try me," the technician said kindly. "I'll see what I can do."

Matt swallowed noisily. "Thank you," he murmured. "I just . . . I need . . ."

There was a place and a purpose for everything, Matt believed—and it was time for his grief to make itself useful. He reached inside his mind to the little box where he'd sealed off his feelings of misery, the memories of Ed's death, and threw himself among them, letting them wash over him in waves. Tears sprung up in his eyes and bands of retching sadness wrapped around his chest, his words bubbling up between heart-wrenching, pitiful sobs.

"It's just . . . Ed's parents . . . they . . . they asked me if I could m-m-make . . . make them a v-v-video, something to r-r-remember him by, for Thursday, for the . . . the . . . the . . ." As he tried to say "funeral," Matt's voice wavered and broke, his grief spilling in hot, damp rivers out and down his face. The taste of salt mingled in his mouth, the tears staining wet throughout his words. He shuddered, sucking in air, and forced himself to go on.

"For the funeral," he continued, his voice still unsteady but nevertheless pressing determinedly forward. "And I was . . . well, see, I don't have much of him, and I wondered . . . if there was any chance . . . I know it's a long shot . . . but I remembered a lady working on the cameras, and I thought . . . maybe just . . . whatever you had . . . whatever we could . . .

to remember him by . . ." And he broke down into tears again, his breaths coming in mangled, sobbing gasps.

"Hey, hey, come on," soothed Warbrook, his concern audible on the other end of the line. There was a pause on the officer's side while 90 percent of Matt continued to sob into the phone, the remaining 10 percent keeping a close ear out for whether the technician would take the bait.

"I know you're really busy," Matt said between hiccups. "And I know I'm asking a lot, it's just . . . it's all I can do, and I just want to do the best I can, and . . ."

"Look," Warbrook conceded. He let out a long, heavy sigh. "Let me see what I can do. I don't think we've got much, mainly just the few hours before"—he hurriedly trailed off—"but I'll see what I can find, all right, and I'll send it through. What's your email address?"

Between shaky, sniveling breaths, Matt told him. Then he proceeded to stutter mumbled thanks over and over again to the sympathetic technopath.

"It's nothing, it's really nothing," Warbrook assured him. "Really, anything I can do to help. I'll send through something soon."

"Thank you so much," sniffled Matt.

"You're really welcome, buddy. And again, I'm just so sorry for your loss."

The call ended. Matt drew a long, shuddering breath, then exhaled and promptly sat back up, dabbing his eyes on his sleeve. "Video should be coming through shortly," he informed Jane matter-of-factly, any trace of unhappiness dispersed and his voice returned entirely to normal. Jane—who'd been sitting beside him the whole time looking increasingly uncomfortable and hovering awkwardly back and forth as if unsure whether to be giving Matt space or support—recoiled like she'd been stung.

"The hell was that?" she yelped.

"What?" Matt answered with a shrug, his eyes a little red but otherwise nonchalant.

"You can cry on command?" she asked incredulously, gaping at him.

"What? You can't?" he replied.

"No," spluttered Jane. "I'm not a psychopath!"

"Your loss," said Matt. He glanced from her to his open in-box. "Because it pays off."

Jane reluctantly turned back to the computer, still slightly perturbed. "Well, what now?"

"We need to know more about psychics," Matt replied. He clicked open Google, but to his surprise Jane stood up, her eyes bright and a wry grin spreading over her face.

"Stay there," she said, heading for the door. "I've got a better idea."

It took a little more than an hour, but Warbrook was true to his word. An email heavy with video files *ping*-ed its way into Matt's in-box. He'd just finished downloading the last of the attachments when there was a knock on his door.

"He's busy with a workshop," Jane said briskly, stepping through the door the moment Matt opened it without any preamble. "But he can meet us later, room 324."

"Who is?" asked Matt. "Who're you talking about?"

"Wally," she replied, as if that should have been obvious.

"Wally Cykes!" he cried incredulously, turning to follow her as she pushed straight past him and sat perched on the side of his bed.

"We need an expert," she said with a shrug. "He's an expert."

"He's a psychic!" cried Matt, appalled. "Who lives here! In this building! Where Ed was killed! By a psychic!"

"Was maybe killed by a psychic!" Jane countered, realizing a second too late that she was arguing the wrong point. "Come on, you really think Wally's a murderer?"

"Well . . . no," Matt conceded, but then he immediately snapped back. "But we don't know, Jane, that's the problem." He made a noise somewhere between a sigh and a groan and pinched the bridge of his nose. "What did you tell him?"

"Nothing," She scowled. "I'm not an idiot." Matt opened his mouth to argue that last part, but she cut him off. "I just said we wanted to talk. He seemed fine with it."

"Awesome," despaired Matt. "Subtle. Great."

"Shut up," she snapped. "Better than getting fed garbage by some backwater webpage."

"Backwater . . . ? Whatever," he said with a sigh, giving up and sitting down. "The videos came through."

"Great," said Jane. "Have you taken a look?"

"Was waiting for you," he told her, which was only half true. She nodded at the screen, and Matt opened up the first file.

To their disappointment, what footage there was of Ed was unremarkable. The largest and primary file Warbrook had sent them was the video from the computer lab—a grainy black-and-white recording that showed Ed entering a little after eleven, sitting down in his usual chair and typing steadily in the dark for the next five hours, the only light coming from his monitors. Even on fast-forward, it was dull viewing— Ed unmoving from between the screens, the time stamp rolling progressively forward, nothing really changing. His back to the camera, it was impossible to get a clear look at Ed's face, and the quality of the footage was too poor to make out what he was doing. At a little past three, he appeared to sit up a bit straighter, like an idea had occurred to him, but whatever it might have been, pursuing it seemed only to involve further typing. Finally, at three fifty, Ed's hands paused over the keyboard. He sat unmoving for a little under a minute, then without a word got to his feet and walked calmly out the door. That was it—the footage ended. The next videos, glimpses of him walking through the corridors on his way to the roof, yielded no further insight.

"I don't get it," said Jane, once the recordings had ended. She stood with her arms folded and her eyebrows furrowed, absentmindedly chewing her lip. "Did we miss something?"

"I don't know," replied Matt, deflated. The disappointment was tangible. He'd been so sure they were going to find answers on the videos, the notion that this could be a dead end had barely crossed his mind. It was a struggle not to give in to despondence. "It looks like nothing."

"That's what I thought."

"But maybe that's just it. Maybe the nothing means something. Maybe it's a clue." But Matt didn't feel particularly certain.

"Yeah maybe," said Jane, sounding similarly unconvinced. "We'll see what Wally says."

They had an hour or two until Wally had said he'd be able to meet, so the two of them headed down to the hall for dinner, half to eat, half to burn time. Initially, Matt simply sat, waiting, casting subtle, suspicious glances at the psychics around the room. But eventually, the troubles weighing on his mind weren't enough to erase his body's needs, and the fact that he hadn't eaten all day coupled with the sight of Jane gnawing on a rack of ribs caused a rumbling in his stomach Matt couldn't bring himself to ignore. It was a strange sensation, he thought as he finally ate, feeling something as petty as hunger, so soon after someone had died. It felt wrong, like the world should have stopped and waited, life paused to show its respects. But it didn't. Nothing substantial changed. The lights of the hall stayed bright, its occupants loud—unaffected, it seemed, by the thought of someone among them, who'd sat among them, being murdered.

Or being a murderer.

They found room 324, a small, disused classroom on the upper levels, without difficulty. Jane led the way, having obviously been there before. Wally was already sitting waiting inside.

"Well, it's good to see you two made up," he said, standing as they entered. He grinned, hands in his pocket, the white of his teeth matching the frangipanis on his shirt—though the smile seemed somewhat strained. "I was afraid Jane was going to chicken out."

"Chicken out of what?" Matt asked, shooting her a curious look.

"Nothing," Jane growled through clenched teeth, glaring at Wally, who blinked. "It doesn't matter. We're not here for that." She dropped into the chair beside when Wally had been sitting, her arms crossed. "We want to know a few things about psychics."

Wally looked slightly taken aback. "Um, okay," he said with a shrug. "What did you want to know?"

"Can psychics control people?" she asked without preamble or hesitation. Matt quietly shuffled beside her into his own seat, internally despairing at Jane's complete lack of tact. They'd agreed over dinner that Jane would take the lead on questioning—a decision made against Matt's better judgment, which he was now beginning to regret. Personally, he would have opted for a long, disarming conversation, maybe even with drinks involved, before casually weaving in some discreet inquiries and extracting what he wanted to know without the telepath ever realizing. Jane, on the other hand, had all the subtlety of a battering ram and half the charisma. Nevertheless, if Wally found her question strange, it wasn't enough to stop him answering.

"Of course," he replied, nonchalant. "Mind control is a step above mind reading, but it's pretty basic."

"Can you tell if someone's being controlled?" Jane continued. Wally frowned.

"Well, I mean to me, yes, it'd be obvious. To an outsider . . ." He grimaced slightly. "There might be some shaking, delayed reactions, slurred speech—although they're preventable. Smaller stuff—tension, dilated pupils, nervous ticks"—he held up his fingers like he was counting off a checklist—"only the best can stop those. And obviously the bleeds, but everyone knows about them."

"And when you mind control someone, can you make them do anything?" Jane pressed.

"Sort of," Wally replied, shrugging. " It depends." He paused, looking from one to the other. "What's this all about?"

"Nothing," Matt started to say, but Jane cut him off.

"We think Ed was possessed when he died," she said bluntly, ignoring Matt's silent protests. Wally recoiled like he'd been slapped.

"You . . . what?" he spluttered. He turned between the two of them, his pale face suddenly even whiter. "You're joking."

"Just look at this," Jane commanded, and she opened Matt's laptop on the desk in front of him.

By the time they'd gone through the photos of Ed's last moments on the roof, Wally's incredulous rejection had turned to stunned shock.

"Where did you get these?" he whispered. He looked up at Jane and then at Matt, his eyes wide and disbelieving.

Jane ignored the question "You see it, right?" she asked. "Look at his eyes. Tell me that's normal." The psychic stayed mute—just staring at the final picture still frozen on the screen.

"Look," Matt said, pointing to the image of Ed on the roof. "Right there. He's bleeding. Which means . . ."

"I know what a nosebleed means," Wally murmured. He closed his eyes and shook his head. "What it . . . what it can mean. It doesn't . . . it could be the angle. A trick of the light."

"It's not," Matt said bluntly. He watched closely as Wally once more stared at the screen, looking for fear, recognition, any sign that the red-headed psychic was in any way involved. All he saw was ashen-faced horror.

"Why are you showing me this?" Wally eventually whispered, tearing his eyes away from the screen to glance between the two of them. His hands were shaking.

"We want you to believe us," Jane answered before Matt could say anything. "And we want you to help us figure out what the hell is going on. There's more," she added, unprompted. Wally nodded silently and Jane loaded up the security footage Warbrook had emailed through. The three of them sat watching Ed's final hours without a word. When they reached the end, where Ed stopped typing and walked off, Wally let out a soft hiss.

"Play it again," he requested. "Just the last minute." Matt complied, and they replayed the video in silence. Wally swore.

"You see something?" asked Jane.

"Maybe," murmured Wally, narrowed eyes peering at the gray-scale image frozen on the screen.

"Maybe?" Matt scowled. If his impatience was audible, Wally didn't notice.

"See how he tenses?" the psychic pointed out. "See how his fingers lock, stop moving on the keyboard? That . . ." He forced out the words with some difficulty. "Could be someone overpowering his mind. I don't know, the picture's not clear . . . and it's fast." He leaned back and exhaled. "Very fast."

"But that's got to be it then!" Matt exclaimed in a rush of excitement. "Ed was mind-controlled; he didn't want to do this!"

"It's impossible," Wally said quietly.

"Come on, Wally, like hell it's impossible," demanded Jane. "You said it yourself, if a psychic controls your mind, they can make you do anything!"

But Wally shook his head. "You don't understand," he told them. "Forcing someone to kill themselves isn't something a psychic can just *do*. It's not like making them spout gibberish or bake pancakes. You're literally forcing the brain to go against self-preservation, its most basic instinct." He paused and glanced at the two of them. "This isn't conscious thought we're talking about. Survival is a subconscious, primal drive, forged through hundreds of millions of years of evolution. It's hardwired into the very foundations of our brains. You can't just flick some switch and override it."

"But is it doable?" Matt pressed on. Wally's face looked strained.

"Well, I mean, it's not impossible, I suppose . . ." he conceded, reluctantly, "but not by just anyone. It's absolute apex stuff—why do you think you don't hear about psychic suicides all the time? There'd be . . ." he struggled for words, holding his hands up halfway exasperated. "Four, five telepaths, in the whole of North America? Half a dozen, max, who'd be strong enough to pull this off? And Natalia and I are two of them."

"Really?" Matt replied, eyes narrowing. "And where were you around four a.m. on New Year's Day?" Jane made a noise in protest, but Matt held out his hand to silence her, staring intently at Wally. The psychic stared back at him with a deadpan expression.

"Seriously?" he asked flatly.

"Hey," shrugged Matt, although his gaze never wavered. "You admit you could have done it, and you were here. I'm just covering my bases."

"Matt, don't be an idiot," Jane snapped.

"I'm just making sure," he growled.

"It's fine, Jane, it's understandable," interjected Wally, waving her concerns away. "I wasn't here, actually," he informed Matt.

"Then, where were you?" Matt demanded.

To his surprise, the psychic's face went slightly pink. "I was at the beach, actually. In Barbados," he informed them. He sat up straighter and ruffled his collar slightly, averting his eyes. Matt frowned. This was not the answer he'd been expecting.

"Can anyone vouch for that?" he asked.

"Will can," Wally answered, his chin held high. "Since he teleported me. We stayed there for a few hours."

"Both of you?" said Matt, raising an eyebrow. "What were you doing?"

Wally's face grew slightly pinker, but he nevertheless resolutely met Matt's puzzled gaze. "We got cocktails. We talked a lot. We watched the sun come up. We . . . um . . ."

The lightbulb suddenly clicked. "Ah," said Matt, abruptly shutting his mouth. Wally looked slightly relieved.

"Will can confirm it," he said. "If you want—"

"No, no, that's fine, I, um, I just didn't . . . you know . . ."

"No, that's fine, we didn't . . . you know, on the down-low . . ."

"Yeah, of course, that's fine, you don't need to . . ."

"Didn't get back until at least seven . . ."

"Great, no that's all good, I, um, I believe you . . ."

"Hold on," Jane snorted derisively, still not having caught on. "I don't get it. What were you and Will doing in Barbados?" She looked at Wally, who simply gazed back at her with a blank, patient expression. Suddenly, the shoe dropped. Jane's face froze. "Oh," she said, in a very small voice. Then she blinked. "Oh," she repeated, louder, gaping at Wally. "Oh!"

The psychic shrugged sheepishly. "Yup."

"Um," stammered Jane, fumbling, "all right. Okay then. Of course, that's . . . well, um, there you go."

"Natalia wasn't here either," Wally told them, turning to Matt, still smiling slightly at the stunned look plastered over Jane's face. "She's been at a consultancy job in London all week."

"Right, but maybe one of the other psychics you mentioned—"

But again, Wally shook his head. "None of them were here. Remember Ed's retinal scanning system? It would've gone off the second anybody unregistered entered Morningstar."

"Right, but maybe from a distance, they—"

"No," the psychic said flatly. "Impossible."

"I've heard of psychics entering people's minds from halfway across the country," Matt persisted stubbornly.

"Yeah," replied Wally, "as a vision. To pass a message." He explained patiently. "Our influence decreases exponentially the further we are from the mind we're interacting with. From any kind of distance, sure, if you know what you're doing, you can pop into someone's head. But you appear as little more than a ghost, an annoying distraction. You can't actually read someone's mind, let alone exert any kind of influence." He shook his head. "Especially without eye contact, eye contact is huge. For this stuff? Even if I believe this . . ." He pointed at the screen, at the frozen image of Ed's stiffened shoulders. "I don't know, whatever the hell this is, even if I believe that someone's assuming control, it only lasts"—Wally's fingers moved over the mousepad, and he replayed the last snippet of video—"forty-five seconds? Forty-five seconds to break someone's mind and suppress their most basic instinct, all while preventing them showing practically any physical signs?" He shook his head again. "There's maybe seven psychics in the entire world strong enough to pull that off, and not one of them could do it without being in the same room. Without a direct line of sight? Impossible. Straight out, one hundred percent impossible."

"What if a bunch of psychics worked together?" Jane asked over her shock and coming back into the conversation. "What if they, like, merged their powers? Pooled their resources?"

"Does tying two horses together give you one, faster horse?" Wally responded, a little sarcastic. Jane scowled and crossed her arms, muttering something under her breath about "legitimate question." Matt shook his head.

"But that just takes us back to square one," he muttered, feeling a fresh wave of frustration creeping up. "The room's empty, there's no one there."

"That's definitely what it looks like," Wally agreed. But his words gave Matt a sudden, horrifying inspiration.

"We can't see anybody," he whispered, staring at the screen. "But that doesn't mean no one's there."

It took the other two a second to grasp his meaning. "Invisibility?" said Wally. He appeared skeptical. "Well, that's a great idea, except if they were invisible, they wouldn't be a psychic. You get one or the other."

"Unless you can have both," Matt said quietly. Slowly, slowly, his stomach filling with a cold, sickening dread, he turned his eyes to the girl beside him—to Jane and the black E tattooed onto her cheek. She met his gaze and then suddenly the implication dawned on her.

"You don't . . . you're not saying I . . ." she spluttered, and then her face split into fury. "You think it was me?"

"Was it?" cried Matt, getting to his feet. "Because only an empath could be invisible and telepathic, and you're the only empath the scanners wouldn't have picked up!"

"How dare you!" Jane shouted, standing up as well, glaring into his face, an inch or two taller. "How can you even suggest that? How can you even think I'd do something like this, after all this time, you stupid piece of—"

For a moment, Matt thought she was going to hit him, and in a single, mad instant he felt himself tense, readying for a fight—but then the sound of soft laughter broke through the madness and both Matt and Jane snapped around to find Wally, still seated, chuckling at the sight of the two of them yelling at each other.

"Matt," he said, laughing. "It wasn't Jane. I promise."

"How do you know?" Matt demanded. He ignored Jane's vicious glare.

"Um, apart from the fact that I know her?" replied Wally, raising an eyebrow back. He threw a smile at the empath. "Look, Jane has many talents," he said kindly. "She's really very amazing in a lot of different ways. But"—his smile turned slightly sad—"unfortunately, well, mental discipline just isn't one of them."

He patted Jane gingerly on the sleeve. "You've been trying really, really hard honey and you have improved, I swear, I'm not saying this to be discouraging." He turned back to Matt. "But I wasn't kidding about how difficult something like this is. Most psychics couldn't manage it, and Jane—well, Jane's still working on the basics. Even if she had stolen telepathy and invisibility—and I think someone probably would've noticed that—she just doesn't have the juice. Not that that's a bad thing, sweetheart," he added kindly, looking up at Jane. He glanced between the two of them. "So how about you both sit down and stop being stupid?"

There was a pause. Matt suddenly felt profoundly idiotic. "Sorry," he murmured to Jane, dropping his gaze.

"Ass," she replied, although with more annoyance than outright hatred. They both shuffled back into their seats, their arms folded, leaning fractionally apart.

A slow silence stretched out across the room, only to be broken again by Wally.

"I don't know," the psychic said, sighing. He stared at Ed's image frozen on the screen, his freckled, boyish face looking distressed and worn. "It could be nothing. People get nosebleeds for other reasons. People act weird before they die."

"Wally, come on!" demanded Matt, incredulous. "You can't seriously believe this is all just coincidence?"

"Matt, I don't know," Wally replied, turning to him. "I'll admit it's weird, but what you're suggesting is impossible. Ed was alone. Heck, the door doesn't open the entire time he's in there. No telepath could force someone to kill themselves remotely, no one, period. Not this cleanly, not this quick. It's just not possible."

"Everything's impossible until someone does it," Matt countered doggedly, refusing to concede. "People are always popping up with new powers, making breakthroughs, breaking records. Someone did this, someone took control of Ed's mind." He shook his head, gritting his teeth. "Maybe they've found some new technique. Maybe they've come up with a drug, maybe there's a machine. But they did it. Somehow, someone killed him."

For a few seconds, Wally said nothing, his finger on his lips, pale face unmoving.

"I don't know," he finally admitted. "But I'll tell you this much. If there's someone out there who can attack a mind with this much force from a distance"—he hesitated—"then nothing we do matters." His face grew dark. "Because nothing anyone can do could stop them. No one, anywhere, would be safe."

It was almost eleven. Matt and Jane sat in silence, the cold from the roof where Ed had jumped, from the whispering wind, seeping into their hands and legs. The world had faded to black, to gray and blue—the only light the glow from odd windows, hints at warmth interspersed among frozen stone, and the crescent moon, its shape intermittently obscured by thin patches of cloud, a flock of wisping sheep herded before a shepherd's half-closed eye.

"He's wrong," Matt murmured after a while, his chin resting on his hands, his knees tucked to his chest. He gazed out across the grounds, at the fields of cold gray snow, once teeming with activity, now quiet and still. Jane didn't respond.

"You know he's wrong. You know Ed didn't do it."

"I don't know Matt," she said, sighing. A loose strand of her bronze hair, broken free from its usual tie, fluttered silently in the breeze. Jane rubbed a knuckle into the bags under her eyes. "I don't know what I think anymore."

They lapsed into a dull, painful silence, their words swept up in the gentle rustling of the wind. They'd come up here . . . well, who knew really? Ostensibly to look around again, in case darkness revealed something. But, of course, there was nothing visible in the daylight that was not less so come night. And so, they'd just ended up sitting—watching, waiting, contemplating the cold world go by. It was a beautiful, lonely view, a sad place for a man to die.

"I know he didn't do it," Matt muttered again. He said it quiet-like and Jane didn't know if he was saying it to convince her or himself. "I know he didn't kill himself. I just know it."

"How?" she asked, rolling her head over to look at him. It wasn't a derogative question, but she wanted to shake his persistent faith a little, to see if it was grounded in reality or a dogged, grief-born delusion. "How do you know?"

Matt fell silent, staring straight ahead. His eyes shone slightly, but he didn't cry. "Because it's stupid," he said finally. He shook his head, still gazing out over the fall. "Maybe Ed got rejected. Maybe he was depressed. But he wasn't stupid. Above all, if nothing else, he wasn't stupid."

Matt paused and pulled his knees in closer. "And suicide is stupid. Fundamentally, at its most basic level, it's a stupid, stupid idea. Life can suck, sure. Life can be horrible, painful, miserable. But no matter how bad it gets, no matter how bleak things might be, there's always the possibility—no matter how tiny—that it'll get better."

"But once you're dead, you're dead! It's over, hope extinguished, and that possibility is gone. No matter how miserable you are, choosing to die is picking an eternity of nothing over the chance of life improving. You're swapping something for nothing. And that's not a smart choice."

He shook his head. "I don't care how low Ed got. I don't care how many girls rejected him. He was the smartest guy I knew, and he would've realized this was a stupid choice before he got halfway up the first staircase."

He turned away slightly and fell silent, resting one cheek upon his knee. Jane didn't know how to respond. She thought it might not have been as simple as all that. But her thoughts were the kind that didn't go easily into words, and she didn't know if words would be any help. So, she just sat, looking up at the stars.

It was getting late. They had a funeral tomorrow.

It was a big funeral. Probably bigger than Ed ever would have anticipated, had he given the topic any thought. He hadn't left a will—just some old clothes, several boxes of robotics scraps and soldering irons, and a top-of-the-line computer tower whose digital contents had now automatically liquefied into a useless slurry of zeroes and ones. Another indication that he hadn't planned on dying, Matt thought. Another glaring oversight by a so-called suicidal genius.

Matt almost didn't go to the funeral. Going there, putting on a black suit and somber face and listening to some priest drone on about life and death and tragic loss while Ed's real killer was still out there felt like a manifest betrayal of their friendship. Matt could imagine Ed standing there, shouting at them for being so stupid, demanding to know how they could think so little of him, wondering why nobody could connect the dots. Except he wasn't, of course, because Ed wasn't saying anything. Because he was dead. His corpse was right there, forty feet away, in a mahogany coffin. Apparently, the healers had done well repairing the body into what could be considered good condition—apart from the whole death thing, which remained incurable—but the casket was still closed. That was fine by Matt.

Most of the Academy had turned out—less, Matt thought, because of who Ed was and more for the part of their institution he had been. To Matt's eye, they all looked stricken with an appropriate level of grief— solemn and somber, with the occasional sniff or damp eye—with the exception of Natalia, who looked bored, and Wally, whose thousand-yard stare marked him lost in his own thoughts. Only Ed's mother, a squat, dark-haired woman, and his father, a pock-marked, rigid man, seemed genuinely, heartbreakingly upset. Matt had to mentally block out the sight and sound of them breaking down as the priest prayed over their son, for risk of losing control and falling into his own grief.

The only notable absence was Giselle Pixus. Matt had overheard on the walk over that the speedster had barely left her room in days— though out of guilt, grief, or some ridiculous fear people would blame her for Ed's death, he didn't know. A large part of him wanted to bring her into the fold, let her know what they'd found—but a smaller, sharper corner of his brain knew that the more people knew about their suspicions, the harder they'd be to confirm. Giselle's pain, however awful, would have to wait until they had something more.

Because right now all they had were straws to grasp at. All through the funeral—while the coffin was telekinetically floated down the aisle, while the priest gave his commiseration and discreet reminder of the need for love, while Ed's parents bade their tearful farewell, while the terramancers split open the earth, while two hundred black-clad voices rose together in "Amazing Grace"—Matt stood among the Acolytes, staring straight ahead, turning the pieces over and over. The footage, the photos, the paparazzi and the blue-eyed child, Cassandra, psychics, the word *Dawn*—individually, they were suspicious. Together, they were too much to be a coincidence. But together they made no sense. If Ed had been killed by a psychic, then why message about Dawn? If a psychic hadn't been involved, then who killed him? And how had they done it? And what had the point of his ambush been? And where did the kid fit in? Was he trying to help or mislead them?

He tried to think—to force himself to ignore his friend's face on the projector screen in front of them, the hot, clutching pain in his chest; the coffin being lowered into the ground. His best . . . he drew a deep, shuddering breath. His best theory revolved around an exceptionally powerful psychic—a prodigy, able to—to hell with what Wally said— remotely assault another person's mind. "Dawn," then, could be a warning from Ed that Captain Dawn was in danger, or maybe already under this mysterious assailant's control. After all, all the power in the world meant nothing once the fight shifted to the mind. The only problem with this theory was that it seemed strange—and he was perhaps a bit uncomfortable to admit, a little uncharacteristically selfless—for Ed not to name his attacker but another potential victim. And as Jane had immediately pointed out when Matt had suggested this theory, Captain Dawn had been taking Psy-Block to protect against this very threat since the late 1980s—the stuff had been invented with him in mind. So, it just seemed odd that Ed's final act would have been to worry about psychics on Dawn's behalf. And it still left the mystery of the clairvoyants and the kid.

Or maybe there were no psychics. Maybe the photos were fakes. Maybe the photographer in the woods had been there to throw him off. Maybe it was all meaningless.

They entombed Ed in a small, nondescript grave beside the monument, marked only by a black marble headstone. Then one by one, of their own accord, the Acolytes turned and left, forming a steady stream of mourners that grew less and less mournful the closer they got back to the manor. Matt walked alone in the middle of them, following the wide path the pyromancers had cleared through the snow—head bowed and quiet, not really listening, as respectful silence gave way to the usual whispers, questions, and chatter of the crowd.

His friend was dead. And he was no closer to understanding why.

After a few minutes, a shadow fell over the ground beneath his feet, and Matt looked up to see the huge figure of James Conrad lumbering alongside him. They walked together for a while in silence.

"Sucks, doesn't it?" the giant said eventually, without any prompting. "Losing one of our own." He paused and glanced down at Matt. "Really sucks."

Matt just nodded mutely. James glanced back down again.

"You hanging in there all right?" he asked.

"Yeah," lied Matt, who didn't feel like having this conversation right now, or ever. The strongman's blank gaze lingered for a few seconds, but eventually he must have realized Matt wasn't going to say any more. He gently rested a gigantic, plate-sized hand on Matt's shoulder.

"Well, if you ever need to talk," he said. "Let me know. I can find someone." His hand lingered for a few seconds, only removing it after Matt gave a short, sharp nod. They continued on in silence.

"Of course, now we got a world of trouble for the Academy." James sighed after a while. "Have to find someone new to take care of IT. Not to mention security. Cameras, firewalls, scanners. Ed ran half the systems in this place. Geniuses," he added mournfully, with a slow shake of the head. "You never really appreciate everything they do until they're gone."

"Ed was a great person," Matt replied stiffly. James Conrad nodded, not really listening.

"Yeah, definitely. Real shame he's gone." Suddenly, the big man smacked his palm to his forehead, making a sound like two raw steaks slapping together. "Ah, nuts. That's what else he was doing. Damnit." He looked down at Matt. "Don't suppose you'd do me a favor? Ed said he'd organize it, but, well . . ." James's voice trailed off.

"Sure." Matt sighed heavily, too weary to care. "What is it?"

"Not much. Just a little party. I figure, hey, you're the party guy, you'll probably do a better job anyway and—"

"Wait," said Matt, a little confused. He looked up. "Ed was organizing a party?"

"Well, more of a reunion, really," replied James, peering over at a group of girls, their black dresses fluttering in the breeze. "Just whoever you can round up. And then I don't know, some cheese, wine, canapés, I don't know, whatever old people like." He tore his eyes away from the girls and glanced back down at Matt. "So, can I count on you?"

"Um, sure," mumbled Matt, not really sure how else to respond.

"Excellent." James threw him a quick smile. "Thanks, man, I really appreciate it." He turned back to the girls and his pace quickened. "I'll catch you later."

"Hold on," interjected Matt before James could lumber too far. "What was Ed organizing? Who's the reunion for?"

James Conrad stopped in his tracks and barked a short, meaty laugh. "Right! Ha! That'd probably help." He guffawed, smacking himself on the side of the head and grinning. "It's a surprise party. Sixtieth. For the captain. Captain Dawn."

PANDORA'S LIST

Captain Dawn
The Champion of Light

Strength	★★★★★
Speed	★★★★★
Agility	★★★★★★
Stamina	★★★★★★
Durability	★★★★★★
Intelligence	★★★★★

With the power of unlimited energy, the invincible Captain Dawn is the Legion of Heroes' steadfast leader and strongest warrior. Said to wield the power of a hundred suns, in times of peril he's the first person the world turns to and the last one the bad guys want to see. The relentless force burning inside Captain Dawn protects him from any harm, and lets the hero hit as hard as any strongman, fly as fast as any flier, and unleash devastating blasts of golden energy against his foes. But in the end, his greatest strength lays not in his powers but in his love for his friends, his dedication to peace, and the limitless courage in his heart.

"For truth. For justice. For the dawn."

Legion of Heroes Trading Cards No #1 (Limited Ultra-Rare Holofoil)
Booster pack $8.95

* * *

"Jane!"

He found her in the library of all places, sequestered in a corner behind an huge medical textbook with sheets of paper strewn across the desk. She glanced up, looking mildly irritated as he approached.

"What?" she hissed, halfway between a whisper and a *shush*. Matt ignored her annoyance and slid down into a free seat.

"I know what it is!" he whispered. "The message! I know what Ed was trying to tell me!"

" 'Dawn'?" Jane whispered back, her irritation instantly vanishing. "What, what was it?"

"It's his birthday," Matt told her, making sure to keep his voice low so as not to be overheard. "Jane, Ed wasn't telling me to get Dawn; he was giving me a lead!"

"His birthday?" echoed Jane. Her face scrunched into a frown. "But his birthday's not 'til May third. I don't get it. That's ages away."

"How do you just *know* that?" Matt wondered, shaking his head. He waved the question away. "Never mind. The point is: Ed was organizing a party. A surprise party for Captain Dawn, because he was turning sixty."

"Why wasn't I invited?" Jane laughed, a little too high and a little too forced. Matt rolled his eyes.

"Really?"

"It was a joke," she said defensively.

"Oh yeah, sure. Be sure to stretch your back out, don't want to cramp up carrying that torch."

"Shut up."

"You shut up. Just listen for a second, stop frothing over your boyfriend—"

"He's not my—"

"Jane!"

"Fine!"

"Thank you." He rubbed his temples. "Ed had been tasked with organizing this surprise party. But not so much a party, James said."

"James, as in James Conrad?"

"Right. He's the one who told me. He called it a 'reunion,' and then mentioned something about stuff 'old people like.' So, I'm thinking, Ed must've been tracking—"

"Tracking down Captain Dawn's old friends and relatives," Jane finished, touching a knuckle to her lips. Suddenly, she snapped up, a look of understanding splashed across her face. "And you think he found something."

"Or someone," Matt said, nodding. He glanced around the shelves then back to her, leaning close. "Someone from Captain Dawn's past, or, or, I don't know, a whole group of someones. I don't know who, I don't know why, but somehow it got Ed killed."

He could see the gears turning in Jane's head. "Like what?" she muttered, the concentration in her eyes boring a hole in the desk. "What the hell did he find?"

"I don't know," Matt admitted. "Maybe he didn't even find anything, maybe he was just getting too close, but either way it must have been something enormous—something worth killing over."

"Something that could threaten the entire world," whispered Jane.

For a few seconds, they just sat in stunned, horrified silence, Matt trying to steady his breathing, Jane slowly, unconsciously, shaking her head.

"So, what do we do?" she asked finally, looking across at him.

"We do what Ed did," said Matt. "Whatever Ed did. Follow his footsteps, track these people down. Try to do what he did until we find whatever he stumbled on."

"Great," Jane said sarcastically. "So repeat the workings of a genius. That'll be easy."

Matt shook his head. "Ed may have been able to think a hundred times faster than us, but he wasn't insane. We've just got to go step by step, work this out this logically."

"Right," agreed Jane. Then she hesitated. "But not right now, I've got to finish this report on concussions for Lum by tomorrow, and I've got dwnagintonit . . ." She trailed off in an incomprehensible mumble.

"You've got what?" asked Matt.

Jane coughed unnecessarily and suddenly grew very preoccupied with a spot on the ceiling. "Dawn, I've got a, ahem, lesson with Captain Dawn tonight," she mumbled quickly, her voice low and discreet. Matt rolled his eyes so hard it felt like they were going to fall out.

"Oh well, that's just *great*. Make sure to use protection!"

"It's not like that!" she hissed at him, low and furious.

"Right, sure," Matt spat. "Are you serious? A man is dead, the world could be in danger, and you're worrying about classes?"

"Don't be an idiot," Jane snapped back. She kept her voice low. "We don't know what's going on. We don't know what the kid or Cassandra mean. We don't know if we can trust them. Hell, we don't even know if they were being metaphorical! It could take months to figure this out, and I can't just drop everything, put my entire life on hold just because you have a hunch. I know you don't care about being here," she continued, cutting off his protests, "but I do. And you should at least be subtle. If this is real, if someone killed Ed because he got too nosy, what the hell do you think they'll do if it looks like you're searching for the same crap?"

Matt opened his mouth to argue—then reluctantly forced himself to swallow an angry retort. For once, Jane was actually right.

"Keep up appearances," he muttered, the words tasting unpleasant in his mouth.

"Exactly," said Jane, sounding a little relieved. Matt shook his head.

"Fine," he conceded. "But in the meantime, we've got to keep this quiet. Don't talk to anyone."

"I'm not stupid," she said, scowling.

"Not even Dawn. No, *especially* not Dawn."

"For the last time, he's not involved," snapped Jane.

"I'm not saying he is," Matt growled back. "But until we know what's going on, it's safer to keep this to ourselves. Deal?"

Jane glowered at him, but eventually she relented.

"Deal," she agreed. "Now go away, you're distracting me. I need to finish this essay."

"Right," Matt muttered under his breath as he got up and strode toward the library doors. "Don't want to be late for the captain."

"You're early."

Dawn's voice hummed through her as soon as Jane walked through the auditorium doors. She looked up to find its owner floating effortlessly in the middle of the room, sitting calm and composed ten feet off the ground, his cape rippling as though moved by some invisible wind. Jane tried to hide her grin.

"So are you, sir," she responded. He smiled at her and her heart leaped.

"Come, join me," he commanded, and so she did—flames licking at her heels, cold air nipping at her head, she flew over to where he sat and then likewise sat hovering opposite him—although with a lot more effort and a lot less grace. She felt so noisy, so clumsy, wobbling as she tried to hold still, struggling to stay balanced with fire rushing down and lightning crackling everywhere. Dawn could just sit, serenely, floating without a sound.

They sat, master and student, hovering for ten long minutes, until the sound of Jane's labored breathing must have penetrated Dawn's thoughts and the captain opened his eyes. "Enough," he instructed, seeing her sweat-drenched face, and the two of them floated gently to the floor. Jane struggled to keep her descent from turning into an open fall. The second her feet hit solid ground, she doubled over, sucking in breath.

"I apologize," said Dawn. "That was not intended to be a test." Though his green eyes twinkled as he said it, and Jane had the momentarily insane thought that he might be teasing her. "Though if it was, you passed admirably."

"Thank you, sir," she panted, wiping her face on her sleeve. She allowed herself three full breaths before straightening back up and standing at attention.

"Your week was pleasant, I trust?" he asked, mirroring her pose, hands clasped loosely behind his back. Jane hesitated.

"Well . . . yes, sir. Pleasant enough. Except for the, um"—her hands fidgeted slightly—"the death. And the funeral."

"Ah, yes," murmured Dawn, his mouth twisting in a grimace. "I heard. Such a senseless waste."

"Yes, sir."

"Did you know him? The deceased?"

"Yes, sir," repeated Jane. "We were acquainted."

"Ah," lamented Dawn. "Then all the sadder for his passing." He glanced up at the distant ceiling. "Still, the dead need not our mourning. They are beyond our reach. The future is clay, but the past is stone."

"Yes, sir," Jane said with a small tinge of sadness. She dropped her eyes. This must be how he coped, she realized, with everyone he had lost. Keep moving forward; don't ever look back.

There was a cold, quiet silence. Then Dawn spoke more firmly than before.

"Do you know what is ahead of you, Jane?" he asked, his voice strong and clear, like great bells tolling across the land. "What is ahead of all of us?"

"No, sir," she answered, feeling a jolt of excitement pulse through her at the purpose with which he spoke. "I don't."

"Maybe we should ask the clairvoyant," said Dawn, allowing himself a small smirk, but then the lightness turned to steel. "For ten years, I've been waiting, preparing for rebirth, for the next step. I want to forge a new Legion—the chosen few, the strongest of the strong. I think, I hope, I am almost ready. And when the Legion is reborn, Jane, I want you to be a part of it. Would you like that?"

"Yes, sir," Jane replied, suddenly breathless, suddenly trembling, the blood in her head rushing through her heart. "More than anything."

"Good," said the captain, surveying her eagerness, her shaking face and pleading eyes. "Then prove yourself. Become stronger. Show me the height of your power—not just in here but out there." He raised a gloved hand and pointed at the far wall, the door leading to the rest of Morningstar. "Against them. In the coming months, leave no doubt in mine or any mind that you are what I believe you capable of being." He paused. "Then—and only then—when the time comes, will you be worthy to stand among my Legion."

"Yes, sir," she murmured, and for a second all the visions from her old life, from those countless nights spent laying alone in the dark, came pouring back—her, standing victorious over everyone around her, donning the armor, the Legion's crest, triumphant and unstoppable, alongside her hero. Respected, feared, loved by all. Suddenly, they were so close, so real, she could almost touch them—all she had to do was—

"I'll do it," she whispered, and without even realizing it, she'd twisted her hand across her chest, a fevered salute. "Everything. Every day. I'll prove it. I won't let you down."

"I know you won't," Captain Dawn said simply. He stared down at her, his eyes twinkling like emeralds in the night. "I believe we have a great future together, Jane." And for an instant, a single moment of desperate elation, she saw a small smile dance across his powerful, chiseled face—a smile that maybe, just maybe, in her wildest, wildest dreams, meant more than he said.

"Now prepare yourself and let us begin."

* * *

The bedroom was dark, the blinds closed. The only light came from the lamp on the desk, a yellow circle that streamed out and cast warped shadows over the unmade bed and clothes on the floor. Matt Callaghan sat alone, bent over the wooden desk, silent and unmoving save for the occasional keystroke or mouse click.

Where would Ed have started?

Captain Dawn was almost sixty years old. He'd been married once, to his high-school sweetheart—but his wife had died. Everyone knew that. He'd spent decades assembling the original Legion of Heroes—but they were all dead as well. Everyone knew that too. What did that leave? *Well,* mused Matt, *power of a hundred suns or not, everyone came from somewhere—everybody had a family. Who better to invite to a party but relatives? Especially for an old person, they loved that kind of stuff.* That's where Ed would have started.

The miracle of the Internet was that there was such an amazing wealth of knowledge so well indexed and freely available, all within the touch of a few buttons. Unfortunately, in this case, the information Matt uncovered was not particularly useful—he only had to travel as far as Captain Dawn's Wikipedia page to realize that this train of thought didn't have much track laid out. Both of Captain Dawn's parents were deceased—which, given their age, Matt didn't find surprising—and of his two siblings, older brother, David, and younger sister, Amelia, one had died childless in the Year of Chaos, while the other had managed to have a child before dying of a stroke in 1991. That boy, Captain Dawn's nephew, Matt thought might be worth finding—but a few pages deeper into Wikipedia and he was greeted with the news that young Angus McDonald had apparently felt his mother's death particularly hard and taken his own life not long after his she'd lost hers.

So not the luckiest family, the Dawns, Matt was forced to conclude. If he'd been Ed (and there was a lot of ifs coming off that statement) and he'd been trying to organize a surprise party, Matt thought he now would have reached the small hurdle that Captain Dawn seemed to have no living partner, friends, or immediate family, somewhat stunting the guest list. Then again, he mused, Mr. and Mrs. Dawn Senior might have had siblings, and it was conceivable that, low on loved ones, Ed might have tried to track down some of Dawn's distant relatives. He pulled an unused notebook out of his desk and began scribbling the outlines of a family tree. Aunts, uncles, cousins, maybe even cousins' kids . . . beyond that, he'd be entering "first-second-third-once-twice-removed" territory, which he secretly hoped—already feeling the familiar lethargy of study settling over his brain—Ed had not been dedicated enough to get into. Still, he made a little note on the side of the page to check out the greater family forest, should he run out of ideas.

I need a plan of attack, Matt thought grimly to himself as he surveyed the rough sketched lines and realized the potential enormity of his investigation. Family members, old friends, enemies, dignitaries, acquaintances—any one of them might be involved, any number of them could be important. A single oversight might mean missing the entire answer, and Matt wasn't prepared to let that happen. He had to be methodical. He had to think like a genius, who had been thinking like a recluse. Great. Where the heck did he start?!

At the beginning, Matt decided. And so, the light of his desk lamp burning bright into the darkness, he bought a digital copy of Captain Dawn's most comprehensive biography and began to read into the night, pencil in hand, tapping the tip on his notepad.

Slowly, January shifted into February. The snows began to recede, which the wind made up for by howling with renewed bitterness—an excellent modifier said Mac and several of the other range instructors, to help those who still didn't understand that sometimes you had to lead your target. For no amount of wind, hail, or snow could halt or impede training at the Academy—those that complained about the conditions were politely informed that they were most welcome to take their leave, and the Legion would call upon them to serve only when the fighting was taking place somewhere weather didn't exist.

The new year seemed to have brought with it new vigor to Morningstar Academy—a renewed tension and excitement once the small hiccup of Ed's death had been passed over. This year would mark the fifth anniversary of the institution's reopening, and speculation was running high that this would finally be the year when the Legion of Heroes would be officially reformed. Thus, the Acolytes were in nothing short of a frenzy. Throughout the ranks, from juniors to seniors, every person of every power was pushing to be harder, better, stronger.

It was commonly accepted rumor that the new Legion would only be taking a limited number of members, so competition was fierce—to the point where Daniel Winters had to take to the podium one morning and forcefully remind all present that any Acolyte caught attempting to sabotage another in any way would be immediately and irrevocably removed from the program. Ironically, the effect of this explicit ban was a sharp increase in training-related injuries—to the point where the Infirmary healers were getting almost more practice than anyone else— as everyone's focus and frustration funneled into the permissible violent activities.

"It's like they've all gone mad," Matt commented to Wally—seemingly one of the few people immune to the mania—over breakfast one morning, as news trickled through that a supervised battle between Hannah McKillop and Mohammed Abdellmessiah had resulted in an earthquake devastating a nearby town. "Anyone who messes with this new Legion is going to get steam-rolled."

"I think that's the point," Wally replied quietly, sipping his orange juice and thumbing through a text from Will.

There was, however, one exception to the redoubled enthusiasm: Giselle. For weeks after Ed's funeral, the speedster had barely left her room, and when she did, it was obvious that something inside her had changed, and not for the better. Her spark was simply gone. The new Giselle spoke very little and looked perpetually like she'd been crying— never joking, never laughing, spending most of her time simply sitting, shoulders slumped, staring off into space. She'd lost all interest in her appearance—stopped doing her hair, wearing makeup—and wore the same, thin black cardigan every day while she sat in the hall at meal times, barely touching the food on her plate or talking to the people around her. Worst of all, she'd stopped running. Before New Year's Eve, there'd been talk of her attempting to break the human land-speed record. Now, she simply shuffled from place to place, staring at the floor, her soft, muffled footsteps making her seem almost invisible. More than a few Acolytes tried cheering her up—invitations, compliments, reassurances that what happened wasn't her fault, but none of it did any good. After a few weeks, everyone, even her hordes of once-admirers, just sort of gave up—and so Giselle Pixus sat in the same spot in the hall, day in and day out, her hair limp and her eyes puffy, gazing numbly at nothing.

There was talk among the Ashes of sending her home, Celeste quietly told Matt one lunchtime, for her health and well-being, on the face of it. But everyone, Giselle included, knew the real reason was more cruel than this—the Academy simply had no place for a speedster who didn't run.

When Matt mentioned this to Jane, Jane—maybe feeling a sense of commitment and comradery or seeking to repay Giselle in kind—went immediately after practice to the speedster's room to offer her strongest support and motivation, which essentially involved yelling extensively at Giselle through her door. Despite giving a prolonged and particularly curse-heavy rant about how Giselle was "better than this" and "needed to get back up and stop being (a bunch of expletives)," to no one's surprise but Jane's this somehow did not have the desired effect.

"Well, obviously that wouldn't have worked on anyone but you," Matt said bitterly the next morning, when Jane informed him of her failure. "And I'm telling you, she doesn't want to listen."

"I don't care what she wants," huffed Jane. "She's too good to waste away like this. She needs to snap the hell out of it."

"And yelling at her is going to help?" Matt responded. "All you'll do is make her angry."

"Better angry than miserable," declared Jane bluntly, slicing butter across her toast.

In a way, had it not been for his desire to find Ed's killer, Matt would have been in a similar state to Giselle. More than at any other point in his life, the so-called clairvoyant felt despondent and uncertain about his future and increasingly, profoundly alone. With Ed gone and Jane spending so much of her time training, Matt was by himself more and more, researching, for a large part, to the best of his ability. But once his eyes grew bleary and the words on his screen started to repeat themselves, he often found himself just sitting, staring at the ceiling, mulling over the general hopelessness of his life. He was in the wrong place at the wrong time, chasing ghosts doing things for reasons he didn't understand. He hated this obsession with the new Legion everyone had around him, and he hated how they were all fixated on becoming stronger, as if strength was the only thing that mattered—hated that this was what "heroism" had become.

"Why is there no morality training?" he asked Jane one evening, when they were sitting together in the library, him trawling endlessly through dates and last known addresses while she powered through *The Art of War*. "What's the point of being strong if you don't know what's the right thing to do?"

"Captain Dawn says being a hero is about being strong," Jane replied, glancing up from Sun Tzu, "strong enough to forge the right path when no one else has the guts to."

"That's not heroism," countered Matt. "That's domination."

The empath shrugged. "History remembers the two as the same thing, if the person's strong enough," she said, turning back to her book.

Matt shook his head bitterly. "It shouldn't matter what history thinks. It shouldn't matter if what you're doing gets remembered, or succeeds, or fails. Only that it's right."

"The only problem with that," said Jane, "is it's hard to do what's right if you don't have the power to achieve it."

"Failing at something doesn't change the truth," Matt said stubbornly. "Doing what's right, even when you know it's not going to work, even when you know it's not going to make a difference doesn't make you any less of a hero. I'd even say it makes you more."

Jane sighed, snapped her book shut and turned to look at him. "I know you're wrong," she told him. "But you're better at words than I am, so I can't explain why. Just take my word for it. Captain Dawn says there's no such thing as a weak hero."

"Well, that's gospel then," Matt muttered sarcastically under his breath, turning back to his endless list of names.

So far, assembling a list of people Ed might have wanted to invite to Captain Dawn's reunion was proving as fruitless as it was frustrating. Matt had managed, after some weeks of trawling through the Registry of Births, Deaths, and Marriages, to accurately account for all of the superhero's extended family—but unfortunately, this had turned out to be completely pointless.

"Because they're all dead," he swore to Jane the morning after he'd finished, eyes so red and dry and tired from staring at a computer that he wanted to pull them out with a blunt spoon and throw them in the sink. Yes, through a combination of the Year of Chaos, a family history of heart disease, and a run of bad luck stemming from what he could only assume was a potent and lingering gypsy curse, the man known as Captain Dawn did not have a single living relative. It would have been impressive, if it hadn't meant weeks' worth of effort culminating in absolutely nothing.

"Because they're probably not killing anyone if they're dead," he added bitterly, after he was done kneading his head into the table and swearing profusely.

"Zombies?" suggested Jane.

"Not helpful," suggested Matt.

In keeping with Jane's suggestion, Matt had been taking care while doing all this to keep up the appearance of normality, to avoid making anyone who might be watching him suspicious. He continued his daily sessions with Selwyn—also one of the few seemingly unaffected by the growing excitement—and continued with his biweekly assessments, which were admittedly easier now. His past successes seemed to have inoculated him against most of Cross's skepticism, so long as he kept up a steady stream of stuff that could one day come true. Even so, he began making predictions of great change and upheaval within the coming months. Matt the clairvoyant foretold a rush of new trials and challenges for the Academy, renewed interest and observance by the media, the coming of "a new dawn," the great cheering of a crowd and "a mighty eagle, spreading its wings wide." Unbeknownst to Cross, these prophecies were based less on second sight and more on what Jane had confided to him in strictest confidence (and with uncomfortable enthusiasm) about her conversations with Captain Dawn, mixed with good old-fashioned extrapolation, showmanship, and common sense.

To anyone watching, in addition to making breakthroughs with his future-seeing skills, Matt Callaghan also appeared to be spending his free time knuckling down and working diligently on the project his senior, James Conrad, had assigned him—namely, organizing a surprise party for the beloved Captain Dawn. He'd printed, embossed, and mailed out several dozen "Save the Date, but Be Discreet" cards to appropriate celebrities, politicians, and figureheads; had a long sit-down with Daniel Winters (who'd been very impressed with Matt's newfound "maturity") regarding seating and catering budgets; and now possessed several folders full of package deal advertising for party decorations. To an outside observer, Matt looked to be doing a thoroughly meticulous job—because he was. That was the point. Putting in a lot of effort researching people from Captain Dawn's past made sense for someone going to a lot of effort in every aspect of organizing a reunion. The best deceptions, Matt knew, were founded not on lies but on truth.

And, Matt admitted ruefully, also so if it turned out Captain Dawn actually had nothing to do with Ed's death after all, he wouldn't get in too much trouble. And the captain would get a nice birthday party. There was that too.

While Matt was working hard, Jane was working harder. Day in and day out, Jane Walker trained, ate, studied, and somehow even slept with a level of single-minded intensity that bordered on psychotic. From five in the morning until nine at night, she was an unwavering, unstoppable force, rampaging through exercises almost faster than the trainers could come up with them, seemingly untouchable by injury or exhaustion. She sprinted through obstacles wreathed in searing flame, unleashed storms of lightning powerful enough to level city blocks, and channeled a maelstrom of ice so cold it temporarily froze a portion of the Firedome. She burned without thinking, flew without slowing, and blasted separate bull's-eyes down range so fast and so reliably, with every one of her powers, that even Mac could find nothing to criticize. Nothing stopped her—not pain, not opposition, not a hundred feet of solid rock and five times normal gravity or weighted clothes and a Category 5 hurricane. Jane's powers hadn't just improved, they'd evolved, and everyone knew it. She was no longer targeted in free-for-alls or picked last for teams—not from any newfound love or tolerance, but because there wasn't a single Acolyte who would voluntarily go up against this one-woman wrecking ball of thermo-electric destruction. If the effortless strength of Jane's powers made them nervous, then her flawless free-flowing between them made them terrified. Fear might not have won friends, but it sure as hell brought respect.

But for Jane, it wasn't enough.

The sky was cloudless on the morning of the Challenge—the first clear day in weeks. If Jane had been the superstitious type, she might have taken that as a sign, but omens were for idiots. She walked to the arena alone, as always—her boots crunching the resilient grass and wavering snow, the dull warmth of winter sun spreading heat through her tattoo. She wasn't the only one going that way. Most of Morningstar now headed through rough-cut paths toward the looming stadium, streaming in dribs and drabs—even the noncombatants, who were presumably going along just to enjoy the show. It was easy, thought Jane, her eyes flicking, to tell who was fighting and who wasn't—the second group chatted merrily among each other, not a care in the world, whereas the first walked either with false bravado or silent looks of mild sickness. Jane felt neither, only clarity. There was a clear, bright line before her, and she would chase it down.

A Challenge was as simple as it was informal—combatants came unarmed and unarmored, they fought, and they learned where they stood. It was more about rank and reputation than training. No prizes, just proving yourself against your peers. And to those watching, Jane knew. One watcher in particular.

The stream of people split into two as they entered the shadow of the arena—Jane marched forward with the fighters, while the onlookers headed up into the stands. The sound of the crowd—murmurs, the chatter of conversation, punctuated by the odd cheer or peal of laughter—hummed and buzzed around her as she took her place along the wall. Jane had never been to a sports match, but she'd have guessed this is what it would've felt like. Up in the crowded stands, a few people had brought signs displaying encouragement, and Jane could swear she smelled popcorn. At present, the white stone square in the center of the stadium was empty. It wouldn't stay that way for long.

There was no formal announcement, no bell, no whistle, no national anthem. Nothing except for the generally accepted rules, and two Ashes and some healers ready to intervene should things get out of hand. You just went up to whoever you wanted to fight, they accepted or refused, then you beat each other out of the ring or into surrender. Simple.

A lean white boy from Michigan about six spots to the left from Jane was, surprisingly, the first. He waltzed down the line of combatants standing with their backs to the arena's inner wall and, grinning from ear to ear, high-fived a purple-hooded Inuit kid of almost identical age, who shook his head and laughed. Each of them started off to their respective sides of the platform, yelling a constant, tongue-in-cheek stream of trash talk about each other's parents, siblings, and sexualities, which carried on long after they'd both taken their places.

"*The showboating*," a voice muttered dryly in Jane's head. She glanced up to see the distant speck of Wally's freckled face grinning down at her from the stands. The psychic made a small, flappy wave. "*Just get on with it already.*" Jane tried not to smirk.

Finally, the supervising Ashes—a thin, beaky-eyed, graying man named Mon Mora—shouted "THREE . . . TWO . . . ONE!" and then the air exploded. A blast of blinding green energy erupted from the Inuit's eyes, rushing the length of the battlefield and slamming into a golden, bubble-shaped force field held out by the other boy's hands. Michigan gritted his teeth, digging his feet into the ground, pushing back against the unrelenting stream, then suddenly he rolled, leaping to the side, the laser careening past him, straight toward the watching crowd, who only laughed as it struck harmlessly against an electromagnetic field raised specifically for the occasion. Eye beams readjusted his aim, but force fields was throwing up barriers left, right, and center, darting from one to the other faster than his opponent could destroy them. The purple-hooded kid gritted his teeth and bulged his eyes, sending a pulsating wave of green hurtling straight through the center of the stadium, breaking through the other boy's force field and hitting Michigan square in the chest. Barrier boy tumbled backward, somehow still on his feet, standing but panting, his shirt rags, his torso splattered with blackened burns, and lasers saw his chance—but he didn't see the glint in his opponent's eyes. A huge blast of energy crackled across the arena, screaming toward the Michigan boy, but the instant before it hit there was a high, deafening *ping*, like the chiming of some colossal bell, as the laser slammed into a clear blue barrier. Before the purple-hooded kid could blink, it ricocheted up, across, refracted into another glass-like field then down again, straight back at its creator, perfectly angled, hitting him straight in the eyes. Lasers screamed, but in the time it took him to stumble, his opponent had crossed the field, hands outstretched—there was a deep, reverberating *boom*, and the Inuit boy was thrown backward by the sudden eruption of a gigantic domed force field in his chest. He hit the arena wall with a stone-crunching crash and slid heavily to the ground.

The crowd cheered. Jane clapped. The kid from Michigan whooped and punched his hand into the air, then quickly hopped off the stage to check how the healers were doing with his friend. *That's nice*, thought Wally.

Next up was a tall Colombian who everyone apparently called Chino with green eyes and green hair to Jane's right. He strode over to a Chinese girl, who Jane knew as Nancy, with a large nose and her hair in a bun, and prodded her square in the chest—the crowd oohed, and the girl's eyes narrowed. Without saying a single word, they took their places.

"Apparently, they used to date," Wally whispered in her mind, of course knowing the gossip. *"He thinks she cheated on him, so he burned a whole bunch of her books."* This time, Jane actually laughed out loud, which made the Acolyte to her left shoot her a funny look.

This next fight was much longer and a lot more vicious. Whatever love these two had once shared, not a single drop remained—both were furious and most definitely trying to kill each other. Nancy could size-shift—growing huge or small almost instantly to dodge or crush with car-sized fists, but her former lover was a floramancer and had brought a pocketful of seeds that sprouted the most messed-up, spike-ridden, pulsating, carnivorous plants Jane had seen in her entire life. Halfway through the screaming, swearing grudge match, it became apparent that the vines were also secreting some type of poison, which was making the girl turn green and stagger as she tore their endless growing, curling tendrils free from her giant arms. Jane thought that might be enough to win the Colombian guy the match, but the stupid idiot decided to get close enough to gloat, and an errant kick from his enraged ex-girlfriend crushed every bone below his waist. So, he lost, but about three seconds later, Nancy threw up and passed out before the healers managed to run onstage. Jane had never seen a thirty-foot titan hurl chunks before and was now positive she could go the rest of her life without seeing it again.

Enough of this, Jane muttered to herself, and before anyone else could move she broke ranks, took three steps out, and turned to face the one person she knew she had to fight. The cheers of the arena fell silent. And the empath nodded at James Conrad.

A shadow crossed the strongman's face. For a brief, insane second, Jane thought he was actually going to refuse—but the world was watching. The moment passed, and James Conrad nodded back. There was no reaction from the crowd this time—no cheering, no boos. Nothing but silence. Dead, frozen silence. Jane turned on her heel without another word and walked toward her position.

The last time she'd stood in this arena, she'd felt confident, headstrong even. Now she just felt calm. She knew what he could do. She knew what she could do. And it was simply a matter of getting it done.

She climbed the seven steps to the top of the cold, open square, and stared straight down the center at the dark, hulking figure of her opponent.

One breath. Two breaths. Three.

A breeze rustled through the space between them. No one made a sound.

"May the best man win," James Conrad called.

"It won't be a man," she replied.

Then she attacked.

Boom! The clap came right where she'd expected it, the shock wave hurtling straight at her, meaning to smash apart her insides—but Jane was no longer flesh. She was fire, fire incarnate, and the air rent by Conrad's hands slammed into the inferno that leaped without thinking from her pores. For a split second, the force tore her fire away, but in that instant Jane was already moving through where it had been. She saw his face flicker, saw the momentary confusion, the disbelief, and right then she knew—he hadn't expected her to go through, he'd expected her to dodge, and when she came out of her dive, he'd have hit her with another shock wave. But he was no longer dictating this fight.

She charged, straight forward, teeth bared, and before he could react, she was halfway across the arena, fire burning around her, lightning crackling from her palms. Jane leaped, slamming her hands together, feeling the air crack between them, exploding in a deafening, focused thunderclap that sliced forward like a wave, straight down into her enemy. Conrad reeled, stumbling back a single step, clutching at his ears; he snarled, spinning, raising a fist to pummel into the ground—

But Jane was already there.

She exploded across, a demon of fire and thunder, slamming into Conrad, pummeling his chest and stomach with sparking, searing fists. James roared and swung wildly, but Jane ducked easily underneath, not giving an inch, crashing her heel down into his foot with a freezing crunch, driving her fists again, again, and again into his ribs, melting, scorching his flesh, feeling his electrified insides spasm and jolt. She was everywhere, in his face, unrelenting, because she'd thought, because she knew—a strongman is most dangerous up close, so up close is where no one ever fights them. But the untrained muscle grows weak, and a single weakness breaks a wall.

She flowed under another one of his fists, rolled around him and into him, pummeling her fists into his side. Reeling, roaring, Conrad swung his huge arms downward, and Jane knew what he was going to do before he did it—unable to properly move, locked into place by the foot she'd frozen to the ground, he raised his free, man-sized leg and slammed it down, pulverizing the stone, sending a bone-shattering shock wave through the ground—

But Jane was no longer on the ground. She was in the air, flying, soaring. She turned, spun, all of Conrad's incredible force smashing downward when she was nowhere but up, behind him, looking down, his head, back and entire body open, completely exposed—

And then she fired. Fired, erupted, exploded, everything she had, a searing, blistering, volcanic cyclone of fire and lightning, focused down between her hands, crashing into him, smothering him, burning, melting, incinerating everything it touched. She twisted, letting the force of it push her back, through the air and across, onto the other side of the field—where she landed, skidding, facing back toward her foe.

Her fists closed. The fire ceased. The titan fell.

And she'd won.

James Conrad still moved. Every part of him blackened, more flesh melted than not, barely conscious—but still alive. She'd made sure of that. He'd showed the same courtesy when they'd first crossed paths, and she wasn't about to be a murderer. As every healer rushed onto the shattered stage, pressing their hands down into Conrad's burns and then yelping, recoiling from the residual, staggering heat, she heard the big man moan—a low, hoarse, gurgling noise, that bubbled out into the frozen silence.

"Congratulations," Mon Mora announced cordially—but Jane wasn't done. She held out her arms.

"Who's next?" she called—to the world, the challengers, the waiting crowd. Jane watched, waited, listening into the silence. No answer came. "Anyone?" she repeated.

Now a murmuring ran through the crowd. The Ashes looked at one another, then up at Jane, standing, defiant, hands on her hips, in the center of the ring. On ground level, the combatants exchanged glances, whispering. Jane carefully watched their heads turn—wondering if any would step up. This part, she knew, was a risk. Suddenly, there was a hand.

"I'll go." A muscular, buzz-cut Egyptian man.

"Me too." A teenager—could've been boy or girl. Long, tattered coat and more piercings than a pin cushion.

A third hand, no callout—a girl. She knew that one. Odette—hyper-voice.

"Challenge accepted," proclaimed Mon Mora. He held up a hand to the new combatants. "Who is going to—"

"All of them," called Jane, cutting him off. "All at once."

Another, larger murmur ran through the arena—but this time, the crowd's noise didn't fade, but gradually grew, built, slowly starting to change. Someone laughed—a few people whooped. Two Acolytes down one end whistled, and a whole section started to clap. Cheers bloomed like sparks in a fire and before long the whole stadium was ablaze. Mon Mora's flinty eyes twitched toward his fellow Ashes, who shrugged, and then to the roaring approval of the crowd he beckoned all three challengers forward. With telekinetic assistance, the healers moved James Conrad's shuddering body off the stage, the worst of the burns already healing. A terramancer groundskeeper placed his palms upon the white central platform and the stone squares re-formed. The three fighters scaled the repairing stairs and took their places, spreading out in a line—Egyptian on the left, Odette on the right, and pinhead in the middle. The crowd cheered louder, and Jane allowed herself a small smile—imagining, just for a second, that it was all for her. Maybe some of it even was. A girl could dream.

"READY?"

The three Acolytes faced off against the empath, stock-still while the world screamed.

"THREE!"

She knew one of them. The hyper-voice. She could plan for that. The other two, well, she'd have to think on her feet. Adapt and survive.

"TWO!"

They knew her powers. Even without the previous fight, she was infamous, it was common knowledge. That meant they thought their abilities were good counters. And they'd seen her tricks.

"ONE!"

Well—Jane smirked, squaring her stance—some of her tricks.

"FIGHT!"

In the space of a heartbeat, Jane dropped to a crouch, her right arm raised, a four-foot lance of ice forming in her crackling hand. Before her opponents could take so much as a single step, she launched, up off her knees, hurtling the spear right and wide—as an instant later a wall of noise, a wave of sonic death blasted from Odette. Jane stumbled, clutching her ears, but an instant later, the screaming wavered as Odette flinched, paling as the ice whistled an inch from her cheek, recoiling just in time, her eyes turning, following the spike as it flew, barely missed—

Except Jane hadn't missed. And that wasn't just ice.

With a deafening crack, the lance exploded an inch from Odette's head, the lightning trapped inside blasting out, exploding in a thousand shards of frozen glass. Odette screamed, so loud the very earth seemed to tremble, and fell to the ground, her voice pitching and rending wildly around Jane, the crowd, her own team, bloody hands clutching her shredded face.

One down.

Jane staggered to her feet, her head swimming, ringing in her ears. She could see her two remaining opponents likewise stumbling, reeling from the unexpected aural assault—their heads turning to glance at Odette's fallen, wailing form, struggling to process the loss of a teammate barely a second into the fight. But an instant later, they recovered from the shock. Before she could react, the punk's coat rustled, and Jane barely had time to throw up a wall of flames as something hissed through the air toward her. For a second, she thought she was safe— but then a searing, burning pain shot through her shoulder and she buckled, crying out in agony. Jane glanced down to see a puddle of boiling, bubbling metal splashed right below her collarbone—super-heated, melted by her own protective fire, sizzling the flesh beneath. She swore, freezing her searing shoulder with her left hand and hurling bursts of lightning with her right, blasting the metal shards out of the air as they hurtled out of the punk's coat toward her—but instead of dropping to the ground, the blades turned and shot back toward her, around and behind, spinning, slicing toward her neck. Jane gritted her teeth and pushed out a field of electricity, encasing herself in lightning an instant before the shards flew at her from every direction, slamming into her barrier. *Magnetic or telekinetic,* she hissed silently, *they were either magnetic or telekinetic.* But a second later, she felt an invisible hand clench around her neck, oblivious to her barrier, and Jane knew the answer. She spluttered, choking, as unseen force lifted her up into the air, her toes dangling an inch from the ground, squeezing the life from her throat. With her remaining good arm, Jane punched a bolt of lightning out through the barrier and toward the telekinetic punk, and the pressure around her neck momentarily relaxed as the kid rolled out of the way—but something else was wrong. As she gulped in air, the electricity around her flickered and wavered, sweat beading on her face as the effort of maintaining the barrier doubled, tripled— her powers suddenly sagging, lethargic, heavy and clumsy. The shards slammed back into the lightning dome, and Jane fell to one knee, the weight closing in around her—and then through a flickering, instant's gap in the barrier, she saw. Standing discreet, unmoving, staring at her, his face hard—the Egyptian man. His eyes focused, his hand stretched out. The electric field around her sagged.

Neutralizer. He was a neutralizer.

She needed to end this, now.

With a mangled shout, Jane pushed to her feet, dropping her barrier and hurling fists of lightning at her opponents. The telekinetic punk dived left, their shards flying back, fanning out into a protective wall in front of the two of them as the Egyptian man crouched, shielding his face with his hands. Jane's attacks grew wilder, desperate now, lightning bolts flying unrestrained from her fingers, branches crackling harmlessly in every direction, into the stone, the barrier, the arena's force field. Suddenly, her arms sagged, and Jane doubled over, gasping desperately for breath as the sparks in her hands crackled and misfired, blackening her fingertips. And behind the telekinetic punk's makeshift wall, she saw the pair exchange glances, then grins. The neutralizing had taken its toll, it seemed—it was all she could do to miss.

Except her powers hadn't actually malfunctioned. And she hadn't missed.

Jane didn't know the science of electromagnetism. She'd never learned the math, couldn't explain how it worked. All she knew was that positive charge repelled positive charge—and by watching her differently charged bolts strike the electromagnetic force field all around them, she'd determined that the field was very, very positively charged.

The punk's wall began to open, and Jane's grimace became a snarl.

In an instant, her hands erupted, a blast of blinding lightning bursting bright as she could make it from her left palm as an enormous crackling bolt exploded from her right. The entire arena flinched, her enemies included—and in that split second, as the telekinetic recoiled and covered his eyes, Jane's second lightning bolt, the last of her power, flew into the protective electromagnetic barrier and ricocheted back off.

Right into the punk's back.

"URK!" The telekinetic's body launched forward, thrown smoking through their own wall of metal shards, which clattered harmlessly to the ground a moment later as their owner's burning, twitching body crashed down upon the stone. The crowd winced—and the telekinetic punk gurgled, fingers tremoring uncontrollably as blue sparks arced between their piercings. They shuddered, eyes rolling back into their head as a healer rushed onto the stage. Jane breathed heavily, her fingers aching, her shoulder screaming, feeling air struggling back into her throat—and slowly, she stood up.

Two down.

The arena roared.

Jane's eyes found the neutralizer—the tall, quiet Egyptian man in dark track pants and an unassuming white shirt that could not disguise his muscle. He stared back, his mouth a hard line. If seeing Jane take down the other two scared him, it didn't show. Instead, he appeared resigned, resolute, as if he'd always known it would come down to this. He strode slowly toward the center of the square, stopping and standing silently only a few feet away from the empath. A hush fell over the crowd.

Jane didn't need to feel the fizzling sparks in her left hand or the spluttering, dying flames in her right to know that her powers were officially stifled. The Egyptian man's eyes still stared into her, through her, unwavering, unblinking, like they had the entire time. Neutralizing was like extinguishing a fire—at first the fire fought but inevitably it died, succumbed to the relentless, smothering oppression. This neutralizer had had time to channel his ability onto Jane, and now the window where she could use her powers was closed. She was completely suppressed.

Neutralizers weren't like other people. They didn't fight using their powers—they used their powers and then they fought. Level the playing field and then have backup step in or take them down yourself the old-fashioned way. The way this guy strode into the center of the ring, confident and self-assured with both his teammates taking dirt naps, made Jane guess it was the latter. One look at the way he stood, and you could tell he was a fighter. Not just any fighter. He was an Acolyte. The best of the best.

"What's your name?" she asked him.

"Omari," he replied.

She nodded. "Jane."

He nodded back. "Well met."

And without another word, they charged.

Omari was half a foot taller than Jane, with greater reach and at least twenty pounds more muscle. She was tired and powerless, with one arm visibly injured. He'd probably trained in martial arts for years with a host of seasoned tutors. She'd taught herself to punch by watching reruns of *The Karate Kid*. He had no weaknesses she could see, and she had no advantages she knew.

Except that she was Jane Walker, and she'd been fighting for her life since she was eleven. And she had no intention of fighting fair.

The instant before they connected, Jane screamed—a piercing, blood-curdling wail that made Omari instinctively flinch just long enough for her to land the first hit, a staggering, crushing hook. The neutralizer stumbled back, recovering quickly, lashing out with a series of blows that Jane blocked, feeling the force of his fists raising bruises on her arms. She lashed out again, punching hard at his head, but this time Omari was ready, and swatted her away, her blows striking only air. He returned fire, punching once, twice, three times as Jane ducked and wove. And then before she could gather her thoughts, he kicked, a savage knee to her rib cage, and it was all Jane could do to spin out of the way a fraction of a second before it connected, panting hard. He was fast—so fast Jane could barely keep up, let alone properly attack. Her mutilated shoulder screamed in agony every time she forced it to move—but with the pain came sudden inspiration. She winced and whimpered, staggering backward, clutching at her arm, held limply by her side—she saw Omari's eyes flash, saw him see the perceived weakness, and within a fraction of a second he charged, swinging his left leg up in a high kick toward Jane's injured right side. The empath's eyes narrowed, and she swung her damaged arm up, crying out as it blocked the kick, feeling something break—but at the same time ripping her own knee up, slamming it with every ounce of force she had straight between Omari's legs. The neutralizer howled and fell to the ground, clutching his groin, and that was all Jane needed. She leaped on top of him, landing a crushing knee into the Egyptian's guts, punching, pummeling him in the side of the head with her left hand, her right hanging limp, genuinely broken and useless now. Again, again, and again, she struck, and when Omari tried to lift his hands to protect his face, she kneed again between his legs. He screamed, lashing out blindly, but Jane leaned back, dodging the blow and then threw herself forward twice as hard, slamming her forehead into his nose, shattering it in a fountain of blood. The neutralizer gave a primal, gurgling roar as she struck, again and again, and somehow, somehow, managed to grab her working hand with one of his, but Jane snarled and bit hard into his wrist, ripping and savaging the flesh with her teeth until the shrieking man let go. She kneed him in the guts, clawed at his eyes, pummeled his throat, until finally, Omari's hand tapped the stone beside her and a small, whimpering word crawled its way from his bloodied mouth.

"Yield."

Jane's fist froze mid-blow. Below her, the neutralizer gazed up at her through broken, swollen eyes.

"Yield," he whispered again, the sound gargling in his throat. "Yield." Slowly, Jane lowered her fist—and then she pushed, panting, every joint agony, up off him, back onto her feet. She stepped backward, stumbling, her right arm hanging useless by her side. The sound of bone striking flesh, of ringing in her head and blood rushing through her ears, slowly gave way to the real world. The arena was silent. Dead silent. As she staggered backward, as she deliriously steadied herself, as her legs threatened to give out, as healers rushed the stage toward Omari, as she glanced upward, as she shielded her eyes from the world, which seemed suddenly so deafeningly silent, so blindingly bright, as the whole Academy looked on with bated breath—no one made a single noise.

For a moment, the world was frozen.

And then somebody clapped.

Somebody, then two somebodies, then three, then more. Slowly, like the breaking of rain, applause spread throughout the stands, until it was everywhere, everyone, the entire Academy applauding her, for her, as if in a dream. It was not loving—no cheering, no hysteria, no joy—but it was still there, still solid, still real. Some maybe begrudging, some insincere, but more rising to their feet, applauding, paying genuinely that respect that had been earned. Bruised and beaten, bloodied and exhausted, her body a mess and one arm hanging broken at her side, Jane Walker suddenly felt huge, felt whole, every fiber in her body trembling in time with the rushing, thunderous applause. She saw Wally putting his fingers to his lips, his lone whistle drowned out among the noise of the crowd. She saw Winters, nodding appreciatively and clapping harder than anyone. She even saw James Conrad, propped up against a wall as healers shimmered his wounds, slapping his huge hands together and nodding at her, his gaze steady, without a trace of resentment—as if to recognize, as if to simply say "well done."

And then, as the strangest feeling washed over her, Jane glanced up into the open sky—in time to watch as a shining teardrop fell from the sun. Without warning, without fanfare, unseen by the crowd, the tiny, glinting star broke from the heavens, falling down to Earth. To her. She watched it fall and then somehow, she knew not how—through her blurred vision, her haze of pain—as if by instinct, as if she'd always known, Jane held out the hand of her one good arm and felt something heavy, something no bigger than a silver dollar, drop quietly, perfectly into her palm.

It was a badge.

A silver eagle, clutching an olive wreath.

The symbol of the Legion of Heroes.

Jane looked up into the heavens, where a distant, white-and-gold figure fluttered high above, shining, flanked by the sun—unnoticed, unannounced, his smile gleaming in the morning light.

And in that moment—that single, glorious moment—Jane thought, she could have died.

As she limped from the stage, healers rushing to her side, the world roaring around her, the silver eagle clasped tightly, secretly in her palm, Jane knew that if she died, right now, it would be okay. It would be worth it—it would all be worth it—for this single, shining moment. Because she'd done it. She'd made it.

And she was complete.

In her pain, in her elation, in her moment of triumph, only one tiny thing nagged at the back of Jane's head, an errant thought, a face she hadn't seen. She glanced over her shoulder as a healer hurried beside her, holding her arm, guiding and supporting as she moved off the stage, the sound of applause still ringing in her ears—but she couldn't see him. Her eyes scanned high and low, across the resonant crowd, and though she wasn't supposed to care, though she supposed it didn't matter, tired and injured as she was, she still couldn't help but let it bother her, couldn't help but feel a small tinge of disappointment in her otherwise euphoric state, a tiny black stain on a shining, golden sea . . . Where was Matt?

"Thanks, Will," Matt said.

They'd arrived in the usual rush of sound and sulfur on a dull green lawn, a gray and overcast sky having replaced the open blue, making it feel as if there'd been an unnatural drop in daylight. Matt shivered, the sudden onset of wind picking at his skin through his coat sleeves, and glanced to his left at the segmented stairs leading up to the old sandstone building they'd teleported in front of. The steel handrail through the middle of the stairs was new. The brown walls, stained with creepers, were not.

"This the place?" asked Will, raising an eyebrow. He glanced around at the prickly lawns and dull, single-story houses spread along the streets, seeming skeptical. Matt waved his concerns away without looking, reading the words stenciled into stone above the building's door.

Coal Point Civic Center.

"This is it," he assured him.

The teleporter's brow furrowed. "And . . . what exactly are you looking for again?"

"I told you," Matt muttered. "Just info. Besides"—he paused and gazed up at the building—"I've got a feeling about this place."

"Oh," said Will, his eyes widening, "you mean like you've had a vision?"

"Yeah," replied Matt. Close enough.

He'd said it more for dramatic effect than anything, but the strange thing was, as Matt glanced at their surroundings, there *was* something funny about this town—something he couldn't quite put his finger on. The streets were quiet save for the wind's rustling, despite it being nearly midday, the sidewalks empty, the roads devoid of cars. Everywhere he turned, Matt saw signs of disuse and desertion, brown grass, rusted chain-link fences, paint peeling from houses. The odd signs of life—the flashing of a TV screen reflected in a window, a clean American flag fluttering on a flagpole in a yard—said the town was still inhabited, but overall, it felt like a ghost town whose townsfolk hadn't realized they were supposed to leave. A nowhere place, not forgotten because it had never been worth remembering in the first place.

Matt turned over his shoulder, glancing at the teleporter. "You don't need to hang around," he assured him.

Will shrugged. "You sure?"

"Yeah, I don't know how long this will take. I could be a while."

"All right well, you've got my number. Holler when you're done."

"Awesome. Thanks again."

"Don't mention it."

They slapped hands, and Will vanished in a puff of sulfurous smoke.

For a few moments, Matt stood watching the fumes twist in the wind. Once they'd disappeared into nothingness, he turned back toward the civic center, hands in his pockets, and trudged silently up the stairs.

A small bell tinkled somewhere as Matt pushed open the heavy wooden doors. The building opened into a small foyer leading to a pair of glass dividers, beyond which Matt could see many rows of brown, book-laden shelves. Matt moved through into the next room, and a pair of old eyes behind large-framed spectacles glanced up at him from behind a counter.

"May I help you, dear?" asked the woman—a kind-looking, flabby lady in her early sixties with a dull pink cardigan, a number of large rings on either hand, and a small jeweled ladybug pinned proudly above her right breast. She was sitting behind an ancient yellowed computer, which looked to Matt's eyes like it still ran on punch cards, with a *Famous* magazine sprawled open to this week's horoscopes across her keyboard.

"Yes, please," replied Matt, with the same nice-young-man smile he used for his grandparents. "Matt Callaghan, clairvoyant. I wonder if you could help me. I'm looking for the library. Or the town archives."

"One and the same here, dearie," Gladys (her name was printed in large, faded font on a name tag pinned opposite the beetle) answered with a kind smile. "Gladys Hardy, elasticizer. Had to move them all after the mildew got into the records room a few years back." She gestured a soft, wrinkled finger at the rows of shelves. "Do you need to find anything in particular?"

"Well, yes, actually," Matt crooned, twisting his hands bashfully behind his back. "If it's not too much bother. I'm from"—he shot a quick glance around the deserted room, then leaned in, shielding his mouth with his hand—"the Legion of Heroes," he whispered, and Matt was pleased to see some excitement light up the old lady's eyes. "On behalf of Captain Dawn."

"Ooh, well," she said, flustered, shuffling in her seat.

"And," continued Matt, leaning in and dropping his voice even further, as if this was a great secret only the two of them could know, "I'm actually organizing a surprise party for his birthday."

"Oh my," fawned Gladys, her cheeks flushing beneath a layer of powder. "How exciting."

"Yeah," said Matt, straightening back up. "He's going to be sixty, you know."

"Oh!" she gasped, putting a pudgy hand to her lips. "That old?"

"Yeah," Matt answered again, still smiling patiently. "I've been looking into his history, for speeches, maybe a slideshow. And so, I thought what better place to start than at the beginning?"

"Oh-ho-ho," Gladys chortled, wagging a ringed finger. "You have been doing your homework." She gazed up at Matt with a sly grin, which Matt returned.

"He grew up here, didn't he?" he asked, already knowing the answer.

"That he did, dear, that he did," confirmed the librarian. "Our most famous resident, and that's counting Mrs. Gordon, whose Pekingese placed best in show three years running at state," she added, looking over her glasses and sounding completely serious.

Matt heroically managed to overcome his monumental curiosity regarding Mrs. Gordon's show dog. "And he went to school here too?"

"Yes, indeed, Coal Point Public School, just down the road, all the way through." She paused, resting a finger on her chin. "I'm surprised we don't get more visitors really. But I suppose this was all back before he was famous."

Matt struggled to keep his excitement from showing. "I don't suppose there's any chance you'd have any old school records?" he asked—but to his dismay, Gladys's old, wrinkled face, formerly uplifted, was touched by a shadow of sadness.

"I wish I did, my dear, I wish I did. But the records were kept in the old school building, and it burned down a few years ago." She shook her head sadly, the chain on her glasses lightly tinkling. "All the trophies, all the photographs. So many years, so many memories, burned to ash." Matt's shoulders slumped, the familiar hollow feeling of disappointment spreading out over what moments ago had been optimism.

"What happened?" he asked glumly. Although at this point, what did it even matter?

Gladys sighed. "Some local kids, we think, though they never caught anyone. You know how those old asbestos buildings are dear—by the time anybody realized what was happening, there wasn't much that could be done." She sniffed. "Such a shame."

"Yeah," Matt agreed, a glum lump in his throat. He rubbed a hand over his eyes. "So, there was nothing left?"

"No," the librarian commiserated sadly. "Everything burned up."

"And you wouldn't happen to know the names of any of Captain Dawn's old classmates, would you? Anybody he knew back in the day?" Matt asked, abandoning all pretense, already knowing the answer. Gladys shook her head again.

"I'm not sure who was with him. I moved here after he left, I'm afraid," she told him. "By then, he was all grown up. Up and off to save the world, never looked back. Bless him," she added kindly. "Him and that lovely wife of his. Both so busy, they never even got a chance to stop by. Well, that's the price you pay for being a superhero. You have to leave your old home behind."

"Yeah," Matt said with a sigh, neither agreeing nor caring. Another dead end. He turned to leave. "Well, thanks anyway for your time."

"Hold on a moment, dear," Gladys called before he could reach the door. Matt glanced back over his shoulder and saw the old woman's face suddenly light up. His heart jumped to his throat.

"Yes?" he asked, his hand midway to the exit, not daring to hope.

"Well," offered the librarian, her old face creased in thought, "there's nothing left from the school, but if you're after names . . . I think . . . give me a moment . . ." She reached out her right arm, which began lengthening, snaking like Play-Doh out across the room and through the dusty shelves. Matt watched with bated breath as her elastic limb disappeared between the rows—waiting for what felt like an eternity until it finally returned, un-stretching back along the same path with a worn crimson book clasped in her hand.

"Here you go, love. This should be it I think." She held the cover out away from her eyes, peering through her glasses, her arm returned to its normal length. "Ah yes, that's the one. This is an old yearbook—1959, if I'm not mistaken." Gladys smiled up at him and held out the red leather-bound volume. "His year, I think."

Matt almost whooped. His hands closed around the yearbook, and it took all the restraint he had not to yank it from the old lady's grasp. His fingers thumbed, shaking, through the pages. "I thought you said the school burned down?"

"Oh, that's not from the school, dear. That was old Janice Carlton's—she was assistant principal at one time or another. They found it in her house after the stroke—apparently, she'd held on to it, after all these years." Gladys sighed, looking wistfully across at the shelves. "It must have had a lot of fond memories."

Matt barely heard her. He was flicking through the pages, photograph after photograph, sepia images of sports teams, line dances, community balls . . . until finally he found it. There. A group of twenty or so young men and women, all suits, skirts, and smiles, seated and standing around their principal—not much older than he was now, it struck him, though the photo seemed worlds away. But it didn't matter, because even after all this time, even after more than forty years, there was still one face Matt recognized, broad and beaming, standing tall among them. Even if he hadn't been studying him so fervently, even if he'd never seen him in person, there was no mistaking—

The young Captain Dawn.

Matt's heart skipped a beat.

"Thank you," he murmured. He forced himself to tear his eyes away from the picture and back to Gladys, not believing his luck. "Thank you so much."

The old woman's face shone. "You're most welcome, young man. I really hope it helps."

"Me too," Matt whispered. His eyes dropped back to the picture, and Matt had to fight the urge to take the yearbook and run. "Do you know where I can find any of these people?" he asked eagerly.

"Oh well, I should think so," she replied happily. "We're only a small town here. Let me take a look." Matt placed the open yearbook down in front of her.

"Which one did you want, dearie?"

"How about him?" Matt asked eagerly, pointing at the man to Captain Dawn's left.

"Dennis Hooper," said Gladys, peering at the grinning freckly man through her spectacles. "Lovely man. A miner born and bred, Dennis— poor soul. Black lung got him almost a decade ago."

"The girl next to him?" Matt pressed, mentally crossing Dennis off the list.

"Oh, Emilia Sparrow," replied the librarian. "My gosh, she was beautiful. But she died long ago, dear, caught up in all that unpleasantness when we were adjusting to the new world."

"The Year of Chaos," Matt acknowledged, slightly impatient. He pointed to the next along, a fit, ruggedly handsome man with light scruffy hair.

Gladys let out a sudden laugh. "Why, that's Willy Harkness! Dear heaven, didn't recognize him that thin. Oh no, dear, he passed away a few years back, heart attack. Butter in the veins and a vacuum for a mouth that one."

"Those two," she continued without any prompting, "the Nikatos brothers. The Year of Chaos took them too, I'm afraid. Dear me." She paused, looking at Matt with a kind smile. "We're not doing well at finding party guests, are we?"

"No . . ." murmured Matt. His eyebrows furrowed slightly.

"Her?" he asked, pointing to the far corner of the group, away from the captain.

"Tracey Holt. Lived three doors down from me actually. A terrible shame what happened, aneurysm at her age."

"Him?"

"Jacob Davies. Crushed underneath his tractor, silly fool, only a few years ago." Gladys shook her head. "Farming is a young man's game."

"Her?"

"Oh well, that's his wife. She's gone now too, bless her soul." Gladys pursed her lips. "Always a bit of a drinker, that one," she continued with some reluctance, "and oh, she took Jake's death very hard. Poor dear. Wrapped her car around a tree."

"Him?"

"That is . . ." Gladys leaned in, peering at the short man with glasses in the back row. "Oh, I believe that's Martin Brown. Now, he's not around these parts any longer. I believe he moved to trade shares or some such down in Austin."

"That's fine," Matt said, feeling relieved. He pulled a pencil and notepad out of his back pocket. "I'm sure I can find him. Do you know whereabouts . . . ?" But he stopped midway through his sentence as Gladys shook her head.

"Sad story, old Martin," she said. "He was quite the talk of the town for some time, for some spinsters. The one who got away. Made quite a lot of money, I heard. But then invested it all in those . . . whatchama-callits, in the mid-nineties. Lost everything. Poor man." She shook her head. "Hung himself in his bedroom. Couldn't take the loss."

Matt stared, dumbfounded, at the yearbook picture.

"Gladys," he said slowly, resisting the urge to pepper his words with profanities, "is there anyone in this picture who's actually still alive?"

"Well, now," the old librarian replied, squinting and adjusting her glasses with stumpy fingers, "let me see. Caitlin Alba, well, she was Captain Dawn's wife, everyone knows what happened to her. Glenn Turner, no, he barely made fifty, but that's just the way of things, his family all went young to stroke. Patty Leech, heart attack—rumor has it doctors had her meds tuned wrong. The Wallaces, their house caught fire a few years ago, poor devils . . . Mr. and Mrs. Kneebone, they headed the Bridge Society, but that was a sad story . . . her going crazy like that, taking a gun to them both . . . hmm . . ."

Gladys's old gray eyes flickered from person to person, her head bent so close to the page her nose almost touched the paper. "You know, now that you mention it, I don't think there is. Apart from the captain, of course. Oh dear, that is disheartening. I'm so sorry. What a shame."

A funny feeling was beginning to creep over Matt. Scraps and seeds, a slow, primordial stew of an idea, churning around in his head, slowly convalescing into something—but no. That couldn't be. That was insane. Slowly, he drew back the yearbook, his fingers cold among the pages.

"Gladys," he said quietly, looking down at the picture in his hands, "I don't suppose I could trouble you for one more favor."

"Of course, dearie," the librarian said with a smile, oblivious to his thoughts.

"Could I see the town records? The births and deaths, the property lists . . . anything about the people living here. Who they were, where they lived. From about"—he did the math—"1940 onward."

Gladys blinked behind her glasses. "Oh well, that's quite a lot of paper dear, are you sure you want . . ."

"If it's not too much trouble," Matt murmured, still transfixed by the yearbook. By the faces of the entire class of people grinning out at him. None of whom could ever look back.

Save one.

"Well, okay, dear," the old lady said, shoulders shrugging underneath her cardigan, both arms stretching out toward the shelves. "Why don't you take a seat at that table there? I'll bring them over."

"Thank you," replied Matt, his eyes following, hard and distant, as the librarian's hands snaked through all that remained of Coal Point's history.

"Where have you been?" Jane asked as Matt fell into the spot beside her. It was late afternoon, and half the hall was still abuzz. Jane couldn't stop grinning. Her wounds were healed, her clothes were clean, and she was eating cake. Real, actual cake. Jane couldn't remember the last time she'd had cake, but it tasted amazing. This was the greatest cake of her life. "Did you see the challenge? I wasn't sure if you saw, I mean I couldn't see if you saw, I just—"

"Come with me," Matt muttered under his breath. His face was as pale as a sheet, but Jane was too excited to pay attention.

"Look," she crowed in a whisper, ducking her head down, keeping her voice low. She opened her hand in her lap, almost quivering with excitement. Her fingers uncurled discreetly, revealing the silver eagle still nestled in her palm, in the same place where she'd caught it hours ago, where it was probably going to stay forever because she was never letting it go. "Look what I got, Matt, look what he gave me!"

Matt's eyes barely grazed the badge.

"I need your help," he whispered, his voice low and urgent.

"Now?" She laughed. "Matt, don't you realize what this is? Don't you know what it means?"

"It's great Jane, fantastic," Matt muttered, not sounding like he heard, not sounding like he understood. "Congratulations. It's really good. Please."

Only now, did Jane begin to notice the tremors in his voice. For the first time since her hand grasped the eagle, her smile faltered. "What is it? What's wrong?" she asked. Matt shook his head.

"I need your help," he repeated. His voice was low, but his eyes were frantic. "Just twenty-four hours, that's all I need, I—"

Jane frowned. "This isn't some stupid party thing, is it?" she replied, sounding skeptical. "They're running dark drills tonight, and—"

"Jane," Matt whispered, and this time she really heard the desperation with which he said her name, "for God's sake. You're done, you've done it. I need you. I'm begging you. Take the day off."

And suddenly, the realization clicked.

"You've found something," she murmured. Matt jerked his head to one side, his eyes racing around the crowded room. He rose from the bench, and Jane followed without a moment's hesitation.

"I don't know," he whispered, his voice low, his words trembling. They strode out the hall, through the corridors, Matt almost on the verge of breaking into a run, Jane struggling to keep up. "I can't tell. I don't know if I'm seeing things or going insane or—"

They scaled the winding stairs to the third floor, two at a time. Matt glanced back at her.

"You know Dawn's history," he said. It wasn't a question.

"Like the back of my hand." Jane shrugged, unashamed. Matt nodded.

"Good," he muttered. "Because we need to find someone."

"Who?"

"Anyone," Matt replied. "Anybody from Dawn's past."

He breathed.

"Anyone who's still alive."

They worked through the night. Matt plundering the depths of the Internet on his laptop, Jane combing through the Captain Dawn biographies she'd read so often as a child. They trawled through old newspapers, public records, files from Coal Point, the State Department, the National Archives, anything, everything they could find. Hunched over in Matt's room, barely a word passing between them, the hours started melding together. Sometime after midnight, Jane brought up a second computer and a whiteboard from the labs—the former she searched on, the latter soon covered in names, pictures, clippings. Missing persons, land titles, coroner's reports—endless databases, articles, searches. Painstaking records of the first Legion's origins, their every move, every fight, every encounter. All leading to the same point, the same result. With every passing minute, every scribbled date, every crossed off name, there grew a greater, darker, billowing sense of dread—of a single, unfathomable, inescapable conclusion—

"They're all dead."

It was after 10:00 a.m. The sun had long since risen, daylight peeking around the blinds, but the room still swelled with the chill of darkness and the burn of artificial light. They were both sitting, surrounded, piles of files and papers strewn everywhere, the whiteboard heavy with marker and tack. Their eyes were red, their hands stiff. Neither had slept a second the entire night. But neither one felt tired.

Matt's face was pale and drawn, and his head shook as his hands ran through his hair.

"They're all dead," he whispered again. "Everyone. Everyone from Dawn's past. Everyone he ever . . . he ever . . ."

Jane said nothing. She didn't know what to say, if she even could say anything. What was she supposed to do, to think, to feel? Her heart was pounding in her chest, a dry, sickly metallic taste on her tongue. The challenge, the arena, the silver eagle—it all seemed like another world, a lifetime away, before this . . . before . . . what was this?

What the hell was going on?

She sat in shaken silence as Matt kept babbling. He'd barely spoke for nearly sixteen hours, but now he'd started, he couldn't seem to stop.

"Everyone," he stammered. "Everyone! His . . . his sister. His cousins. His friends, his classmates! Everyone he grew up with, but, it's not just that, it's—" He held up a list of crossed-out names, his hands trembling. Jane didn't need to see what was on there. She'd help write it. "It's everyone! His, his neighbors, his enemies, his family doctor, his"—Matt unleashed a string of incredulous swear words—"childhood dentist, for crying out loud! They're all dead! There's . . . there's . . ."

He sunk down onto his bed, holding the sides of his head in his hands. "Half the population of Coal Point is gone, and nobody even noticed. How did they . . . how is this . . . ?"

"I don't get it," whispered Jane, her voice hoarse. She felt sick to her stomach.

"It doesn't make sense!" Matt cried out, throwing his hands in the air. "There's, there's no pattern, they're not . . . I mean . . . look at this, listen!" He picked up another list and began reading causes of death. "Heart attack, aneurysm, cancer. Overdose, overdose, suicide, Year of Chaos, Year of Chaos, car accident. Fall off a horse, hit by a bus, building collapse, house fire. Mugging, gas leak, suicide, stroke, stroke, heart attack. What . . ." he spluttered, struggling for words. "There's no link! There's no common cause! These people . . ." He rifled through newspaper clippings. "They're all completely different! They'd moved hundreds of miles apart! They've got nothing in common!"

"Except they all knew the same person," Jane murmured. A cold pit of dread settled over her stomach. She finally looked up. "It's not just his friends. It's not just his family."

"Everyone Captain Dawn ever knew is dead."

THE MINDTAKER

Incident Log, ADX Florence, February 1991

February 2, 1991, 2:52 p.m.
Fire door opened, alarm triggered. Officer Wilcox admits liable, official reprimand. Action: Meeting ADXF staff re: procedure cigarette breaks.

February 8, 1991, 5:23 p.m.
Officer Monahan reports sense presence (TIPh) cell Inmate Mentok. Nil camera presence. Action: Full sweep cell, nil presence.

February 11, 1991, 3:11 p.m.
Inmate Palmer anaphylactic reaction. Doctor present, stabilized 3:14 p.m. Action: Allergy penicillin noted.

February 13, 1991, 8:45 a.m.
Officer Duncan overseen photographing self with Inmate Mentok. Action: Phone destroyed, immediate termination.

February 16, 1991, 2:37 a.m.
Officer Monahan reports intruder in central hall, claims visual confirm (child???). Action: Lockdown, full sweep, nil presence. Recordings review, nil camera presence. Officer relieved.

February 23, 1991, 2:11 p.m.
Inmate Alkozer attack Officer West improvised weapon. No injury. Action: Inmate Alkozer recreation privileges revoked, note meals no cutlery.

February 26, 1991, 11:14 p.m.
Officer Monahan reports intruder cell Inmate Mentok, claims visual confirmation: Caucasian male 10–12, hair blond, eye blue. Claims visual on intruder passing Inmate Mentok "technology." Nil camera presence. Action: Full sweep cell, nil presence intruder or "technology." Officer Monahan claims camera rotation allowing intruder to evade detection. Officer Monahan placed on leave (stress). Refer psych eval.

Matt paced the room.

"This has to be it," he said. He couldn't seem to stop shaking his head, his voice feverish. "This has to be what Ed found. He went looking into party guests, some lighthearted nothing job and then boom. Dead, dead, dead, dead. He was a genius. He would've seen the pattern. He would've made the connection instantly."

Jane nodded her agreement. "But what the hell does it mean?" she asked quietly. She glanced down at one of the scraps of paper in front of her, an obituary notice, Mr. Brian Kitchener, who'd reportedly died last year in his sleep. He'd owned the Coal Point bakery. "Is someone murdering these people?"

Matt shook his head. "It has to be," he said. "It's too much of a coincidence."

"Murdering and making it look like natural causes. Like accidents."

"Or suicide."

They looked at each other.

"How is this possible?" demanded Jane. "How is this not national news? How has nobody figured this out before now?"

"They're old," muttered Matt, staring at one of the files. "Captain Dawn's pushing sixty now, everyone he knew growing up is at least that old." He shook his head bitterly. "Do you really give it a second thought when some eighty-year-old math teacher slips and dies from a fall? Accidents happen all the time. It's just coincidence this was a group of people someone was actually looking into."

"But why?" asked Jane.

"And how?" agreed Matt. "All these deaths, all these different causes? You'd have to be some kind of evil mastermind to pull this off."

"It's got to be a group," declared Jane. "A group, an agency, some . . . I don't know, secret society? No one person could do all this, it's not possible."

Matt was silent.

"It's Dawn," he murmured finally. "It's all about Dawn."

"What do you mean?"

Matt turned to her. "Think about it," he said. "Dawn's practically invincible, right?"

"Well, yeah," replied Jane, as if that went without saying. "Even the Black Death could barely scratch him."

"Right," said Matt. "So how do you hurt someone who's invincible?"

It took a few seconds, but Jane's eyes widened. "You hurt the people around them," she murmured. She looked up at him, her face white. "They're killing these people to get to Dawn."

"More than that," Matt said savagely. "This isn't just personal, it's systematic." He grimaced bitterly. "These aren't just people—they're pieces of Dawn's past. Put together, they *are* his past. Where he came from, who he grew up with, his place in the world. Without them, he's got no one. They're destroying Captain Dawn's entire history."

"Holy crap," whispered Jane. She put her hand over her mouth—then took it away again and stared up at Matt.

"We've got to tell him."

Matt shook his head. "Maybe he already knows. You ever wonder why he's such a recluse? Maybe he's figured it out. Maybe he knows someone's out there targeting people in his life and he doesn't know how to stop them. So, he keeps his distance, shuts himself away on purpose, so that no one else gets hurt."

He turned to Jane. "Answer me seriously. How close are you to Captain Dawn?"

Jane brushed the question away like an elephant shaking off flies. "Don't worry about me."

"I am worried about you!" Matt cried, throwing up his hands. "Jane, if we're right, whoever this is, they've killed dozens of people. Maybe hundreds! They're smart, they're slick, and they're good enough to kill Ed right in the middle of Morningstar!" He clenched his teeth, biting back his frustration. "This isn't a game; this isn't some training exercise. You. Could. Die."

But Jane wasn't backing down. "I'm not running," she declared, adamant. "I'm not going anywhere." She looked defiantly at Matt, then glared at the whiteboard. "We just need to figure out who's doing this before they make their next move."

Matt opened his mouth to argue—but at the look on Jane's face, he stopped and swallowed what he was about to say, resigning himself to merely shaking his head.

"Fine," he said, "so how do we do that?" He glanced at the notes scattered all over the floor, then looked up at Jane, but she didn't seem to have heard.

"What's the motive?" she whispered. Jane stared forward, unwavering, the tired rings under her eyes the same color as her tattoo. "What does someone get out of this?"

Matt rubbed his face with the butt of his hands. "I don't know," he admitted. "Why does anyone murder anyone?"

"Anger," Jane stated, still staring at the board. "Provocation. But this isn't spur of the moment."

"Agreed."

"Then there's profit," she continued. "Killing because you think it'll get you something."

"Hard to see how anyone would make money out of killing Dawn's old dentist."

"Maybe it's blackmail," Jane suggested. "The captain's rich, so is the Legion."

"Could be," admitted Matt. "Except killing everyone someone knows is pretty ineffective blackmail. Seems more like something you'd threaten, rather than do. It doesn't leave any leverage."

Jane pursed her lips. "That leaves idealism—killing for a belief—or revenge."

Matt pondered for a moment. "How about . . . someone hates super-heroes so much, they're so against what Dawn stands for—"

"What, peace, justice, freedom? How can anyone be against that?"

"I don't know," Matt said, exasperated. "Some people just suck. Work with me. They can't kill him themselves, so they take away all his friends and loved ones, in the hope that Dawn will get really, really sad and off himself."

Jane stared at him, her expression deadpan. "That's a terrible plan," she said bluntly.

"Yeah, you're right," Matt conceded. "It's stupid."

"If someone did that to me, I wouldn't kill myself. If anything, I'd want to live more because I'd be really, really mad."

"Yes, well, not all of us instinctively react to every obstacle with rage," replied Matt, struggling to think. The fact that he hadn't slept for twenty-four hours was starting to hit home. "But yeah, point taken, idealism's tough. So that leaves revenge."

"Revenge seems like the best fit," said Jane.

"It makes sense," Matt agreed. "I mean if your only goal was hurting Captain Dawn, if you only cared about causing him pain, this seems like a pretty smart way to do it. Psychotic, but smart." He paused and looked at Jane. "So, the question is, who wants revenge on Dawn?"

"Could be loads," she admitted. "Dictators, communists, supervillains. Anybody with an ax to grind against the Legion. Or it could be entirely unrelated. Maybe someone he crossed paths with we don't know about."

"So, we're back to square one." Matt sighed, frustration tinging the edge of his voice. "Trying to find some mystery person from Captain Dawn's past, when everyone he ever knew is dead."

He closed his eyes.

"Okay," he muttered, rubbing his fingers into his temples. "Let's go back." He opened his eyes and looked at the board, at their mountains of notes. "There's got to be a clue. Something we've missed." Jane murmured indistinct agreement, and the two of them stared in silence at the whiteboard, Jane biting at her knuckle, Matt chewing his thumb.

. . . January 23, 1992 . . . mourn the loss of . . . service held Wednesday, 5th of November, 1995 . . . born April 4, 1943; died September 9, 1991 . . . 1996, blood alcohol reading of . . . witnesses reported smelling gas and . . . Year of Chaos . . . 1932–1993; beloved husband and . . . DAWN . . . house fire at their Redfield residence . . . cause of death: heart failure . . . survived by his . . . July 10, 1997—police called to the scene as . . . SUICIDE . . .

The longer Matt stared, the more it all blurred together—the faces, the photographs, obituary after obituary, a patchwork of words. Presented this way, he thought, death seemed so trivial—an endless sea of details, once so important to someone, now so irrelevant . . . names and dates and causes . . .

Dates . . .

A strange, prickling feeling began climbing its way up the back of Matt's neck.

"Jane," he whispered, his eyes glued to the clippings—to the numbers. Numbers never lied. "When did Dawn's sister die?"

Jane frowned. "Amelia?"

"That's the one."

Jane bent down over Matt's laptop and clicked around in silence until she'd brought up the relevant page. "August 18, 1991."

Matt fell silent, chewing his finger. "And her son?"

"Like, two weeks later?"

"Hmm." Something nagged at him. Maybe it was just the lack of sleep, maybe he was imagining things—but he had to know.

"Can we go through . . . ?" he asked. He glanced back at Jane. "The dates, can we make a list of all the dates when they died?"

Jane frowned, perplexed, but she shrugged her acquiescence, and the pair began going over their notes again.

It took about half an hour to go through the names of every one of Dawn's dead acquaintances and record exactly when it was they'd died—but by the end, Matt knew they were on to something. And that he wasn't going insane.

"It's the last ten years," he muttered, glancing from the whiteboard to the spreadsheet of dates on his laptop. "Ninety percent of them, they were all in the last decade. Look." Jane peered in as he highlighted the entirety of the spreadsheet, some 424 dates, and clicked to convert them to a line graph—a single dot on a time line for every person who had died. At around 1963 to 1964, the Year of Chaos, there was a small group of dots, some thirty or so, which wasn't out of place, but after that, the dots grew sparse, irregular—until the beginning of 1991, where their number exploded.

From there, the line looked like it was swarming with flies.

Jane swore. Matt bit his lip. "What's going on?" he whispered. "Why the last ten years? Is it something to do with Africa, or . . . ?"

He glanced back at Jane, but Jane wasn't looking at him. Instead, she was standing, her eyes wide, her hand over her mouth.

"It can't be," she whispered. The expression on her face was shocked, horrified, but strangest of all . . . almost . . . betrayed?

"What?" Matt asked sharply. "What is it, what can't be?"

"Captain Dawn's a superhero," Jane said quietly.

"Yeah," Matt acknowledged. "So?"

"So," she murmured. "Who'd most want revenge on a superhero?" When Matt didn't answer, she continued. "A supervillain. Someone he'd beaten."

"Right," agreed Matt, still impatient. "But we already ruled that out. All the supervillains the Legion fought are dead, you told me yourself."

"Technically, no," Jane whispered, lost in thought. "But I didn't think . . . it couldn't possibly—"

"Wait, what?" cried Matt, snapping round to look at her. "What do you mean, 'technically, no'? I thought you knew them all by heart! I thought you accounted for everyone!"

"I do know them all," Jane replied. "And I did account for everyone. There's only one, Viktor Mentok, who's still alive." She shook her head, her face pale. "But it's impossible. He's got Scarlett syndrome, he's, he's comatose . . . he can't be the one."

Something about that name rang a bell in Matt's head. He struggled to think. And then, in a flash—

"Ed," he murmured. Instinctively, his hand's fell to the left pocket of his jeans where, nestled in between his keys and wallet, lay the tiny silver disk. The telepathic emulator. He'd kept it on his person, hidden, since the day Ed had died—the second time he'd seen it. Because the first time . . .

"What?" said Jane, looking back at his frozen expression.

"Ed was working with old Mentok technology," Matt whispered. His fingers traced the disk's outline, hidden away in his pocket. "He had accesses to it; he showed me. He was building off it."

"WHAT?" yelped Jane. "Why the hell didn't you say so?!"

"I did tell you," he whispered, suddenly too anxious to care about the anger in her voice. "The device that would give telepathy to non-psychics? That was it, I told you, I just . . . I forgot to mention where it came from."

"Jesus . . ." Jane whispered. She shook her head slowly, breathing hard. "Matt, Mentok was the last supervillain the Legion ever put away.

July 1990. Captain Dawn was the one who brought him in. He stood trial but then he . . . Scarlett syndrome . . . he fell into a coma not long after Africa. A little . . . a little more than ten years ago."

Matt's eyes widened. "Is he still . . . ?"

"Yeah," Jane finished bitterly, her voice heavy with contempt. "He's in a coma. He's still alive."

A horrible silence filled the room. They looked at each other.

"Jane," Matt whispered, "this has to be it. Ed was using Mentok's technology. Mentok is *the only person* from Captain Dawn's past who's still alive! It's too much of a coincidence, it has to be him. It has to be!" A rush of energy, of revelation, of terrible understanding, raced through him and he spun, his hands held out, both ecstatic and terrified, to Jane.

But still, somehow, Jane hesitated.

"I don't know," she said, slowly shaking her head. She made a face. "It just . . . it doesn't feel right."

"Doesn't feel?" Matt couldn't believe what he was hearing. "Jane, he's the only one left! Ten years ago, he gets all 'comatose,' at the same time people start dying? He's a *supervillain,* for crying out loud! A *supervillain!*"

Jane remained unconvinced. "Putting aside the fact that he's been in a coma for ten years," she said, then her voice hardened and she pressed on over the top of Matt's objections. "Putting aside the fact that he's been under guard that whole time, maximum security, under constant surveillance. Even assuming, for a second, you ignore all that . . . I just, I just can't see him doing it."

Matt blinked, incredulous. "I'm sorry," he spluttered. "But did I miss something? Some change to the word *supervillain*? He's the Mindtaker! He's evil!"

But still Jane shook her head. "Viktor Mentok was never evil," she said quietly. She looked at him, a curious glimmer in her eyes. "He was part of the Legion, originally. Did you know that?"

Matt hesitated. "No," he conceded reluctantly. "But that still doesn't—"

"He lived right here," she went on, undeterred by Matt's continued protests, "in Morningstar. Designing the Legion's armor, their equipment, supporting their abilities. All the while creating invention after invention to better the world. Captain Dawn, Ironbound, Zephyr, the White Queen, all of them—they were his friends."

"Until he vanished," countered Matt, who remembered this part of the story, "and turned up a few months later having installed mind-control devices on an entire town."

"Yes," Jane agreed calmly. "He did do that. And do you know why?"

"Because he was crazy?"

"No," said Jane, "because he wanted to keep them safe."

She stared at Matt. "Not many people know this. But when Dawn came to confront him, Mentok didn't fight. He tried to explain. He said that what he was doing was the only way to protect people—that the only way to achieve absolute safety was to remove people's freedom to harm themselves, to make the wrong choices. He didn't care about money or power or anything like that. It was all because he believed, believed so strongly in the Legion's goals. Because he couldn't bear to stand by and watch anyone suffer, not when in his own, warped way, he knew there was something he could do to save them."

She blinked, staring at the whiteboard, her eyes distant—maybe even a little sad. "That's why Captain Dawn didn't kill him. His methods may have been immoral, but he truly believed he was doing the right thing. He was a genius and he believed in the Legion's cause. His understanding of it had just . . . evolved. Some say it was the Scarlett syndrome, his thoughts moving so fast, becoming detached from reality. But no matter what he ended up doing, there was never any doubt about his intentions. He wanted to help. He meant well."

She turned back to look at Matt. "Which is why this just doesn't seem like him. Killing hundreds of people? Murdering Dawn's entire past, deliberately trying to cause him that kind of emotional pain? It's not just cruel, it's pointless. What does it achieve, besides hurting one man?"

"One man who put him away for life," Matt countered.

Jane was resolute. "Dawn argued on Mentok's behalf against the death penalty," she said. "Dawn showed him mercy, Dawn brought him in alive—not to mention, Mentok was doggedly, obsessively devoted to the Legion." She paused and looked at Matt. "I just can't see him doing this."

But Matt wasn't giving in. "Maybe that's the genius of it," he argued. "Maybe the fact that he's above suspicion is exactly why we should be suspicious."

"That doesn't make sense."

"But everything else does! He's a genius, with a reason to hate Captain Dawn, who's had ten uninterrupted years to work on his specialty of, oh yeah, *mind control*, and Ed just *happened* to be investigating his tech when he died!" He shook his head, his hand trembling. "Mentok removed the free will of an entire town. What if he's planning to do it for the entire world? The clairvoyants, maybe they all saw what was coming and were trying to prevent it and the child, the child with his warning . . . Jane, it all fits!"

"Except the part where he's in a coma, in maximum security, under constant guard!"

"You don't think he could fake that?"

"You don't think anybody checked? You think you're the only person who thought when Viktor Mentok went into a coma, 'Hmm, he's a genius, maybe he's faking it'? Believe it or not, you're not the only one in the world with half a brain!"

Matt opened his mouth to unleash an angry reply—but he forced himself to swallow it, seeing the frustration on Jane's face.

"Fine," he said. "Fine. Either you're right or I'm right, but either way, this is too much of a coincidence. I've got to go check this out."

"Check what out?" Jane scowled. Matt began shuffling a handful of papers into a pile.

"Mentok. I'm going to go see him. If he's really in a coma, I doubt he'll mind if I pay him a visit."

Jane rubbed her eyes. "Fine," she muttered. "We can go. If only to shut you up."

Matt looked at her, his face hard. "I said I," he said firmly, "not we. You're not coming."

Jane's lip curled into a murderous scowl. "I swear to God," she snarled, "if you start with the 'it's too dangerous for a girl' crap, I will dangle you out the window until you remember which of us can fly. I'm as much a part of this as you are."

"I never said you weren't," Matt replied. "You're not coming to keep me safe, not the other way around."

Jane glowered. "How does my not being there protect you?" she snapped. "You couldn't defend yourself from an angry goose."

"Say Mentok is behind this," Matt pushed on, doggedly ignoring Jane's goading. "His specialty is mind control. I can keep him out."

"You don't know that," Jane replied, perhaps angrier than she ought to have been. Matt could tell she resented the implication that she couldn't resist a psychic attack—especially since they both knew it was true. "His tech might not work like a psychic."

"You're right, I don't know," said Matt, trying to be placating. "But see, I'm just me. Who cares if I get brain-jacked? Big whoop, what can I do, I'm powerless, he gets nothing. But if he takes control of you? Then he gets *you*—the one-woman wrecking ball, a living weapon, the most powerful Acolyte in the Academy."

Jane averted her eyes and brushed a strand of hair behind her ear, trying not to look too pleased. "So, what the hell am I supposed to do while you're off chasing supervillains?" she complained, though without less vitriol. "Sit around with my thumb up my butt?"

"No," replied Matt, "your job is more important." He stared at her, his expression mixed. "I need you to talk to Dawn."

Jane's heart skipped a beat. "What do you mean?" she asked, but Matt just shook his head. He began to walk slowly, back toward the door.

"Ed learned the truth," he said, "and someone killed him to stop it getting out. I'm not making the same mistake. I'm going to tell every-one—CNN, NBC, ABC, PBS, Fox, the *New York Times*, *USA Today*, the freaking Disney Channel. Everyone I can, anyone who'll listen. Right now, it's us versus them, but once everyone knows the truth, it'll be them versus the world."

He looked at her. "And you're going to tell Dawn. You're going to tell him we know, and you're going to force him to stop hiding from the truth. There's no one left to die anymore. You're going to make him come back out into the open." He paused. "I don't know what we're up against. But I know we need Dawn on our side."

Jane hesitated. The idea of confronting Captain Dawn, of revealing they'd been investigating his past—of forcing him to share his private pain, or worse still, if he didn't know, of being the one to inflict that pain upon him . . . her stomach churned at the thought. But she couldn't escape the truth. Matt was right. Jane nodded, swallowing the lump in her throat.

They waited twenty-four hours—long enough to let their tired brains rest and churn over every aspect of what they were about to do. To their grim, slight, and unspoken disappointment, by the time they met in the hall at ten the next morning, neither had had any further epiphanies. The plan stood. Matt would teleport to ADX Florence with Will to check on Mentok, while Jane found and dealt with Dawn, reporting back at the first sign of any developments. Since Jane didn't own a cell phone, Matt gave her his, preloaded with Will's number, along with the solemn promise that he'd stick close to the teleporter at all times. A few minutes before they were due to leave, Jane—with an expression like she was physically extracting a bone from her finger—gave Matt something in return: her silver eagle, the badge Dawn had given her for winning the challenge.

"It'll help you get inside," she managed to get out, her face contorted in almost physical pain as she passed Matt the pin. "Convince them you're legit." Matt gave her a smile of wordless thanks and went to put the badge in his top pocket—only for Jane to tightly grab hold of his wrist.

"If you lose that," she said in a very quiet, dangerous voice, squeezing so tight it felt like his bones were going to snap, "I will literally murder you."

"I'll be careful," he assured her, forcing a grin over his pained grimace and trying fruitlessly to tug free from her vise-like talons. Jane leaned in, so her grayish blue-eyed, tattooed, and quite frankly terrifying face was an inch from his.

"Literally. Murder."

She let go. "Please don't lose my phone either," Matt added ineffectually, sulking and massaging his wrists.

They still had a few minutes before they were supposed to be meeting Will, so Matt got up and brought over a plate of pancakes and bacon. Jane grunted her thanks, and they sat in silence, picking at the food, neither particularly hungry. With most Acolytes being out training, the hall was relatively empty—a smattering of late-risers and the odd walking-wounded bearing a cast or compress while their injuries knitted together. The only full table was a group of about fourteen older Acolytes seated at the far end of the room, animatedly debating a group assignment, only a few spaces along from where the lone figure of Giselle Pixus sat slumped and staring off into space, unnoticed, practically invisible. Jane watched the speedster sitting alone in her black sweater, feeling a building sense of guilt.

"Should we tell her?" she asked Matt in a low voice, gazing worriedly at the silent, solitary figure. Matt followed her eyes.

"We can't," he muttered—though he sounded unhappy. "Not yet."

"It seems cruel," murmured Jane.

"She'll know the truth eventually. Everyone will. We'll make it right."

"She thinks Ed killed himself because of her. She thinks everyone thinks she led him on."

"Nobody blames her."

"She does."

"We can't tell her before we talk to Dawn."

Jane didn't reply—just gazed unblinkingly at the miserable, silent Giselle.

"Do you think I'm wrong?" Matt pressed.

"No," she replied. "But that doesn't mean I have to like it."

Matt glanced down at his phone in Jane's lap. "Come on," he said, seeing the time. "We shouldn't keep Will waiting."

Will met them at the threshold to the entrance hall, wearing a leather jacket and black jeans.

"Matt," he said, nodding at them as they approached. "Empath."

"Teleporter," Jane replied irritably. Will flushed and began stammering something that might have been an apology, but Jane ignored him.

"Don't get mind-controlled and die," she told Matt. "I don't want my badge smelling like a corpse."

Matt chuckled. "You look after yourself too," he said, rolling his eyes. Jane made a face.

"Please," she scoffed. "I'll be fine. Go see your coma patient."

"Go find your boyfriend."

"I will. And he's not my boyfriend."

"Yeah, I guess he's too old to call a boy, more of a man-friend."

"Please leave," she said, smirking.

"Take care," Matt replied. And then, without really thinking, he hugged her. Jane stiffened—but then, after a moment, briefly squeezed back. The embrace quickly ended and the two broke apart. Then Matt nodded at Will and the pair set off, leaving Jane behind.

"So, what's going on exactly?" Will asked as Morningstar grew smaller behind them. "Why're we going to a prison? Who's getting mind-controlled? And since when does Jane have a boyfriend?"

"It's a long story," said Matt, glancing over his shoulder. "I'll explain on the way."

Jane walked through the empty corridors, sneakers padding on the carpet. It occurred to her as she strode around corners and down hallways, wordlessly searching, that this was the first time she'd actively sought out Captain Dawn and not the other way around. Strange as it was to think, she'd never been the one to initiate contact. It would have been flattering, if it didn't make things difficult now.

She had no idea where Dawn was. What he did with his time, where he went in Morningstar, whether he was even here at all. She knew he had an apartment with an office of sorts, on the highest floor—but that was his sanctuary, strictly off-limits to everyone. She couldn't go barging in there, kicking down the door, or so she told herself. It was a lame excuse to forestall facing an uncomfortable reality—that the conversation she was about to have with Dawn was going to be bad. Either he knew about the deaths and he'd be furious at her for getting involved, or he didn't, and Jane would be telling him that everyone he ever knew was dead. Either way, they were forcing him to go public, shining a spotlight directly onto his private pain. For a man like Captain Dawn, there'd be almost nothing worse. It may have been the right choice, the only choice—but still, she hesitated. On top of all the reasons she was about to give the captain to hate her, Jane couldn't bring herself to add the violation of his innermost sanctum, not unless she was absolutely, positively, 100 percent sure she couldn't avoid it. So, she resolved to check every room, every passage in Morningstar, on the sliver of a chance Dawn was wandering the halls.

Slim though it was.

The blue-eyed boy moved without sound. His feet bare on the carpet, treading only where he knew would make no noise. It was a matter of timing. Too soon and too obvious, too late and unheard. But the child was patient. All it took was refinement.

Tucked into the doorway, shielded from view, he rang a bell.

Jane's head snapped back.

What the hell was that? Three steps down a new corridor, having just turned a corner, for a split second she could have sworn she'd heard something. A bell ringing. But that was ridiculous, there hadn't been, she hadn't seen . . . She backtracked until her head peered around the T-junction, glancing down in the direction she thought the noise had come from, the direction she'd chosen on a whim not to follow. The corridor was deserted, the same as when she'd been walking toward it. Still, Jane frowned. She could have sworn she'd heard something.

"Hello?" she called, her voice at once demanding, curious and hostile. No answer. Jane's frown deepened. Maybe it was just her imagination, maybe she was going crazy. Unless—well, there was a door halfway down. Maybe somebody was in there. Messing with her. Some idiot's idea of a game.

Jane abandoned her left turn and headed straight down the hallway, pausing with mild irritation at the closed door. She turned the handle and pushed the door open—stepping through into a large, sunlit room, lined with bookshelves and scattered through with pillows and incense, in the midst of which sat a large, leathery man.

"Um, hello?" Jane repeated, taking in the man's black clothes, bald head, and dream-like expression. The man's eyes flicked open.

"Hello," he said, his voice deep and calm and not at all like what Jane had imagined.

"Sorry," she muttered, not seeing any bell. "Thought I heard something. Forget it. Looking for someone."

"You found someone," the man said, smiling. His legs were crossed in a way that looked both flexible and uncomfortable. A small line of incense burned beside him.

"Well, I'm looking for a different someone," Jane replied, trying not to let her impatience show. She was intruding, and he was one of the Ashes, judging by his clothes. But the man seemed not in the least bit fazed by either her interruption or her rudeness.

"You have the most interesting mark on your cheek," he mused. Then he asked sincerely, "Is it a letter E or the number three?"

"Um," replied Jane, taken aback. Surely, he wasn't serious. "It's a, um, it's an E. Definitely an E." She paused, frowning. "Isn't that obvious?"

The large man gave a small shrug. "To an observer, it appears one way, but to your own eyes, which will only ever glimpse a reflection, it is another. The truth of its form is yours to determine."

Months of conversations with Matt she'd half been paying attention to came crashing down in the sudden realization of who this man was.

"You're Selwyn," she stated. Selwyn smiled.

"That is what they call me. What guides your feet, young, beautiful woman?" he asked, gazing up at her warmly. "Do I play a part?" Jane peered down at him.

"No . . ." she answered slowly, unnerved by his general niceness. "No, thank you. You can't help me, I'm—" Suddenly, a thought struck her. "Actually," she amended, hurriedly unwinding her distrust, "hold on, you're a projectionist. Can you find Captain Dawn?"

For the first time since she'd entered, a small frown passed over the man's face. "What for?"

"I need to find him," Jane said hurriedly. "To pass on a message. It's my destiny," she added, thinking fast, "the clairvoyant told me."

The moment she mentioned Matt, Selwyn's face split into a huge smile. "I will traverse the halls," he assured her happily, and closed his eyes. Jane couldn't believe her luck.

Ten seconds had barely passed before Selwyn's eyelids fluttered open. "He is in the East Wing," the large man informed her, humming in his deep, kind voice. "Second floor. A passageway running above a room of mirrors, seldom used, where one can observe the goings-on below."

Jane knew exactly where he meant. "Thank you!" she called, already racing out the room.

"Wait, so let me get this straight," said Will, "everyone Dawn knew is dead?"

"Well, not everyone, technically," Matt replied, their shoes crunching on the gravel. "He presumably knows some of the Ashes, maybe some famous people. Plus this guy. But yes, everyone else."

Will swore. "That's insane," he mumbled. The teleporter turned to face Matt. "We've got to tell someone."

"Why do you think I've got your phone?" Matt muttered, not looking up from the screen. "I'm telling everyone." Logged into his email address, he hit Send on the message he'd spent the morning crafting to every major media outlet in the country, attached to which was the most succinct compilation of his and Jane's research. "Just wanted to wait until we were clear of Morningstar."

"You think anyone will believe you?" asked Will. Matt shook his head.

"No," he answered truthfully. "But it'll pique their interest. They'll look into it to confirm I'm nuts and end up realizing I'm right. It's like if you tell someone it's impossible to lick your elbow—it sounds ridiculous, so as soon as you say it, they try to prove you wrong." He glanced over at Will, who to his credit looked too disturbed to try licking his elbow.

They'd warped in a good quarter mile from the front door of the facility, half out of common sense, not wanting to spook prison security, and half not knowing how far the Disruptance fields stretched. The biggest building for miles around, ADX Florence sat square in the middle of a patch of flat, dry Colorado desert, the colors of its walls and towers not far removed from the dust and barren scrub surrounding it on every side. The road leading up to it through which the two of them now walked was little more than a strip of rocks and dirt, ruts weathered through the dry grass by years of heavy vehicles coming and going. At its conclusion sat the maroon entrance to the supermax prison as well as the larger, adjacent lower security yard—both fenced, imposing and looming over the landscape like overbearing tyrants. But it wasn't to either of these that Matt and Will now walked.

Less obvious but more out of place, ADX Florence's third facility looked more like an expensive phone store than a jail. Half the height of its siblings and sitting quietly off to one side, its walls were white, dull and sterile, its front doors and lobby made entirely of glass; a paved, mostly empty parking lot occupied by a half dozen cars situated neatly out front. While it would have been a stretch to describe it as "inviting," the lone two-story building lacked the obvious intentional hostility present in the architecture of its counterparts—more reminiscent of a hospital, truthfully, than a prison. Which was in essence what it was: a maximum-security hospice, built to house those society needed locked away, but who themselves needed medical care. All prisons had a hospital wing—Florence's just stood apart, purpose built around a single great and damaged mind.

It was, if nothing else, an impressive dedication to prolonging a life sentence.

The glass doors *ding*-ed as Matt and Will walked through them, and immediately they were assaulted by a rush of cold, artificial air. Across the room in a small booth beside a glass door blocking further access into the complex, two tall men in tan uniforms paused midway through their conversation and glanced over at them.

"Can I help you?" asked one of the guards, a muscular man with a midwestern accent and sleek crew cut. Will shot a nervous glance at Matt, who did his best to appear unperturbed.

"Hi," Matt said, striding purposefully across the room. He reached the counter, the small, windowed security station behind which both men were standing. "I'm Matthew Callaghan, clairvoyant; this is William Herd, teleporter. We're from the Legion of Heroes." He held out his identity card, and Will fumbled to do the same. "We're here to inspect Viktor Mentok."

Behind a wall of plexiglass, the guards exchanged glances. To Matt's relief, their immediate reaction was not to break out laughing.

"Um . . ." began the second one—slightly shorter, with darker hair, though of a similar style and build. He glanced down at their identity cards. "Why?"

"Surprise inspection," Matt replied. He tried to sound self-assured. "The Legion's been hearing some disturbing stuff. We're here to put the rumors to rest."

"What rumors?" asked the first guard, sounding defensive and maybe a little insulted. Matt stared coolly at him.

"Nothing you need to be concerned about," he replied. "Providing everything's in order. What's the Mindtaker's status?" He looked from one to the other, keeping his face resolutely professional.

The men exchanged glances.

"You say you're from the Legion of Heroes?" the second guard asked skeptically. Matt shot him a scathing, impatient look, as if the question was beneath him. Two pairs of eyes followed his hand as he reached into his pocket and removed Jane's badge, placing it on the counter in front of them.

"We'd appreciate your cooperation," he said dryly.

The two men glanced at each other, wearing mirrored looks of hesitation and concern. As they turned, Matt snuck a glimpse at the back of their necks—which were unadorned, as far as he could see. No invasive neural implants. And so far, no ticks, slurring or any other signs of mental control. If Mentok had somehow overrun this facility, these guys weren't showing it.

One of the guards turned back to him, a worried expression on his tanned face and clean-shaven, well-defined jaw. "I don't know what to tell you, sir," he began. Matt had to stop the corners of his mouth from twitching at a full-grown adult probably twice his age calling him, some baby-faced high schooler sir. "I don't know what you've heard, but on our end he's the same as always."

The guard took a step backward, indicating a panel of security screens on the far wall behind them—the monitor in the center showing an old, sleeping man. "This is a live feed," he said. "Twenty-four hours a day, seven days a week. Plus, we do hourly in-person sweeps of the entire block."

"He hasn't moved," his partner assured them.

"Not in the six years I've been here," the first guard agreed.

Matt frowned. "And there's been no changes?" he asked, looking from one to the other. "Nothing out of the ordinary?"

The two men exchanged glances. The taller one shook his head, and the dark-haired one shrugged and turned back to Matt.

"Nothing we've seen or heard about," he said. "Every other con in this place is ten times more trouble than Vicki. All that security and he just lays there, eating from a tube."

"All the same," Matt said, frowning. "I'd appreciate being able to inspect his cell in person."

Another glance passed between the guards, this time more reluctant than dumbfounded. "We're not *supposed* to . . ." the light-haired man began reluctantly.

"Come on, Angus," his counterpart replied. "They're from the Legion. Let them do their check. Sorry," he said, turning to Matt, "the old man's kind of a unique case, so the protocols are a bit . . . iffy. Plus, this is the first time he's had visitors."

"He is maximum security . . ." Angus said, frowning. "Are you sure we can—"

"He's in a coma," the other guard replied, waving away his concerns, "and even the conscious ones have visitation rights. What's the harm?"

"Gentlemen," said Matt, feigning impatience. "This isn't a social call. Unless Professor Mentok is in lockdown for bad behavior—"

The dark-haired guard chuckled. "Funny."

"—I'd appreciate being able to conduct our inspection." He returned the badge to his pocket. "If you'd be so kind."

The taller guard, Angus, still looked unconvinced—but eventually, he gave in.

"All right," he conceded. "Fine." He reached behind the counter, and a harsh buzzer sounded. The metal lock on the hallway door clicked open. "However, Legion or no Legion, I will have to ask you to comply with our security standards."

"Of course," said Matt, folding his hands behind his back.

"There are no cell phones, cameras, or other recording devices permitted on premises," recited the crew-cut guard. "Additionally, specific power groups are by law required to comply with certain conditions. As a clairvoyant, sir, I don't believe you are restricted, but I'm afraid *he* is." Angus pointed at Will, who recoiled, looking slightly offended. "Teleporters are a class one flight risk."

"Come on," protested Matt. "Surely, this facility has Disruptances."

"That we do," Angus replied coolly. "But policy states that no phase-walkers or teleporters are to enter a federal penitentiary in case our anti-distortion devices fail or are disrupted by an electromagnetic pulse. I'm sorry, sir, that's just the law."

"Secondly," he continued, pressing on before Matt could protest, "in compliance with safety procedures I will need to conduct a routine psychic examination to verify your identity and lack of hostile intent."

"I would expect nothing less," said Matt, who hadn't expected this at all. He quickly readied and smoothed over the surfaces of his mind. Behind him, he could feel Will's worried gaze burning into the back of his head—but he ignored it, focusing instead on keeping firm control over his mental composure.

"With your permission, sir," the dark-haired guard said apologetically.

"Of course," Matt replied, and a second later he felt the tendrils of the man's consciousness extend into his brain. Matt breathed slowly, keeping calm and offering no resistance, letting the telepath explore as he pleased—feeling him glance through his memories of Morningstar, Will, his time at the Legion. But not all of them, just the ones Matt was holding, the ones he wanted the guard to see. That was the trick—to create a facade, a mental mirage of identity, and believe it so firmly that the psychic believed what they were seeing was the real you.

It wasn't hard. Another person's mind was a daunting thing to peer too closely at, easy to lose yourself in. *And,* Matt allowed himself to think ruefully as the telepathic link withdrew, *this was hardly the world's greatest psychic.*

"He's clean," the shorter guard assured his partner. "Is who he says he is. All above board."

Angus nodded, somewhat reluctantly—as if he'd been hoping this was a ruse. Which admittedly it kind of was. "Thank you, sir. Please come with me." He pushed open a small swinging door and stepped out of the security booth.

Matt nodded, then glanced over his shoulder at Will. "You cool to wait here?"

"Hey, man," said the teleporter, holding up his hands, "I'm peachy. Absolutely no problem with staying out of prison. You mind if I step out for a second? Might call Wally."

"Cell reception's best down by the freeway," the dark-haired guard piped up helpfully, pointing at the end of the dirt road they'd just walked down. Will nodded.

"You sure you're going to be all right?" he asked Matt.

"Sure," Matt answered, forcing a smile he didn't feel. "No problem." He stepped into line behind Angus and the guard swung open the plexiglass door leading down the hallway. "Just hang around, okay?"

"You got it," replied Will. Matt glanced back over his shoulder as he followed the guard down the bare and darkening hallway, watching the teleporter's figure grow smaller and smaller. *Well,* he thought, maintaining steady control over his panic, *there goes my phone and my way out.*

He took a deep, shaky breath and stepped into the silver elevator behind Angus, who pushed the button for the lower floors.

The wind was blowing south-south west, six and a half miles per hour, at a bearing of a 192 degrees. The boy watched from a distance as the teleporter strode down the track, his heavy boots kicking up dust with every step. He had his hand to his ear, talking into his cell phone. His attention would be taken—but not undivided. His mind was occupied, but not his eyes.

The child scrunched the paper into a tight-wadded ball and released it, carried by the wind, skipping along the dirt.

"I'm telling you, it's messed up." Wally's voice chatted something half-garbled in his ear, and even though his boyfriend couldn't see him, Will shook his head.

"Nah, nothing like that," he said. His eyes wandered over the scrubland, the sun beating down on dry rocks and desert grass. "Matt's fine, ninety percent the Mindtaker's a dead end. Still though," he pondered out loud, "makes you wonder."

He paused, listening to Wally reply. "I don't see how. Dude's a jailed vegetable. Besides, Matt's a clairvoyant, you'd think he'd know if he was walking into a trap."

Something brushed against his leg, causing Will to glance down. A ball of crumpled paper nudged his leg, nestled against his boot.

"Hold up," he told Wally. He knelt down into a squat and grabbed the paper with his free hand, then stood up, glancing around at the empty desert plains. He looked down, frowning at the scrunched-up ball. Weird. It was so clean.

"What the hell?" He tilted his head, clenching the phone between this shoulder and his ear, using both hands to smooth open the paper—revealing handwritten words.

West Side Tower
11:03 a.m.
Be ready.

"Wal," Will murmured, "I'm gonna have to call you back."

"Sir!"

Jane's voice echoed between the wooden walls. Twenty feet down the hallway, Captain Dawn's shining form turned to face her.

"Jane?" he replied, sounding genuinely surprised. Below them, the sound of Acolytes sparring echoed up through hidden slits in the paneling. The floor was wood here, not carpet, the walls poorly lit, throwing odd shadows off the skirting boards and the small, single picture frames scattered along them. "What are you doing here?" For a moment, his gentle, handsome face looked taken aback and Jane was momentarily terrified he was about to be angry—but then Dawn's face split into a warm smile. "To what do I owe the pleasure?"

"Sir," said Jane, breathless—from running, from what she was about to do, and from him. Just him. "I need to talk to you."

"Well, of course, Jane," he said, smiling. "Anything for you." He hesitated, glancing around at the narrow, deserted corridor. "How did you find me?"

"I, er, someone said you were around." Lying to Dawn's face felt tantamount to sacrilege, but at the same time, getting Selwyn in trouble after he helped her felt wrong. "I really needed to see you." You look great, she almost blurted out, but didn't, thank God. She had to think, she had to not be stupid, not now. This wasn't about her.

"Oh?" said Dawn, tilting his head to one side. He smiled again. Encouraged, Jane took a step closer, wringing her hands behind her back.

"Sir," she stammered, "there's something I have to . . . I need to . . . to talk to you about, but I . . . I don't know how to."

"Go on," the captain said kindly. His smile grew wider. Jane closed her eyes, forcing herself to draw a deep breath. She took another step closer, only a few feet from him now. She could feel her body shaking.

"Sir," she whispered. "Captain. Sir. I . . ." She forced herself to look up at him—past the symbol on his chest, his broad-set shoulders, the cape flowing down his back. Past his calm face, his perfect features. Into his glistening green eyes. "When was the last time you saw your family?"

In the space of an instant, the smile fell from Dawn's face—replaced by blank shock, recoil and . . . fear? "What did you say?" he mouthed, his voice deathly quiet, the words a world away—drawing in, drawing back, his breath tightly held, trapped. But Jane barely saw it, barely heard it.

"Your family," she gushed, the truth tumbling out, the levy broken. "Your friends, your old schoolmates, the people from your hometown, anyone you grew up with? When was the last time you saw them, sir, saw anyone, anybody from your past, I'm sorry, I'm sorry, it's just . . ."

Her voice trailed off, her chest heaving, her hands shaking. She forced herself to look up at him again, forced herself to keep going.

"Sir," stammered Jane. "I know. We found out. I didn't mean to pry, but it just happened. I, we know, we found out that your . . . that you

. . ." She trailed off, unable to find the words. Finally, feebly, she forced herself to say it. "That everyone you grew up with is dead."

The words were a whisper, barely audible above the dull din below. Yet still, the moment they touched the air, something in that corridor changed. Captain Dawn froze. His eyes widened, his expression blank, shocked disbelief.

"What?" he whispered.

The elevator's hum came to a halt. The doors opened, and Matt found himself gazing down a long, sterile corridor. The white plaster walls were punctuated by metal doors facing off on either side, the floor rubber and the color of off caramel. Two floors underground, the only light came from fluorescent tubes running along the center of the plaster ceiling. Fifty feet along, the hall split into a T, branching off identically left and right. Halfway down, there was another security door of metal bars and another guard.

"It's all right, Caleb, he's with me," Matt's escort assured as his colleague got to his feet, throwing a questioning glance at Matt. "He's here to see Mentok."

"Vicki?" the guard named Caleb snorted. He sat back down and reopened his copy of *USA Today*, all interest lost. "Have fun. Should be a riveting conversation." He chuckled to himself and buzzed the gate open, waving the two of them through. Matt followed closely behind Angus.

As they made their way through the hall, Matt discreetly glanced through the small windows built into each of the metal doors, into the well-lit rooms of white and fiberglass beyond—some small, some larger, all clinical and clean. Through one on his left, there was a single bed and a man with a clipboard, a half-drawn curtain and a thin, dark-eyed woman in a wheelchair. To his right, they passed a larger room with more doctors doing (what at least looked like) normal doctor things—taking blood, glancing at charts, talking to patients, while in the middle of it all stood a broad-chested, bored-faced guard, his arms crossed, one booted foot resting against the wall. As far as he could see, nobody was behaving unusually. None of them shook when they moved, save for the odd frail patient, and none bled from their eyes. Nobody even spared him a second glance—too caught up in their duties, too busy with their work.

The knot of fear and trepidation that had been twisting around Matt's stomach began to loosen—but every inch it gave filled up with confusion and concern. Was he wrong? This place seemed . . . well, it was hard to use the word *normal*, since it was an underground prison hospital, but definitely . . . benign? He'd been afraid he was walking into some hellish pit, a nightmare of trapped souls and broken minds . . . but if anything, Nightingale was quiet. Empty. Two-thirds of the rooms he passed had no one in them—just neat, ready-made beds and unused racks of monitors.

They took a right at the hallway's end. "This is it," Angus informed him. The guard indicated to a spot ten feet further along where for the first time the uniform plaster wall ended, replaced by a sixteen-foot-wide, ceiling-to-floor plexiglass window—clear as crystal and providing a perfect, unbroken view of the lone bed inside and the man in it.

His eyes closed, motionless beneath hospital sheets, barely recognizable.

Viktor Mentok.

Or what was left of him.

He was sick: that was Matt's first impression. Sick, old, and frail. Gone was the Mentok whose picture he'd seen online, the hawkish, cold-eyed Russian who'd stared down the world at his trial, all leather skin and wiry muscle; replaced by a husk, a worn, shriveled skeleton with eyes sunken beneath wrinkled eyelids and arms almost thinner than the drips and wires stuck into them. In his mind, Matt had pictured Mentok as unchanged, unrepentant, a murderer—standing hands behind his back or strapped to a wall, staring out at him with cruel, dead eyes. But the evil he'd expected, maybe even hoped for, was nowhere to be seen. There was only an old man.

Gone was the fierce intellectual energy, gone was the superiority, the defiance. Matt watched, feeling a mixture of pity and despair as the old man's frail chest rose and fell. The machines around him beeped, wires running to his arms, chest, and head, their lines of heart and mind flowing in a steady, static rhythm. God, Jane had been right. How could this be their killer? No one, no matter how vengeful, would choose this existence. No one would spend their life like this, wasting away in a bed, if they could be something more.

"Can I . . ." The request was only half-hearted. "Can I go in?"

Angus shook his head. "Sorry. Staff only. You understand."

"I understand," said Matt. He sighed heavily and dropped down onto a bench propped up against the wall directly opposite Mentok's room. A viewing seat to look through the glass like this poor, pitiful person was an exhibit in a zoo.

"You mind giving me a moment?" he asked, glancing up at the guard. "Just to . . . to check things over." Because what was the rush. He may as well wait awhile. He had come this far.

His escort shrugged. "Suit yourself," said Angus. "You know the way out. Just don't touch the glass."

"Alarmed?" Matt mused.

"No," replied Angus, "because then I'll have to clean it." He turned and walked back the way they'd come—leaving Matt alone, leaning his elbows on his knees, staring in silence at the old man in the hospital bed who the world had once called supervillain.

The minutes ticked by.

What am I doing, Matt wondered. He rubbed his eyes—feeling the culmination of months of late nights and bleary hours rushing up to greet him all at once. This was stupid. This was pointless. He was wrong, again. There was nothing funny going on here, no secret conspiracy, no evil lair. Just an old sick Russian in a hospital gown, kept alive by machines.

Matt shook his head, the sound of his sigh the loudest thing in the long, empty hallway. He'd been so sure. It'd made so much sense. Viktor Mentok, the Mindtaker, genius supervillain—like something out of a cartoon. It tied together so many threads, made such a nice picture from the pieces. But seeing this man, this sad, frail man, laying in a sterile room, forever forgotten and unloved, all dreams of glory and legacy faded . . . well, it made Matt realize the world was rarely so black and white. Even now, knowing everything he'd done, suspecting him of doing so much more, Matt couldn't help but feel a deep pang tugging at his heart.

Sympathy for the devil. A sure sign of a sentimental fool.

He sighed again, leaning his head back on his hands and staring up at the ceiling, wondering what the heck he was supposed to do now.

The machines beeped their steady rhythm. The prisoner's chest rose and fell. The drip of his feed, the tube running into his weathered arm, wizened by age. All of it a pulse, a pattern, a ticking metronome, easy to count, easy to follow. The child saw the instant between the beeps, saw the moment when the human looked up and away, his eyes wandering from the room. Timing was everything. The boy stepped through, silent and unseen.

His hand unlocked the door. And then he stepped back, away, and was gone.

Click.

Matt glanced down, his brow furrowed. He could've sworn he'd heard a—

And then he saw it. The smallest gap, a fraction of an inch.

The door to Mentok's cell was open.

"Hello?" he called. He swung his head, glancing either direction down the deserted hallway. There was nobody there. Matt's heart skipped a beat. His eyes moved back to the door.

"Hello?" he called again. Still no answer. He glanced up and around, looking for a sign, a security camera. Maybe the other guard on the front desk had disagreed with Angus, unlocked the latch remotely. Maybe this was them being cooperative.

Yeah, Matt tried to convince himself, his heart starting to race, maybe that was it.

"Hello . . . ?" he tried a third time. But the silent halls gave no answer.

Okay, he whispered to himself. He pushed off the bench, glancing around the bright fluorescent corridors. *Okay*. The door, a thin frame of the same thick glass as the window, hung still, silent, decisively unlatched. It had definitely been locked. He definitely hadn't opened it. Maybe one of the staff . . .

Slowly, as if in a dream and against his better judgment, Matt slowly tiptoed forward. His hand clasping gingerly around the latch, and he pulled the door gradually open, shoulders tensed, poised to panic at a sudden eruption of blaring alarms.

Nothing. Matt glanced around, straightening up. No alarms, no sirens, no release of hounds. He turned to inspect the open room, wary of anything previously unseen, any signs of impending doom or sudden revelation that it was Mentok himself who'd let him in, spider to fly. But there was nothing. Apart from a slight musty old-man smell, the soft sounds of the life support, and the Mindtaker's shallow breathing, everything in here was exactly the same as it had seemed from the other side of two inches of plexiglass. Matt stood, frozen a step through the doorway, staring at the comatose genius.

"Hi," he half-called, half-whispered. No response. "Did you . . . um . . . the door?"

The body didn't move or otherwise give any indication that it had heard him or done anything except lay perfectly still and drink food through a tube for ten years. Matt took a further step forward, head turned skeptically to the side.

"I'm not here to hurt you," he assured the silent Mentok, uncertain if he needed to give that kind of assurance. No answer. "I just, ah . . . have a few questions. I just want to talk."

Funnily enough, the man who'd been in a coma for over a decade didn't say much to that either. Matt straightened up, starting to feel slightly stupid.

"Are you awake?" he asked bluntly. Then when the sleeping figure again gave no response, he rubbed the back of his head. "Well, I mean, of course you're not going to . . . Duh. Sorry."

He paused, gazing down at the sad, lifeless body underneath the white linen sheet. A second passed, then ten. Then thirty. Nothing moved.

Finally, Matt sighed, rubbing his eyes. He slumped down into the one plastic armed, fabric-cushioned hospital chair, which was sitting alone and unremarkable by the supervillain's bedside.

What am I doing? he muttered to himself. He glanced over at the silent figure of Mentok, motionless save for the ragged rise and fall of his thin chest beneath the hospital gown. "Yeah, go ahead, laugh it up. Like you're so smart."

He leaned down, placing his head in his hands. His fingers were cold against his forehead, numbed by the omnipresent air-conditioning.

"I don't know what I'm doing," he admitted out loud to no one in particular. "I don't know what's going on. Am I going insane? Is that what all this is?"

"Seeing phantom children. Almost getting blown up. God." Matt sighed, leaning back against the wall. "I don't know any more man. My friend Ed see," he said, not knowing why he was explaining. Maybe it was the captive audience. Maybe he just liked having someone who couldn't judge. "My friend Ed—you'd like him, he's a genius too. We were at Morningstar together. You know Morningstar, the Legion of Heroes." He glanced at Mentok, then waved a dismissive hand. "Sure you do. Anyway he"—Matt took a short breath—"well, a few months back, he jumped off a roof. And see, everyone just assumed he killed himself, but me, well, I . . . I guess I . . ."

Again, he sighed and shook his head. "I guess I just couldn't accept that. And then, well, everything's just snowballed from there. Because if he didn't kill himself, then someone must've killed him, and there must be some reason, and so on and so forth . . ."

Matt paused. "And now, here I am, two stories underground, talking to a vegetable, not sure if I've made it halfway down the rabbit hole, or dug a pit and called it a burrow. Suppose either way, I'm in deep."

He glanced at the silent, shut-eyed supervillain. "Right, yeah, sorry, like you care. The famous Mindtaker, evil genius. Sure, you've got better things to do than listen to me." The air hissed between Matt's teeth, and his head dropped into his hands. "I don't know, man. I don't know what I expected to find here. I don't know if I'm chasing ghosts or dead ends, drawing patterns out of stars. Because you're right you know, Jane's right, Wally's right, it could all just be a coincidence, all just a truckload of nothing. People die all the time—they just do. Lives end without meaning, without justice, without resolution. People kill themselves. People talk crazy. People see things. Maybe that's the deep dark truth I've been fighting so hard to avoid this whole time. I want there to be a conspiracy, because then there's someone to fight. Then there's someone to blame." He leaned back and sighed, holding the back of his head, a dry stinging in his eyes. "Then my friend didn't kill himself over something as stupid as a girl."

Matt slumped forward again, resting his cheek on his wrists. He gazed over at Mentok, laying still and silent beneath white sheets, on a shifting bed of semi-solid, shining, aquamarine gel—an invention of his own design, Matt had read this morning, designed to prevent bedsores. Used by hospitals worldwide.

"I don't know," he muttered. "My friend doesn't think you're evil. Seeing you like this, it's hard to argue. Maybe you are just misunderstood. Maybe I'm just crazy. Clutching. Desperate for excuses. A part of me wonders if I'm doing all this to impress a girl." He gazed up at the roof. "Sure, you know what that's like."

He paused for a moment. Ed had known. Ed had—

No. The cold, oily melancholy inside him ignited with frustration, and Matt leaned forward, squinting hard at the crystal window, fists clenched together, teeth gritted, fiercely shaking his head.

"Except I'm not," he insisted, fervently. "I swear to God I'm not seeing things. I'm not making this up. Everyone Captain Dawn ever knew is dead, that's the truth, that's a"—he swore—"fact, and putting aside Ed, photos, children, psychics, and Albania, that's not . . . that can't just be nothing. It can't."

He shook his head, his mouth set into a hard line. "Something's going on, I swear it. Whether I'm a mile off on the reason, it just . . ." Matt stared at the lifeless Mentok and slowly shook his head. "I don't know. It was all because of this party, see—"

"A reunion," Jane explained, her voice trembling at the look on Dawn's face—the blankness, the mask, devoid of emotion, that could be hiding fury. That could be hiding despair. "This, this, surprise party, the Academy wanted to throw one for you. So, we were looking into it and by accident we found . . . Captain, we found . . ."

She paused, struggling to keep her voice level. Get it out. Keep going. "Deaths."

"Hundreds of deaths," Matt explained. "Hundreds. From, from a dozen, a hundred different causes. If I hadn't researched it myself, I'd have said it was impossible. There's no pattern. I don't understand, it doesn't make sense, but I thought—"

"Matt thought it was Viktor Mentok," Jane stammered, her hands shaking. Captain Dawn still standing there, frozen in place. "I thought he was wrong, but he's the only one from your past still alive and he thought . . . well, he's gone to check, just in case, though I don't see how . . ."

"I don't see how it could be you," Matt mumbled. He shook his head. "I mean, yeah you worked on mind control, and Ed was looking into your designs, but it's just . . . Jane's right. Seeing you here, like this . . . you couldn't have done it. Not this," he said. "Not a decade of systematic

SUPERWORLD — BOOK 2 223

killings. I thought I'd figured it out, thought it made sense." He paused. "I guess I was wrong."

Jane's voice trailed off. "But it doesn't matter," she said firmly, resolutely shaking her head. "Because even if it's not him, it's something, someone trying to hurt you, or blackmail you, or *something*." She looked up at Dawn, pleading. "And we've got to do something, so we have and I'm so sorry, but we didn't have a choice, it's already done, Matt's already—"

"So, we've gone public," Matt murmured. He stared at the still, sleeping figure. "Or at least I've gone public. Emailed every news station, newspaper, and website I could think of." He paused, pursing his fingers on his lips. "Figured about the stupidest thing you could do if you know the truth about a conspiracy is to keep it to yourself. So now . . . I guess now we see what happens. Now the whole world starts trying to figure it out. A whole lot more people smarter than me start investigating."

"Now, one way or another," said Jane. "We'll get some answers."

She looked up at Captain Dawn—at his wide-eyed, frozen face—silently begging, pleading for him to understand. The seconds passed like hours as they stood there—so close, yet, separated by an endless divide.

And then slowly, slowly, Dawn looked down on her, his blank face split into open horror.

"What have you done?" he whispered.

"So that's about the gist of it," Matt said, sighing. He slouched into the hospital chair, leaning into the plastic armrest. It felt cathartic, saying all this aloud, even to a living corpse. "The bit I don't get is the ten years thing. I mean when I thought it was you, it made sense. Ten years of you in here, ten years of death out there, sort of fits, right? Right." He chewed his thumb. "And the other thing I don't get is why. Why do this? I mean as far as I can see, you're the only one left with any real cause for revenge, and apparently, you're not even the vengeful type . . . So why bother? Why kill so many people connected to one man?"

He glanced at the coma patient. "Don't suppose you've got any genius ideas?"

The only response was a beep from the brain-wave monitor.

"Figures," said Matt. He rose to leave. "Well, thanks for listening. I should probably get out before a guard sees me in here and thinks I'm trying to spring you, gets overzealous with a taser." He paused, giving the silent figure one last look. "Anything you want me to tell the Legion?"

It was, of course, a rhetorical question. Matt turned on his heels toward the door—but as he did, the brain-wave monitor let out another, sharper beep.

And then another. And then another.

Slowly, Matt turned, his eyes widening, toward the screeching screen, back toward the bed—

As, to Matt's shock, amazement, and terror, Viktor Mentok began to stir—

As his eyes flicked open, and his cracked lips drew apart—

As he whispered—

"Help."

"What have you done?" Dawn whispered again. He stood staring at her, stock-still, his teeth clenched, his hands balled into fists. Jane flinched at the anger in his voice. The anger and fear.

"Sir, I didn't, I'm sorry, I—"

"Who knows?" he muttered, cutting her down with a word. "How many, who are they?"

"I-I-I . . ." Jane stammered, "I don't know. Lots, I think, Matt sent the message to everyone we could think of, journalists, newspapers . . ." Her voice trailed off into a whimper as the captain's shoulders began to shake. For a moment—for a wonderful, terrible moment—she thought he was about to cry.

"Sir, I -I-I was just trying to help, I, I care about you, I -I-I love you." Jane gasped, caught her breath, tried to take the words back as soon as she said them. She gazed up at the hero with trembling eyes.

But Dawn wasn't looking at her.

"I know you do, Jane," he murmured, distracted. His eyes burned into the empty space in front of him. "I know you do." He strode ten paces away from her, golden cape shimmering behind him. Then he stopped and breathed deep, drawing himself up as if he'd made a decision. "Fine," he whispered.

And before Jane could think, his hands sparked blue—and in an instant, a pulse of electric energy exploded from his body, rushing through Jane, the walls, the floors—

And suddenly, they were engulfed in blackness. Suddenly, Morningstar was dark.

Electromagnetic pulse, a little voice said, in the back of Jane's sluggish, reeling mind.

Then faster than a blur, Dawn hit her.

Jane didn't have time to move, time to breathe, time to flinch. Faster than a heartbeat, faster than should have been possible, he flew across the hall, slamming into her, fist driving into her gut. She gasped, gulped, crumbled, feeling her ribs crack, the world blinking bursting specs of darkness, shuddering before her eyes. She tried to cry out, tried to scream, but her air was gone, and there was a hand around her neck, a gloved hand, holding her as the floor spun, as the room swirled around her, swallowed and collapsing in smothering black—

And then there was light.

She fell to the ground, knees catching, heavy in the dirt—dropped spluttering, wheezing, chest screaming, gasping for air, the strong iron bands released from around her throat. Her vision wavered. She tried to look up, tried to see . . . where . . . how . . . she couldn't understand . . .

And there, his shadow falling over her, his face shrouded in darkness, golden cape shining in the open sunlight, rippling in the desert breeze . . . there stood Dawn.

"I'm sorry I had to hurt you, Jane," he said quietly. "I didn't want it to happen like this."

She struggled, pushing herself to rise, hands pressed into the dirt, blood seeping through her teeth. But Captain Dawn merely stepped over her, away from her, a single golden movement.

"Stay away," he told her, gazing out at the horizon, far and away.

And in a rush of sound and sulfur, he vanished.

"JESUS TAP-DANCING CHRIST!" yelped Matt. He stumbled back, his hands scrambling for the door handle, heart hammering a million miles an hour as he—

"Please."

The word, barely a whisper. Halfway out the door, Matt froze. Against his better judgment, against the skittering nova of panic in his chest that was screaming at him to get out, to flee, he turned around. Mentok was staring at him, his body shaking, his wrinkled head lolled uselessly to one side—but his bloodshot, bleary eyes were focused. Unwavering. Burning into Matt.

"Please," he croaked, voice cracking, the word gurgling in his throat.

Matt knew he should run, knew he was in danger, knew he had to get out of there, as fast as he could, get the guards, get help. But he couldn't. Something about the old man's whimper—the desperate pleading in his voice. Something held him.

The old man shuddered. His frail chest heaved, his throat struggling to push sound through a mouth that hadn't spoken in ten years.

"Dawn," he murmured, and the hair on the back of Matt's neck stood on end.

"What did you say?" Matt whispered.

"Dawn," Mentok repeated, his voice quavering, hoarse. His dry tongue dabbed like sandpaper over cracked lips. Every word was painful, the effort shaking his frail frame—but his eyes still burned. "Help."

"Help?" echoed Matt. The brain-wave machine was beeping wildly and somewhere vaguely in the distance he knew any second there'd be alarms, shouting—but he couldn't turn away. "Help Dawn, that's what you're saying? Help Captain Dawn? Get help, get Captain Dawn? I can do that, I can be right back, give me two seconds, I—"

"No," the old man croaked, and there was urgency in his gasping, his ragged, rattling breath. "Not . . . Dawn . . ."

"Not Dawn," Matt stammered, trying to think fast, struggling to understand. "Not Captain Dawn, don't get Captain Dawn to help? Why not, what's going on, I don't understand what . . ."

"Dead," gasped the genius.

"Dead? Who's dead? Dawn's family? The Legion? You? Is someone going to die? Tell me who!" Matt took a step closer without even realizing, away from the door, his body electrified, hanging on to every word.

Mentok shuddered. His eyes rolled back in his head and his eyelids fluttered. Then slowly, with incredible effort, he forced them open. "Dawn," he whispered finally. "Dawn."

"Dawn? Captain Dawn's dead? Or . . . or he's dying?" Matt shook his head, desperate, trying to understand. "No, you're wrong, you're confused," he explained. "He's fine, he's alive, I've seen him, Dawn's alive—"

But the rasping sound of Mentok's voice struck him silent. "No . . ." he uttered, and his eyes burned into Matt's. There was fever in them— but not madness. A pit of icy dread opened up in Matt's stomach.

"What do you mean?" he whispered.

"Dawn . . . died . . ." rasped Mentok, his eyes bulging, a lone, weak vein pulsing in his temple. "Africa . . . lost . . ."

"You're insane," cried Matt. "If Dawn died in Africa, then who's at the Academy?! Who's walking around wearing Captain Dawn's uniform and . . ."

His voice trailed off. It hit him. It suddenly, finally hit him.

"Oh God," he whispered.

Mentok stared at Matt, breathing hard and ragged—every word shaking with certainty, with truth—

"That's . . . not . . . Dawn . . ."

YERSINIA LAZARUS

"And lo, I hang my head in shame; for if this morning, God looked upon the world and asked, 'Hast Satan wrought this calamity?', would must I answer, 'No. It was but a man.'"

—Bishop Desmond Tutu, October 10, 1990.

He dropped from the sky and stepped into the building without ceremony or fanfare. The glass doors parted for him as they would any other, no louder than the soft swish of his cape or the padding of his golden boots on the fresh-cleaned carpet. Yet the instant he entered, all other noise ceased—as if his towering figure, striding forward without a second's hesitation or a sideward glance, had absorbed it all.

One guard snapped to attention so fast he pulled a muscle saluting. The other could only stand there, slack-jawed, speechless, his mouth hanging open. The tall, shining figure took notice of neither—his face hard, his eyes forward. He reached the security gate and stopped.

"One of my students," he demanded. "The clairvoyant. Where is he?"

The gaping guard's mouth worked silently, unable to form a reply. His rigid companion was faster.

"Downstairs, sir!" he yelped. His eyes flickered out of their disciplined lock, stealing a frenetic glance at the man's face. "Should I escort you?"

"Open the gate," the caped figure said quietly.

A thin drop of sweat beaded down the guard's forehead, though the air inside was cold.

"Yes, sir. Of course, sir. Just give me a moment to perform the routine security checks, and I'll—"

The man they called Captain Dawn's lip curled.

"Help me."

Mentok's voice quavered as he struggled to rise, and before he could even think about it Matt was at his side, sweeping away the wires, patches, and blankets that hung like lead weights against the old man's body. He wrapped an arm around Mentok's frail, wheezing chest and pulled him upright.

"How long have you known?" he asked. Mentok didn't reply. Breathless, he hung his head, panting, his free hand feebly swiping at the cannula drip still stuck in his left arm. Matt only hesitated for a second, then leaned over and drew the needle from Mentok's vein. The old man moaned.

"Sorry," said Matt, but the genius just shook his head, sucking air through his teeth. He clutched the wounded arm to his side and crooked the other behind Matt's neck.

"Always . . ." he croaked, "knew." Matt pulled him from the bed to his feet, which dangled uselessly against the floor. "All wrong. TV, jail. Moment I saw."

He tried to stand, to take his own weight, but his shaking knees buckled beneath the hospital gown. Matt caught him, holding them both upright, his teeth bared. Even reduced to skin and bones, Mentok wasn't light.

"Two fight. One emerges. Process of elimination. Heydrich, abilities. Shapeshifter."

"Why didn't you tell anyone?" grunted Matt, struggling with each step, the old man dead weight—like carrying a corpse.

"Would have . . . forced hand. Killed me. Everyone. Out in the open," replied Mentok. He drew a long, ragged breath. "Needed . . . find a way . . . stop him. More . . . time."

"So you faked a coma? Scarlett syndrome?"

Mentok shook his ragged head. "No. Real. Scarlett's . . . misunderstood. Thoughts . . . move too fast, but . . . I . . . had to . . . learned to . . . focus . . ."

Underneath his arm, Matt felt the old man stiffen and straighten. Among the fear and the fever, the worn skin and sunken cheeks, a hint of pride glinted in the Russian's eyes.

"I am master of my mind," he said quietly.

They were only halfway across the room.

"So, what's the plan?" Matt asked, his heart racing in his chest. "Get you out of here, then what, what do we do, how do we stop him?!"

There was a pause—a dreadful, horrible pause. Matt stared wide-eyed at Mentok's ashen face.

"I don't know," he mumbled.

For a moment, Matt's heart stopped beating. "What do you mean you don't know?" He felt his voice growing high, panicked. "You're a genius, you're *the* genius, you've had ten years, you—"

"Too strong," Mentok said softly. They'd stopped moving, Matt standing, watching, horrified, while the old man gazed forward, his eyes blank, staring into nothing. It was the clearest Matt had ever heard him speak. "No way. Can't stop him."

The words hung in the air—in the stillness, in the silence. The room felt suddenly small, Matt's head suddenly light.

"Okay," he murmured. Then louder, "Okay. We just need time. You need . . . you need time." He moved toward the doorway, striding into a loping run, pulling them forward, pulling them both forward. "Clear your head, get you better, let you . . . there's still time, we just need to get you out of here, give you time to think, time to figure out a way to—"

A distant boom rippled through the complex. All around them, the lights flickered. Slowly, Mentok looked upward as a line of dust breathed from the ceiling.

"Too late," he whispered.

Will heard it.

A far-off rumble, like an earthquake, coming from the inside of the building. He stopped in his tracks among the dust and scrub, fifty feet from the fence, a hundred feet from the west tower—staring at the building. Suddenly, there was shouting, movement, the wailing of sirens. Will swore under his breath. He didn't know what the hell was going on.

But he knew Matt was in there.

"Run," croaked the Mindtaker. In the lifeless room, the lights flickering in the ceiling, Matt looked down at the sallow, twisted body he was carrying, and the blank, curious expression on the old man's face.

"But—"

"Go," Mentok uttered, gasping for breath. He retracted his arm from around Matt's shoulders, sagging, half-falling to the ground.

"I won't—"

"No time," the old man groaned. "Warn the world. Warn the Legion. Find a way."

Again, the walls trembled. The lights failed and outside the halls fell to black. For a moment, all was darkness—but then from the gloom came a glow. Emergency lighting, swimming like ghostly fireflies in the black. The last remnants of the dying light.

A tightness pressed around Matt's chest. He loosened his grip, and Mentok slid from his grasp onto the floor. The sound of the Russian's shallow, labored breathing heaved out into the dark.

"Run," he hissed.

But before Matt could move, there came the screaming.

Horrible, blood-curdling screaming. The sound an animal makes when it's dying. Coming from above them, from the elevators, the end of the hall. From the guards, from grown men.

And an instant later, there was nothing.

Matt's hands began to shake.

"Not that way," murmured Mentok. "Not that way."

"Where?" trembled Matt.

"Other way. Fire escape. Electric. Unlocked. Go."

"If I leave, you die."

"Yes," Mentok said quietly, staring into the coming dark. "But you live. Run."

And so, with only a single glance of wordless thanks behind him, Matt ran.

The old man lay facedown on the cold floor—breathing, listening, dying. A million thoughts shouted in his head for supremacy, endless chains spiraling into eternity. They clashed and pulled at him, dragging him down, apart from the world, away from the real. They spoke fast—but the man listened slow.

There was a resounding crash, the sound of metal rending, tearing in two. Shouting, then banging, then screaming, then silence. Viktor Mentok listened and knew.

His legs were too weak to walk. His arms were too weak to crawl. Death was coming for him as surely as it had come for those it had just taken, those who had guarded, pitied, maybe even cared for him. He could not save them. He could not save himself.

But he could save the boy.

One last secret. A tiny neural implant drilled into the back of his neck, hidden beneath a layer of false skin. His eyes rolled back and his shaking fingers fumbled, but they found it and it came alive at his touch. Flashing green and red and calling for him to sing. Sing with it, call out, speak into the darkness.

Three words: Heart of Ash.

And from the walls, from the floors, from this room where he had spent ten long years, where he had hoarded a million moments of clarity—from this room, came his machines. Built in secret, built from scraps, from the gifts of a silent stranger. His creations, neither grand nor glorious, slamming roughly into him, his arms and legs, pieces piercing and drilling into place, a second skin, a second skeleton, as strong as his body was weak. Cabling around his chest, steel along his spine. He took one shuddering step forward and then another, armor sliding into place. Bleeding. Agonized.

Alive.

For the first time in ten years, Viktor Mentok rose, tall and alone— hero and villain, machine and man. He walked from that room, his withered head held high, iron gauntlets around his arms, steel pistons beneath his feet, once more a titan, the eagle upon his chest. From the walls more pieces flew, his armor growing, crude weapons forming around his hands—hands he raised defiant at the figure of Death that turned around the corner, untarnished, unbeatable, shining in the dark. Wearing the face of his fallen friend.

Come, Siegfried. Let us show them who we are.

"*Dlya moyey sem'i,*" he whispered to Death, and he knew Death understood.

BAM!

Matt shoulder-barged through the fire door and into the stairwell, a tight concrete spiral straight up. He ran, chest heaving as behind him came the sound of crashing, tearing, metal rending metal. Suddenly, there was a deep, resounding boom, and Matt's hand gripped white-knuckled around the railing as the entire staircase shuddered.

Don't look back. Keep going.

He flew up the steps two at a time, breathing in starts, heart hammering—one floor, two. The sounds were getting louder. A crackling, something like gunfire, then worse—silence. Matt blocked it out, had to block it out, keep running. He reached the top of the stairs, slammed open the door, and ran, sprinted out into the blinding daylight—

"MATT!" Three hundred yards away, beyond the fence, a man, a friend, a familiar voice—running toward him, shouting, waving—

"WILL!" But in an instant, behind him, two floors down, the fire door exploded off its hinges, and Matt looked back, horrified, awestruck, as something flew up toward him, not around the concrete but through it, an unstoppable force, a blur of white and gold and—

There was a bang—a rush of sulfur—and suddenly, a hand had grabbed Matt by his arm, and he was hurtling through the blackness, through the tunnel of nothing, through the howling abyss toward—

Bam! Countryside. Green fields and cows and him and Will, tumbling through smoke, the teleporter's face clenched and grip tight, the world roaring around them, pressure in his ears, as a second later—

Bam! Snowfields. The top of a mountain. Gray-black clouds and chilling, biting cold crashing over Matt's exposed skin, squeezing the air from his lungs before he could even breathe, stand, before he could gather his bearings, work out where they—

Bam! A beach somewhere. Matt's shoes caught on sand and he staggered, stumbling, catching glimpses through blurred vision of palm trees, sky, the endless ocean and Will, his eyes wide, his hand still locked in a vise-like grip around Matt, gasping, sweating, but once more scrunching up his face to—

Bam! A desert. A different desert, not tan scrub like the plains around ADX Florence but hard, dry dirt, red and brown rocks and towering stone formations. The grip around Matt's arm faltered, and Will fell to his knees, pale and panting, his arms shaking, struggling to breathe as Matt staggered forward, his hands outstretched, fumbling against a stone wall for support.

"Is he behind us?" he cried. He turned around to face the teleporter, coughing and wheezing in the dirt. "Will, is he coming?"

"I don't know," Will panted. "I don't think so, I think, I—" His eyelids fluttered and he heaved, doubled over, clutching his stomach. For a second, Matt thought he was going to hurl—but after a moment, the teleporter uncurled and looked up at Matt with terrified eyes, his teeth clenched and chattering. "Matt," he whispered, "it was following us."

"I know," Matt mumbled. He stepped forward, numb, his mind still reeling, head spinning, his legs feeling like they would give way at any moment. He gazed down at Will who was staring up at him with a slow-dawning horror matching his own.

"Matt," he cried, "it was following us!"

"I know, Will, I know!"

Will pushed up, staggering to his feet, reeling, his eyes wild. "Only a teleporter can tunnel through jumps," he muttered, still clutching his chest, still fighting for breath. "Only a good one, only . . . but that wasn't . . . it couldn't . . ." His head snapped up, his face terrified. "Matt, what was that?!"

"Will, it's Heydrich."

The teleporter fell silent—abruptly silent, as if Matt had hit him in the face. "No," he breathed. Matt nodded.

"The Black Death's alive."

Will mouthed some shaken reply but the desert wind turned the words to whispers. They stood there, among the sand and stone—the sun beating down on them, together and alone. Matt stared into nothing, a tight pain around his chest.

The teleporter spoke.

"Okay," he muttered, and the way his voice shook made Matt wonder who he was trying to convince. "It'll be okay. We can go back to Morningstar. We can get Dawn. We can—"

"Will," Matt said bluntly, cutting him off, "Dawn is dead."

This time, Will let out an actual, physical moan.

Matt pressed on. "He killed him," he said. "The Black Death, he killed him, back in Africa, he . . . he killed him, and . . . and took his place, and nobody . . . nobody realized he . . ."

There was silence. A moment's terrible silence as the truth of Matt's words—the implication of what he was saying—sunk in.

"He's going to take over the world."

"He's been killing the real Dawn's family."

"Nothing can stop him."

"I told everyone. They're going to figure it out."

"The Academy, rebuilding the Legion, it's all a lie."

"There's no more reason for him to hide."

"He's got every power imaginable."

"There's nowhere we can go. Nowhere he can't find."

"Jesus," whispered Will. He cupped his head in his hands. "Jesus, Jesus, Jesus, Christ. What the hell are we going to do?"

Matt drew a long, shaky breath, staring at the dirt, the cracks and pebbles, the rocks on the ground.

And then—in tinkling, generic tones—a phone rang.

Matt glanced over at Will. Will glanced back at Matt. They both glanced down at Will's pants, at the vibrating, buzzing, glowing cell phone in his front pocket. Will gingerly pulled it out. His dark brow furrowed.

"It says it's you," he said stupidly, holding up the screen for Matt to see, confused. Matt shrugged.

Then at the same moment, they both clicked.

"Jane!" Will shouted, his fingers scrabbling to answer, the phone flying up to his ear, as through the receiver came Jane's frantic, panicked voice. "Jane!" he called. "Where are you? We're in trouble, Dawn's . . . what? Hold on, slow down, you're not making any—"

Suddenly, Matt's mind woke up. Suddenly, the world became clear. "Get her," Matt commanded, pointing his finger. "Get her now, get the Legion, get . . . get anyone! Go! Now!"

Will hesitated, lowering the phone a fraction, Jane's words still bubbling through. "What about you?"

"Who cares about me!" Matt roared. "Leave me here, I'm useless, I'm just a . . ." Then suddenly, he stopped. The words faded on his tongue—as a terrible, shining thought captured his mind.

Matt breathed the final word. "Clairvoyant."

His head snapped up, his heart racing. He understood.

"It's me," he said, the words racing from his mouth before he even knew what he was saying, the truth erupting as it dawned. "It's all me." Will started to speak, but Matt cut him off, driving over his protests. "Heydrich," he told him. "He's after me, that's why he attacked Nightingale, that's why he chased us. He wants my power. He wants my blood . . ."

He trailed off, then laughed, mirthlessly, shaking his head without a single shred of humor. "The power to see the future. The ultimate protection. One more power and he's safe forever." His voice dropped to a whisper. "One more power and he's invincible."

He spun to face Will, standing there, stunned, his mouth hanging open. "Go," he commanded. "Leave me here. Get Jane, get the Legion, get anyone, get . . . he'll come for me. Before he comes for the world. I know it. I'll buy you some time."

Will opened his mouth to argue.

"GO!" Matt roared, causing the teleporter to flinch. For a moment, the two of them locked eyes. Then with a small, curt movement, Will nodded, eyes swimming with pity, with fear, with wordless thanks.

"Wait." Matt reached into his pocket. He held out Jane's silver badge. "She'll want this," he said. Need it, maybe. He tossed the badge to Will, who caught it with a nod—then he raised the phone to his ear, spoke three words, and vanished into thin air.

Leaving Matt alone and waiting to be found by the greatest murderer in the history of the world.

He hated the suit.

So gaudy, so shiny. A circus outfit to dazzle the bleating crowds—no function, all form. What was the point of a cape? To get pulled on, to get trampled. A misused relic of a long-dead age—once, a blanket for a traveling warrior, now the hallmark of an adult's body lumbered with a child's mind. A child's morality. Good and evil. Black and white.

Pathetic.

The man who wore the face of Captain Dawn stood silently in his parlor, in the study of the fool he'd killed—inspecting himself, turning his broad body slowly in front of three long, adjacent mirrors. The symbol, the insignia on the chest—that was the one part he liked. Klaus Heydrich knew the value of symbols, their effect on lesser minds. The breaking day—new beginnings, a reprieve from the dreaded, primal darkness. He was almost tempted to co-opt it as his own. But there was no need for that.

Slowly, his face changed. His cheeks narrowed, his hair drew back. His eyes returned to their natural brown—their sockets shrunk, ever so slightly. His mouth spread out into a hard, firm line, his skin almost unnaturally smooth. His chin and neck were hairless, and finally devoid of the ridiculous jut that was so prominent on Captain Dawn. A smaller body, a proper body, with a young man's face—a strong man's face. A face he'd only allowed himself to view for sixty fleeting seconds, once a day, for ten long years, while he waited, while he searched. A single, sweet taste of the truth.

And now, once more, that truth could be reality.

He held out his palms and the long-dead captain's rags undid themselves from his body. They fell to the floor, discarded, forgotten—as from the depths of his sanctuary, from within a wooden panel sealed and hidden in a forgotten wall, his true colors emerged. Black. The black of his father, of his people, of their strength, their pride—what had once been, what would be again. The black armor, the synthetic, silken fabric, covering neck to ankle, flowed over him first—then the uniform, the black-collared shirt, pants, and high boots of an officer. Then the coat. The long, flowing coat, gleaming and leather, the color of charcoal. The buckles on his boots, the straps around his chest, the buttons on his gloves, all laced, pulled, and pressed themselves—as he stood there, thrice reflected, marveling.

He was a symbol. Far from any crest, his sign was all that he was, his entire being, a living, breathing symbol of truth, of superiority, of indomitable legacy. He was as he had been, as his forefathers had been— unfaltering, unchanging, unapologetic. The irresistible pull to betterment. To perfection. To a united, stronger world.

Only the weak feared the dark. The strong ruled it.

There was nothing they could have known, nothing that could have told them they were about to die. This day was no different to any other, save for a strange power outage that minutes ago had knocked the electricity offline. But to the Acolytes, the optimistic young minds of Morningstar Academy, this posed more inconvenience than threat. The sun was shining; the sky was bright. Their needs were not so pressing to warrant panic, not after barely a quarter of an hour. So, they went about their business. Eating, laughing, talking about whatever pointless irrelevance momentarily captured their desires. Trusting. Oblivious. Unaware.

It was almost a shame, the man they called the Black Death mused. They all had such potential. But the inescapable truth was that the legacy they had brought into was a legacy opposed to his own, the latest growths on a slate that, now it could not be repurposed, needed wiping clean. It was not their fault, but the world was not fair. And a symbol created was equally as powerful as a symbol destroyed.

His boots made no noise as he stepped slowly down the stairs. His coat brushed no wall or carpet. Like a phantom in a theater, he walked down the solemn spiral staircase connecting the parlor to the hall, out the discreet exit, the unassuming doorway pressed back against the shadows of the stage. He surveyed the sea of shining faces before him. It was midday; the hall was packed. Two hundred "heroes," the last infection of the Legion—grinning, laughing, conversing as they fed. Not watching. Not aware.

It only took an instant.

Time seemed to stand still as the man in black took a single step forward, a lone foot over the threshold, a minute, invisible intrusion. He removed his glove and raised his left hand, held out his index finger, the tip wisping energy, beginning to glow. To pulse. A twisted, sickening, electric violet—raw atomic power, compressed and infused through flesh. The air sliced—and the Black Death smiled to himself. He closed his eyes—the wound already healing—and vanished.

Leaving behind only a glowing, pulsating shred of skin where his finger had been, falling slowly toward the floor.

The work of a moment.

Unseen by the Acolytes.

Save one.

Giselle Pixus. The girl who stared at nothing, but who today alone saw everything.

Her eyes widened.

Her face hardened.

And she ran.

Faster than a bullet, faster than a blur. She grabbed the nearest person and raced with them outside. Then back. Another girl, another boy, out, then back, another, another. Acolyte, Ashes, rival, friend. Faster than sight, faster than sound, the girl ran with the Legion on her back.

And the bomb kept falling. And the girl kept running.

Faster, faster. In the space between heartbeats, as her legs burned, her feet bled, and her muscles screamed under the weight of people twice her size, as one by one the hall cleared, as she pushed, harder than she'd ever pushed in her life, as the tiny scrap of glowing flesh fell, inches from the ground, still she kept running, up into the halls, through every room and corridor, carrying them out, carrying them all before—

The bomb exploded. A ball of white light, for a microsecond no bigger than a fingernail but then growing, erupting, consuming everything in its path—

And still the girl ran.

Up into the dormitories, the gymnasium, the labs, wherever people lay, up stairs, out windows, and back in again, around the swelling, burning ball, the growing explosion, until it was too big to go around, and so she went through. Through the fire and the flames, through heat and death, her skin blistering and her hair burning, still she ran, carrying, clutching, roaring a defiant soundless scream. Faster than thought. Faster than anyone.

Giselle Pixus ran. Leaving no one behind.

BOOOOOOOOOOOOOOOOOOOOOOMMMMMMMMM!

James tumbled through the grass, suddenly thrown, suddenly falling, suddenly stumbling with enough momentum to send him skipping like a stone through the dirt. He rolled, coughing, skidding to a stop, his thick fingers digging tracks through the wet earth. His head snapped up—his senses assaulted by a shock wave, a sudden blast of heat and sound hot enough to smell, close enough to feel reverberating through his ribs. He looked up, his eyes wide, at the flaming, billowing explosion. At the smoking ruins of Morningstar.

He yelled, a strangled, wordless yelp, half anger but whole confusion as all around him people stirred, staggering to their feet, thrown like he was thrown, a sudden, inexplicable crowd, hundreds of acolytes, gasping, winded, crying out. What was going on? How were they outside? They'd been in the foyer, he'd been walking, he'd been—

A cry—a mangled, whimpering sob. James looked to his left—and there, blackened, red, hairless, her skin dripping off, burned almost beyond recognition, was the body of a girl.

"Giselle," he whispered.

And then he roared.

"MEDIC!" He scrambled to his feet, racing to her, his feet tearing up the ground, sending chunks of dirt flying with each step. In that moment, he didn't care about anything else—not himself, not the explosion, not the Academy. Nothing mattered except she lived.

"MEDIC!"

The crowd was parting, someone was running toward them— a woman, he thought, one of the healers. He looked down at Giselle, red and charred, her breathing coming in stiff, shallow rasps, then up at the hill where flames flickered through the ruins of the place he'd called home—at the clouds of ash raining down upon them, the pillars of smoke billowing upward, blackening the sky. Hell on Earth.

A sudden *pop* twenty feet away and James looked up to see Will the teleporter and Jane the empath appearing from the ether.

"Oh my God . . ."

"What the hell happened?"

"WALLY!"

"Giselle?"

Will was off and running through the survivors, shouting the psychic's name. Jane pelted toward them, staggering to a halt three feet away from Giselle's corpse.

"Oh God," she whispered, a hand going to her mouth. She and James exchanged glances. And then a healer shouldered past and was on her knees in the grass beside Giselle, her hands flinching from the heat as she forced them onto the speedster's burning flesh. Giselle moaned.

"Here, sweetheart, come on, it's going to be all right," the small healer soothed. She looked up at James, her face hard. "She needs a hospital."

"Take her," James commanded. He didn't need to think. "Will!" He snapped his head around, through the chaos and the carnage, gritting his teeth. "Where the hell is that *goddamn teleporter?*"

"I'll find him," shouted Jane and she was off, sprinting through the crowd, who were pulling each other to their feet, shaking, crying, trying to account for lost friends, trying to understand what had happened, what was going on.

She was back in less than a minute, Will and Wally in tow. James had never seen the psychic's face so white.

"Giselle," he cried. "Oh no, please no, hang in there, baby, hold on—"

"Get her to a hospital!" James barked, climbing to his feet, his eyes wild. "Go, now!" Will nodded.

"I'll go too," said Wally, choking back tears. The three of them, him, Will and the healer, locked arms around Giselle's body. Will gave James one final, frightened look.

And then they were gone.

Leaving James and Jane behind, in the shrieking silence—the sky still black, Morningstar still burning. Phones were starting to ring; people were clustering around. Some looking at the empath with suspicion, a few even hostile, like this was somehow her fault—most just looking scared or blank. Shell-shocked.

He turned to Jane—her arms wrapped around her shoulders, her hands shaking. "What happened?" he demanded. "What the hell is going on?"

Matt wandered for ten minutes before finding the shack. At first, he thought the silver glint in the distance was a car, but that'd seemed strange for this far out in the middle of nowhere. He'd walked toward it anyway. He had nowhere to run, anyway—nowhere to hide.

But the moment the shack came into clear view, Matt knew this was the place.

It wasn't much more than a shed, if he was being honest. One room, corrugated iron roof and walls, a small shaded porch, solar panel on top, a reclining deck chair out front. Maybe a hiker's pit stop or a hunter's retreat. Either way, there was a small round table inside and a work-bench laden with a few tools, jugs, cloth, that sort of thing. There was even a small TV inside and—to Matt's amazement—a small running bar fridge, stocked and loaded. Matt helped himself to a cold beer—he didn't think the owner would mind, given the circumstances—and sat outside, stretched out on the deck chair with his hand pillowing his head. Waiting.

It didn't take long.

There was a *pop*, the familiar rush of air and sulfur—and a man in black, a man he'd only ever seen in history books, stepped out from nothing.

He was bigger in real life. Somehow the photos always managed to look down on him, but now, in flesh and bone, the reality of his presence was apparent. He wasn't big like Captain Dawn had been. Not overlarge, not forcefully muscular. But strong. Strong and hard, fast and lean. His hair was slicked back, his lips flat, his skin pale and oddly smooth. He looked almost like a fake man—a perfect imitation of a person who nevertheless still lacked some vital feature, some intangible piece of humanity. A flawless doll, unreal for how close it scraped to reality. Maybe it was his eyes. Small but piercing, dark to the point of being black. No picture he had ever seen, no news footage, had ever properly captured those eyes—the way they twisted, burning with fierce, vicious intelligence. Looking at you, staring through you, as if you weren't even there. The eyes of a creature that could destroy you, would destroy you, without an idle thought.

But Matt didn't allow himself to feel afraid. He didn't show any hint of surprise.

"You changed," he commented. He tilted the tip of the beer bottle toward the man's black uniform. "I guess capes aren't for everyone. Looks hot though. For a desert." He took a short, slow sip from the bottle, keeping his voice steady and his heart slow. He was choosing to be calm. Not to act calm—to be calm. Because right now, calm was what he needed to be.

The Black Death titled his head, ever so slightly, to one side.

"You're not going to run?" He smiled, a twitch of the mouth that showed no teeth.

"Pfft," Matt snorted. He dismissed the notion with a wave of his hand. "What would be the point? Where can I go you can't catch me?"

The Black Death's smile twitched again. "Smart."

"Realistic," corrected Matt. He took another sip of beer and glanced up at the mass murderer. "Know your strengths."

There was a pause. A gust of wind rustled, whipping a breath of dust between them. The Black Death, peering down, imperious, inspecting. Matt, nonchalant, gazing up.

"Do you want a beer?"

"I don't drink."

Matt shrugged. "Suit yourself." He took another swig, making no attempt to move.

"So," he said after a pause, "you killed Captain Dawn."

"Yes," the Black Death replied simply, gloved hands folded behind his back.

"Killed him, then shape-shifted so you looked like him, so nobody would suspect the truth." Matt gave a small nod. "Gives you time to rest, recover . . ." He paused and made a face. "I mean, if people knew you'd won, the whole world would've been after you, and heck, you never know . . ."

The Black Death said nothing—but merely stared down at him with the expression of a scientist viewing a particularly novel strain of mold. Matt continued unabated.

"Here's the part where I'm fuzzy though," he asked. "Why'd you stay? Why not reemerge or fake your death? What made you go, after being Dawn for a few weeks, 'Hey! There're some perks to these pajamas'?"

"It didn't take weeks," the Black Death said softly. "The second he died, I'd formulated my plan."

"Impressive."

"Thank you," Heydrich replied sardonically. He rolled his head in a full circle, idly cracking the bones in his neck. "The Legion presented an ideal place to collect and process"—his eyes flashed over Matt, still laying comfortably on the deck chair—"*rare* individuals, without anyone becoming suspicious."

Matt let out a long, slow breath. "Which is why I was accepted in the first place," he murmured. It all made sense. "Clairvoyants are pretty few and far between. You wanted my power. You wanted my blood." It wasn't a question.

The Black Death smiled. "The power to see the future . . ." he breathed, as if savoring the taste of a delicious steak. "It was the last one, truthfully, the only one I ever needed after Africa. I have the power to slay a God, but with your sight . . . I'll be unbeatable. Truly, perfectly unassailable. There'll be no enemy who could touch me, no threat I can't anticipate. The others, they saw me coming, clearly, destroyed themselves rather than grant me my prize, but you . . . you are an amateur, fumbling blindly with your gifts. I will perfect your power. I will control fate."

"We'll see," Matt said softly.

"Yes," replied the Black Death, "we will." He fell momentarily silent. "You have no idea how long I searched," he whispered finally. "Year after year. Denied time and time again. But then I found you. And you walked right into my Academy."

"I really did." Matt laughed dryly, his suspicions confirmed. "It's the perfect front. Rare powers. Unlimited time. Unlimited access." He paused. "All while influencing promising young minds."

"I'll admit that was my hope," the Black Death drawled. "Dawn had his band of fools he'd tricked into following him. Why couldn't I? Imagine it: a new Legion, a true Legion, forging a new world empire." His voice trailed off, and he shook his head. "But that was always a secondary consideration." He sighed. "And it's over now. I had thought to work under Dawn's name a while longer, make use of his goodwill to begin shaping my better world. But you and Jane scuttled that by going public. Forced me to play my hand."

"Sorry," said Matt.

"Don't be." The man smiled, his eyes gleaming black against the desert sun. He breathed slowly without a single drop of sweat. "An army may have been useful, but in the end a leader's role is tiring. It's easier to do things yourself. Simpler. Purer."

"Other people just weigh you down," Matt agreed. "Can't rely on anyone these days."

"Exactly."

"So what?" Matt asked. "What was the plan? Reinstate the Legion of Heroes, bring Dawn out of the darkness—only a little more forceful this time? A little more controlling?"

"Baby steps," Heydrich murmured. A part of him seemed almost pleased to be talking, to finally be saying these things out loud. "People follow those in authority. You have no idea how far humanity can be led in the name of the greater good. If you're willing to be patient."

"And patient you were," said Matt. "Ten years patient." He paused. "Didn't you ever get bored?"

The Black Death smirked. "I have come too far to rush. What are years, compared to eternity? I am ageless, child."

"Of course," Matt continued mildly. "Ageless, invisible, intangible, supersonic, telekinetic. You could practically be a ghost. Cut me, the others, anybody, drink whoever's blood you like. Piece by piece. Drop by drop. So many day-to-day wounds, so many injuries at a place like the Academy."

He paused and put a finger on his cheek in mock contemplation. "Of course, ten years is a long time. Even as a recluse, there was always the risk someone who knew Dawn before he was you would blow your cover. Someone who, I don't know, knew him, or knew something about him or had shared some memory with him, which, of course, you couldn't know. The face would only carry you so far."

Matt laughed, dull and dry. "The whole time, I thought someone was killing everyone Dawn ever knew to get at the captain. But it was the opposite, wasn't it? You were removing anyone with any connection to who Dawn really was."

The Black Death chuckled. "You're clever, Clairvoyant," he murmured, and there was just the slightest hint of bone white teeth in his smile. "I like you."

"But then comes Ed," continued Matt, wrapping his fingers neatly around the bottle. "Completely by accident. Some do-gooder wanting to organize a surprise party, starts looking into your past."

"Of course, he could churn through the data a thousand times faster than I could. He would have made the ten-year connection right off the bat. What happened ten years ago? The title fight of the century, which everybody knows Dawn won. Except . . . well, it's a crazy possibility, borderline unthinkable, but he's a genius, so it crosses his mind. And then everything falls into place. And suddenly, without you making a single mistake, someone's figured you out."

Matt shook his head bitterly. "Wally was right. No psychic could have made Ed kill himself from outside the room. But you were inside the room, weren't you? Invisible, levitating, able to move through walls. And, of course, telepathic. Able to break into Ed's mind and make him jump off that roof." He paused, glancing casually up at the Black Death. "How'd you know?" he asked. "How'd you know he'd found out?"

"Luck," the Black Death said simply. He gave a small, idle shrug, as if they were discussing house prices. "I was nearby. I sensed his wild panic, his thoughts of me. The boy was ill-disciplined—his mind practically shouting. I took care of it. Quickly, quietly. He did not suffer. I am not cruel."

"You kill people on a whim," reminded Matt.

"There is no inherent value in human life," Heydrich stated, neither defensive nor passionate. "It is one of the greatest lies of this era. The strong survive, the weak do not. It was the way of the world, before our simpering outgrew our sense. Is the human race any lessened for what I have done? Was anything of value lost?"

"Far be it for me to argue philosophy," Matt said calmly. He took another slow sip. "That's not what we're here for."

"Oh?" replied the Black Death, merriment touching the edges of his voice. "Then please, do tell, little clairvoyant, what are we here for?" He paused and his smile widened. "Are you trying to stall me? Maybe give the Legion of Heroes time to formulate a plan? Clever, but I'm one step ahead. The Legion has already been destroyed."

It took every ounce of control Matt possessed to stop his heart racing or his stomach dropping. He stared up at the man—at his smooth face, his small eyes, his wide, cruel mouth. And then, suppressing the dread in throat, the sickness in his guts, he forced himself to smile.

"Well, that may be," he said. He was certain. He was calm. "I couldn't tell you. Not the way this works, unfortunately—it isn't mine to know. But either way, it doesn't change anything."

A small frown creased the Black Death's pale lips. "Change what?"

"Change the choice you have to make," answered Matt.

"Change your future."

"What the hell do we do?" someone whispered.

Jane didn't have an answer. They knew all she knew. The Black Death—alive. Captain Dawn—dead. The man she'd trained with, strived for, pledged herself to—a lie. All a lie.

"We should run," a boy suggested, and there was an instant cascade of voices disagreeing, agreeing, answering.

"He might come back!"

"Get the police!"

"What're they going to do? What's anyone going to do?"

"We have to go!" Celeste pleaded.

Jane said nothing. Felt nothing. Everything was gone. The Legion of Heroes. Her dreams—her home. Any hope for the world. The man she'd thought she'd loved. Who she thought had loved her. All ashes. All destroyed.

"Go where?" murmured James. He was standing off to the side, not far from Jane—but when he spoke, the eyes of Morningstar Academy turned to him.

The crowd's muttering faded as James shook his head.

"There's nowhere we can go. Nowhere in the world. Because that's what he's going to take."

No one laughed. No one scoffed. As dumb as it sounded, it was true. The Black Death could conquer the world—one man, alone. Because no one alive could stand against him and live. No one alive could stop him.

James let out a long, mournful sigh. "So, I suppose we've got no choice," he said. He looked up at the sky, at the black smoke still pouring from the ruins of the Academy, blotting out the sun, and breathed in through his nose. "We've got to take him down."

"Are you insane?" hissed Natalia, pushing her way through the crowd, her face scrunched up in a scowl. A sickle-shaped cut ran down the side of her forehead and the sides of her jacket were singed and tarred. She didn't notice. It was a miracle Giselle had gotten as many out as she had. "He destroyed the previous Legion! The real Legion!"

"I know," muttered James.

"He had every power we knew back then, and he's had ten years, *ten years*, to get stronger!"

"I know!" James shouted. He turned on the psychic, his face twisted in the darkness, in the shadows of the firelight. Natalia recoiled, paling before the strongman's bulk. "I know," he repeated. "I know all that. Every bit of it. You don't think I'm scared?!" He struck a thick finger into his broad chest. "Because I am. We all are."

James looked around at the crowd. At the sea of blackened, anxious eyes. "How many of you came here because you wanted a job?" he asked after a moment. No one answered, so he continued. "How many because you thought it was a 'smart career move'? Because of good grades?" He paused, looking down at his hands. "Because I know I didn't," he whispered. Then his voice rose. "I came here because I wanted my life to mean something. Because I wanted to be part of something bigger. Because I watched those *goddamn* cartoons every morning!" he shouted, and then his voice dropped—and he gave a small, sad laugh. "And I thought, That's who I am. That's what I want to be. I want to save the world."

"And now it's real," he called out, his arms held wide, speaking out to the crowd, through the drifting smoke, through the thinning darkness. "All the stories, everything we grew up with. Real death. Real evil. There is a man out there with the power to conquer the world. Who *will* conquer the world, who'll kill millions. Billions. Unless someone stops him."

James Conrad paused—and he looked at them. At all of them. At her.

"You say, maybe we're not strong enough," he said quietly. "But I say, we're what the world's got. And I don't know about you, but in ten, twenty, a hundred years' time, I don't want them saying that we just gave up. That we didn't fight, that we ran away. That the Legion of Heroes didn't even try."

"The Legion of Heroes is dead!" shrieked someone, and a chorus of voices agreed with her.

"We're not real members!" echoed a second.

"We are real!" shouted James defiantly over the dissenters. His voice grew, raising up into the smoke. "Screw the titles, screw the badges—this, here, is what we trained for! This is what every second, every breath of our lives has been about! It doesn't matter that we didn't graduate. It doesn't matter that Morningstar's destroyed." He took a deep, steadying breath—then locked his jaw. "It doesn't matter that Dawn is gone. None of that matters. None of that changes who we are. What we believe. Life. Freedom. Justice. I still believe in them. And I still believe in you. We're *real.*" He thumped his fist on his chest. "And as long we're here, the Legion endures. So long as I breathe, so long as any of you breathe, the Legion survives."

The crowd around was silent.

"Never give up. Never give in. Because this is our world. And I'll be damned if I stand by and watch it burn."

"They need you." He looked at them—from boy to girl, from young to old. And finally, to her. Lingering, on her. Jane's hand reached in her pocket and closed around the badge—her silver eagle. "All of you. The world needs us."

"Answer the call."

Matt fingered the beer bottle idly in one hand, watching the sun reflecting off the brown glass.

"Do you know I used to have dreams about this cabin?" he told the Black Death, who was standing unmoving, six feet away, watching. Certain, unafraid—yet, ever so slightly, wary.

Matt pointed a finger at the rusty silver shack. "For years, I dreamed about it. This desert. This place. No idea where it was. No idea why." He paused. "Knew it meant something though."

Deep down inside, he believed every word he was saying. "And now we're here. And it all makes sense. This is where I've been heading. This whole time. This is my purpose." He paused. "I sit here and you stand there, and I tell you the future."

"Really?" the Black Death said coldly. His lip curled.

"Yup," replied Matt, unconcerned. "I didn't know—it wasn't clear until today. But now it's simple. You"—he pointed a finger at Heydrich's chest, not aggressive, not forceful, just to emphasize—"have a choice." He paused. "You've been walking down a path, a path you started on, which you've been on your entire life. You were born on it, you thrive on it, and you think you know where it's going—but you're wrong. And now you're at a crossroads. Because," Matt said simply, "if you take my blood, you lose."

There was silence. Matt gazed up at the Black Death, who stared back down at him, his face frozen.

The midday sun beat down between them. The wind rustled. Somewhere, an eagle called.

And then slowly, horribly, Heydrich began to laugh.

He laughed, a cold, terrible sound, soft at first then harder, throwing back his head and cackling, his voice echoing up and out through the rocks and stones. On the top of some cliff, a flock of birds flapped away, startled, but the Black Death paid them no heed. He just kept laughing, brutally, manically, doubling over, his teeth bared, eyes watering, clutching his sides. He laughed and laughed and laughed.

And all the while, Matt said nothing—simply looked on, watching, sitting, impassive.

Slowly, the cackles dried to chuckles. Slowly, the laughter died. And slowly, the Black Death looked down at Matt Callaghan, his insane smile fading to fury. To stone.

"How?" he demanded, his smooth face twisted with rage, contorting into a scowl. He threw up his hands, his eyes never leaving Matt. "How is that possible? How can I lose?"

"I don't know," Matt said simply. "But you do." Suddenly, the Black Death was upon him, his iron fingers around his collar, his face inches from Matt's.

"I have more powers than most people can name," he hissed. "I can go anywhere, heal anything, kill anyone. I can slaughter armies, raze cities with a single thought. I. Destroyed. Africa." He released his hold on Matt's shirt, letting him fall back down against the deck chair. "So, tell me, wherein lays my disadvantage? Where is my weakness?"

"I don't know," replied Matt. "I can't tell you how it happens. I'm just telling you what I see. I'm just the messenger. And the message is, beyond a shadow of doubt: if you take my blood, you'll lose."

"You're lying," snarled the Black Death, but still he hesitated. Still, he paced. Matt sat perfectly still, watching the conflict play across the murderer's face. He held up his hands and spoke.

"If you want it," Matt said with a shrug, "take it. I can't stop you. Heck, far as I know, there's nobody alive who can stop you. Not the army, not the government, not the Legion. The only power strong enough to even hurt you, you snuffed out ten years ago."

"This isn't a threat. Heck, how can *I* threaten *you*? You're *Klaus Heydrich*, you're the *Black Death*. I can't do anything to you, you could kill me by snapping your fingers. I'm not going to run. I'm not going to fight. I'm not even going to pretend to know what you're going to do, because I don't. All I know is the truth. And all I can do is share it, so your decision's informed, so you can choose." He looked up at Heydrich with clear, steady eyes.

For almost a full minute, the Black Death just stood there, his hands balled into fists, his jaw working, grinding soundlessly back and forth. And then, without warning, his face darkened, and he thrust out his hand, a gloved finger on his temple.

But Matt was ready.

My name is Matt Callaghan, and I am a clairvoyant.

He felt the vast, sharp, violent mass of Heydrich's consciousness come tearing through his mind—a dark, sweeping presence, huge, cold, brutally intelligent. An ocean storm made of black glass, a swarm of voidling stars. Yet Matt did nothing to resist, made no effort to keep him out.

My name is Matt Callaghan, and I am a clairvoyant.

He saw it, believed it. The truth of it. The memory of him standing in line at the registration office getting his card. The endless hours he'd spent in practice, prediction after prediction, all right. This was his life—the simple truth of it. He remembered the first time he'd seen Jane, knowing she wouldn't harm him, knowing that she was his friend; feeling strange about being at Morningstar, untrusting of Dawn. Knowing he'd survive Albania. Knowing, right away, that Ed's death was more than it seemed. He felt the Black Death rolling through, turning the pieces over, sliding through the streets, the cathedrals and alleyways, of the city that was his mind—away from the past, toward the part he wanted to know, toward the present. So . . . Matt let him see.

My name is Matt Callaghan, and I am a clairvoyant.

He showed the memories of this place, pieced together from blurred dreams—showed Heydrich arriving, the final stone in the mural, the illusive man in black who had long haunted his visions. Saw the truth stretching out before him, vast and strong, a mighty, muddied river— unable to see what it contained but knowing with perfect clarity where it flowed.

He knew it, he believed it, and in his mind, and thus in Heydrich's, he made it true.

My name is Matt Callaghan, and I am a clairvoyant.

And slowly, he felt the Black Death's sweeping, cavernous consciousness retreat.

He opened his eyes, not remembering having closed them, and looked across at the man who would be king. Matt smiled a plain, simple smile.

Klaus Heydrich didn't move.

For what seemed like an eternity, he stood there, his face frozen in place as Matt reclined against the deck chair. He stood stock still, a twisting, tormented fight flickering across his face, as the desert wind whipped through between them, dancing on the heels of his coat. His eyes darted between specks in the ether, then froze on nothing. On the ground. And then finally on Matt. He twitched, a sudden movement forward, and it was all Matt could do not to flinch. But in the same instant, the Black Death retracted, undid the motion as fast as it had come. He breathed, long, hard and slow, the shoulders of his uniform rising and falling. His teeth gritted; his hands balled.

"No," he finally whispered. And he jerked out his hand.

In an instant, an invisible force wrapped around Matt's arms, dragging them out and pulling him up from his chair. Matt yelled, but a second later, his shout of surprise turned to pain as deep gashes sliced open across his wrists. He gasped, shuddered, tried to fall—but the invisible force around his arms held tight, and he hung there, upright, feet not touching the ground, a puppet dangling from a pair of strings, blood pouring from his veins, splattering out into the desert air.

And there it stayed. Before Matt's horrified eyes, his blood pooled in midair, a steady crimson stream, flowing in gentle, glugging waves toward the Black Death's open hand. His fingers stretched, the glove removing itself, exposing the bone-white flesh beneath. Matt felt his heart punch a staggering, desperate beat, his eyes stinging, the world blurred. But he couldn't look away. He watched in morbid fascination as his lifeblood streamed toward the red, pulsing tips of Heydrich's fingers—and as it flowed, like water through a sieve, into, under, through his skin. A river of blood, drunk greedily by five pale worms. They guzzled and guzzled and guzzled, until the Black Death and the desert floor swam hazy in Matt's mind, shadows creeping against the corners of his vision and his eyes began to flicker, struggling to stay open—the pain in his wrists, the plan, all of it forgotten, as he drifted further and further away, closer and closer to the dark . . .

Then the bleeding stopped.

The pressure around Matt's hand vanished. His arms dropped and he fell, slumped back into the deck chair. Matt's eyes flicked open. Above him a dark figure towered over, tilting his wrist with mild amusement, examining his pale, gloveless hand.

Then he reached down and the tip of Heydrich's fingers brushing lightly over Matt's wrists. And the wounds began to heal.

"Waste not, want not," the Black Death whispered. His lips twitched in the start of a smile—but then Matt looked up at him, his face a blank question, and any trace of joviality fell away.

"Stay here, Matt Callaghan," he said quietly. "Stay away. Perhaps I'll return once I've finished. Perhaps we will talk again once the world is brought to heel. Perhaps we will discuss my future."

He glanced at the open sky and a small smile slid over his smooth features. "But until then, enjoy the show."

"This is my world now."

DARKNESS

Curriculum Vitae
Leyton Poole, 38 (Flight): Camera Operator and Photojournalist

Notable Achievements:
- 15 years' independent operational experience
- 12-time nominee for Featherdale Prize for Outstanding Coverage of a Live News Event
- Winner of 1991 Featherdale Prize for Outstanding Coverage of a Live News Event (Mount Pinatubo Eruption)
- Winner of 1994 Featherdale Prize for Outstanding Coverage of a Live News Event (O. J. Simpson Pursuit)
- Winner of 1998 Featherdale Prize for Outstanding Coverage of a Live News Event (Bangladesh Landslides)
- Current holder of fastest top speed for mounted flying camera
- Husband and father of two

"How big an explosion?" asked Frisk.

He leaned over the desk, one hand on the glass tabletop, the other around his coffee mug. Fifty-six, overweight, balding, and in denial about all three of those facts, the station head looked attentive, though hardly excited.

"Big, according to the source," said Whitebridge. She clicked the silver pen in her hand a few times while Frisk made a face.

"It's Morningstar," Dutton said with a sigh, sounding bored. He leaned against the wall, not looking up as his fingers tapped away at his phone, his suit as crisp as always. Vanessa didn't understand why their head of social media was so adamant about his clothes always being neatly pressed—it wasn't like he ever fronted a camera. "There's crazy stuff coming out of there all the time. It's by the by."

"Source says this looks different," argued Whitebridge. Frisk looked at her.

"How close is the source?" he asked.

"Ten miles," she replied. "Visible smoke." Her boss took a moment to chew his lip. Outside the glass walls of his office, the hum and chatter of the broadcasting station bubbled on, running as it always did, oblivious.

"I don't know," he said after a few seconds. "They're very anti-press at the moment. We don't want to push them if it's not worth it. Reach out to Winters, see what he's saying. Then get back to me."

"I already called his landline," Whitebridge told him. "He's not answering."

Frisk's brow furrowed. "That's unusual. Man's never been shy for a statement."

"I'm telling you," insisted Vanessa, "something's going on."

"You're starting to sound like one of those conspiracy nuts," chided Dutton. He pocketed his cell and glanced up at Frisk. "Did I tell you about the nut job who emailed through this morning?"

"The one about the Chinese death twins?"

"No," Dutton chided, "not that. Some wacko claiming everyone Captain Dawn grew up with is dead. Stupidest thing I've heard all week."

Vanessa frowned, a hand on her hip. "They're not, are they?"

"No," snorted Dutton. He rolled his eyes. "I mean, I don't know off the top of my head, but come on." He went back to his phone, dismissing Whitebridge with a wave of his hand. "The intern will tell you, I put her on it, I'm sure it's bull."

"You mean Abby," she said irritably.

"Whatever."

"She's been here two weeks."

"Yeah," Dutton scoffed. "And she's minimum wage, so—"

The room exploded.

Suddenly, everything was sideways. One second Vanessa was standing in the center of the room talking to her boss, the next she was on the floor against the far wall, coughing, spluttering, ringing in her ears, her hands cut through with shards of glass from Frisk's broken desk. Frisk . . . the chief of broadcasting was gone. Pulped, blown to pieces by the explosion that had decimated the office's outside wall. The wall and everything within three feet of it just gone, disintegrated to a gaping wound torn through concrete and cabling.

And as Vanessa struggled to stand, mind stuck in a dream-like stupor, seventeen floors above the wailing traffic, through the dust and the debris and the bus-sized hole leading out to open air, floated the Black Death.

"Hello," he said calmly, his hands upturned. "I'd like to send a message."

Vanessa screamed.

Dutton screamed, reeling against a cabinet and turned to run.

The Black Death flicked his fingers.

And Dutton fell to the floor, his neck slit open.

Vanessa's screaming stopped—her hand trembled across her mouth, her eyes wide as saucers. Just like Dutton's. As he lay there. Twitching. Blood pouring into his suit.

"That's better," the Black Death said simply. And he smiled at her with a flat, dead smile. He raised his other hand, and Vanessa jerked into the air—choking, writhing, her chipped red nails scrabbling at the invisible force curled around her neck. "Now, where would I go if I wanted as many people as possible to see me?"

It broadcast live on every one of their channels. An override of the entire network, the largest in the country, all 116 stations. At the start of the transmission, it was just their company, just one unannounced emergency broadcast from central control, but by the end every network in the country had picked it up.

The face of one man, live, in front of a plain blue screen.

"Ladies and gentlemen, children, governments of the world. My name is Klaus Heydrich. You know who I am."

"Easy now," soothed the doctor, moving her hands over scorched skin. She looked up at Wally. "You can't be in here," she ordered.

The redhead looked at her, incredulous. "Try and make me leave."

They glared at each other. On the stretcher bed between them, Giselle moaned in agony.

"You know what I can do."

"Will someone shut that damn thing off?!" the doctor roared, glaring at the TV. But Wally's eyes widened. That voice. He slowly turned, horror spreading over his face. His hand clutched Will's.

"Oh, God," he whispered.

"Reports of my demise, as you can see, are greatly exaggerated. I am alive. Captain Dawn is dead. I killed him ten years ago, assumed his identity, and scorched Africa with his remains."

"How many stations?" murmured the secretary. The only one who dared speak—everyone else standing deathly quiet around him, watching the same face on a hundred different screens. The entire Pentagon brought to a standstill.

"All of them," the man beside him whispered. An aide stepped to his side.

"We've got the location."

"Get the Joint Chiefs of Staff," muttered the secretary. "Everyone, now."

"Since then, I have acquired more gifts—become more powerful. And I have watched this world, as I have for a lifetime, as it has continued down the path of weakness. Of stagnation. We have been blessed with the knowledge, the power, to shape a better future—and yet we rot in mediocrity, weighed down by inferiority, by the mewling of human scum."

"You have abandoned virtue. You have abandoned the natural order. You fear the superior who should be revered and shackle them with the burden of those who offer nothing. Invalids and imbeciles and incompetents. Their infection has drained our society of purpose, of drive. What should be humanity's golden age has become a mongrel breeding ground."

The plant had stopped work. The machines hissed and steamed, but no one cared. A hundred blackened workmen stood silently together, every eye fixated on the screen of the tiny television.

"Turn it up," the man next to Peter Walker whispered. So he did.

The Black Death stared back at them.

"No more."

* * *

"My message is simple. Every government on Earth will submit them-
selves to my rule, immediately. Anyone who resists will be killed. As a
show of compliance, submitting sovereigns will start by exterminat-
ing all human vermin possessing traits I deem unworthy. A list will be
supplied."

Matt Callaghan shook his head, his hands white on the bench, tremors running through his chest. This couldn't be happening. This wasn't
real. Any second now he'd wake up.

But the Black Death just kept on speaking, and the nightmare didn't
end.

In front of the camera, as the entire studio watched on with shaking
breaths, Klaus Heydrich paused, unblinking, his eyes cold.

"I realize this may be difficult to accept. I realize, too, that some may
not like the idea of ceding their autonomy or may not believe me capable
of doing everything I claim. I do not care. Every half hour, I will annihilate
a major city in a country that has yet to accept my authority, starting with
the United States of America and continuing until all living people submit
themselves to me. That is my proposition. I will not negotiate. I cannot be
stopped. Fight, and die. Surrender and live.

"Citizens of the world, embrace your new order. In thirty minutes, I
destroy Detroit."

He raised his fist and clenched it, shattering the camera—the sound
of splintering metal and glass causing every person in the room to flinch.
The Black Death stood up, brushing dust from his shoulders.

"Now then," he announced, light and conversational, "where can I
find Mr. Leyton Poole?"

It was scorched, and it was buckled. But with its body sunk deep into the
ground and its walls thick steel, the Legion's armory stood intact. James Conrad swept aside the rubble over the entrance, and the Acolytes, the Ashes,
anyone who was willing, anyone who was left, all followed him inside.

Leyton Poole's hands had never shaken. Never once in his entire career.
Not in blizzards or hurricanes, not when he was sleep-deprived, not
when he was sick.

But today, waiting outside the outskirts of Detroit with his camera on his shoulder, feet floating off the ground and the greatest murderer in human history patiently counting down the minutes by his side—today, he shook.

"Careful of that," the Black Death said mildly, sliding over his trembling with an imperious eye. The first words he'd spoken since he'd teleported them from New Mexico. "I want it as clear as possible. I want everyone to see."

Leyton nodded, swallowing, clenching his jaw. Sweat, or maybe tears, stung his vision.

"Don't worry," the Black Death assured him, his arms behind his back, "you're not in danger. So long as you remain by my side doing your usual, exemplary work, you and your family will live."

"Y-y-yes," he stammered. His fingers squeezed white around the camera.

"Yes, what?" Heydrich said quietly.

"Yes, yes, sir!"

"Good," he said with a smile. The alarm on Leyton's watch beeped, and the Black Death got to his feet. "You learn quickly." He glanced with an expression of mild boredom in toward the city, at the crowd gathering in the streets. "Others, it seems, resist the lesson."

His head turned to the cameraman. "Turn it on." Leyton's fingers fumbled and the broadcasting light flashed red. "I take no pleasure in this," he announced into the lens, shaking his head, "in the arrogance of fools. I do this to better the world. A gardener, pulling weeds."

He started toward the crowd. "Stay close, Poole," he instructed, striding forward. "Let the world bear witness." They walked without speaking—the Black Death first, his hands behind his back, humming a tuneless tune, coattails flapping in the breeze, the cameraman six steps behind, his pale blue shirt and jeans stained with sweat. The waiting crowd made no noise to greet them—no shouts of anger, no cries of fear. They stood, the wall of them, a formless mob turning to distinct human figures as the Black Death and his witness drew closer.

Police and military uniforms, clerks and office workers, punk kids and tradesmen. Lightning crackled and fire sparked; knuckles cracked and light flickered. Some turned larger, some turned to stone, young and old, rich and poor. All came, all stood together, defiant, to defend their

city. A wall of people against him. An army of the superhuman. Against
one man.

The Black Death stopped, fifty feet from the first of them. Then he
held out his hands and spoke to them, to the whites of their eyes.

"I will give you one more chance," he called, and his voice echoed
through the streets. "I am merciful. Leave now and go unharmed. Stay
and perish."

The wind rolled through behind him, between the silent houses and
among the waiting crowd. Fists clenched. Throats swallowed.

But no one moved.

"Screw you," someone called. A shout rang out amongst the fighters—and then, together, they attacked.

A wall, a tidal wave of ice and lightning, metal and earth, acid and
energy, flesh and flame, charging, unleashed.

The Black Death smiled. And in his mind's eye, time slowed to a
crawl, and he moved to superspeed.

In the space of a second, he flew up, twenty feet above the crowd.
His pupils flashed sparking green and, in an instant, a shrieking blast
of energy surged out from his eyes. It hit the assembled, a searing deluge slicing through them, blasting half of them back, turning half to
ash—and then he flew, faster than sound, down through the middle of
them, his body turned to iron, a bullet train carving through meat. His
hands crackled and erupted forth a storm of lightning, arcing out into
the backs of those still alive—as within the space of the same heartbeat,
the wall of people fell in slow motion apart, disintegrated, shattered,
and bleeding. He slammed his hands into the road, rending the earth,
turning it to his bidding, raising a thousand shards of splintered rock,
launching them out, an unstoppable, gleaming wave, piercing, shred-
ding everything in its path.

And then, so few remained. Then, he only needed to clean up.

Another speedster had escaped, moved aside from the blast, eyes
widening with terror as he ran, his mind alone moving fast enough to
comprehend the devastation. As he whitened at the sight of slaughter, the Black Death raised a hand, telekinetically pulled the speedster
beneath his boot, and split his skull against the asphalt. A woman made
of metal still stood, naked, her arms over her eyes and her body glowing red from the onslaught. The Black Death sighed, moved alongside

her, turned a fingernail to diamond, and patiently slit her throat. Then he turned similarly to a man of stone and crushed his head to powder between his palms.

Then he slowed down, stepped back, and returned to walking calmly down the road, whistling the same tuneless tune—as three hundred corpses, a field of ash and blood, fell apart in his wake. He raised his hands, palms out toward the buildings lining the street on both sides, magnetically gripping the metal inside them. The walls cracked and the buildings groaned.

"Come along, Mr. Poole," he called pleasantly. "Do keep up."

Less than ten seconds had passed.

They stood in the colors of the Legion.

Crimson and gold, Kevlar weave and ballistic plating, some with weapons, some without. From every corner of the globe, every color and creed, but to the same place, for the same reason.

Some stood pale and steadfast, their faces blank. Some sweated, some shuddered, some rocked with heavy rage. Some sobbed, their faces tracked with tears—afraid to go, afraid to die.

But still they stood, as one by one, a hand closed around their shoulder and they vanished into the air. As one by one, they appeared in the city. As together, united, the Legion's last battalion, the best of mankind, they looked up at the smoke and listened to the sirens, the screaming and the cries.

"Let them know we're here," James Conrad said quietly.

And in an instant, Celeste took to the air, arms shimmering to wings of tawny feathers. And as she flew, as her head stretched to a bird of prey's proud, imperious face, she grew. Higher and higher, she flapped above the rooftops, growing, changing, become the eagle—soaring, free. She lifted her head and spread her wings, twenty, thirty feet wide.

And side by side, Charles Farrington of the Ashes, his body aflame, and Jane Walker, the silver badge pinned to her breast, raised their hands into the air and sent forth a blazing wreath of fire, a hundred feet above the city skyline, an arc beneath Celeste. The eagle screeched a bellowing, defiant scream and every person in the city, every fearful face who'd turned and run heard it, looked up and saw—the symbol of the Legion, living, burning in the sky.

The Legion of Heroes had arrived.

Come to save the world, one last time.

"Tsssssrrrr!"

A piercing, distant cry. The Black Death raised his eyes. His face hardened, passed over by a shadow, a flicker of annoyance. Leyton Poole followed his gaze with the camera, to up above the other side of the city where the fifty-foot eagle soared above a wreath of flame. His breath caught in his chest.

"Survivors," the Black Death murmured, and there was within his words the barest anger. "Fools."

He floated upward, boots drifting from the ground. "Come, Poole," he said softly. "Let us offer them sense." And then they flew toward the burning symbol.

A figure rose up and toward them, a dark speck against the sky. Jane's breath tightened. This was it. She could feel it—the radiating evil. The void around him, sucking in the light.

James Conrad knew.

"Spread out," he ordered, waving out his giant hands. "Loose formation. One of you is a distraction, a group is a target. SPREAD OUT!" he roared, and the Legion fanned out behind him, filling the street, a crescent moon of faces and armor, crimson and gold. James breathed heavily, his jaw clenched, staring without blinking at the approaching shadow of Death.

"Hit him together," he shouted at them. "All together, everything at once. Everything you've got." He shook out his hands then scrunched them into fists. "He's stronger than all of us alone, but together we can take him down."

"You really believe that?" Jane said quietly, standing at his side. Watching as the shadow flew closer. James grimaced.

"Last time, the Legion had no idea what they were up against," he muttered, the words black with anger. "This time we do."

He glanced at her out of the corner of his eyes. "I'm counting on you, Empath."

The dark shape drew near. The murderer, the imposter, the man who'd deceived her in the deepest, most personal way. Every nerve hurt to look at him. Every part of her ached with loss. Betrayal.

"I'll kill him," she whispered.

The Black Death descended, alone save for the camera at his back.

"I'll never let you down." Jane's shoulders clenched, the silver eagle gleaming in the sun.

Without sound or ceremony, the Black Death touched down at the very outskirts of their circle, forty feet away.

For a few moments, no one spoke. Armor creaked, feet shuffled, breaths drew shallow. The wind whistled between them, oblivious. The fiery crest extinguished; Celeste returned to the ground.

Finally, the Black Death spoke.

"So," he called, holding out his hands, surprisingly calm. "I have to say, I am impressed. So many of you survived."

Beside her, James Conrad gritted his teeth. "We're stronger than you think," he snarled.

"Obviously," the Black Death replied with a smile. He paused, his dead eyes surveying the assembled crowd. "I'm actually pleased. This way, we get to talk."

"None of us want to hear anything you've got to say!" James roared.

But the Black Death was unmoved.

"I'm building a new world," he told them, his voice ringing through the empty distance. His eyes slid off James's shoulders and around their ranks, surveying the many faces of the Legion—some clammy, some hateful, some set. All, though they might try to hide it, afraid. "Where the great will not be constrained by the small. Where the natural order will be restored. Where the strong will rightfully rule."

Slowly, he started to pace, his black boots treading sure, silent steps. His pale chin held high. "You are all exceptional examples of your gifts. Superior beings, worthy of a place in this world and of standing at my side. Think of me what you will, but I am not evil. I hold no grudges. I have no quarrel with any of you. I warn you. I will kill you now if you stand against me, but I will take no pleasure it. The senseless waste of your talents." His black eyes flicked to Jane. "So, I ask you. Walk with me into the future. Help me shape, help me better the world. Don't be fools. Don't throw your gifts away in defense of this sick society's lies."

He stopped and turned his head, gazing back at the assembled. "I am offering this to you and no others. Think for yourselves, think of your families. You could be royalty." The Black Death paused. "Or you could die now, painfully, in some nameless, pointless street. The choice is yours."

His voice fell silent, the space between them filled once more with the sound of rushing wind. Through the rows of crimson and gold, friend glanced at friend—student looked to teacher. For a few seconds, no one said anything—the Legion holding its collective breath, waiting to see if anyone would accept the offer. Waiting to see who would break ranks.

Until finally, in front of everyone, James Conrad's shoulders slumped.

"How do we know?" he asked quietly. "How do we know we'll be safe?" His eyes dropped to the ground. "That you won't hurt us."

A murmur rushed through the crowd, and Jane stared up at the strongman in disbelief—but James avoided her gaze.

"No," she whispered.

"My good man," the Black Death hummed pleasantly. "I am many things, but I am not a liar. I give you my word: stand with me now, and you will not only live, but thrive. I swear it."

There was a brief, terrible silence.

Before James Conrad quietly nodded. His eyes still on the ground.

"Okay," he mumbled.

"What was that?" The Black Death smirked, holding a hand to his ear.

"Okay," James repeated louder. Still seemingly unable to look up—an expression of resignation, of defeat, fallen blankly over his face. "I'll join you." He took a step forward from the circle.

"James!" cried Jane, and her calls were echoed all throughout the Legion's ranks. But the strongman just kept walking forward, toward where the Black Death stood grinning broadly.

"It's no use," James said sadly. His gaze trailed along the ground. "We have to face facts. We can't win. We shouldn't throw our lives away."

He glanced at the Acolytes, his comrades behind him, his face blank. "I'm going to join him. We all should." His great head swung back around. "We have to save ourselves. We have to be smart." He paused, and his gaze dropped. "Like Giselle."

And in that single, fleeting instant, Jane saw the glint in his eye.

James stopped, a few feet away from the Black Death. He looked up and then held out his giant hand. "To the future," he said. For a moment, the Black Death hesitated—but then he, too, smiled and took a step toward the strongman.

"To the future," he agreed, and reached his gloved hand out to shake James's.

The glint in their leader's eyes became a fire.

"NOW!" he roared and in an instant he slammed his palms together. BOOM!

A thundering, rippling shock wave exploded through the air, slamming through the Black Death's outstretched hand, into his body, concussing through his chest with a sickening, squelching crunch. Heydrich cried out, stumbling sideways, pushed backward, his right arm suddenly hanging useless, his insides turned to mush. In a heartbeat, his eyes were ablaze, crackling with green energy that erupted, screaming out toward them—

But the Legion was ready.

A golden forcefield the height of a school bus bloomed in front of their lines, holding the streaming laser as around it the Legion charged, fire, light, earth, and sound blasting out from a hundred hands, eyes, and mouths, a hundred streams of searing destruction all racing toward one man, one man who staggered, barely able to move, barely able to throw up his own force field in time to save himself from the assault, his teeth gnashing, his knees buckling, struggling to hold his barrier against the relentless, pounding waves of power. He roared, the sound swallowed by the noise of the attack, pushed back, his boots tearing rocky tracks through the pavement, the earth around him twisting, forming into stone spikes that slammed up into the rear of the Black Death's force field as it shook, as it wavered, but still, somehow, held, the man inside it shaking as the combined might of the Legion pressed in around him—

And as James Conrad charged.

Six foot eight. Four hundred pounds. An unstoppable wall of superhuman muscle, his feet pushing cracks into the earth as he ran, alone, unarmed, toward their cowering foe—as he leaped, forward, his giant shoulders shattering the Black Death's force field, his face contorted, his arms outstretched, never losing step, never losing focus, oblivious to the burning energy searing all around. Through the hurricane of light and noise Jane saw him go, not daring to hope, not daring to believe. She watched as the strongman flew through the chaos, toward the paralyzed

Heydrich, the eyes of the entire world upon him, as mighty hands closed around their enemy's head, as James roared—and as he twisted, wrenching his arms, and snapped the Black Death's neck.

The shooting stopped.

The Legion froze.

And the body of Klaus Heydrich, the man they called the Black Death, fell soundlessly to the ground, his head crushed and lolling like a rag doll, turned a full 180 degrees.

Nobody moved. Nobody breathed. James took a step back, his eyes as wide as saucers, staring at the body, staring at his hands.

"We did it," he whispered.

For an instant, all Jane could feel was her heartbeat. All she could hear was her breath.

And then time unfroze and James Conrad spun around, his face electrified, ecstatic, punching his enormous arms into the air.

"WE DID IT!" he shouted as a cascade of cries, shrieks, and celebration went up among the Legion. Everywhere around Jane, Acolytes were yelling, screaming, grabbing, hugging one another, laughing, hysterically, some literally jumping with joy—

But then suddenly a cold voice chuckled. And all noise ceased.

"I'm sorry." The Black Death laughed, floating back up off the ground, his head still turned the wrong way. "That was cruel." And with every eye on him, with the entire Legion rooted in place, there was a sickening crunch and his neck whipped back around.

"I shouldn't play." He smirked, then his eyes flicked over to James Conrad, standing four feet away, and his smile darkened.

ZAP!

Time seemed to slow. James's eyes bulged. He looked slowly down, down towards his heart—where a sparking silver hand gleamed out from his chest, dripping in blood. James's mouth opened, his eyes rolled back—and as if in slow motion, he fell, lifeless, to the ground, a gaping, sucking hole burned clear through his chest.

Where he lay, unmoving, before the Black Death's feet.

Somebody screamed. The Black Death's smile widened.

And all hell broke loose.

Suddenly, spires of earth erupted from the ground around the Legion, launching up behind them, into the force fielder, skewering the boy from Michigan through a hundred different places before anyone could move or blink. The ranks broke—the Legion swarmed, some forward, some back, some firing, chaos, but their enemy was everywhere, nowhere, supersonic, untouchable. Jane launched forward, bellowing a wordless roar, and suddenly alongside her raced Natalia Baroque, swearing, her fingers flying to her forehead, her eyes burning into the Black Death, power streaming from her mind. But her curses turned to shrieking an instant later, and she fell, blood spurting from her eyes and nose, unconscious, shut down. Jane saw the Black Death's fingers drop from his temple, the work of his antipathic abilities done, his eyes shifting to her as she flew, a bullet of fire and lightning, straight toward him, screaming, deadly. Faster than she could react, he opened one palm toward her, one hand behind him, and all at once between them was a red, pulsing ellipsis, five feet tall and half that wide, inches from Jane's face, and she was hurtling into it, through it—

And suddenly, she was no longer in the battle, no longer in the street, no longer flying toward the Black Death but moving through open sky, tumbling headfirst out of another red portal. Jane dropped her powers, spun, flew to a halt, her head spinning around wildly, trying to get her bearings, and figure out where the hell she was. Far below her, somehow almost a mile away, she saw it, the crimson mass of the Legion and the lone figure of the Black Death moving through them. She clenched her teeth and swore, burning hard with everything she had, rocketing back toward them, despair bubbling in her chest, willing herself to get there, to rejoin the fight—

But she was too far, and he was too fast. Jane flew like she'd never flown before, but it was too late. All she could do was watch.

Faster than a bullet, the Black Death sped through the Legion's ranks, ignoring everything they threw at him, focused solely on one target— the neutralizer Omari, standing at the back, his eyes struggling to track the racing blur. There was no pause, no sound, no warning—the Black Death simply grabbed the Egyptian man on either side of his chest, and suddenly he was in two pieces instead of one. A shadow loomed—the Black Death's eyes flicked up, and he flew backward as a car-sized fist slammed into the ground where he'd been only seconds ago. Nancy bellowed, thirty feet tall, but before she could even raise her fist, the Black Death flung out his arm and a road sign tore free from the pavement, instantly re-forming, melting into a three-foot metal spike, flying up and through the titan's forehead. The girl fell, but the Black Death was already moving, ducking under a withering ball of fire, hands moving up, a gash opening in his palms, projecting a stream of hissing clear acid ten, twenty feet, cutting a swath through the Legion, melting skin and armor and everything it touched. But aimed squarely at one man, at the head of a group of Acolytes—the burning form of Charles Farrington. The clear stream hit the Ashes pyromorph squarely in his flaming chest, and for an instant Charles looked down in shock, the attack seemingly doing nothing, evaporating harmlessly against his impenetrable barrier of fire—only to begin screaming, a second later, as his lungs filled with acidic gas.

Half a mile away, Jane could only look on in horror as first her teacher, then everyone around him, fell to the ground, clawing at their throats. The Legion reeled. The Black Death moved.

And nothing they could do against him worked.

Chino, the floramancer, erupted vines around his feet, but the Black Death simply flew up, telekinetically pulling him into a blast from the Inuit Acolyte's laser eyes. Celeste, morphed into a dragon the size of a school bus, launched at him with crushing jaws but he flew under her bite, grabbed a hand on either side of her scaly jaw and snapped her neck with superhuman strength. Still airborne, he rolled, a thick cable-like cord shooting from his wrist and wrapping around a terramancer's waist, pulling him up and straight into the Black Death's other arm, turned to a blade—the man struggling helplessly as Heydrich infused his body with sickening violet light and then threw him down into a clumped crowd. The man exploded—a blinding flash—and through the smoke and stifled cries Jane's eyes found Mac, his grizzled fingers throwing bolt after bolt of lightning at the black, supersonic shape hurtling toward him, flying around his attacks. Suddenly, the Black Death's face was an inch from his, split into a manic, inhuman grin—Mac's eyes widened, weathered lips twitching in some final word, as the Black Death touched two fingers underneath the old man's chin and shot his own bolt of lightning directly up.

Then he was gone—vanished, as Odette Dodecan's hyper-voice screamed through the air where he had been. No, not vanished—split into two identical copies, who in unison raised their hands and pulled the building behind Odette down on top of her. Then the copy flickered, and again there was only one. One man, slamming his fist down into the asphalt, splitting the earth, raising from the fissure a swarm of broken, jagged piping that flew out, indiscriminately sinking into the wounded, the fleeing, the fallen. Anybody, everybody. Anyone who was left.

It took Jane only seconds to get back.

But in the space of those few seconds, it was over.

The Legion had already lost.

Jane landed, her powers flickering as she skidded to the ground, falling to her knees—her body numb, her mind hollow. The street suddenly, horribly quiet. The air whirled, billowing brown and gray, streaked with curling trails of dust and smoke. Ground broken, walls blackened. All around her, destruction, death. Frozen faces, empty eyes. Lifeless piles of splattered crimson and broken gold. She tried to speak, to call out, to cry, but nothing came. Only choking, mangled sobs. There was nothing. No one. She was alone—alone among the dead.

And against it all, standing in the center of the slaughter, the Black Death slowly turned to face her.

"Poole," he ordered quietly. "Turn off the camera."

The red light on the camera the flying, trembling man was holding faded and died.

Over a motionless maroon body, the Black Death stepped toward her.

"Jane," he murmured. Then a pause. "I'd hoped it wouldn't be like this. That when we finally met, it would be different." He shook his head. "But the world is so. Now you know the truth."

Jane sucked in a wet, retching breath. "I'll kill you," she whispered. She promised. She pushed to her feet, her hands clenched, her arms shaking.

"Stop," the Black Death pleaded. He held out his hand. "Think." He motioned to the broken buildings, the bodies, the smoldering ruins of the Legion of Heroes. "Don't be like this. Don't be like them. Don't throw your life away."

"Shut up!" shouted Jane, her chest heaving, her eyes blurred. "You're a murderer! You're a monster!"

"No, Jane," he implored, "I am necessary. I do what I must so that the good in this world might thrive. Please see that."

"You're evil!" she cried, taking a jagged step forward, her teeth trembling. "You used me, you lied to me, you tricked me into . . . into . . ." She staggered to a stop, the horrible words, the betrayal, sticking in her chest.

The Black Death's voice was soft. "I never lied to you, Jane," he said. "Yes, I wore another man's face. But the words I spoke were always mine, and I meant every one of them. This world wants to tear the great down; it needs strong people to forge a path . . . everything I told you was true."

"Shut up," she hissed, clenching her teeth. "Shut up, shut up, shut up!"

"They couldn't accept it, Jane," the Black Death cried, pointing with a sweeping gesture at the dead around her. "But you can. You've seen it! The hatred, the injustice of this world! These people, this broken society that spits on you, when they should be worshipping you as a queen!" His voice stopped—a heartbeat's pause. "My queen," he added quietly, "if you would have it."

For a second, the earth fell away beneath her feet. Her stomach churned and her arms trembled, a feeling of corruption, unclean, spreading through her every bone. "You're sick," she hissed. "You're insane."

"You are perfect, Jane," he told her, fixing her with his pale lips and dark eyes. "Everything my new world stands for. Beauty, ambition, strength . . . Do you think it was coincidence that you were sent to me? We are the chosen few, meant to rule. Imagine it—imagine what we could achieve together. Imagine what we could do. Imagine a world where empaths are not looked down upon but revered as the gods they are. No more waste, no more fear—no more suffering." He reached out toward her. "I know you're strong enough to see through the lies they've told you. Strong enough to see that this is your destiny. Come with me," he pleaded. "And I can give you everything you ever wanted. Everything you rightfully deserve."

And for one brief, delirious moment, Jane saw it.

A new world. Everyone who'd ever wronged her brought to justice. The people who'd hit her, mocked her, hated her for existing, tried at every step to tear her down. All of it, righted—all of them, punished. And not only them, not only justice, but beyond that she saw the future, the endless possibilities. Whatever she wanted—whatever she dreamed. The power to make changes, to force real good, to lead . . . She saw a sea of faces, a world of bettered people, looking up at her without hatred, only respect, only devotion, only fear . . .

All except one.

One single person, standing alone in the back. A woman's face, black and white, gazing up at her softly. Lovingly—quietly. Sad.

My beautiful girl.

A memory. A picture on her wall. All she had left.

But worth a thousand worlds.

And in an instant, Jane's heart throbbed painfully, seeding her body through with aching warmth, and the vision of conquest vanished—replaced by her mother's eyes.

"Burn in hell," she whispered, and in that instant, she attacked.

Her arms flew out, and she launched toward him on jets of flame. A pillar of thunder erupted from her hands, faster than thought, in milliseconds, a searing storm screaming toward where he stood—but the Black Death was gone, vanished into thin air.

"Jane," he said from behind her. "Please. Try to reconsider."

She roared and slammed her fists into the ground, sending trunk-sized spikes of ice erupting through the street. And then before the Black Death could speak another word, she clenched her arms, infusing them with lightning, exploding the ice out in every direction in a hail, an unstoppable shock wave of slicing shards. In every direction, no matter where he'd run or try to hide. The ice flew outward, slamming into windows and walls.

"Jane," came the Black Death's voice, and Jane's head snapped up to see him floating, his arms crossed, thirty feet above her, showing the soles of his boots. His face was a mask of disappointment—he sounded tired. "This is foolish."

She shot upward, her left fist full of lightning, her right full of flame—launching everything at him, around him, a cyclone of heat and death with the Black Death in the center, cutting off his escape. Her face grew hot, her body burning, fire head to toe, a human rocket flying toward him, through the center of her own assault. As his eyes narrowed and as she closed the gap between them, mere feet away, she forced everything she could muster, everything she had into the flames around her, super-charging the very air—

With a deafening BOOM, the barrier around Jane's body exploded, erupting in a wall of fire and lightning, the air cracking and roaring under the pressure, the sudden drops and spikes in heat throwing a rippling wall of searing force out in every direction—inches away from her, from where the Black Death floated, trapped. The world spun before Jane's eyes, and she fell, spinning, thrown back by the sheer force of her own attack, but out of instinct, out of training, she threw out her hands, stabilizing herself in the air thirty feet above the ground, a steady jet of flame burning from her hands, holding her in place. Her head snapped back, panting, desperate, to where the Black Death had been, to where she'd exploded.

Nothing. Only empty space. For an instant—a hysterical, delirious instant—she thought she'd won.

And then he spoke. "Clever," a voice said from behind her. Her eyes wide, Jane spun to see the Black Death, his arms by his side, traces of sulfur scattering to the breeze, twenty feet behind her. Alive and unharmed. Save for a small burn, the size of a dime, on the leftmost corner of his cheek.

"I commend your effort," he said quietly. He touched a black, gloved finger to his face, tracing over the mark, without a hint of pain or fear—only disconnection, as though the skin he touched was a distant source of interest rather than his own. Before his fingers fell, the damage was healed. The Black Death's voice grew hard. "But that is enough."

And then before she would blink, his hand was on her throat and his knee was in her guts. His fist slammed into her face, through her fire like it was nothing, hitting again, again, again, and again in the space of a second with the force of a sledgehammer—too fast to see, too fast to stop.

In a single moment, everything she'd learned, all her training—all of it became useless. The steel hand crushing her windpipe threw, and Jane Walker fell, crumpled, tumbling into nothing, her thoughts fading and her face streaming blood, patches of light and dark flickering before her eyes. Down and down, she fell. The fire faded from her palms, a sick, squelching ringing in her ears, face down, the wind whipping back her hair, as the earth rushed up to offer its final, breaking embrace—

But before she could hit, her fall halted—a smooth hand clenched firm around the back of her collar, jerking her to a halt. A loose sack of meat held inches from the ground.

Through delirium and pain, blackness encroaching on the edge of her vision, the hand pulled her effortlessly up, and a cold voice hissed in her ear, "Jane."

Her eyes flickered, her swollen lips murmuring something indistinct. Her hands twitched limply by her side. "You're not going to die, Jane," the twisting voice whispered. "I haven't given up. You're stubborn, but I know you'll understand. I know you'll see."

There was a rush of darkness, an assault of pressure and sulfur, and then Jane felt her broken and bloodied body thrown loosely in the dirt. Her mind swam, delirious—but still, she forced herself to look up. To look at him, standing there staring down at her. Unscathed.

"Don't resist me, Jane," he said quietly. He stood, his back to the city, his figure blotting out the sun, flooding her flickering consciousness with shadows. A being of pure darkness. "Don't sacrifice your future— what we could have. Think about it while you lay here. Think about that I didn't kill you when I could have, with a thought." He glanced back at the city behind him. "Watch what's about to happen. And think about what you want."

Jane tremored and tried to rise—but the pain and darkness came crashing down. As she fell into unconsciousness, the Black Death turned and flew back toward Detroit.

He landed, his boots tearing twin trails through the road.

"Apologies, Poole," he called out and the cameraman jumped, his eyes wild at the sound of his master's voice. "Rude of me. Personal business." The Black Death stopped and rolled his neck a full circle. "Resume broadcasting. And take to the air. You'll want some distance for this." His eyes flicked lazily upward to where other cameramen were now flying and news helicopters hovered, taking in the scene. "Ignore the competition," he added. "They won't interfere with our exclusive. Let them see." The Black Death spread his palms against the ground as Poole flew hurriedly up. "Let them all see," he murmured under his breath.

He inhaled, long and slow—then opened his eyes and pressed his arms down.

The ground split around him with a mighty, shuddering crack. Fissures raced from his hands, jagged lines opening across the earth and deep, deep underground. A web of cracks through rock and stone spread out underneath the city, breaking along every fault, every tectonic seam, until the entire city stood undermined, shaking yet still standing—as if for an endless, terrible second, it could only hold its breath—

Before the Black Death shifted and pulled the magma up from below.

A thousand miles away in a desert with no name, Matt Callaghan watched his friends being slaughtered and watched half a million people die. He stood stock-still against the workbench, his face frozen in horror, unable to watch but unable to turn away from the grainy images streaming through on the tiny, fuzzy screen—the live footage, bird's-eye-view, as the earth opened up and swallowed the city of Detroit. The buildings buckled, the skyscrapers fell, sinking, melting, into the gaping, molten maw. Fires burning, smoke belching, steel, ash, and death—hell on Earth, brought up to mankind. Mankind who stumbled. Mankind who screamed. Mankind, who the cameras could only watch helplessly as they tried to run, tried to escape as their city sank into a pit of searing, bubbling stone. The watching world saw everything—saw parents running with children, friends trying to fly away with friends. Strangers, trying to save strangers.

And in the center of it, the black figure of Klaus Heydrich, raised aloft upon a pillar of earth, smiling as the city around him died. Untouchable and alone. Slowly, his boots lifted from the ground, and he floated gently into the air, a lone shard of black against a boiling sea of red, indifferent to the hissing, the smoke, the screaming beneath him.

His work was done. As every nation on Earth watched on in horror, Klaus Heydrich drew in close to the camera, his face momentarily obscuring the devastation behind him.

"Thirty minutes," he stated. "Then Chicago."

His pale smile widened. And, black coat whipping, he flew away.

Matt's hands clutched the bench.

"God."

It wasn't an exclamation, but a prayer. Matt had never prayed before in his life. He'd never believed in the divine. But right now, he had nothing else. No plan, no power, no hope. His friends were dead, his world falling apart, and all he could do was beg.

"God," he whispered. His face scrunched up, tears leaking from his eyes. "Please. I don't know if you're listening but please. Please."

He looked up at the sky, pleading.

"Help."

Heat.

Heat and dust, everywhere, rolling over. Distant rumbling in her ears. The taste of blood in her mouth.

Jane tried to breathe. To suck in air where he'd struck her, through the pain in her chest, her sunken guts and lungs. Everything was blurry. Smoke crinkling down her crushed throat, dark blotches flittering at the edge of her vision. She tried to stand but couldn't. Tried to move her arms, her legs, anything. But everything just lay there. Everything hurt. She closed her eyes.

"You need to wake up."

A voice. Not the Black Death. Soft and young. Oddly calm.

Her eyes flicked open.

There, in front of her, stood a boy.

Pale and small with a quiet, round face and hair a color between white and gold. He stood there as still and silent as a statue, watching her, unblinking, unmoving, as dust and darkness whorled around them. Pure, plain, and untarnished, while she lay bruised and broken, covered in dirt and ash and blood. It was like something out of a dream. Jane forced herself to blink. But the boy didn't disappear.

And then, as her eyes refocused, she saw what was behind him.

"No," she whispered. Detroit. The entire city, sunk into the earth— the tops of its tallest buildings, still sinking slowly down into the red, violent glow. Curtains of ash, pillars of toxic smoke, raining down, rising up from within its cavernous depths, blotting out the sun. She pushed unsteadily to her feet, taking a step forward, two, the pain forgotten—before sinking back down, her knees stinging in the dirt. Homes. Schools. The Legion. All gone, all extinguished—swallowed by the tides of fire. Turned to nothing in the dark.

"I can't . . ." she uttered, choking. "I don't . . ."

But there were no words to say. She put her head in her hands, unable to bear—unable to watch any more.

Then the child behind her spoke.

"He'll destroy everything. Everyone. The entire world."

Jane opened her eyes a fraction. She looked up, through her fingers, her chest heaving, half coughing from the smoke. What was . . . there was something about his voice. The way he spoke. He couldn't have been more than ten, maybe eleven, but he wasn't scared like a child that age should be with the devastation swirling around them. He was quiet, almost serene—and when he spoke, it was without urgency, without inflection. Out of place. Like he was.

Slowly, she lowered her hands and stared back at him as he stood there, gazing into the sinking storm—the choking clouds, the crater of melting earth. His face blank, his small mouth set, his eyes distant.

His eyes. The deepest, sapphire blue.

"Who are you?" she whispered. Was she dreaming? She'd been concussed, hit in the head a lot. Was this even real? "Where . . . where are your parents?"

The pale child looked at her, his blue eyes steady and piercing. Eyes that didn't blink or waver. Eyes that seemed to know her.

"*I am watcher and wanderer,*" he said softly, and it was as though his voice echoed through a veil. "*Eternity and instant. I am no one and everywhere. I tug at the life threads.*"

"I don't understand," whispered Jane. She was unconscious. This was a dream. The child turned back to the fallen city.

"*I led you here,*" he said simply, "*to this point.*" He looked back at her, his young, smooth face—but the words he spoke were not a child's words. "*To stop this. But the time for discretion has passed. I have stacked the deck. But I cannot stop him. Only Dawn can.*"

His words rang in Jane's ears, his voice a half-forgotten memory. But the truth stuck in her throat.

"Dawn is dead," she whispered, despaired.

But the child shook his frail head. "*No,*" he murmured, voice echoing in the wind. "*Not always.*"

He turned to her and held out his tiny hand. "*Take my power,*" he offered. There was no fear in his voice. Jane stared at him, unmoving—her knees still grazed in the dirt, her armor cracked, hair run through with ash, and temple slicked with gore. The battered empath, beaten and bloodied, kneeling face-to-face with the small white child. For a moment, they just sat there, the girl staring, the boy's thin arm outstretched—dust and smoke billowing, the world brown and ocher gray, swirling in spirals around them.

And slowly, as if a dream, Jane reached up and took his hand.

Instantly, she felt it. Under his skin, echoing—a gaping, cavern-ous feeling, stars studded through the singing abyss. A heart beating backward, a sense of falling, up into the sky. The warm, frozen infinite. Words and sounds and color, humming through him, like nothing she'd experienced, nothing she could comprehend. She reeled, not knowing or understanding, for the first time truly afraid, wanting to let go, want-ing to run away—but when she looked up, she found herself looking face-to-face with the boy. Jane froze, terrified, seeing only his eyes—the swirling sapphire galaxies, opening up into eternity, deep enough to lose yourself in, to swim forever through.

But then her gaze widened, and she saw the greater truth. The boy's eyes were of his powers—alien, unfathomable—but what was in them was not. In his eyes, across his face, in his small, sad smile, there was only compassion. Only tenderness. And in an instant, she knew some-how that he was only there to help her. That he wasn't going to hurt her, now or ever. That all he wanted was to be kind.

Somehow, he reminded her of Matt.

"*Don't be afraid,*" he murmured gently. Young and hopeful. Old and knowing.

She closed her eyes, closed her fingers gently around the child's soft, warm palm, and felt the power underneath it flow into her.

"*Concentrate,*" the child whispered. "*Remember this place, this moment. The sound, the smell, how the earth felt beneath you. Remember, so that you may return. Then listen. And think.*

"*The numbers sixteen, three, five, and seventy. A square opening into a circle.*" Jane felt it moving within her, the new coin between her fingers, rolling into place. Eyes still closed, listening, breathing, following the boy's words. "*The smell of leather and sawdust. Warm rain in your hair, the sound of starlight, soft wool beneath your skin. Focus on them, all of them, compressed, a single point. Hold it in your mind and walk through it,*" he told her. And Jane felt the wind around her churn, the sounds and smells swirling out and away into a warm, singing, shining blue darkness—felt her body falling forward until there was nothing around her but a wrapping, threading tunnel and an echo, the boy's voice whispering in her ear. "*And bring back the Dawn.*"

"UGH!"

Jane lurched, stumbling, the spell broken, suddenly unbalanced. She threw out her hands, shouting, bracing herself for the impact as a wall of brown and crimson came rushing out toward her.

But no impact came.

Gingerly, wincing, Jane snuck a peek through squinted eyes. The wall stared back, indifferent to her presence. Jane opened her eyes a little wider, lowering her hands. The world around her was suddenly very still and very silent, no longer a rushing, hurtling blur.

She took a deep, steadying breath, forcing herself to blink, now thoroughly awake, feeling like she'd just run her face under hot water. She flexed her fingers, this odd almost-current running through them, flighty and strange, as she glanced confusedly at her surroundings. It wasn't . . . had she teleported? Because she sure as hell wasn't where she'd been a second ago. The dust was gone, Detroit was gone, the sky was gone—she was inside. Somewhere.

She held up her hands in front of her face, rippling the nonexistent coin between her fingers back away from the new power—which sat there, between her pinky and ring finger, an entire tiny universe, invisible, vast, swirling, and light, almost alive, humming with kaleidoscopic energy. Jane shook her wrists, her heart beating rapidly, the intangible ability singing softer than a whisper—patient, all-knowing, terrifying. She glanced around her, looking to see if the strange child had come with her—but she was alone.

Alone, and in a corridor she knew.

Jane took a step back, her head snapping in every direction. This was Morningstar! This, this was the entrance hall, the opening foyer, she . . . she knew these walls! These doors, these pictures, this . . . well, not this carpet. This carpet was red, burgundy, the color of spilled wine, whereas she knew for a fact that carpets she'd walked along just this morning were green.

But this was impossible. Morningstar had been destroyed. Jane had seen it, seen the smoking ruin with her own two eyes. There wasn't anything left, charred wood and ash and a few stones and . . . nothing like this. Nothing this intact, this pristine, this . . .

She ran her hands through her hair, glancing around, breathing fast, pain still pulsing through her body, a ringing in her ears. What the hell was going on? What had she . . . how had she . . . ?

Okay. Jane forced herself to calm down, to take stock. There was an explanation. There had to be an explanation. She was likely concussed. The boy—the boy had said to bring Dawn back. Dawn, okay, Captain Dawn, and now she was at Morningstar, okay, that made sense, except Dawn was dead. But then, this manor was supposed to be too. She glanced around at the sandstone walls she'd seen torn down, the roof she'd seen turned to ash. And this stupid red carpet, which was just plain wrong. A damn biohazard that was, you'd never know to clean it when someone tracked in blood. But apart from the ceiling, the carpet, the pictures, and the walls, there wasn't anything to see. No one was around. No Acolytes, no Ashes. The hallway was completely deserted.

Hello? Jane wanted to call—but something about being here, about her sudden, unexplained presence, made her throat lock tight. Clutching her bruised rib cage, her Legion body armor cracked and torn in more places than not, she limped as quietly as she could along the hallway and through the double doors to the Grand Hall.

The hall lay dark and deserted—but as Jane's eyes adjusted to the low light, she realized that wasn't the weirdest thing. The long tables were gone, replaced by a table, singular—an enormous, perfectly circular wooden ring taking up almost all the space in the room, two feet thick, with high-backed, studded leather chairs spread evenly along its outer length. Jane froze, staring open-mouthed and furrow-browed at this wrongness, this bizarre change to a place she'd been sitting in for months. It was so big, from where she stood in the doorway, you almost couldn't see the far end of it in the unlit dark.

And then it hit her. The dark. It was night outside. But in Detroit, it'd been midday and . . .

What in the burning, unholy hell, Jane whispered to herself. She added in a few stronger swear words for good measure.

After shaking her head to no one and taking a moment's pause, Jane's eyes flicked over to the stage on the far side of the hall—and the doorway she knew was tucked in against it that led up to Captain Dawn's quarters. Screw it, she decided—the Black Death was on the warpath, cities were sinking into the ground and buildings where she lived were unexploding wrong—she'd weather the consequences of violating Dawn's privacy. The empath skirted, still clutching her chest, half-limping, quiet as she could, around the left-side edge of the table, to the far and looming wall. She grunted as she lifted herself onto the stage, most of her body still crying in pain—but nothing she hadn't taken before, and nothing the sound of her heart racing, the adrenaline kicking through the madness, wouldn't dull. Her hand clutched the side of the slim, open doorway for support, and she pulled her dirty boots step by step up the narrow spiral stairs.

It was difficult to judge how high she climbed—the staircase was dark, the walls uniform, leading nowhere but up. Three stories, maybe four. Her breathing grew steadier as she climbed, her bruised lungs slowly taking back in air, though her head continued to pound. She was lucky. Apart from some ribs and what felt like one or two small cracks near an eye socket, she didn't think anything was broken.

Jane reached the top of the stairs to find an unassuming wooden door with an old metal handle. Gingerly, she thumbed down the latch and pushed the door silently open into a warm room of oak and cedar. Jane's eyes swept over a leather lounge, a messy bookcase, and a darkened doorway leading to a pitch-black walk-in wardrobe—then a second, lighter chamber with three tall, adjacent mirrors affixed to one side, reflecting an entire wall of framed medals, certificates, and commendations. Beyond that the room transitioned into a quiet, simple study, with a floor-length glass case in one corner displaying a familiar garb, a woman's uniform, the matching white and gold once worn by Captain Dawn's wife, and in the other corner an antique wooden desk and a brown leather chair.

And in that chair, sitting silent and alone in the dusty light, sat Captain Dawn.

Jane froze—her hand still clutching the latch, the tip of her foot barely peeking around the door. Her cheek pressed against the lacquered wood, holding her body back in darkness, one eye staring wide into the light. She felt like she was going to faint, like her heart was going to explode out of her chest. He was alive. She closed her eyes, begging, pleading with whatever gods might be watching her—please let this be real. After a few seconds, she opened her eyes. And Dawn was still there.

Still there. Still strong, tall, and radiant, the air seeming to glow bright around him. His hair, his face, his uniform—all of it, all like the pictures, all like she'd known. Somehow, inherently, she knew: this was no imposter. This was the man she'd grown up worshiping. This Dawn was real.

She stood there, breathing deeply, her heart trembling, just watching him. Sitting at his desk, golden cape shimmering down his broad shoulders, leaning forward, ungloved hands in his lap, eyes forward, shining like a star, a statue. For a single moment that seemed to hang for an eternity, Jane didn't move, didn't speak—only watched him, breathed in the sight of him. In that instant, it seemed like doing anything would break the spell, so Jane just stood there, watching Captain Dawn, this perfect, golden hero, frozen in time, gazing at him from afar in a strange, dreamlike trance . . .

As he raised the barrel of the six-shot revolver to his temple and pulled the trigger.

"NO!"

BANG!

Every road out of Chicago was packed. Bumper-to-bumper, cars, trucks, and buses as far as the eye could see—half trying to push past the others, half abandoned, their occupants running through the gridlock on foot. Horns blaring, shouts and sirens—from the air, this far up, it was almost melodic. A writhing symphony of chaos.

But it wasn't only the roads out of Chicago that seethed.

Into the city, along every highway and overpass, rolled the military. Tanks, mounted artillery, long-range missile launchers, and even a few the Black Death had to admit he didn't recognize. All alongside the jogging troops and trucks, the commanders and carriers, the pomp and panoply of war. Khaki green, pumping in through the city's veins.

There was a distant bang and the bullet of a far-off sniper stopped dead in the air two feet from the Black Death's face. Three more cracks immediately sounded, and three more bullets as thick as a thumb froze in midair the same distance away, floating at different heights and angles.

"Fools," he hissed. He twitched his fingers and the magnetic field around his body pushed out another ten yards, the caught bullets dropping harmlessly into open air. Far below, a shout went out among the soldiers—and in a matter of seconds, a thick, unnatural fog rolled over the city, low and gray, obscuring the Black Death's vision of Chicago's streets and the soldiers moving through them. Below, there came the sound of gears whirring, barrels moving, weapons adjusting—the creaks and calls of an army taking aim, rendered invisible and almost inaudible by the thickening cloud.

It was an admirable strategy, he thought—shield their positions from view while they could see him clearly through infra-red, radar, or thermal imaging. A clever fusion of weaponry and power. But as with all things American, it was ignorant and arrogant. Even if he, too, couldn't control the weather, even if he couldn't have blown the fog away with a single thought, even if his eyes couldn't change to see outside the visible spectrum, even if his superhuman senses didn't let him hear the creak of every bolt—even then he could still feel them, scurrying around, little bumps in his magnetism. Metal men with metal guns driving metal machines. Preparing, as he floated, as he waited, to launch metal artillery.

He could have destroyed them. All of them, in an instant. Blasted them from on high, collapsed buildings upon them, crushed them with their own crumpled steel weapons. But instead, he did nothing. He'd let them expend their effort. Let them try. After all, this was going out live. He was putting on a show.

And there was nothing more demoralizing than watching your best plans fail.

A thousand hissing, echoing booms exploded out from Chicago's streets and through the cover of cloud shot the offerings of an arsenal—screaming, hurtling toward him in the blink of an eye, too fast for any human to see or dodge. But the Black Death didn't move, didn't disappear. He merely held out his hands—and as if time had frozen, hundreds of shells and missiles, bullets and bombs all thudded to a halt in a wall of explosive steel, twenty feet away. Floating, as he floated—some stopped, some sizzling, some spinning. All held in place before his outstretched hand, balancing in limbo.

A small smirk twitched over the Black Death's lips. Pre-Aurora weaponry. Really. What did they expect? His right hand gave a lazy twitch and as one, the military's gifts flew back to their masters in a repurposed, deadly rain. He cracked his knuckles, stretching the bones in his fingers as a wail of screams and explosions echoed up from the street below. Before whoever he'd hit had time to die, more shots were being fired, more missiles launched, any semblance of unified assault forgotten as every man down there retaliated as fast as he could, sending a constant stream of fire screeching up through the clouds. The

Black Death did not waver. Every piece of munitions that flew too close he threw straight back, not caring where it fell, raining indiscriminately on the soldiers. Many exploded before they reached him, showering the sky with shock waves of fire and shrapnel, but the Black Death's left hand stayed steady, projecting a force field around him that no chemical explosion would ever penetrate. Then his ears twitched, hearing something new moving below. Suddenly, out through the clouds, a tremendous, invisible force screamed up at him, a pummeling torrent of shuddering sound. The Black Death laughed as a blast of deafening noise slammed harmlessly into his force fields. Sonics. They had a machine that shot sound. He shook his head and unleashed a barrage of energy from his eyes, incinerating the mounted device and silencing its infernal wailing.

"Enough of this." He laughed. His magnetic fields closed around a few dozen shells and missiles that were hurtling toward him. Without a backward glance, he started climbing, flying straight up into open sky, the shards of deadly metal trailing obediently in his wake.

"Sir."

The president's head turned, as did the eyes of every man in the stuffy, dim-lit room.

"Sir," the adviser repeated, "he's heading into orbit."

They could all see it. On every screen in front of them, the black speck of a man, rising higher and higher against the darkening blue. Some of the camera feeds followed him but many backed off.

"He's running," someone whispered, their voice rising with strangled hope. But nobody else seemed to hear them.

"Status report."

"Heavy casualties, sir. Divisions three through five reporting loss of at least sixty percent of their armor."

"And Heydrich?"

"Multiple shots on target, sir. No confirmed damage. Sir"—the analyst paused, turning around to the commander in chief, sweat beading on his glasses—"I think he let us hit him. I think he's sending us a message. Showing off."

Someone swore. The president's knuckles tightened around the back of the metal chair.

"Sir," muttered General Armstrong, leaning in, unblinking, "this is our best chance. We have to do it now."

"Christ, Bradley," Clarke whispered. He ran a hand through thinning hair, his face gaunt. "We've got soldiers in there. It's right over a civilian population!"

"There's no guarantee it'll stop him" agreed McCulvic. "And that high up, the radiation could spread to—"

"We don't know what will happen—"

"Sir," implored Armstrong, blocking out the dissenting voices, "if we act now, some people may die. If we do nothing, we all will."

The room fell silent. All eyes fell to the president, who pinched the bridge of his nose, breathing unsteadily through his hand.

"God help us."

"NO!" Jane screamed.

She lurched forward, her eyes wide, her arms thrown out—but too far away to stop it, too far away to do anything as Captain Dawn set the gun an inch from his head and pulled the trigger.

BANG!

Plink.

"NO!" she screamed again—but then her cries abruptly died. Halfway across the room, she stumbled to a halt, stunned, as Captain Dawn turned his head around to stare at her, a morose, curious look on his face.

"Who're you?" he mumbled. "What're you doing? You're . . . you're . . ." The gun flopped down into his lap. "You're not supposed to be in here."

Her feet frozen in place, her face contorted in strangled, dissolving horror, Jane's eyes flickered from the captain's miserable expression to the smoking pistol in his hand to the squished, compacted bullet laying harmlessly on the floor.

"What . . . what am I . . . ?" she spluttered incredulously. Then her brain regained proper use of her tongue and her voice rose to righteous anger. "What am I doing? *What are you doing?* ARE YOU OUT OF YOUR GODDAMN MIND?"

"Stop shouting . . ." murmured Dawn. He sniffed and rubbed his wet nose with the back of the revolver. He looked down at the gun. "It doesn't hurt me," he said glumly. "Nothing does."

"I . . . uh . . . my . ." stammered Jane, words having temporarily abandoned her. All she could do was keep shaking her head and staring, disbelieving, at the man in front of her. "Then . . . then why?" she got out finally, her teeth gnashing every word. "Why? Are you shooting yourself? In the head?"

"See if it works," Dawn replied miserably. He swung his big head back around away from her, staring blankly at the desk in front of him, at the pile of reports and newspapers. "Maybe one day, it will."

"What! What!" Jane spluttered, her hands held incredulously in the air. Her mouth worked furiously, struggling to form a coherent sentence. "One day? I . . . Are you . . . Give me that gun!" she demanded. Dawn just sat there, slumped over, not looking at her.

"Please leave," he whispered.

"Um, no," Jane replied sarcastically, pausing in faux consideration. "No, actually, I don't think I will."

"Suit yourself," Dawn mumbled. He flopped his hands on the desk and lay his chin on his arms.

A dusty silence stretched out between them—the captain laying with his head in his hands, resting on a newspaper, the empath shaking her head, blinking rapidly as she struggled to comprehend what she was seeing.

"Why?" she got out finally. "Why, for the love of . . . EVERYTHING are you trying to kill yourself?"

"You wouldn't understand," Dawn moaned softly. He rolled his head to the side, refusing to look at her.

"I—" Jane pinched the bridge of her nose and unleashed a flurry of violent swear words under her breath. This was insane. She was going insane. First the kid, then Morningstar, now . . . How hard had she hit her head?

"Try me"—she swore—"just"—she resisted the urge to swear again—"try me."

Captain Dawn rolled his head on the side, looking up at Jane, the edges of his green eyes tinged with red. For a moment, she thought he was going to yell at her—but when he finally spoke, his voice was soft and sorrowful.

"Have you ever been in love?" he mumbled.

Jane hesitated.

"No," she said finally, her voice little more than a murmur. "I don't know."

The superhero shook his handsome head, his dark hair barely moving. "No. You'd know. There's no way you couldn't, no way . . . when you love someone, when you find someone perfect, and the world stops moving around you, and they're . . . they're everything, and—"

"Captain," Jane, hating herself for doing so, but unable to shake the burning image of Detroit from her mind. "Look. I'm sure this is all really important, but I need you to come with me. I need your help, the Black Death is—"

"Who?" mumbled Dawn.

"The Black Death!" she repeated louder. "He's destroying cities, sir. You need to stop him. He's going to destroy the world if you don't—"

But to her horror and amazement, Captain Dawn just turned away.

"I don't care," he muttered.

Jane felt like he'd slapped her.

"You don't . . . you don't . . ." she stammered, stumbling over her words. She squeezed her eyes closed and open again, sure she'd misheard him, positive she'd explained it wrong. "Sir, Captain, he's killing hundreds of thousands of people. He's going to take over the world, you need to—"

"I don't care," Dawn said again. Face down on the desk, he rolled his head back over on his muscular arms, his lips drawn, angry yet miserable. "There's always something. Some . . . villain to fight. Some . . . people to save. It doesn't matter." A single tear, a glistening drop of sunlight, leaked from the corner of his eye. "None of it matters anymore."

Jane just stood there. Unable to speak, unable to move. The gears in her mind grinding through blank shock. After a few seconds, when she didn't respond, Captain Dawn kept going.

"She's dead," he said, and his chest shuddered with the words as he said them, as though they caused him physical pain. Jane stared blankly.

"Who?" she asked. Dawn's head snapped around, his eyes shimmering with disbelief.

"Caitlin!" he cried. "Caitlin, who else?!"

"Right, okay, Caitlin," said Jane hurriedly, holding up her hands to placate the captain, who was suddenly halfway off his chair, his face a mask of mangled fury. "No, of course, Caitlin, your wife, who else?" She kicked herself for missing the obvious. "Sorry, sir, I'm really sorry."

The anger on Dawn's face faded as quickly as it had risen. "I . . . I don't . . ." he sobbed. He slumped back into the chair. "Now that she's gone I . . ." Dawn let out a long, heartbreaking moan. "I don't know what to do, I don't . . . none of it matters. Not anymore."

"But . . ." murmured Jane, unable to grasp it, unable to understand, "but, sir . . . just because she . . . Caitlin . . . is dead, doesn't mean you need to stop . . ."

"You don't understand," Dawn mumbled. He raised his head from his hands, staring blankly down at the desk. "It was all for her. Everything I did, I did it to make her happy, I . . ." His voice gurgled. Then he straightened up, shaking his head, unable to meet Jane's eye.

"She was the one," he said miserably. "She was the one who wanted to be superheroes. She was so passionate, so forceful, with all these dreams about changing the world and helping people and I . . ." Dawn's voice wavered. "I just wanted to be with her. I just . . . I loved her. I loved her so much and I was scared. I just wanted her to love me and so I . . ." His voice trailed off, and he sniffed, staring down at his hands.

Jane's mind was blank. "But . . ." she started, but her voice caught in her throat. She tried again. "But you . . . that's wrong! You started the Legion of Heroes! You're a legend, the power of a hundred suns, you, you intervened in dozens . . . hundreds of conflicts, you've saved thousands of lives!" She stared at him, her face ashen, aghast.

Dawn shook his head. "It was all Caitlin's idea," he mumbled. "She came up with everything. The Legion of Heroes. The name Captain Dawn. Even the costume," he added miserably, gazing with painful longing at the glass case in the corner where his wife's uniform stood empty, perfect partner to his own. "Everything. She would talk in my mind, tell me what to do, she . . . she cared about these things, about the world, about"—he made a face—"politics and people and human rights . . . being a hero . . . all of it. And I just, I had the power, and it just made her so happy, and I just wanted, I . . . I just didn't want her to leave."

Jane's heart dropped to her stomach, but she didn't believe it. She couldn't.

"We will do what we must, we few, we great," she recited. Memorized, word for word. "We, who have the power to save the world, and who will not, cannot, stand idly by while its peoples suffer. We are servants of no nation but the protectors of humanity." She looked at him pointedly. "You said that."

Dawn shook his head again.

"Caitlin wrote it," he mumbled.

"But you're . . ." Jane whispered lamely. Underneath her battered armor, her shoulders drooped. "You're a hero. You're Captain Dawn."

The golden man, slouched over, glanced at her out of the corner of his eye. "That's not my name," he murmured. "Everyone always calls me that but I'm not . . . I'm just Walter," he said pathetically, "Walter Reid." His face crinkled. "Caitlin, she's gone and . . . nobody ever calls me by my real name."

And then, before she could do anything, the hero of legend's shoulders hunched over, and he began to genuinely, openly cry—as Jane just stood there, watching golden tears stream down his perfect face.

"Oh God." Her knees buckled. Jane doubled over, a dry, retching sickness spreading through her chest. She wanted to collapse, to scream, to beat this giant, miserable man—hit him, again, again, and again until he gave in, until he retracted these lies and admitted that he really was a hero, the hero he had to be . . .

Oh God. Everything she'd believed in, all those years of hard work, and now . . . this man that she'd . . . she'd *worshipped*, who she'd looked up to since she could walk, was saying these things and just . . . moping, sobbing, and crying there in front of her like some shining overgrown baby . . .

No. She straightened up, forcing herself to draw a long, shaking breath, trying to focus, to drag her mind back to why she was there. Detroit, the fire, she had to, there wasn't . . . there wasn't time for this.

"Sir," she whispered. Her voice shook, and her eyes seemed too heavy to ever leave the floor. But she pushed herself onward, forcing the words out. "Captain," she said. "Captain Dawn. Walter. I"—she took a deep breath—"I know, you might not be the man everyone thinks you are. I know you . . . you miss Caitlin, and I'm so, so sorry she's gone. But I . . ." Her voice trailed off and she looked at him, slumped over in front of her alone in this attic. "But I need you," she pleaded. "Right now, I need you. I need you to use your power, I need you to be a hero, I . . . I need you."

A heaving sob caught in her throat, but she forced it back down. "Please," she begged him, "I can't do it. It's just me and I don't know how to . . . the Black Death, he's back and he's going to destroy the world—"

Captain Dawn—Walter—barely looked up from crying. "I don't care," he snapped sulking miserably. Then, with a hint of anger, he added, "And I'm telling you, I don't know who that is."

Jane's fists clenched in frustration. "What do you mean?" she demanded, feeling so exasperated she could cry. "How is that possible? How can you not know who. . . ?"

She fell silent. For a few seconds, both she and the most power-ful man in the world stood stuck in place—her trying to collect her thoughts, him sobbing like a baby, his arms dangling either side of the chair. Finally, after a full minute of her groggy mind reeling while . . . Walter . . . bawled into thin air, finally the man's crying ended. He sniffed and exhaled, drawing a shuddering breath in between his teeth and star-ing across at Jane through bleary red eyes.

"Who are you?" he asked finally, sucking in a wet sniff. "One of Elsa's new . . . ? Why are you even . . . ?" The words fumbled on his tongue. "She's supposed to tell them, they're not supposed to, to come in here . . ." His eyebrows furrowed, dull confusion scrawling over his features as his eyes took in Jane, seeming to really see her for the first time. "What happened to you? Are you . . . are you hurt? What's . . . why is there an E on your face?"

"It's my—" started Jane, her hand flicking instinctively to her tattoo—but then she hesitated, the true meaning of his words hitting her. "Wait, Elsa?" she queried, peering forward at him, confused. "Elsa Arrendel? The White Queen? She's alive too?"

Captain Dawn stared at her, tear stains still fresh on his cheek. "Well . . . I think so," he said with a slight hiccup. "I mean I haven't heard . . . wait, what do you mean *too?*"

Jane blinked, her mouth stuck open, trying to process. The White Queen—alive? And Captain Dawn . . . Morningstar . . .

And suddenly, her eyes caught the top of the newspaper on Dawn's desk, the bottom half covered by his arms. Jane squinted, reading the headline upside down—something about the Lakers beating the Celtics, she didn't know, she didn't follow basketball—but the date . . .

June 12, 1988.

"Do it," the president mumbled. He closed his eyes. "Send a nuke. The fastest, the biggest payload we've got. Order the military to evacuate, get as many people out as we can. We need to end this."

"Sir," Clarke protested, "it's a violation of the disarmament treaty with—"

"I'll deal with the Russians," the president murmured. He shook his head, not looking up from the blur of Heydrich, speeding through open sky. "I'll deal with the fallout. I don't care what I have to do, if it brings this son of a bitch down, so be it."

"Ready the launch," he commanded, and the room moved on his orders. "Bring me the codes."

He shook his head, staring helplessly at the screen and city. "May God have mercy on us all."

Jane stopped breathing. She stared, open-mouthed at Captain Dawn.

"Nineteen eighty-eight," she whispered. And suddenly Morningstar, the carpet, the table, Elsa, the captain, everything—all of it clicked into place. Jane staggered, her hands reaching out, catching on the side of one of the mirrors, the room spinning before her eyes. She was . . . the boy . . .

"Not always."

Her head snapped up to Dawn, heart hammering in her chest.

"Sir," she whispered, her voice trembling, her entire body electrified, shooting through with a giddy, electric rush. "Holy hell, sir, Walter, I mean, I get it, I understand now, I—"

She paused, shaking with excitement. "Sir," she gushed, "my name is Jane Walker. I'm an Acolyte, part of the Legion of Heroes, except not this Legion, the Legion from the future, from 2001."

Dawn's blank expression opened into a slight frown. He leaned back, looking at Jane like she was crazy.

"What?"

"I know it's hard to believe," Jane continued, talking so fast it felt like she was going to trip over her own words. "But I swear it's true. I've come back in time—I think, I'm eighty, no, ninety, no a hundred percent sure—because we need you, sir, the world's in danger and we need you, right now, well, not *now*, but right now in my time and . . ." Her voice trailed off at the captain's blank expression. "Is any of this making any sense to you?"

Walter hesitated. "You're . . . you're from the Legion . . . in the future?" he sniffed.

"Yes!" Jane almost kissed the air. "Yes! I know it's insane, but look, look at what I'm wearing, look at my armor!" She pointed her hands wildly at the cracked and torn crimson-and-gold Kevlar-woven plating. "And look! Look, I've got the"—she stuck her shoulder out, leaning enthusiastically forward—"I've got the badge, I've got . . ."

"We can travel in time?" Dawn whispered slowly, his eyes glazed over, not seeing the silver eagle the empath was thrusting in front of his face. Jane hesitated.

"Well, it's less *we* can so much as *I* can," she conceded. "And I mean, barely, I've got no idea how it works, I just sort of got led here, I don't actually know how to . . ." Again, she trailed off, shaking her head, trying to flush away the doubts. "But it doesn't matter, sir, you've got to help us," she pleaded. "You've got to stop him, Klaus Heydrich, I mean, the Black Death, you haven't heard of him yet, but he killed you and now—"

"He what?" yelped the captain, sitting up like someone had stabbed him in the spine.

"Yeah!" rambled Jane. "He killed you, and then he destroyed Africa, and now he's back and—"

"How?" Dawn interrupted her with a strangled cry. Jane blinked.

"How what? How'd he destroy Africa? He supercharged his cells with energy and—"

"No!" he cried. "How did he kill me?"

"Oh," said Jane, a bit taken aback, "well . . . he's an empath. Blood-based." She huffed impatiently at the blank look on the captain's face. "He absorbs people's blood and permanently gets their powers."

"And he copied my power?" said Dawn, his face scrunching in skepticism. "I don't even think I have blood anymore."

"No, I don't think he—" began Jane, before she realized what he'd just said. "Wait, you don't have blood? What do you have in"—she stopped herself—"you know what, never mind. No, the Black Death didn't get your powers. He just managed to combine his and . . . and defeat you, I guess, he was more powerful."

Captain Dawn looked horrified.

"When did this happen?" he whispered, his green eyes wide.

"Ten years ago," answered Jane, then corrected herself: "Okay, ten years in my past, two years in your future." She pressed on, recounting her history. "He started killing people in Africa. The Legion went to fight him, and he killed them all, and then you went and fought him too, and everyone thought you won." She averted her eyes slightly. "But we were wrong. He killed you, stole your identity, then . . ." Her voice trailed off. "And now he's back," she finally managed to get out, "stronger than before. And he's going to take over the world, my world—and you're the only one who has any chance of stopping him." She looked up at Dawn's blank, horrified face, her eyes pleading. "You're our only hope."

There was a long pause.

"So, let me get this straight," Captain Dawn finally said, his face inscrutable. "This man—this 'Black Death'—killed me once already. And now he's stronger."

"Yes," began Jane, "but—"

"And you want me to go fight him again?!" yelped Dawn, retreating up and out of his chair, recoiling away from her. "He'll kill me!"

The rush of excitement that had been racing through Jane's mind came to an abrupt, crashing halt. She gaped up at the giant, simpering superhero. "What?" she cried, unable to believe what she was hearing. "What do you mean 'he'll kill you'? We're talking about the fate of the world!"

"I-I-I-I-I-I can't," stammered Walter. "I can't do it, you don't understand. I-I-I don't want to die!"

"You just tried to kill yourself!" cried Jane, in utter disbelief.

"That doesn't mean I'm just going to throw my life away!" Walter wailed like some white-and-gold child. He retreated a step further away from her, lips trembling. "I can't, I can't do it, not without her, not without Caitlin, I—"

And before Jane's despairing eyes, he fell to his knees and once more began to cry.

"I can't," he sobbed, golden cape heaving against his shoulders. "I just can't. I can't fight him, I'm sorry, I'm not brave, I don't—"

"You have to!" Jane implored. She dropped to one knee in front of him. "You . . . you're the only one that stands a chance. I believe in you. You have to do it. You . . ." A tightness spread across her chest. "You have to try."

"But I'm scared," whispered Walter, tears streaming silently down his cheeks. "You said it yourself. I'm not strong enough. He kills me. I can't . . . I can't . . ." He sniffed quietly, his eyes on the floor. "What if I can't do it? What if I fail? What if I die? I . . . I'm supposed to be a hero." He gazed up at her through shaking eyes, his face wet and frightened. "Heroes never lose."

Jane looked down at him—at this glowing, broken man, wracked with fear, paralyzed because for the first time in his life, he might not be strong enough. And she remembered being where he was, feeling what he was feeling. Seeing Morningstar burn. Walking, waiting to confront the Black Death, her and the Legion, even though they'd known they couldn't stop him, even though they'd known it was probably hopeless. She thought about James, Mac, Celeste, all of them, how they'd all stood while he'd slaughtered them—how they'd never given up, never given an inch. About Matt—loyal, loving Matt—who'd never once stood down, never once backed off. Not for Ed. Not for her. Not when it was someone he cared about. Even though he had nothing, even though he was the least powerful person in the world.

And slowly, like it was someone else talking, she started to speak.

"Being a hero, it's . . . it's not about winning or losing," she said softly. "It's not about being the strongest. It's . . . it doesn't matter how strong you are. Whether you succeed, whether you fail, who you are, what you can do. Being a hero isn't about strength. It's about doing what's right." She swallowed and looked up. "And knowing you're going to fail," she said defiantly, "knowing you'll change nothing, knowing you'll be forgotten, but trying anyway . . . it doesn't make you less. It makes you more."

Jane shook her head and smiled, sniffing back the sadness tugging at her heart—because suddenly, she understood. Suddenly, she knew what she had to do. She took a deep, ragged breath—feeling the cracks in her face, the pain in her chest—and with a single step, turned away from the man she thought she'd loved.

"I'm going back," she said quietly. "I'm going to fight. I can't stop him. I know that." She looked back at Dawn, still standing in his corner, paralyzed with fear. "But I'm still going to try." Her beaten face moved into a small, sad smile. "Even if it kills me. Even if I'm going to die."

"But why?" the man whispered. "If you can't win, what's the point?"

"Because I have to," Jane replied simply. She shook her head. "Because I can't just stand back and do nothing. Because it's right."

There was a long, empty silence.

Slowly, Captain Dawn lowered his eyes—the fear on his face fading to stillness. Fading to shame.

"You sound like her," he said quietly. "Like Caitlin."

Jane closed her eyes, feeling them growing hot and blurry. Her mouth quivered in a weak smile. But she didn't falter. Even now, even at the end, she could say that much. Hold her head high.

She opened her eyes and looked back at Dawn.

"I'll ask you," she said to him, "one last time."

She held out her hand.

"Come back with me."

DAWN

The Black Death rose.

Ten miles. Twenty. Climbing higher and higher, straight up, alone against a sky turning blue to black, leading a trail of captured weaponry.

One by one, his followers wavered—each of the flying cameramen turning back as the air grew too cold, too thin. But the Black Death needed no air, no warmth.

Thirty miles above the city of Chicago he halted, hanging in emptiness. The shells and missiles he was trailing rose up to join him, orbiting in a perfect circle, a ring of steel satellites. The Black Death held open his palms, face up, and the metal of the munitions melted into a solid, silver mass—lengthening, hardening, re-forming into a single, man-sized spike. His palms pressed against his cold creation—but then suddenly, the Black Death stopped. He glanced down—his eyes narrowed. And then his smile widened.

For, from the Earth, something was coming. Something sleek, something metal, something with letters down the side and chemical propellant spewing from one end. A speck on the horizon, growing larger and larger by the second, heading straight for him.

A nuclear missile.

Oh. Well, now.

He had been planning to use the spike. Infused with explosive energy, shot like a pin, a man-made meteor to fall upon the city and unleash a wave of devastating force. Maybe climb even higher, crush and remold a satellite, simply let gravity do the work . . .

But this was so, so much better.

The Black Death spread his hands wide, his white teeth gleaming.

"Ten seconds until detonation," called the analyst. Nobody in the bunker spoke, nobody breathed.

"Nine."

"Eight."

"Seven."

"Six—"

And then the control panels flashed red, blaring lines of errors running down the screens.

"Sir, we've lost control!"

"Navigation's not responding."

"We've lost power."

"Some kind of electromagnetic pulse."

"Firewall's down, we can't—"

"Get it back!" demanded the president. "Someone, tell me what's happened, give me a report! Do we have detonation, did it . . . ?"

"Sir," whispered Clarke, "the feed . . ."

And one by one, every head turned to watch the news screens, the live footage streaming from the skyborne cameras. Up in the stratosphere, with the cameramen unable to follow any higher, the Black Death was little more than a distant dot.

But what drifted beside him was unmistakable.

The world watched on in horror as the dark figure of Klaus Heydrich floated through empty space, his hands outstretched, slowly rotating a disabled, seventy-foot missile.

Pointing its payload straight down.

The president's face whitened.

"Oh God," he whispered.

". . . as it comes around now, and we can see . . . it is indeed nuclear and it appears . . . it appears the Black Death has assumed technopathic control . . ."

"Oh no," Matt whispered, his hands white around the bench. His eyes were glued to screen, the grainy sight of the revolving missile, the commentator's panicked words, coming live through the TV. . .

"Urged to evacuate . . . the two million people, living in Chicago . . ."

The missile creaked as it swung.

Hundreds of pounds of metal, machinery, fuel, and payload. He focused, his arms out, magnetically, telekinetically, technopathically pulling the warhead into place. A giant, heavy thing—so much to kill one man.

Far better to kill many.

His teeth bared, and he pulled harder—feeling the weight of the rocket, breathing a little faster . . . starting to feel, ever so slightly, the strain . . .

And suddenly, his eyes widened. His breath caught, his face warped, frozen in fear and disbelief. His hands slackened, and the missile ceased turning—as slowly, slowly, the Black Death raised a shaking hand, slowly reaching to his forehead . . .

To the trickling drop of sweat.

His head snapped round, his eyes bulging. The tiny, glistening bead of liquid floated, held, telekinetically suspended between his thumb and forefinger, a single traitorous drop. The Black Death stared at it, stock-still, unmoving, unspeaking, his face warped into a mask of horror . . .

And deep inside, he felt it.

The darkness.

Thirty miles above the ground, the Black Death floated, staring at a drop of sweat, frozen, ashen-faced, alone—and without a word he turned and flew away, shooting down toward Earth, leaving the warhead, the city, all of it behind, seemingly forgotten.

Matt's heart leaped to his throat.

"Leaving and we . . . Ladies and gentlemen, I don't know what to tell you, it's unclear why but this is confirmed, the Black Death is leaving Chicago, I repeat, the Black Death is leaving Chicago and appears to be heading south . . ."

Even on the shack's tiny, fuzzy screen it was visible—the missile stopped revolving, the dark figure frozen, then speeding away, a rippling trail in his wake. A cheer went up through the studio, crackling live through the TV speakers. Relief spread through Matt's body and he stumbled backward, grabbing the little table for support, his head suddenly light, his knees weak.

"And we're get . . . yes, it's confirmed, the Pentagon has reestablished . . . reestablished control of the missile and it is . . . auxiliary controls . . . going to touch down in Lake Michigan and . . ."

He didn't understand it. There was seemingly no reason, it was impossible, Matt didn't care. It was a miracle. He swore and prayed and thanked everyone and anyone, whoever or whatever had done this, all together at once—the words all jumbled, falling out in whispers beneath his breath.

"Unclear where Heydrich is headed, flying overland at supersonic speeds, camera crews attempting to follow . . ."

He needed air. Matt pushed open the shack door and stepped out into the blazing sunshine, his light-headed feet almost tripping down the single step. He closed his eyes, ran his hands through his hair, feeling the wind on his face, his heart hammering in his chest.

Thank you, he thought. Not knowing who he was saying it to, not caring. Thanking them all the same, tears on his cheeks, with every fiber of his being. He opened his eyes and looked up into the daylight, taking a long, steadying breath, blinking, as something up there caught his eye—

And without warning, a dark shape hurtled from the sky, and the world around him exploded.

Suddenly, he couldn't see. Suddenly, the air was black with dust and debris, the shack obliterated into a million pieces, flying chunks of earth and metal, a sandstorm blotting out the sun. The ground shook, the force of the impact throwing Matt backward, knocking him to the ground. He rolled onto his belly, his ears ringing, blinded, crawling, scrambling, trying to get up, trying to get away—

But before he could move an inch, an invisible vise wrapped around his throat and Matt was lifted off his feet, choking, helpless, pulled through the whirling wind, towards the center of the crater, toward a black figure, panting, crimson with rage—

"WHAT DID YOU DO?"

Heydrich screamed, demented, the instability in his voice tearing the very air asunder. His arm raised, three feet away, hand rigid, holding

Matt suspended, his shoulders heaving underneath his coat. His dark eyes bulged; his face contorted into twisted lines of hate. Matt coughed, spluttered, his fingers clawing pathetically at the invisible bands around his neck.

"I . . . don't . . ."

"YOU SAID IT!" shrieked the Black Death, and the force around Matt's throat tightened, his legs thrashing, spots dancing before his eyes. "You said if I took your blood . . . you said I'd lose, and now . . ." On the other side of the crater, behind the Black Death, people were dropping from the sky, men holding cameras. But the Black Death didn't notice, didn't care. There was madness in his eyes and every ounce of it burned into Matt.

"My powers," he whispered, and his eyes twitched to his arms, his shaking hand, "I can feel them . . . fading and there . . . there's something inside me, and it . . ."

He pulled Matt's helpless body closer. "WHAT DID YOU DO?" he shouted, eyes bulging, sweat streaming down his cheeks. "WHAT'S HAPPENING TO ME?"

And in an instant, Matt knew. Suffocating, his brain screaming, the world swimming before his eyes, he saw visions of a conversation with Ed, a lifetime ago—and in that moment, he knew. As he looked into the Black Death's desperate, darkened eyes and saw panic, real, honest fear, Matt knew he had one card left to play. One final thing to do. Live, with cameras glistening in the desert sun, before the eyes of the entire world, his family, and 4 billion people, Matt Callaghan told the truth.

"I'm . . . not . . . a clairvoyant . . ." he choked.

And he smiled a weak, savage smile.

The Black Death's face froze. The force around Matt's neck slackened, though still held him, dangling in the air. And Matt kept talking.

"I . . . am . . . human . . ." He grinned, forcing his lungs to breathe, forcing his teeth to bear—in raw, trembling defiance. "You took . . . my blood . . . your body . . . is . . . absorbing . . . becoming human . . ."

And he looked down at the Black Death with vicious, triumphant eyes, as everything the man in black was came tumbling down, live, in front of the world he had broken.

"You . . ." hissed Matt, "lose."

For a few seconds, nothing moved.

Matt hung, suspended in the air, struggling for breath. The wind whipped through the desert, swirling grains of sand. The cameras turned, zooming in on the Black Death's twisted face, his bulging, frozen eyes—standing there, unmoving. Unblinking. For a moment, the world seemed to hold its breath. For a moment, time stood still.

And then finally, almost too quietly to hear, the man spoke.

"I'll kill you," he murmured.

And suddenly, there was a snap, a severing, sickening snap, and Matt screamed, screamed as his legs crumpled in half, the bones cracking and shattering, splintering like twigs.

"I'LL KILL YOU!" the Black Death screamed. Suddenly, there was an explosion, a storm of fire, earth, and lightning, a hurricane of darkness rushing all around. The Black Death roared, spit flying from his mouth, his eyes bulging with unchecked insanity as his rage took form and split the sky in two.

"I'll kill you!" he screamed. "I'll kill everyone, I will BURN THIS WORLD TO THE GROUND BEFORE I LET YOU HAVE IT. I'LL KILL THEM. I'LL KILL THEM ALL!"

And as the madness in his voice reached fever pitch, his eyes fell back to Matt. His open hand clenched and Matt's body flew toward him, shrieking as the Black Death squeezed again, crushing his femurs, forcing the ends of the bone upward through leg muscles and skin, holding Matt two inches from his crimson, twisted face and his raging, psychotic eyes.

"But first," he whispered, "I'll kill you."

The Black Death raised his hand.

And suddenly, there was an earth-shattering boom and a blast of golden light.

The Black Death launched back, rolling, tumbling, his hold on Matt extinguished. The boy dropped instantly as the man in black slammed down, crashing through the earth before skidding to a halt, one hand on the ground, one knee in the dirt, his shoulders singed and smoking. Every camera followed as he turned, as he stared, his eyes widening, his face whitening, his mouth forming a single, whispered word.

"Impossible."

The cameras swung. Matt looked up.

And there in front of him, where the Black Death had been, stood a being of gold and white.

Gold boots.

Golden cape.

White body.

The symbol of breaking day.

Gloves curled.

Jaw clenched.

Face hard.

Eyes burning with golden light.

And golden light streaming from the mark on her cheek.

Jane, the empath.

Lady Dawn.

There was a moment's pause.

Wide-eyed, the Black Death's mouth opened.

"Jane."

With a wordless roar, Jane attacked.

She streaked forward, a burning golden comet, hurtling into the Black Death, driving him backward, her fists pummeling him once, twice, then on the third time nothing, her hand striking thin air, the Black Death vanished, intangible. There was a bang, a shout, and suddenly a fist slammed into the side of her head with the force of a sledgehammer, the Black Death teleported behind her, hitting again and again and again. But as he raised his hand, Jane grabbed it, held it, straining against his superstrength, her eyes glowing, teeth bared. The Black Death struck again with his free hand, Jane leaning out of the blow and grabbing his other fist, struggling, their arms locked, pushing against each other, the air burning, the ground cracking beneath their feet—faces inches apart, mouths locked in identical bloody snarls . . .

Then Jane snapped her neck forward, her forehead crunching into the Black Death's nose, and Heydrich cried out and fell back, rolling as he fell, driving both boots up and into Jane's stomach, launching her back, tumbling skyward. He spun, screaming, a searing beam of green energy erupting from his eyes toward her, but Jane twisted and turned through the air, and with a ringing shout shot back, a torrential blast of golden light scorching from her hand, racing downward, meeting the Black Death's attack in midair.

There was a boom, a blinding shock wave and Heydrich hurtled back, a ball of black tumbling in the dirt. He threw out his hands, his fingers tearing tracks through the earth, dragging himself skidding to a halt, shaking, glaring across the barren plain as Jane landed, the gashes on his face healing—and before Jane could blink, he shot forward, a silver blur, slamming into her at superspeed. His body now solid steel, he hit with the force of a bullet train, driving her back, pummeling her arms, her chest, her face with supersonic steel fists. He was everywhere, too fast to see, too fast to dodge, hitting Jane over and over as she tried to shield herself, push back against the relentless, pounding assault.

But then her eyes burned, and in an instant, light exploded around her, throwing the Black Death back, up into the air. Jane roared and fired, launching blast after blast up after him, bursts of golden energy crashing against his force field, cracking through the shield. Then her hands came together and out, unleashing a single, relentless beam that seared upward, toward the Black Death as he fled, the beam chasing as he flew, dodging and circling, barely missing, his eyes wild, his black coat smoking as he weaved desperately under and aside, up through the clouds, pursued by the scorching pillar of light.

And then Jane was streaking upward after him, the cameras following, a meteor of gold, bursting through the clouds as the Black Death turned and flew toward her, a burning deluge of fire streaming from his hands, searing the very air. But Jane didn't stop. She flew, up into the inferno, pulsing with golden light, a sunlit needle piercing through the flames, untouched, unstoppable, hurtling toward Heydrich. Once more, the two collided, and once more the Black Death fell, plummeting to earth, body whistling through the air, slamming into solid ground in a shower of broken stone, a giant crater, bigger than any normal man . . .

Because the Black Death was growing. Widening, shooting upward, growing twenty, forty, eighty feet, a bellowing, colossal titan who pushed to his feet and lunged, punching a fist the size of a house toward the miniscule, flying Jane who strafed, rolling, streaking by an inch from the surface of his freight-train arm, cape fluttering behind her, a golden bullet hurtling toward Heydrich's face. But instead of hitting, she kept going, passing right through the giant head as if it was an illusion, the Black Death momentarily intangible, her eyes wide, suddenly careering toward solid rock.

At the last second, Jane spun, bracing her knees as her feet slammed into the ground, the momentum of the impact spreading cracks through the bedrock, her legs bent, head turned, glaring up—as a giant fist, moving superhumanly fast, slammed down on top of her, smashing her a full foot down into the earth. The Black Death rumbled a thunderous roar and faster than lightning his ten-foot fists struck down, blurring, pummeling, again, again, and again, hammering Jane further and further down into a crater of dust and rock.

And as the cameras followed, as the world watched on in horror, the Black Death shrunk, his body shimmering, splitting into two, three, ten, twenty copies, panting, blinking into existence around the staggering Jane, a different power erupting from each—fire, lightning, lasers, sound, hails of stone and ice, streams of air and acid, the Black Death reborn two dozen times over, surrounding Jane on all sides, an unrelenting avalanche of energy and death, forcing Jane to her knees as she threw out her hands, the barrier of golden light around her wavering as the replications fired, over and over, without pause or mercy, pummeling her further and further down until there was nothing left to see, until her gold and white were gone, until all that remained was dust . . .

The cameras twisted their lenses. In hospitals, schools, factories, all around the world, people stood breathlessly, not daring to move, watching. Rich, poor, adults, children, Wally, Giselle, the president, her father—all looking on horrified as the Black Death's copies stopped attacking, panting, collective shoulders heaving, staring into the blackened crater at the center of their relentless assault, the billowing cloud of dust, where surely nothing could have endured, nothing could have survived . . . For a second, it was as if the entire world held their breath, held each other, the Black Deaths' unified eyes bulging, victorious, manic . . .

And then inside the dust, something shone.

Her face bloodied, her outfit torn, her cape in tatters, burned, scarred, and bruised—but alive. Her legs braced, her arms locked, holding out her glowing barrier, her jaw clenched, her face furious and defiant—with golden fire burning in her eyes and through the mark on her cheek.

From the ashes, Jane rose.

She hurtled, blazing gold, slamming into the Black Deaths, tearing through one, kicking another, spinning through the air and burying her fists in two more, the clones vanishing as she broke them, blasting one coming at her from behind, grabbing another as it lunged with bladed arms, throwing its body into its brethren. In an instant, she braced, unleashing from her hands a shining golden beam, sweeping through the crowd of copies, vanquishing every one of them it hit, cutting through their ranks—until only one remained. Jane charged, roaring, light streaming from her hands . . .

Only to strike nothing as the pale figure vanished into the ground.

Jane skidded to a halt, rocks flying underneath her boots, panting, turning, eyes darting around the dust, stones, and craters, the open desert expanse—empty save for the cliffs a hundred yards away, the inconsequential cameramen. She spun on the spot, teeth bared, glancing in every direction, ready for an attack—but she couldn't see, the Black Death was invisible, maybe intangible, somewhere in the air or underground, she didn't know . . .

So, with a deep breath, she closed her eyes. And slowly, she began to glow.

Ripping, echoing, pulsing—wave after wave of energy pushing out, a surge of golden force, growing, growing, harder and harder, until the wind whipped around her and the very air throbbed with burning light. She rose, an inch from the ground, her body vibrating with pure power, a building torrent of energy flowing out in a perfect circle, a perfect sphere, roaring, a relentless, golden thrum . . .

And out of the corner of her eye, she saw him. An invisible shape, a void, straining toward her, pushing against the rushing light, a man with blades for arms against a hurricane—struggling with all his might but unable to get closer, unable to push forward through the waves of energy crashing around him, the billowing golden wind. Jane's hands flew out and the Black Death was thrown back, his body suddenly visible, skittering through the dust, coming to a halt forty feet away. He looked up at her, hate and terror in his eyes, his face bruised, bloodied, glaring—Jane stepped forward, triumphant, preparing to launch . . .

And the Black Death's fingers flew to his temple.

Suddenly, the desert grew dark.

The sky black, the sun overrun, turned gray with seething cloud. Jane glanced around her, suddenly lost, suddenly afraid, the sunburned land flattened to pale and barren wasteland, spreading out into eternity. This

... this wasn't right, it was a trick, it ... the Black Death, she had to ... Jane spun around wildly, the colors drained from her clothes and cape, unable to see him, unable to see ... anyone, she was alone, everyone had vanished, she had to ...

Fight it! This isn't real!

Jane tried to focus, tried to think, but there was this pit, this great billowing pit of emptiness opening inside her, and her heart was racing and she was shaking, shaking though she wanted to ... she had to ... she had to save the world ... but this place ... there was no world left to save. Everything was already dead.

Keep him out, keep him out of your head!

Remember, remember, remember—she closed her eyes, trying to hold on to her thoughts, she had to ... she had to think, all those lessons, an eternity ago, far away from this place drained of all life and color, and where the very air cloyed with dust and death ...

Focus! Don't ...

Weakling!

She tried to breathe, but all that came out were petty, sickly shudders. Remember who you are, Wally had said—remember who you are. Who was she? She ... she was Jane Walker. Jane ... Jane Walker and she lived ... her home, where was her home, she ... it was ... and she did ... she was a fighter and, and a ... a ...

Failure.

No. No, no, no, no, no. Jane held out her hands, trying to fly, but to her horror nothing came—she was powerless, she was worthless, some- how she'd lost it, everything, their only hope, the power of Dawn ... She turned, bare feet racing across the empty landscape, breathing so fast it hurt, hands clutching at her chest, running somewhere, anywhere, nowhere, just away, away from the memories, the voices, the ...

Coward.

"No," she whimpered. "No, please, no." She stepped forward, and there was a crack, a soft, pale crunch. "No," she pleaded, begging not to see but unable not to look, unable to stop herself from staring down, trembling, at the bone white dust, at the fragments of tiny skull she'd crushed underfoot as they scattered, blown away, whispering in the wind ...

"You failed us." The tiny, fragile voice of a child. "Failed everyone."

"No," pleaded Jane, gray dust in her eyes, on her hands, breath coming in wrenching sobs. But as she said it, she looked around and finally saw the wasteland's truth, the endless fields not of gray, but of cold, dead white—of ashen bones.

"No, no, no . . ."

"Look what you did," came a voice from behind her. Jane spun around and suddenly she was standing in the crater of a house, the blackened shell of someone's home, broken posts and husks of wood, the roof gone, the clouds swirling with ash. Only one charred wall of splintered wood remained half-standing behind her—and against it leaned a figure, a withered corpse. Unmoving, undying, trapped in soft agony as it spoke.

"You said you were worthy," it stated plainly, full of neither sorrow nor rage but only tired, empty deep. "You told us you could be more than we thought you were."

"No, please." Jane fell to her knees. But she knew there was nothing she could do. The world was dead, scorched, and gray. Only ruins, only bones, only voices left. She was alone.

"You were wrong," the dead man murmured. "All you're good for is hurting people and you couldn't even do that right. You're worthless."

"No," whispered Jane, "I tried, I—"

"Stood back and watched us die? I'd expect nothing less. Parasite." Suddenly, the voice coming from the corpse was James Conrad's, his shrunken face hanging loosely from its weathered head like a mask. "It should have been you," he whispered, "not me. I was a leader, I was part of something, but you . . . ?" He laughed. "The world loses nothing if you die."

"Even if you won," murmured the body, and suddenly it was Giselle, her face twisted and burned, head lolling to the side, eye sockets empty, "it wouldn't have mattered. We hated you. Everyone hated you."

"Always, hated you," another ghost whispered in her ear.

"And why not? Who wouldn't hate such a worthless, pathetic creature? How could it ever delude itself into thinking it could be loved? It just can't accept the truth, that there's a reason it's alone, now and always."

Jane dropped to her knees, sobbing, squeezing her hands over her ears. She shrunk, curled up, tiny and alone on the cold ashen floor, all light, all color, all warmth within her flickering and dying as she listened—as she finally heard the truth.

"Animal, monster, parasite. Your mother left you, your father hates you, people flee from your very sight—and it'll never change, it will never, ever change, no matter what you say or try or do. Because you're broken. An abomination."

"You're not supposed to be a part of this world," Giselle said softly. "No one will ever want you; no one will ever love you. Pathetic, worthless child."

And she was. She was a child, a little girl, whimpering in the dark, clutching at her chest—defenseless and alone, as the shadows swirled around her, towering over her, taking form. They twisted, rising up into a hulking being of pure thought, jet-black knotted glass, with eyes the color of burning blood and teeth of glinting knives. It stood over Jane as she lay in darkness, a broken, weeping child, staring down with black satisfaction—and between its hands it thought a crimson, darkened blade.

"Goodbye Jane," it whispered. And it raised the sword, the point hanging over the broken babe.

I AM HUMAN I AM HUMAN I AM HUMAN I AM HUMAN I AM HUMAN I AM.

From the ether of Jane's mind came an avalanche of force, and before the Black Death could strike, it slammed into him, pummeling his thoughts, a tidal wave of will that rammed and roared and hammered into Heydrich's mind, a giant of green and white that locked its arms around the being of black and drove it back, driving it into the ground, pushing it away.

"ARRRRRGGGHHHH!"

In the real world, the Black Death's eyes bulged, his body frozen, fingers locked to his forehead—unable to let go, unable to break free, his eyes swung around, disbelieving, terrified . . .

To see Matt Callaghan.

Broken. Bleeding. Powerless, laying in the dirt.

But alive. Holding himself up. And staring at the Black Death with unyielding, burning eyes.

As between his fingers, next to his temple, shone a small gray disk.

"AAARRGHHH!"

The Black Death screamed as he struggled, as roared, as he pushed with all his might against the titan, the hurricane of howling consciousness driving him away from Jane, blasting into him with a single, unstoppable thought ...

I AM HUMAN.

Years of secrecy. Years of lies. Years of pent-up truth and frustration, of deception and denial, finally unleashed in a tidal wave of fury, of certainty, of unrelenting, perfect identity and acceptance of a single ringing fact ...

I AM HUMAN.

This was not a belief. This was not a story. This was him, the whole of him, his truth, his very core. It was undeniable, indestructible, and it slammed into Klaus Heydrich without fear, without mercy, pushing back against the darkness, pushing back against death, because his name was Matt Callaghan and ...

I AM HUMAN.

He drove, green sinews of thought locked against Heydrich, shoving him back, holding him at bay, slamming a mental fist into the creature's twisted consciousness, hammering him again and again, tearing through the gray dust and darkness as he swung, as he focused, as he roared ...

I AM HUMAN.

As he put everything he had into a crushing blast, a staggering torrent of thought ...

I AM HUMAN I AM HUMAN I AM HUMAN I AM.

But then slowly, slowly, the Black Death pushed back.

Bit by bit. Inch by inch. Matt's hands started to shake, his eyes watering, his jaw clenched.

I AM HUMAN I AM HUMAN I AM HUMAN I AM HUMAN I AM HUMAN I AM.

But his focus was wavering—primal, unstoppable thoughts intruding, the real world, the blood loss, the pain ...

I AM HUMAN—pain—*I AM HUMAN I AM HUMAN I AM*—pain—*HUMAN I AM HUMAN.*

His legs were broken, the pain from them leaking through, unable to be ignored any longer, red flashing cracks appearing in the green giant's thighs. The black demon's razor teeth clenched and its sinews bulged.

I AM HUMAN—pain—*I AM HUMAN*—pain—*I AM HUMAN I AM HUMAN I*—pain—*AM.*

"JANE!" he called out, frantic. The monstrous darkness pushed hard, and Matt felt himself sliding. He roared and drove forward with everything he had, his mind locked with Heydrich's, desperate to keep him away from her, desperate to hold him back.

I AM HUMAN I AM HUMAN I AM HUMAN I AM HUMAN I AM—pain pain pain.

"JANE!" he cried again, and this time the Black Death managed to break free, momentarily throwing him aside, before Matt once again rose up and charged, holding back the twisting dark.

"JANE!" he cried, shouting through the grayness, through their minds. "YOU HAVE TO GET UP!"

But the girl could only lay there, curled and shaking, the sound of her sobbing echoing in the dark—broken and unreachable, cold and alone.

I AM—pain—*HUMAN*—pain—*I AM HUMAN*—pain—*I AM*—pain—*HUMAN I AM HUMAN*—pain—*I.*

"JANE!" he begged. "PLEASE!"

And to his horror, the black of Heydrich's mind split into two—one coiling around Matt, dragging him down, holding back his shrinking, wavering thoughts, the other stalking slowly, back over to the darkened corner, to where remained the last shred of Jane's soul.

"JANE!" Matt tried to scream, but his words were cut off by the sinews of smothering darkness, his concentration broken, his strength failing. All he could do was watch, helpless beneath the weight of the Black Death's abyss, as the demon standing over Jane smiled savagely. Its crimson eyes flickered to Matt.

"Strong," it whispered, "but not strong enough."

And for the final time, it raised its sword.

Whoosh.

Something hit the Black Death, like a gust of air, a ghost, a spectral figure blasting past him, causing him to flinch, making his head snap around, his eyes wide as—

Whoosh. Whoosh.

Two more, striking on either side, transparent figures appearing from nowhere and brushing past him, making him yelp, more distracted than pained, spinning around and slashing after the specters, who vanished as quickly as they'd came . . .

Whoosh. Whoosh.

And suddenly, there were hundreds. Thousands of transparent figures, men, women, and children, emerging from nothing, rising up in a crowd, a mountain around Jane, around the Black Death, around Matt, ghosts of every age and country, every race and religion, a swelling illusory army, striding into their minds. And as the phantoms multiplied, Matt heard them speaking, and he saw, connected to them as they were to him, saw through their eyes, saw the incredible truth . . .

Matt the human.

In schools and offices, libraries and prisons, newsrooms and slums. Groups of dozens, hundreds, gathering around psychics, projecting their collective minds across the world.

Lady Dawn.

Natalia Baroque and the few, bloodied survivors of the Legion. Will, Giselle and Wally, determined and unwavering with every doctor, every patient in the hospital, joined together. Laying on hands.

We are with you.

The president, the politicians in their bunker, gripping one another tight. The whole of Northridge High School, assembled in the cafeteria, teachers holding students, friends joining friends. And in the middle of a steaming factory, a group of workmen, standing silently in a circle— each one of their hands reaching out to the man in the middle, Jane's father, his eyes closed.

You are not alone.

On their own, they were nothing. Noise, voices, distractions, weaker than a thought, little more than ghosts. But they were not on their own— they were united, thousands, tens of thousands, rising up, surging forth.

They were legion.

And as they fell like rain upon Klaus Heydrich, swarming over him, the Black Death screamed and tore at them, each one he destroyed replaced by two more, and the darkness around Matt lifted and the human's thoughts bellowed a defiant roar. The green giant rose and once more slammed into the Black Death, knocking loose his razor teeth, the sea of souls around him drawing away Matt's pain—and as a hundred, thousand minds moved together to attack, one, alone, ran the other way. A single, dusty man, who flew toward the darkened corner, to the body of the tiny, whimpering girl. Who knelt over his daughter and looked down, tears leaking from his eyes.

"Jane?" he whispered. He reached out his shaking hand to touch her, feeling the hurt, the suffering, the pain, her frail and fragile heart, with all that was broken inside.

"Oh, Jane." And without another word, he took her in his arms.

There was light—blinding, golden light. The Black Death screamed, helpless, overrun . . . as Peter Walker's memories flowed into his daughter's soul.

A playground. Swings. Laughter. His hands on the small of her back, pushing her, the wind in her hair, flying higher and higher. Gumboots and autumn leaves. Her mother's face, bending over, lifting her up, holding her close, cradling her head.

A birthday cake. Candles in the dark. A funeral. A deep, shaking sadness—but in the middle a tiny hand, seeking comfort in a bigger one. Instinctual, twin sorrows nesting together for warmth. Together, underneath a blanket, eating microwaved dinners while it rained, watching TV.

I love you.

Her face, growing, hardening, changing as she strode, out and through that door a thousand times, into fights, into failure, into hate— but never letting go. Never giving up. The weight, the aftermath of their arguments, anger hanging around his neck—but never at her. At himself. She was everything he couldn't be. She was perfect. Strong and fierce and . . . her. Every day more like her. The light, flickering late in her room, her head resting on the desk, exhausted from all she had to endure. His beautiful girl, his young woman. He stands there for a moment watching and then he turns off the light—his hands underneath her legs, lifting, carrying her the few feet to her bed. She mumbles, nods her head against his chest. She never remembers. She barely stirs and he never tells her. Never says what he needed to say, what he should have been telling her, every single day.

I am so proud of you.

Her face on the news, fierce and lean. Sitting there on Thanksgiving, hard and defiant, a proud warrior, her eyes only for him, not seeing the eyes only on her. The pride at seeing her stand there in the front rows of the Legion. The terror at watching her fight. And the awe as she returned, as she fought to save her friend, glowing with golden strength—but still afraid. So heart-breakingly afraid that something would happen to her. That she'd be hurt. Not seeing the costume, the goddess—just seeing his little girl. Alone and fighting. Perfect and flawed.

Now get up.

Jane's eyes flew open.

In her mind, and in the world, she rose—eyes burning with sunlight, tears streaming down her cheeks. The woman in white and gold, cape falling out behind her, her cheek ablaze with day. Whole, unbroken. Rising slowly, a being of light. Reborn, to bear the weight of the world.

Lady Dawn.

The Black Death screamed in terror, and his mind pulled free from hers. His hands clenched inward, his flesh writhing with hissing energy, unnatural violet that spread throughout him with a sickening glow. Even in his weakened state, even as the blood of the human coursed through his veins, pulling him down, still he would do it. He would destroy the world, if he himself was to be destroyed.

But he would destroy nothing.

And as the clouds parted, as the sun streamed through her veins, Jane Walker pulled her hands together; and with a single step forward, before the man named Klaus Heydrich could harm another soul, and with a hoarse, strangled cry, she unleashed the power of Dawn.

There was a blinding, billowing, all-encompassing light . . . and the Black Death was no more.

The room erupted. A dozen men, shouting and clapping, sinking wearily into their chairs. The president of the United States let out a deep, shaking breath, cupped his mouth in his hands and closed his eyes.

The hospital shrieked. Manically, ecstatically, powers erupting everywhere, people crying, kissing, Giselle punching the air so hard she tore her skin grafts.

The news station cheered. The cameraman practically toppled over as tears streamed from one anchor's eyes, while the other ran his hands through his hair and swore, loudly and profusely, live on national television.

All around the world, people laughed and cried, shook their heads and thanked their gods, hugged one another and swore from this day forth to live every day of their lives.

And alone in the desert, blood streaming from his legs into pools of crimson dirt, Matt Callaghan's eyes rolled up into his head. And he collapsed without a sound.

The world was blinding—light, cold, and warm. Somewhere in the distance, Matt felt strong arms wrap gently around him, cradling his broken bones.

And then he was flying.

I'm dying, he concluded. The angels are carrying me away. His eyelids flickered in the wind and warmth. Rising up into the sunlight.

Finally, finally flying.

It was okay. He could go now. This was the end.

The angel, sunlight streaming through her hair, carried him up.

Matt closed his eyes and drifted away.

EPILOGUE: MATT THE HUMAN

"One week since the criminal known as the Black Death . . ."

"The incredible heroics of . . ."

"Memorial service held outside what was once Detroit, but will now . . ."

". . . federal inquiry into how a known terrorist managed to bypass all security checks and personally meet numerous political figures . . ."

" 'I got it because, you know, it's a bad law, it's prejudice, and I say enough with the hate, enough with the fear.' The man pointed to the letter E freshly tattooed on his face. 'We've been down this road before and I say I'm with you Lady Dawn, a hundred'. . ."

". . . begun rebuilding of the Eastchester Academy, overseen by newly elected leader of the Legion of Heroes, Giselle Pixus . . ."

". . . issued a warrant for the family's genetic material, an order already being contested by . . ."

"I think she's dangerous, I think she's unstable, and she can't just keep flying around with this kind of power and . . ."

" '. . . world keeps spinning, you know? We try and pick up the pieces, and even though we've lost so much, I guess . . .' The old man shook his head, smiling sadly. ' . . . I guess I just want to say thank you. Thank you, Matt the Human. Thank you, Lady Dawn . . .' "

The TV blared in the background, but nobody paid it much notice. There were more important things going on.

They had the room to themselves. The whole floor actually. The hospital board of directors were staunch, unanimous supporters, and had taken every precaution to ensure their privacy and well-being. So, for almost two weeks, the halls had stood largely silent, save for the one room with the sea-green walls—where seven people came intermittently in and out. Two veteran doctors, one trusted nurse, and the entire Callaghan family.

All of them there for Matt.

And now it was time to say goodbye.

His bandages had come off days ago—the twin pink scars sitting midway up his thighs now the only indication of how close he'd come to death. The doctors had offered to heal them for him, but Matt had declined. They were a part of him now, a testament, a reminder.

Something he'd probably need in the days to come.

He dressed, then hugged them, one by one. Shook his father's hand, Michael Callaghan's eyes a little red. Listened as his mother held his shoulders and whispered how proud she was. Punched Jonas lightly on the chin as his brother hugged him. Picked Sarah up, her small arms wrapping tight around his neck, not really understanding, not wanting him to go.

But this was something he had to do alone.

Matt's footsteps echoed through the hospital corridor, walking steadily, his eyes firmly ahead. His heart beat fast, but his hands didn't shake. It was all right. He breathed. It would be okay.

His secret was out. No going back now—not after announcing it live on international television, not after having thousands of people hear him shout it inside his head. His hands moved almost without thinking to his wallet. His ID.

Matt Callaghan, Clairvoyant.

He tossed the card into a silver bin in the hallway and kept walking.

Until he stood at the hospital's exit.

Matt glanced up at the green Exit light, at the steel, push-bar double doors. He closed his eyes and drew a deep, steadying breath. This was it. No turning back.

He opened his eyes, placed a hand on either side of the doors and pushed.

Taking his first steps into the outside world, greeted by blinding sunlight . . . and a bellowing roar.

Matt held up his hand, shielding his eyes, momentarily dazed. As his pupils adjusted to the outside light, the flashing camera lenses, he looked down and he saw, gathered there, waiting for him, at the bottom of the hospital steps . . . People.

A crowd, a sea of people, maybe thousands. Clapping, chanting, calling out his name. Waving banners bearing the Legion's symbol, holding signs saying, We're Human Too. All there, all for him—all on his side.

And at the top of the stairs, from beside the door, alone and oblivious to the crowds, stepped Jane.

The same as always. In her gray hoodie and faded jeans, her arms crossed. The black E shining proudly on her cheek. Smiling. She stepped beside Matt. He turned to her and smiled back.

"So," he muttered so only she could hear, beneath the crowd's roar, "this is new."

"You get used to it," she replied, grinning.

They stood there for a moment at the top of the hospital steps, a thousand cameras flashing, looking down at the sea of shining faces. Then Matt glanced back at her.

"So, what do we do now?" he asked. "Morningstar's destroyed."

"We'll rebuild," Jane said calmly.

"Can you even be in the Legion without powers?"

"We might need a secretary."

"Not to mention the government wants to take my blood," Matt said with a grimace.

"Mmm," Jane mused. She hesitated; then her fingers wrapped through his. "They can try."

They paused.

"I mean you'll probably be off," Matt said after a second, heart racing, but still with an overly dramatic sigh. "Kicking ass. Saving the world. Probably won't have much time for me."

"You're an idiot," she said softly.

"And you're amazing," he replied, meeting her eyes.

"No," she corrected, leaning close, "we're amazing."

And in front of the whole world, they kissed.

Kissed long and hard, his hands cupping around her cheeks, her arms wrapping around his head, their eyes closed, soft and then deeper, pulling each other close—and as the crowd shrieked and the cameras flashed, as her hands closed tight around him, as their lips pressed together in guiding warmth, Jane's mark shone and her eyes flew open, ablaze with shining gold.

And in a rush, a wind raced through the sea of onlookers, a wave of breathless, billowing light—as they rose, spiraling, embracing, intertwined, the sunlit air swirling around them as they kissed, as they held each other, oblivious to the world.

Then slowly, the light faded, and the wind died. Slowly, they descended back to earth, their feet touching softly on the ground. Their lips gently parted, breaking an inch away—breathing slow and warm, looking into each other's eyes. His hand squeezed hers, and they exchanged stupid smiles. Then Jane glanced at the flashing crowd.

"Hang on." She grinned, wrapping her arm around his waist. Then she bent down, glanced up . . . and in a rush of light they flew away together, into the open sky.

EPILOGUE: THE WATCHER

The couple flew.

The shouting grew.

The fever faded.

The crowd dispersed.

And then, eventually, everybody was gone.

Save one.

A blue-eyed boy, waiting as the world fell to twilight, sitting alone atop a stoop.

Though he made no sound, he was happy for them. These brief, fleeting moments, this togetherness, this joy. A connection neither knew they wanted until the moment it fell into place. Life was, on occasion, surprising like that. Or maybe it wasn't. There was nothing like near death, he'd found, to make one blink and see new colors.

The child leaned back on his hands, feeling the cool air against his skin, the stone beneath his legs, and allowed himself to indulge in this time. The quiet of it. The cold. The lack of immediate, pressing problems—of burning, consuming concern.

And yet.

Almost against his will, the child glanced back over his shoulder, at the shadow lurking beyond.

One thing at a time, he tried to reassure himself, *one thing at a time.*

They had cleared the first hurdle. It had taken ten thousand efforts and cost half a million lives, but he'd threaded the star-silk pathway, found an "acceptable" solution, in the end. Hamstrung, bitterly, by the pins set in place, limited by harrowing conclusions he had to walk back from. From here, it was easy to see the end as the beginning. He knew what needed to happen, what should happen, what he wanted to happen from now. Hindsight was the vantage point of a god.

And yet.

And yet.

Now it was no longer just his choices to contend with. Now, though she did not know it yet, a second will was loose.

Now, it was far harder to undo.

The boy glanced back again at the ever-present darkness and again pushed the fear back down.

So far, her thread was steady. For now, she remained divested, a toddler laying by the pool. The path was still clear in the steps to follow. But it was different, now she'd dipped her toes in—things unable to be undone. Reaction had become probability; margins crinkled with mistake. Ripples feeding into ripples, until maybe—just maybe—the ocean would shift upon its surface, and the painted doors he'd dripped so carefully would cease to be the spaces she'd dive through.

Fear nibbled like a dormouse.

How long before she'd attempt it? How long before she took that unguided step, until she lay in bed, unable to sleep, and wondered what could have been? The pain, he knew, would dissuade her, the incomprehensible vertigo of standing at the precipice of time and thought and space. But eventually, she'd surmount it. Once they had time to catch their breaths, once they cleared their way through more linear problems—well, they both had questions which lay unanswered. Even now, in celebration, they both wondered how they'd won.

They would know, eventually. The boy's pieces were in place, and they would—should—fall where he needed. But until then, he had to watch them. Had to guard for thoughts unseen. Be ready to interfere on the edge of an instant.

He would not let the Weave claim her, as it had claimed and annihilated him.

The child turned back to reality, to the soft blue world around. His eyes flew out, over the city streets and sweeping night, over the fate lines spreading bright across the endless sky. The countless paths, the life threads, pulsing ceaseless toward the horizon, twisting technicolor intertwined. He watched as they shone, as they flowed, as they drifted together, oblivious, toward what destiny had in store. Toward a future only he could see.

Toward the blackened pit that consumed everything in its yearning, voiceless maw.

They had cleared the first hurdle.

Soon, the boy whispered. *Soon.*

The darkness swirled.

ABOUT THE AUTHOR

Benjamin Keyworth is an Australian author born and raised in Newcastle, New South Wales, and currently living in Sydney with his partner and dog. A lawyer by day, Ben has wanted to be a writer since he was five years old (before which he wanted to be a dinosaur). He is pursuing a master's degree in creative writing at the University of Technology Sydney, and in his spare time he enjoys baking and playing video games and *Dungeons & Dragons.*

DISCOVER
STORIES UNBOUND

PodiumAudio.com

Manufactured by Amazon.com.au
Sydney, New South Wales, Australia

12096878R00196